"You have to watch these Louisiana boys. They can drink you under the table, and some of them can write you under the table. Ken Wheaton can do both. He's a wild one, and this is a sparkling debut."
—Luis Alberto Urrea, author of *Into the Beautiful North*

"Warmed my chest faster than a double shot of Wild Turkey and kept me laughing through the night. This is a rollicking, wonderfully irreverent debut. It's also a charming love story with a heart as big as Louisiana. I am a huge Ken Wheaton fan."
—Matthew Quick, author of *The Silver Linings Playbook*

"A frustrated priest who smokes, drinks, and curses like a sailor, a loveable centenarian matriarch whose appetite for Crown Royal is matched only by her busy-body compulsion to counsel on any and all matters, a feisty flock of Cajun gals and gents who know how to get any ball rolling—all are unforgettable characters on a mission that's not so holy and that gives new meaning to the notion of Southern Gothic. Add a carnival, the aroma of gumbo and fried turkey, and a little Zydeco dancing, and it's easy to see why Ken Wheaton has produced a highly original yarn that is hilarious, beguiling, and, at times, warmly moving."
—James Villas, author of *Dancing in the Low Country* and *The Glory of Southern Cooking*

"Ken Wheaton's fictitious story of a real small community in Grand Prairie, Louisiana, will keep you entertained and laughing out loud! Wheaton thoroughly describes the tradition and passion for the Cajun French way of life. Strap on your waders and get ready to trudge through some of the most colorful characters in the South."
—Helen Pursell, Fifth Annual Festival Du Lapin Queen

The First Annual Grand Prairie Rabbit Festival

KEN WHEATON

Craig,
Thanks for Reading.
Hope you like it.

KENSINGTON BOOKS
www.kensingtonbooks.com

KENSINGTON BOOKS are published by

Kensington Publishing Corp.
119 West 40th Street
New York, NY 10018

All Kensington titles, imprints, and distributed lines are available at special quantity discounts for bulk purchases for sales promotion, premiums, fund-raising, educational, or institutional use.

Special book excerpts or customized printings can also be created to fit specific needs. For details, write or phone the office of the Kensington Special Sales Manager: Kensington Publishing Corp., 119 West 40th Street, New York, NY 10018. Attn. Special Sales Department. Phone: 1-800-221-2647.

Kensington and the K logo Reg. U.S. Pat. & TM Off.

ISBN-13: 978-0-7582-3852-8
ISBN-10: 0-7582-3852-5

First Kensington Trade Paperback Printing: January 2010
10 9 8 7 6 5 4 3 2

Printed in the United States of America

For Susan . . .
and Mawmaw

Acknowledgments

This novel would never have existed if not for a drunken bet proffered by Jason Primm on New Year's Eve in 2001. Also providing proper motivation for that long-ago first draft were Lynn Jones and Erin Gallagher. Thanks to all three for giving me the push necessary to move on to a new, more readable project.

Thanks to Jacquelin Cangro, not only for publishing me in "The Subway Chronicles," but for providing excellent editorial feedback to take this work from a shoddy second draft to something someone might read.

Thanks to Jeff Moores, formerly of Dunow, Carlson & Lerner, for rescuing me from the slush piles, and to Peter Senftleben and the gang at Kensington Books.

Of course, I'd be remiss to skip Mama, Daddy, Gardiner, Amber, Brian, Seth, Jennifer, and Daniel, who've made me what I am and remind me where I'm from, and my son, Nicholas Jones, who gives me something to look forward to.

And, finally, thanks to my wife, Susan, who also provided invaluable editorial feedback and who, more importantly, puts up with me, motivates me, and believes writing silly books about silly subjects isn't a silly pursuit

Author's Note

A note about "yall": While most consider y'all a contraction of you all, in all my years growing up in Louisiana, I never once heard the phrase "you all" uttered. Regardless of what the fancy-pants dictionary might say, yall is one word, a second-person personal pronoun used to address two or more people (never one person, despite what crappy TV writers and third-rate comedians would have you believe). Therefore, for the purposes of this book, yall is written as . . . well . . . yall.

Further, while there is a St. Peter's Roman Catholic Church in a town called Grand Prairie, Louisiana, and, there once was something called a Rabbit Festival, this book in no way reflects reality—or any research—on my part. In other words, the whole thing's a damn lie.

Chapter 1

The counter clerk at T-Ron's Grab 'n' Go doesn't bat an eye when I ask for two packs of Camel Lights, a bag of pork cracklin's, and a pint of Crown Royal. Is it every day she's confronted with a priest—black pants, black shirt, white collar and all—buying whiskey and cracklin's before lunch?

The cigarettes are mine, the rest is for Miss Rita, who's finishing out life in Easy Time Nursing Home, where the staff frowns upon booze and pigskin. Before I walk in, I place my purchases into my black leather satchel, alongside a Bible, a *Daily Missal,* and last week's copy of *People* magazine.

"Hey, Father Steve," the receptionist says when I enter Easy Time's lobby, which is covered in the chintzy sort of Thanksgiving decorations you'd expect to see in a preschool or kindergarten. She's a short, chunky girl with a curly helmet of dull brown hair and an overly pleasant smile. She strikes me as the type who, unable to find a suitable man and unwilling to settle for an unsuitable one, has come to a place where she'll be appreciated and adored, where she can dole out a little of that love pent up in an otherwise lonely life. I wonder if she lives in a trailer full of cats.

"Hi, Marie. How you doing today, cher?" I don't know why I put on the Cajun schtick for her, but I do.

"Aw, I'm doing good, and you?" she chirps. I swear her teeth just might explode right out of her head.

"Comme ci, comme ça," I answer. "Can't complain. How's Miss Rita doing today?"

"Oh, she's good today. She's awake and sitting in her room."

As opposed to what? Hopping around the grounds on her one leg? Playing roller hockey in the parking lot?

"Good, good. I'll see you later, Marie."

Miss Rita, as far as anyone can tell, is somewhere between 105 and 117 years old. No birth certificate. Her "birthday" rolls around in late November, early December and seems to fall on whatever day is convenient for Easy Time and the reporters who cover the occasion. Her grandchildren don't mind. Miss Rita doesn't, either, as long as someone makes a fuss over it.

Aside from one dutiful grandson, I'm Miss Rita's only regular visitor. She's not a member of my parish—St. Pete's doesn't have a single black parishioner—but she's practically a member of my family. Miss Rita was "the help" Pawpaw hired for Mawmaw back in the days when it was still acceptable to call people "the help."

I remember Miss Rita and Mawmaw sitting in Mawmaw's kitchen, in a pair of old wooden rocking chairs, Miss Rita shiny black to the point of being purple, Mawmaw white and liver-spotted. They rocked in a counterrhythm, black forward, white back, white forward, black back, all day long watching soap operas. Soul poppers, Miss Rita called them. I guess there was plenty Miss Rita helped Mawmaw with—folding laundry, shelling peas, collecting eggs from the chickens, peeling shrimp. But I remember them most clearly in those chairs, rocking away and arguing about the existence of evil twins.

Mawmaw died when I was twelve and Miss Rita went right on living. Now Miss Rita spends her days in a nursing home, sitting one-legged in a wheelchair, watching TV alone. The newspaper reporters invariably describe her as slightly incoherent but happy, like a retarded child who doesn't know she's been handed a tough lot in life.

Daddy used to visit her a lot, which is where I picked up the habit, but not so much since he remarried fourteen years ago. I asked him about it once, but he didn't want to talk about it.

I walk into Miss Rita's room. She's facing the window, her head thrown back on her shoulders, eyes closed, mouth opened, a little string of drool hanging down onto the T-shirt she's wearing—a wet splotch sits right in the middle of Malcolm X's forehead. Not quite what he had in mind when he uttered the words printed on the shirt: "By any means necessary." The left leg of her jeans is rolled up and pinned to where the knee should be. It's what she's worn since the amputation ten years ago. The orderlies would prefer her to wear a robe or a housedress, but I'm sure they found it easier to let her have her way. Her skin's faded in her old age to the color of dirt, and sitting there like that, she looks like a piece of discarded furniture.

A rap song blurts from the radio; every other word is bleeped out for airplay and I can still make out the phrase "Bitch, I'ma kill you." One of the orderlies must have been listening to it. I twist the radio's volume knob and Miss Rita moves.

"Boy, you better put my program back on." Her voice is a whisper of its former self, but it still demands respect. She told me once when I was a child, "Never, ever fear no man. You fear God, but no man. God. And Miss Rita, too. Boy, you better watch out for me, too."

"You sure you don't want some Cajun or zydeco music, Miss Rita?"

"Yeah, I'm sure I don't want no Cajun or zydeco music. Your mawmaw made me listen to that for thirty years. Tired of that noise. Now put that radio back on 95.5 before—" she says, but falls silent as the door swings open and Marie pokes her head in. "Yall doing okay?"

"Just fine," I say. Miss Rita's head falls to her chest. She's all smile and drool and babbling while she picks at some imaginary spot on her T-shirt. "Just having ourselves a little visit."

When the door closes, Miss Rita's head snaps back up. "You bring my stuff?"

"Yeah, I brought it. You sure you should be drinking this?"

"You sure you should be putting your pecker in them little boys' behinds?" she shoots back at me, and starts cackling.

"Now, c'mon, Miss Rita," I say, blushing for no good reason.

"Now, c'mon nothing. You quit bugging me about my little medicine, then. Same thing every time. I'm the one a hundred years old. Think I know what I should and shouldn't do. Lotta good not drinking did your mawmaw."

"But what about the cracklin's? All that salt and fat. You don't even have teeth to chew them with."

"I got gums. All I need. Now give." I hand her the bottle in its little purple sack and the brown bag already going transparent from the grease. "All them years of dumping them bowls of okry gumbo your mawmaw tried to force you to eat and this is the thanks I get? You getting on my case all the time?"

She has me there. She was my only ally in the battle against Mawmaw and her okra gumbo. Any other gumbo I loved—chicken and sausage, gizzard and hearts, seafood, squirrel. But okra? No way. I could write sermons about the pure evil that is okra. Fry it, sauté it, cover it in sugar and chocolate, or wrap it in bacon, but no way is anyone going to convince me that okra, especially in its slimy gumbo manifestation, isn't concrete proof that Satan walks the earth.

Miss Rita's hands stop trembling after she takes possession of her gifts. I half expect her eyes to bug out and for her to start hissing and talking about her "precious."

Strong from years of work—picking cotton, shelling peas, snapping beans, smacking kids—her fingers make quick work of the plastic seal and cap on the bottle. I remember those fingers taking hold of my ear and dragging me off for a switching.

She takes a slow pull, says, "Ahhhh," and smacks her lips before placing the purple Crown Royal bag into a cookie tin with a nest of others like it. I wonder who her connection was while I was away at seminary, but I don't bother asking. "None of your damn business," is the reply I'd get.

She takes another pull from the bottle and pops a cracklin' into her mouth, rolls it around, and sucks on it noisily.

"Mmmmmmm-mmm. Never get tired of that," she says, slapping her knee.

Our little ritual over, she turns her full attention to me.

"Now, what's your problem, boy?" She nods at a calendar on the wall. A twenty-something black man in a fireman's hat and a Speedo lies stretched out on a rock. "You a week early for your regular visit."

"I can't come at other times?" I counter.

"You can come any time you want, as long as you remember to bring me something. Now, what's your problem?"

"I don't know," I say. And I don't. Well, I do. Kind of. Three months into my first solo assignment, just twenty minutes up the road in Grand Prairie, Louisiana, I've grown bored. Absolutely and utterly bored. But I didn't come here to whine about malaise to a woman whose mother was born a slave.

No. The problem is boredom leads to other problems of the heart and soul and mind—or, in my case, the optical system. I've been seeing things. Well, one thing in particular: a red blur flitting around the church, always near the edge of the grounds, in the trees or by the road. I'm pretty sure it's not a ghost. If it is, it's a peculiar one that avoids the cemetery and the inside of the church. At first, I told myself it was simply a trick of the eye—a butterfly flitting by, a red leaf on the wind. Lately, I've grown partial to the theory that it's a symptom of a massive brain tumor. I can all too easily imagine how Miss Rita's going to respond.

But there's no need—or time—to explain. She's quick with her own conclusion: "What you need is a woman." She points a bony finger at me.

A woman? Mama doesn't even bring that one up anymore. Besides, that's the last thing on my mind. A woman? That part of my mind has been cauterized.

"Can't have a woman," I say.

"Don't matter. You still need one."

"Well, it does matter. I'm a priest. Can't have one."

"Them Baptist preachers over at Zion got women. Hell, that main one there got him three or four from what I hear."

"Them Baptist preachers don't let their people drink."

She pauses for a moment, takes another sip, and fixes her eyes on me. "I bet you a woman do you a lot more better than a beer anyway."

"Hmmph," is all I can think to say.

"You not one of them likes men or little boys?"

"No, Miss Rita," I snap.

"Hey, now. Just checking. You never know these days. You never know. But Lord, it'd kill your mawmaw if she wasn't dead already."

"Well, she'd be fine because I'm not."

"There's your problem, then. Need a woman. Ain't natural for a man to be without a woman. Bible says so."

"The Church says—" I start.

"The Church nothing. I had the Bible read to me about five thousand times in my life. Ain't a damn thing in there about priests not getting married."

When did she become a theologian? Of course, she's right. Nothing in the Bible about it at all.

"Look. I can't. Okay? It's the rules. That simple."

"Hmmph. Rules say you can't have altar girls, either."

She glares at me. I glare back. I never told her about the altar girls. Which means I've become a rumor already. The new priest in Grand Prairie adding another chapter of crazy to that little town's history. She pops another cracklin' in her mouth and takes another swig of whiskey. She wipes her mouth with the back of her hand, bobs her head in rhythm with the hip-hop coming out of the radio.

"There's nothing in the rules against altar girls," I say. "Besides, I couldn't find any boys."

"Wonder why," she says. "Some strange man living alone in the woods without a wife. I wouldn't let my sons go around him, either. People read them stories, you know."

"But they trust me with their daughters?" I say, knowing full well what the response is.

"Probably didn't even cross their mind you'd be interested," she says, laughing again.

At this point, she's already enjoying herself at my expense far too much, so I decide to save my ghost story for another time. "I'm sure there are other good explanations," I say, not entirely convinced myself.

"There always is an explanation, isn't there? Well, I got a simple one for you. You need a woman."

The last thing I want lousing up my life is a woman. I don't want one and don't need one. Miss Rita is wrong about that. Wrong as a Scientologist. Forget the rules of the Church. I like my life simple, and simplicity is the last thing I associate with women.

Yet now, at this very minute, I have two women-in-training traipsing about my altar, their fruit-scented shampoos making it next to impossible to stay in that space I inhabit when I'm saying Mass—the zone, if you will.

I'd waited a month, an entire month, before asking for altar boys. To be honest, I don't really need them. But the altar felt naked without them. Besides, the priests in all the other parishes have them. So I put a notice in the church bulletin and made a few announcements during Mass.

The following Monday, a young girl with strawberry blond hair knocked on my door.

"Yes, my child?" I asked in my most priestly voice, immediately feeling like an ass. Thirty-two years old and there I was saying, "Yes, my child?"

"Mama sent me to help you. Daddy said it was okay."

"Help me? With what?"

"I don't know," she said, shrugging. Her thick accent made it sound like a one-word question, Ahduhno? "With the altar and stuff, I guess."

"Really?" was the only thing I could think to say. I had her write her name and number down and told her I'd call. Denise Fontenot. She dotted the *i* in Denise with a heart.

Five more girls followed, all about thirteen. Two for each Mass. Not one single boy.

And now, instead of focusing on the Blessed Sacrament of the Eucharist, I'm overly aware of my surroundings.

This is not a good thing in St. Peter's Roman Catholic Church in Grand Prairie, Louisiana. Doubly so at the Saturday evening Mass, when the old-timers stroll in out of the woods.

For example, in any other congregation, the old man burping in the fifth pew, on my right hand side, would send a ripple of arched eyebrows, turned heads, and covered giggles through the church. But not here. Mr. Boudreaux can sit there and let one rip, his big owl eyes blinking away like all's just peachy keen.

Then a fart echoes from one of the pews to my left.

No one seems fazed by this. The only two people in St. Peter's who seem to notice at all are the Smith boys, who attend twice a month when they're visiting their father out here in the sticks. I feel for those two boys, spending a Saturday night in the Grand

Prairie wilderness while their friends are getting pizza delivered to their front doors in Opelousas.

Opelousas, twenty minutes down the road via the Ville Platte Highway, is where I grew up. With a population of fifteen thousand people, we were a veritable metropolis. And we had a name for places like Grand Prairie: Bumfuck, Egypt. Bumfuck. A good word to be thinking while saying Mass. Good work. The Lord, no doubt, is smiling upon me.

Luckily, the seminary doesn't just toss you into the world without a lot of practice, and the words coming out of my mouth are holy, sanctified, and expected.

"Bless and approve our offering. Make it acceptable to You, an offering in Spirit and Truth." (And please, God, forgive me for my wandering mind and for Your sake, my sake, the congregation's sake, get me back on track here. Have that little white bird of yours flit back down here and roost in my head.)

But the truth is, once I lose the path, it's hard to regain. While my mouth keeps motoring along, my mind wanders.

The church building itself doesn't help. Of all the churches in all the towns in Louisiana. I was hoping for a cathedral; I got stuck with a gussied-up bingo hall, one of those unfortunate low-ceilinged '60s constructions. The heavy timber beams bracing the roof are the only things even remotely "majestic" about it. Threadbare carpeting covers creaky wooden floorboards. The Way of the Cross marches down either wall in simple formation. There they are, the last, most painful hours of Our Lord and Savior Jesus Christ done up in fourteen plastic "sculptures" all made in Taiwan.

Near the main entry is the church's namesake, St. Pete, concrete done up in paint, his eyes directed woefully toward the scrawny but suitably gruesome crucifix suspended by wire directly above me.

"Let it become for us the Body and Blood of Jesus Christ, Your own Son, our Lord," I say.

St. Pete's eyes bug me. Too much like an understudy watching the lead actor onstage, mesmerized by his idol but hoping for a tragic accident all the same. I'm tempted at times to wheel that statue of St. Pete out to the front of the church, where an older version of himself, this one done in white plaster, is nailed to an upside-down cross. That'll show him. But who knows? Maybe he'd be glad to see it. Maybe it would tickle him to know that when we were kids we were convinced the upside-down crucifix was the welcome shingle for a satanic cult. But I doubt it. St. Peter never struck me as the type to have much of a sense of humor.

To my right and facing the gathered flock is Mother Mary. Now, her, I like. She's the one truly beautiful thing in the church. Carved out of cedar and stained rather than painted, she still manages to be more realistic than the rest of the lot—like her husband shoved off in the corner, an afterthought done up in faux marble and chipped paint. In the right light, Mary outshines the tabernacle, which comes as no surprise. I'm not going to admit this sort of thing to some born-again Pentecostal, but in these rural parishes, Mary carries the load. In her simplicity, she sits above that enigmatic Trinity of her Son, His Father, and that little white bird—or whatever it is people imagine the Holy Ghost to be. I spent kindergarten through twelfth grade at a Catholic school, went to seminary to become a priest, and I still have problems wrapping my mind around the Holy Trinity. But everyone understands a mother's capacity for love and forgiveness—and her power over her child.

Mr. Boudreaux burps again, and the Smith boys look at each other, eyes wide and betraying thoughts of strangling their daddy while he sleeps. Divorcing their mother was one thing. Dragging them to this place is unforgivable.

Mr. Devillier, one pew in front of Mr. Boudreaux and three people over, jams his pinky into his ear and gives it a good shake before pulling it out and studying his fingernail.

"Take this, all of you, and eat it," I say.

So much for the miracle of Transubstantiation.

I wrap up the Eucharistic Prayer, lead the flock through the Lord's Prayer, and make it to the Breaking of the Bread with no incident.

"This is the Lamb of God who takes away the sins of the world," I say. I hold up the jumbo wafer for all to see. "Happy are those who are called to His supper."

"Lord, I am not worthy to receive you," they all reply like good little lambs. "But only say the word and I shall be healed."

I break the wafer into the platter that holds the smaller, uniform ones I'll administer during Holy Communion. I chew and swallow my piece and I feel a calm working through me. I wouldn't expect some random heathen or some Bible-thumping Tammy Faye to believe or understand. A runner, maybe. I've heard of runner's high and that's how I try to describe it, although I've never run anywhere near far enough to experience anything more than runner's aches, runner's cramps, and runner's vomiting. But whatever it is, it's working. I can feel I'm slipping back into my zone, my plane of worship.

I reach for the wine chalice, bring it to my lips, and, *bam!* I've lost it again.

Grape juice! Son of a bitch!

It's all I can do not to wince. I never did like grape juice. Vile, nasty, sickly sweet purple scourge of the fruit-juice set. Yes. I know. By this point in the ceremony, it's supposed to be the blood of Jesus, and the flavor shouldn't matter.

But still.

I shoot a glance over the chalice rim at Denise Fontenot, standing there decked out in the white robes that belong on a nice, obedient, unscented altar boy.

She's the one, the thorn in my side. The very picture of innocence if she weren't Satan incarnate. I swear she was watching me for a reaction just now. There's no other explanation.

She had to have switched it purposely. Or else she somehow, impossibly, after being told twice before, confused my cardboard box of Franzia with one of the plastic bottles of grape juice that dear departed Father Carrier left behind.

I suffer through the rest of the grape juice. It's not even good grape juice—if there is such a thing. It's that Sam's Choice garbage from Walmart. I shudder to think where Walmart gets its grapes.

Bad wine I can stomach. I belonged to a group in seminary who theorized that Transubstantiation was all the more miraculous if you had to turn really cheap wine into the Blood of Christ. One guy, who was probably a self-flagellating Calvinist in a previous life, planned to torture himself weekly with Thunderbird (Fortified by Christ!) even if it did render him blind within a year. Grape juice was the last resort of recovering alcoholics, God have mercy on their souls.

As I wipe the rim of the chalice, I look over at Denise again. Is that a smirk? I look over at the other altar girl, Maggie Deshotel, for some sort of comparison. But as usual, she simply seems sleepy. I worry that one of these days she's going to pitch right over, split her head open, and I'll have little-girl blood pooling all over the sacred altar of Jesus. I look back at Denise, who seems very pleased with herself.

Denise has been acting a little weird lately. Squirrely, maybe? Or kittenish? Is that the word I don't want to acknowledge? She's been bumping into me on the altar. Her palms have been a little clammy, her grip a little too firm, a little too slow on the release during the Sign of Peace. Or maybe I've just lost my mind. Maybe I'm just imagining these things.

I manage to conclude Mass without verbalizing anything I'm actually thinking. I hate to run things on autopilot, but at the moment I'm more than thankful for the ability. I follow the two girls down the aisle and through the front doors. Denise hugs me around the waist—a new development—says "Bye, Father Steve," and runs off with Maggie.

I make my usual round of handshakes, hugs, and headpats. The old men say little. A handshake and maybe a "How you, Father?" or a "Comment ça va?" before going to their trucks and Suburbans, where they stand around talking the serious business of farming, hunting, and dirty jokes. Their wives stay behind, clucking with each other and fighting for my attention.

This is a fine art, this making old women happy, playing to their individual egos without permanently offending the rest of the gaggle. In a way, I'm their rock star, they are my groupies.

Tonight, I have to thank Miss Robichaux for the pork roast she dropped off this afternoon. While I'm doing this, I notice Denise and Maggie, now in jeans and baby tees, being chased through the parking lot by Sammy Guidry, a gangly boy still at an age where he hasn't figured out why he's been chasing girls his whole life, an age where he wouldn't know what to do with one if he caught one. Both of the girls are laughing, their cheeks red. I'm watching this action over Miss Robichaux's head when Denise looks directly at me.

"I'll tell you a secret, Miss Robichaux," I say, returning my eyes to hers, stage-whispering loud enough for her friends to hear. "That was the best—and I mean the best—piece of pig I ever had in my life. And don't you go repeating that anywhere near Opelousas, because my mama'd like to kill me if she heard me saying that."

Miss Robichaux blushes and giggles. Even through the Avon base she has caked on, her cheeks turn the same gaudy red she's died her hair. It's the same look Mawmaw wore to church when she was alive—Louisiana old lady.

"Aw, now, Father. You stop that," she says, and makes a show of slapping my chest, a bit of the teenager she once was apparent in that gesture.

* * *

After the crowd departs, I stand alone in the parking lot watching the sun set over the graveyard, a small intimate plot just to the west of the church. Only a few of its bodies are shelved aboveground. The land here is high enough, the water table low enough, that we don't have to worry about flash floods filling the graves and squirting fifty-year-old caskets out of the ground like watermelon seeds from the mouths of children.

This has become common practice for me, standing here after Saturday evening Mass, watching the sun set through the moss-draped live oaks, painting the headstones a soft salmon color.

A car pulls into the lot behind me. I don't turn to face it. I know it will stop five inches from me. I can feel the heat of its grill on the back of my legs. When the door opens, I hear the distinctive *bling-blong, bling-blong* of a mid-'90s Buick.

"Hey, Vick," I say as she slides up next to me. She hands me a lit cigarette.

I give her a once-over before turning back to watch the sunset. She's wearing jeans and an unbuttoned man's jacket over a white tee. Her blond hair just barely reaches her shoulders and her dark skin looks good in the dying light. She's a smidge taller than me, but I don't hold it against her.

"What's on the agenda tonight?" she asks.

"Just a silent moment of reflection."

"Mass a bit of a distraction?"

I don't know how she does this. I've known her for only three months, but she seems to have the ability to read me like a book, a book not all that complex or layered, a catalog maybe.

"Denise give you grape juice again?" is her follow-up question.

"Yup."

"I told you to throw it all out."

We watch the top edge of the sun slip below the horizon.

"She hugged me tonight."

This, Vicky finds hilarious.

"Don't know what we're going to do with you, Padre." She likes to do that, use cute little priest names for me. She's a little over-comfortable around priests, probably because she's the daughter of the last one who worked here.

I'm still trying to wrap my head around that one. Vicky's my age. We'd heard rumors of her existence over in Opelousas when I was a kid. But rumors are a dime a dozen the world over and go at an even cheaper rate down in these parts. It's one thing to hear a rumor, another to meet one.

It's her old man I replaced, so she's been helpful, my own Encyclopedia Grand Prairieca, Chamber of Commerce, and default St. Pete's church lady.

But she can also be a big pain in the ass.

"I told you not to try getting altar boys," she says, pulling a beer out of her jacket pocket and offering it to me. "Daddy didn't use any."

"I figured Father Carrier didn't use altar boys because he saw it as an unnecessary luxury."

"Daddy? Ha."

Daddy. The word didn't sound right coming out of her mouth. It sounded like the wrong answer to a bad brain teaser. What can always be a father but never a daddy? A priest. Then Paul Carrier went and screwed everything up (not that he was the first by any stretch of the imagination). When I heard Vicky say Daddy, I imagined some sort of reverse virgin birth, something out of Greek mythology. Father Carrier still full of youth, but lonely in his marriage to Christ, shuffling to the tabernacle on Sunday morning wondering if he can stand an entire lifetime in this profession. He opens the tabernacle door and, lo, within is a girl child, cooing and giggling at him. Of course, that's not the way it happened at all; Father Carrier preferred to conceive his child the old-fashioned way.

"Daddy," she was saying. "He might have said something like that. But he would have had seven or eight of them little bastards up there at one time if he could have found them. Hell, this was the same man who replaced the priest's chair with a La-Z-Boy."

"Why didn't he use girls?"

"I think Daddy had enough on his hands with me. Also, it's just not a bright idea to put pubescent girls in the same room with a horny old goat."

"Now, just a minute," I protest.

"Simmer down, sailor," she says, laughing again. "I was talking about Daddy. Then again, them little girls running around that altar seem to get your blood boiling." Her hands are in her pockets now. She rolls up onto her toes, then back to her heels a couple of times. It's sort of a mannish gesture, one that says, "Yes, my boy, I know you're in a pickle and I'm just pleased as I can be about the whole thing."

"Give me a little credit, Vick."

"All I'm saying is it can't be easy."

"That's part of the point, I think. It's not supposed to be easy. Besides, I made it this long, I think I can make it another thirty years."

"You expect me to believe you've gone your whole life without?"

"I expect you to believe what I tell you," I say, giving her what I imagine to be a rakish grin.

"Okay, stop that. You look like you're in pain. But, seriously, another thirty years? You're not giving yourself a very long life."

"I'm hoping the equipment will give out by then and I won't have to worry about it anymore."

She laughs. I laugh. But I'm not joking half as much as she thinks I am.

"Well, I'm going inside," I say. "Going to watch *Touched by an Angel* or something."

"So that's what angels are for?" she says, trying to keep a straight face but failing miserably. I would have laughed—I walked right into that one—but she's so pleased with herself that she's bending over at the waist and laughing too hard at her own joke.

"Shit, Padre," she says. "Sorry. I couldn't help myself."

I turn away and face the one streetlight in the parking lot, where the nightly drama of bats chasing moths is unfolding.

"Aw, c'mon, Steve. Look, I'm sorry. I'm just messing with you. That was a good one. You have to give me that much." She's almost pleading.

"Okay. It's a good one. Ha. Ha. Now I'm going inside. You're more than welcome to come in."

She stands straight. "I'd love to join you, but I have to head into town. Big Saturday night."

When was the last time I had a big Saturday night? When was the last time I had a Saturday night?

She picks a moth off my shoulder. After releasing it, she smoothes out the spot on my robe where it was sitting. "Yeah, I promised Mama and the girls I'd go play cards with them."

Oddly enough, I find it harder to imagine her mother, a woman I've actually met, than her father. Grace was never more than a minor character in the rumor, so maybe that's why it's hard to deal with her in terms of reality. It would be like running into Jesus one day and when he introduces you to a parent, you get stuck with Joseph instead of Mary.

We say our good-byes and she drives off into the night. As she's pulling out of the driveway, I see the flit of red again, this time across the highway about half a mile down in the gathering shadows of dusk. For a second, it looked like a girl wearing a red cape and hood. But just like that, it's gone. I rub my eyes, blink, and look again. Nothing. Probably just residual red in my eyes from Vicky's taillights.

I go to the vestry and help myself to a large glass of un-blessed Franzia before putting away my overlay, taking off my collar, and heading to the rectory.

Chapter 2

They told me before my placement to expect such moments, that I'd get a little loopy sometime around the fifth month, sooner if plopped into a small rural parish. I'm nothing if not punctual. There's even a hotline I can call.

One of the seminary instructors, Father Benjamin Snyder, had warned me of the "dangers" of working in a small parish.

I laughed in his face. "You're kidding me, right? Priests back home are minor celebrities," I said. "They get fat on the meals cooked just for them. Besides which, every town in Louisiana has more than one church. I can always just hang out with the other priests. Just like here."

"You'll see," Father Snyder had said, with a thousand-yard stare that should have been warning enough. "You'll see."

Oh yes, I have seen.

First, I saw my blind spot. Yes, proper towns have more than one church. But if Louisiana lacks one thing, it's an abundance of real towns. How could I have forgotten this? As a kid, I was dragged around the state to one godforsaken hamlet after another in the service of visiting distant relatives with my dad, the family's self-appointed missionary. Those little towns. Three intersections, one convenience store, and, halfway between one village and the next, the church they shared. It inspired in me an overwhelming claustrophobia—or was it agoraphobia?—and a need to escape to something grand.

I got grand all right.

Grand Prairie. Plenty of horses. One church. We don't even have a convenience store. I have to drive fifteen minutes to get a Coke and a pack of Camels.

And yes, I'm a minor celebrity. I was right about that much, at least. I don't cook for myself because these old women can't get enough of me. They send their husbands to take care of the church lawn, their grandkids to wash my car.

But what's becoming increasingly clear is that I'm the shepherd of a flock that does little more than the requisite bahhing. They're good people. Good and simple. Good and simple and boring. My Dear Lord, forgive me, but, man, are they boring!

I suspect that's what Father Snyder, who himself had served a small-town church for twenty-five years, had been trying to warn me about.

If nothing else, I expected to be tutored in the ways of the common man, schooled in the philosophy of folk wisdom. But either movies about common folk are far, far off base or the good people of Grand Prairie aren't living up to their part of the bargain. They farm, go to work in Opelousas, eat too much, sleep just enough, and spend time with their families. Some have an easy time of it, others make a mess of it. But no one seems to be following a secret code of simple people.

And other priests? Of the four in Opelousas and the three in Ville Platte, five are too busy with their big fancy parishes, with all those weddings and baptisms and confirmations and funerals. Another is about as stimulating as decaffeinated coffee and carries on way too much about his mother. And the seventh is a black separatist trying to break from Holy Mother Church while still keeping the church and school buildings for some sort of Black Power commune.

So it's just me. Sometimes Vicky. Sometimes the red thing. I attend to my duties, flirt with the old women who drop by, and stay up too late watching bad TV or surfing the Web. Then I'm up at the crack of dawn for prayers and morning Mass, which is always attended by the same four people: the Holy Trinity and me. It's actually rather nice, the ritual of it, the familiarity of it. But to be honest, I get a little creeped out by the echo of my own voice bouncing around the otherwise silent church. Every time the building settles, I flinch and look around to spot the source of the sound, as if I'll find a ghost in a red sheet bumping around the place or one of the statues taking a leisurely stroll through the pews.

When I first started at St. Peter's, a couple of the hard-core biddies showed up for morning Mass. But there was something slightly embarrassing about it. In a cathedral of appropriate size, there's enough room for each person to create her own personal buffer. But in St. Pete's it feels like we're sharing an intimate moment. The prayers take on the hushed tones of a seduction, the call-and-response portion of some sort of holy, private flirtation. One morning, I made eye contact with Miss Emilia Boudreaux and a blush bloomed from her neckline straight up to the roots of her hair. They'd all rather flirt outside of Mass, I guess, because she quit showing up after that, and so did the others.

So now I have the Masses all to myself. It took some getting used to at first. Sitting alone and silent for the Adoration of the Eucharist is one thing—chilling with the J-man, we called it back in seminary. You sit or kneel in private with the Eucharist, wrapped in silence, contemplating Christ—or, depending on your lack of focus, the art on the wall, how funny chimpanzees are, or whether ghosts really do exist because you swear you just heard something moving in the dark corner of the church for the fifth time.

Mass is different. It involves at least thirty minutes of formalized religious ceremony and public speaking—minus the public. When I first did it alone, I was overly conscious of my movements and how silly I must look, raising my arms up into the air, praying out loud, and saying, "Peace be with you," the only response the dead-eyed stares of the sculpted saints. As time went on, it felt less like mental masturbation and more like meditation. Now it seems an especially tranquil way to start the day.

This morning starts out no differently and finds me standing in an empty church reading aloud to myself from 1 Corinthians.

That's a meaty one, all about spiritual perception and receiving wisdom and those in the world who are limited to believing only what they can see with their eyes, touch with their hands. Some folks always think of scientists when reading this passage, but in my limited experience with scientists, many of them seem to feel like the more they learn, the less they know.

The Gospel reading is from Luke, in which Jesus goes down to Capernaum and starts casting demons out left and right.

Then I see it.

A little girl, all in red, her pale white face pressed to the door, her dull eyes staring, staring.

"Son of a bitch," I say, dropping the Bible to the floor.

"Shit," I say, and bend immediately down to pick up the Good Book, my hands shaking violently. When I stand up, it—she—is gone. I run to the front door. Another flash. Off to the left on the highway. That's it. I'm getting to the bottom of this. I run out to the car. I don't have my keys. I always take them out of my pocket so that they don't jingle during Mass. "Fuck," I whisper, and run back into the church. As I'm doing so, I hear a faint clopping sound drawing near. "No, no, no. Not today," I mutter, casting about wildly for my keys. But once I find them and get back out to the car, the clopping—hooves on asphalt— is distinctively clear and growing closer.

By the time I have the car backed up and turned around, it's too late. Lem Landry and his horse-drawn hay wagon are upon me, cruising down the highway at a blistering five miles per hour. Bastard. Once a year, a reporter-slash-photographer from the *Daily World* will trek out from Opelousas to take a picture of Lem going down a dirt road in his wagon. And Lem, in excruciatingly broken English, will smile and tell the reporter how Lem's granddaddy made the wagon by hand and how he, Lem, lives in the woods and survives on the squirrel, rabbit, and catfish he kills or catches and whatever his wife grows in the backyard. And he always apologizes for his bad English " 'cause we don't got much use for it back here."

I wonder why the paper doesn't just keep the story on file instead of sending someone out every year to be lied to. Because it is a lie. And not just a little lie. To borrow an expression common to the area, it's a *damn* lie.

As anyone in Grand Prairie could tell any reporter interested in doing more than a fuzzy feature piece, Lem Landry bought that wagon at a flea market in 1972 and pulled it home with a truck. In fact, sitting in Lem Landry's driveway at this very moment is a sparkling red Ford F-250 Super Cab, which complements his true sweetheart, a 1973 Thunderbird that he drives once a week to Walmart, not half a mile from the offices of the *Daily World.* Once he gets to Walmart, he sits in the concession area with a bunch of other old farts and shovels the bullshit until it's knee-deep. Furthermore, said shit-shoveling is done in perfectly fine English, the only flaw being that Lem never did get a firm grasp of correct pronoun usage, referring to everyone and everything as "he," even if speaking about a "she" or an "it."

Lem prefers Popeyes fried chicken to squirrel and, from what I hear, will only eat squirrel if someone else kills, cleans, and cooks it for him. His wife grows nothing in any yard, gardening being a tough hobby for a woman who's never existed in the first place. Lem, in fact, had been an incorrigible womanizer well into his fifties, taking advantage of the fact that many of the men around here worked two-weeks-on/one-week-off schedules in the oil fields during the boom years. One of the truly amazing things about Lem is that he'd never been shot and left for dead in the woods of Grand Prairie.

Even calling the hay wagon horse-drawn is a bit of a stretch considering Lem insists on using the most stubborn mules he can find. It's as if he goes to farmers' auctions with an eye for the slowest unmovable animals created by God. He even admits that if mules could be bred, he'd get in the business and breed the stubbornest animal he could create just because the entire idea, like suckering newspaper reporters, strikes him as a great laugh.

What also strikes him as a great laugh is driving his buggy down the center line of the highway, seeing how many cars he can get to pile up behind him. Today he's already got a string of six. So even if I got on the highway behind them, it would be nearly impossible to pass them all. That's assuming the red thing is something real, something that can be followed.

So I get out of the car and wave at Lem and the passing parade. Then I head back into the church to finish the interrupted Mass. I mutter my way through the rest of it, embarrassed that I'd let myself get so scared. Even so, I can't help but keep one eye on the door to see if it comes back.

After Mass, I clean up the altar, then halfheartedly clean up the rectory before heading over to the home of Miss Velma Richard for an early lunch.

I've been dreading this one, using all my other invites as excuses, putting off Miss Velma again and again until finally guilt got the better of me.

The thing is, Miss Velma smells familiar. Mothballs, cigarette smoke, and canned cat food. It's the smell of old, the smell of loneliness, the smell of defeat. And the Avon perfume she douses herself with for church can't hide that. It's something worse than nursing home; it reeks of shut-in.

Even the other old birds sort of shun her. They're polite, sure. But after Mass, Miss Velma is always that person just outside the group, standing on tiptoes to see over the back of whoever is blocking her entry into the circle. She listens to the gossip but is never invited to participate. If hyenas roamed the grounds of St. Pete's, Miss Velma would be lunch.

If I haven't exactly done my part, I have an excuse.

When I was a kid, Daddy, good old Steve Sr., dragged me to the outlands to visit an assortment of crazy old aunts and uncles. But there was one in particular, Aunt Gladys, that I've never been able to shake. Daddy always brought Aunt Gladys two cartons of cigarettes along with her inhaler and prescriptions for emphysema.

"It's all she has left," he used to say. And when I whined about going, which was every single time, he'd respond with, "*We're* all she has left."

"Can't you just buy her an extra carton of cigarettes and leave me at home?" I'd said once. His elegant and fitting response was a backhand to the side of my head.

A kamikaze had taken Aunt Gladys's husband, Uncle George, in World War II, leaving her with one child and a hatred for Asians that bordered on the pathological. That child, George Jr., grew up and ran his pickup into a school bus. Drunk and dead at eight o'clock on a Monday morning. With a Vietnamese hooker bloody-faced and babbling in the passenger seat.

But I didn't care. None of that was my fault and it had nothing to do with me. Those trips terrified me.

We'd pull up the dirt drive to a tar-paper shack with a sagging porch. Aunt Gladys would shuffle to the door in a threadbare floral-print housedress and tattered open-toed slippers. She wore no stockings and the sight of her varicose-veined legs is burned onto my retinas to this day.

"Yall come in," she'd say after unlatching the screen door, inviting us into her lair. Cats, like roaches under a light, rushed off into the other rooms, leaving only their fleas behind. Damn cats. We'd sit at the kitchen table under an exposed bulb and I'd immediately start scratching my ankles. I learned after the first time not to wear shorts, but jeans weren't much better. I always prayed I'd get ringworm and Mama would make Daddy stop bringing me around.

While she poured coffee, Aunt Gladys would get the conversation rolling. The same one every time. Dead relatives. No shortage there. And it always ended with her damn fool son. At least George Sr. had died in battle. Why not talk about him? But no, it was always George Jr. "I just thank the Good Lord above he didn't kill any of those kids on that bus," she always said. Never mentioned George Jr.'s passenger, who died later at the hospital.

And the smoke. I like a cigarette now and again. But I don't see how she didn't die of smoke inhalation. She'd blow the first plume of each cigarette straight up into the haze hanging just below the ceiling. I've seen college bars with less smoke in them. For whatever reason, she never opened her windows. Perhaps she was one of those old ladies who thought the elements—rather than three packs a day—made a person sick. The place was always shut down tight. During the summer, it was freezing from the unit rattling away in the kitchen window. Worse was during the winter, when the wall-mounted gas heaters hissed away, backed up by two or three electric space heaters.

All things considered, it was only fitting that one cold winter night, the house blew up with Aunt Gladys in it.

"At least it was quick," was what Daddy said.

Yeah, if you didn't count the twenty-some-odd years of sitting alone in that kitchen, waiting to die. God have mercy on her soul.

So when I pull into Miss Velma's dirt drive and park behind her '70-something Toronado, I ask God for an easy afternoon, for Him to instill in me whatever spirit had moved Daddy to make those trips all those years ago.

"It's your job," I remind myself as I consider the squat house on its stubby concrete blocks. I know that after all is said and done, I'll feel better for having visited, feel that inner glow of a job well done, of doing something no one else wants to do, bringing joy into another person's life. The porch isn't sagging at least.

A cat darts out from under Miss Velma's car and dashes under the house.

"Christ," I say.

"Please help me," I add as an afterthought, but I'm not fooling either of us.

I skip the front porch and walk to the door just off the driveway. Miss Velma answers wearing a pantsuit. Not a varicose vein in sight. Her hair is combed neatly and she has a light dusting of makeup. She's even wearing shoes.

As she holds the screen door open to let me in, an orange cat runs up the steps and into the house.

"Uh-oh," I say.

"Aw, that's Meenoo. I can't keep that one out of the house," she says with a laugh.

I step into Miss Velma's kitchen. Bright light reflects off the recently mopped linoleum. A cigarette burns in an ashtray next to the sink, but a small fan is blowing the smoke out of the window. Meenoo rubs against a door opening onto the rest of the house and Miss Velma opens it a bit. The cat disappears into the darkness of the other side. I wonder if Miss Velma simply cleaned up the kitchen, shoved all of her mess into the other part of the house.

"I hope you don't mind the smoke," she says.

"Not at all," I reply. She's trying. "I just might join you," I add, reaching for my pack. I don't like to smoke in front of the flock, but it might make her feel a little more at ease.

She offers me coffee. I scratch my left ankle with my right foot out of some conditioned response. The smell of mothballs and cat food is here in the kitchen, but it's being held at bay by candles and incense.

I notice, too, that the stove is bare. Nothing bubbling or simmering or warming. The oven knob is in the off position. Nothing in the sink and nothing in the draining board. That's just not right.

Miss Velma hands me a cup of coffee and puts a Tupperware bowl of sugar and a jar of powdered nondairy creamer on the table. Coffee is good. I like coffee. But I swear she'd said lunch. My stomach growls as if in agreement.

I say nothing about the apparent lack of food and sip my coffee. We start talking and it isn't long before her story comes spinning out. Born and raised on a Grand Prairie farm, married young to a good man, a farmer who later became a bus driver for the St. Landry Parish school district. They had no children, something wrong with one or both of them. They never bothered to look into it. It was a different time then—just after the last of the orphan trains rolled through south Louisiana and before fertility treatments were as common as cold remedies. If you were barren, you lived with it until God sent down an angel to change you, perhaps striking your husband dumb in the process. Still, they were happy with each other, one of those couples that could have lived forever without the rest of the world and been happy as clams.

Mr. Richard died ten years ago.

"He had a heart attack," she says, blowing out a cloud of smoke. "Right there in bed. It was bad, bad, Father. Thirty-five years I was married to that man and I never seen a look like that on his face. Never seen him cry."

"It must have been hard on you," I say, reaching over and

patting the back of her hand. The move surprises me. I'm not the touchy-feely type, but it strikes me as the right thing to do. It's what priests do in the movies.

She stares down at my hand on top of hers.

"You get used to a person after that long. And then they're gone. You know?"

I don't. I absolutely don't. I live behind a church, by myself. I don't even have a dog. I've only been alive thirty-two years.

But I need to say something. That much is obvious. In the space of seconds, Miss Velma has seemed to shrink. Her shoulders are slightly hunched now and I swear the room gets dim, the smoke starts to collect around us, the old smell of defeat gets stronger.

"I'll tell you what. I'll remember you both in my prayers tonight. And I'll light a candle for Mr. Richard over at the church."

It shouldn't be that simple, but it is.

"Thank you, Father Sibille," she says. "That's so nice of you." And her smile comes back. It's a little weaker, sure, but a couple of kind words from the priest and it was all a little more bearable.

She pats my hand now, stands up, and goes to the fridge.

"I don't cook too much since he's gone, but I still like to make chicken salad. That was his favorite."

"That sounds great," I say. And I mean it. It's not just that I like chicken salad—and I do—but the thought of a light lunch, something cold served on white bread, is somehow liberating. The conversation was heavy enough.

Miss Velma places the large ceramic bowl on the table. The chicken's been shredded down almost to a paste, just the way I like it. She grabs two plates and a loaf of Evangeline Maid bread and is making the first sandwich when someone knocks on the door.

"Miss Velma, what you doing in there, girl?"

"Oh, it's Vicky," Miss Velma says. But I'd recognized the voice immediately.

"Well, that's nice," is all I can think to say.

"Come in, come in," Miss Velma says.

"Hey, folks. Hey, Padre, thought I saw your car out there. Figured I'd stop in and see what kind of party I was missing."

Miss Velma giggles. "Father Sibille, Vicky stops by all the time to say hi," she says with a hint of pride.

"Really?" Well, there goes my beatification, I guess.

"We're just having some lunch, Vick, so you gonna have to stay and eat you a little something," she says, grabbing another plate from the cabinet.

"Okay, but only if you sit down," Vicky says, pulling a chair from under the table and motioning to Miss Velma, who doesn't put up an argument.

With that, Vicky takes over, makes two sandwiches for each of us, fetches a pitcher of iced tea from the refrigerator, and lunch is on. Smiles all around. It's that simple.

Following lunch, Miss Velma and I are enjoying a post-meal smoke and Vicky is washing dishes when she suddenly says, "Little Red Riding Redneck!"

I practically fall out of my chair. "What?"

"A little girl in a red hoodie just rode by on her bike," she says. "Red jacket and long skirt. Weirdest thing. I've never seen her around here before."

"Which way was she going?" I ask, already at the door.

"Toward Ville Platte," she says. "Steve, what's the matter with you?"

"Bye, yall," I shout, and offer no further explanation before running out to the car and nosing it onto the road heading toward Ville Platte. I'm not even a mile down the road when I see her ahead of me, steering her bike with one hand and swinging a stick at the tall grass growing from the ditch running along the shoulder. I drive by at forty miles per hour and glance at her through the rearview mirror. She looks like a normal kid riding her bike on the side of the road. A ghost, she's not. But Pentecostal she does appear to be.

The long hair tied up in a bun. The ridiculously impractical denim skirt. Where the hell did she come from? I didn't think there were many—or any, for that matter—Pentecostals back here.

I keep on driving. I never come down in this direction. All of my house calls so far have been in Grand Prairie proper (as loosely as that's defined) or on the road toward Washington. I slow down to thirty and keep an eye out for a house or gravel road heading off into the woods that could conceivably harbor a nine-year-old Pentecostal girl.

I'm about to turn back after four miles when I see in the distance a large yellow bulldozer worrying a mountain of dirt off the side of a newly laid gravel road in a recently cleared field. A handful of trees—four stately oaks and three pecan trees—have been allowed to live. The trunks of the fallen—those that haven't been hauled off yet—are stacked neatly on timber-hauling beds waiting only for the trucks to come and cart them away. Toward the back of what appears to be a twenty-acre piece of land are the burning remains of pulled stumps.

Sitting under the biggest oak is a double-wide trailer. In front of it are a wine-colored Cadillac, a brand-new Chevy Suburban, and a child's jungle gym. Swinging from the monkey bars is a small, pale redheaded boy.

"What is this all about?" I ask myself.

I'm not exactly proud to admit it, but Pentecostals bug me. Unlike Baptists and Methodists or any other Protestant faith, they simply strike me as traitors. Why? Because my perception, right or wrong, is that many of them—the ones in south Louisiana, at any rate—were born and raised Catholic and then, one day, they turned tail and ran.

And they took Timmy with them.

* * *

Timmy was my best friend in grade school. Before he suddenly changed. Kindergarten through fifth grade we were as thick as thieves. Then one year, he was a week late coming back from Christmas vacation. When he did come back, he told me bluntly: "We ain't Catholics no more. Mama and Daddy switched us to Pentecostal and they say the rest of yall are going to burn in the fires of hell."

How's that for a conversation starter? The details at the time were fuzzy. His parents had converted and adopted a whole slew of weird rules. Out went the TV. Out went the movies. Out went any music other than approved Christian stuff. No more cursing. In other words, out went everything twentieth-century American kids based their friendships on. Hell, Timmy couldn't wear shorts anymore. His sister and mother couldn't cut their hair or wear makeup. On top of that, he had to go to church twice during the week and another two times on Sunday.

Even more mystifying was that he seemed happy about all of this. How could he be? Everything enjoyable in life had been taken from him. Worse, as the weeks went by, as he grew into his new religion and learned its language, he started talking about the Holy Ghost more and informing me that I was going to hell for listening to Eddie Rabbitt's "I Love a Rainy Night." When we went to Mass once a week for school, he'd sit there and watch the priest intently as if expecting him to burst into flames.

"He's the one who's really gonna get it," he'd tell me.

"God, Timmy. Shut up!" I remember telling him one day. "Why do you even come to this school anymore if you're so full up on Holy Ghost? Why don't you go talk in tongues somewhere?"

My words didn't seem to make an impact. "Because it's halfway through the school year, that's why. Once summer rolls around, I ain't ever coming back to this school and I'm never going back into one of those churches. All them false idols drive me crazy."

"False idols? What are you even talking about?" I wanted to know.

"Statues and stuff, dummy. All them saint statues ain't any better than a golden bull."

And that was pretty much the end of it. We tolerated each other until the end of the school year, and I spent more and more time with other friends talking about Transformers and Smurfette and whether country music was even worth listening to. And at the end of the school year, Timmy bid us all good-bye and we never really saw him again.

Of course, with half a lifetime under my belt and a library of gossip at my disposal, Timmy's happiness at the time isn't such a mystery anymore. His parents hit a rough patch when the oil market went under in the '80s. Daddy started drinking. Mommy started yelling. They both started smacking Timmy around. Then one day they realized they needed help or someone was going to get really hurt. Their twice-a-year Catholicism really didn't do much for them. They probably felt they'd have the eyes of the whole parish on them if they started going to church more often. "There's the drunk and his beat-up wife," they'd whisper. A friend of a friend told them about this new church, which just happened to be filled with rules—no drinking, for example—and structure and a whole community of people trying to get their acts together.

As far as Timmy knew, Daddy caught the Holy Ghost and he quit being a mean old drunk. Now, those are results. And it was certainly more than all those statues in the big brick and marble building had ever done for him.

Good for Timmy. And good for the Pentecostals.

Still, they took my friend away from me, the bastards.

* * *

And now they seem to be setting up in my backyard. Across the gravel road from the big trailer under the oak tree where the little boy is playing, there are four more—all double-wides by the looks of them—set at fifty-yard intervals from one another. Each trailer is on its own concrete slab. On the right side of the path, groups of men are knocking together wooden braces where I assume more slabs will go. Clusters of gas and water pipes sprout from the dirt like wildflowers telling me it's just a matter of days before the new slabs are poured and more trailers moved in.

How does this happen? There's a suburb going up back here without me knowing about it?

The bulldozer comes to a jerking halt and the driver climbs out of the cab and stands on the passenger-side tread of the machine. While he considers my car, he pulls a red bandana out of the bib of his denim overalls and wipes his brow. Like meerkats who've detected a hawk, the men working on the slab frames for the trailers all pop their heads up, look to the stopped bulldozer, look at my car, and settle their eyes on the bulldozer man. He waves his bandana at them absently and they go back to their work.

He then flicks a wave my way in hello and motions me over. I ease up on the brake and inch down the drive, watching him the whole way.

I stop the car and walk across the fresh dirt of the field. I feel it sticking to my shoes, but don't look down. I don't want to come off as prissy.

This guy's a mountain of a man, central casting's idea of a Midwestern farmer: barrel-chested, beer-bellied (though if he's Pentecostal, he doesn't drink), a long-sleeve plaid Western shirt poking out from his overalls and wisps of blond hair sneaking out from under his camouflage baseball cap. The cap is the kind with the mesh back, the kind worn ironically by cool kids in big cities. But irony isn't in this man's vocabulary.

He's probably well on the other side of fifty, but despite his age and his size, he hops spryly from the tread of the bulldozer and meets me halfway, offering his hand as he approaches.

"How you doing?" I say.

"Hoo-boy, I tell you. If things got any better, it just might kill me," he answers in a twang much more traditional Southern than the local Cajun. His eyes practically twinkle. He gives my hand a vigorous shake. "I'm Reverend Paul Tomkins," he says.

"Reverend? Is that right?" I say, smiling like an idiot.

"Well, soon to be. Once this here church is finished." He waves his hat back at the bulldozer and mound of dirt behind him as if it's all just some little task to finish in an afternoon, like cleaning the attic or emptying out the garage. "But you can just call me B.P. Brother Paul. That's what the brothers and sisters back in Church Point called me."

"Is that so?" I respond.

"Yup," he says, casting an eye out over the property and hooking his thumbs into his belt loops. "Oh, shoot," he says. "I'm plumb forgettin' my manners today. I didn't even ask your name."

Now it's my turn. "Father Steven Sibille. From St. Peter's just up the road in Grand Prairie. Everybody just calls me Father Steve."

The smile remains fixed on his face but something changes in his eyes. He's examining me now. I've gone from a potential member of his flock to some sort of alien species.

"Is that right?" he says. He looks over at the men working farther back in the field, as if I might run back there and snatch their souls. He turns back to me just as quickly and asks, "Where's your uniform at?" The joke seems to put him back in his good mood.

I force a chuckle. "I left it back at the church."

"Afraid to get a little dirt on it?" he asks.

What's that supposed to mean? I look at him. I can't tell if he's joking or if he's making a statement about the Church. "All that black gets a little hot," I respond. "Besides, I find it makes introductions a little stiff, makes people a little nervous."

"Yeah, funny how that works," he says. He's still smiling at me. I wonder suddenly if he was born Pentecostal or if he's an ex-Catholic with an ax to grind. I smile right back at him.

"Anyway," I say, trying to brush off his comment, "I don't make my way out here that often, but I saw your daughter in the woods behind my house the other day and didn't know quite where she'd come from."

Storm clouds gather in his eyes and suddenly I regret ratting on the child. She'll probably catch a beating tonight. Corporal punishment is one of the few things not forbidden by the faith. Spare the rod, spoil the child, and all that. But his eyes clear up and the smile's back on his face. "Oh, Cindy-bell? She ain't nothin' but a goat sometimes. I swear, that girl will wander all the way to Baton Rouge one day if we don't keep an eye on her. I hope she wasn't botherin' you none."

"Oh no. Absolutely not. She just ran off. I think I might have scared her." I'm starting to realize just how ridiculous this might sound. "And I saw her head out this way, so I followed." Ridiculous or dirty. "So I drove out here to . . ." To what exactly? "To, um, make sure there was somewhere she was running back to."

"Is that right?" he asks, not really expecting an answer. "Just so you know, you don't have to worry about her. She'll always find her way back home no matter how far she wanders. But I can tell her to stay away from there if you want me to."

"No, not a problem at all. She'll just want to watch out in them woods with squirrel season going."

A real smile comes back to his face. "Heck, Father. I'd bet that's what she's doing back there. Practicing."

"Is that so?"

"I've been taking that girl hunting with me since she was knee-high to a grasshopper. And this is the first year I'll let her use her own gun. Her mama ain't too happy with me. But it was pretty much the only way I could get her to move from her little friends in Church Point without her pitchin' a fit and hatin' me for the next six months." He shakes his head. "But that's family for you," he adds.

"Yeah, that's family for you," I say, as if I have any clue at all what he's talking about. Family. So I try to change the subject. "Pretty impressive progress you're making out here."

"You ever hear of the Amish, Father?"

"Certainly. I went to seminary up in that part of the country."

"Ever seen them throw up a barn?"

"Yeah, pretty impressive stuff," I say. In fact, I'd done just that one day. A Catholic farmer down the road from the seminary told us he'd hired a crew of Amish to build a stable and he invited us over to watch. We woke up at dawn and drove down to the site to find them already working. Sunup to sundown with a half hour for lunch. Hammers pounding all day. It was exhausting just watching them.

"I like to tell people we're just as good as the Amish, but twice as fast because we use power tools."

"Well, it definitely isn't a union schedule," I add.

We both laugh, and I hope we're done trying to one-up each other. I don't know if I can compete.

"So what are you planning out here?" I ask. "You building a trailer park?"

"Certainly looks like that, don't it? Just family, though. Me and Christine in that trailer, there. My oldest son and his wife and baby in the next one. My sister and her family in the next.

And her oldest son and his wife in the next. On this side of the street, it's going to be Christine's family."

"Wow. That's a lot of family," I say, impressed and maybe even a little jealous.

"Certainly is. We drive each other crazy every now and then, but I wouldn't have it any other way."

"I bet," I say, but really I have no frame of reference for the things coming out of his mouth.

"That's my boy and some of his cousins getting the slabs ready. And I'm just leveling ground for the church. Once everyone's set up and comfortable, we'll get rocking on that."

"And the church?" I might as well get all the bad news at once.

"Nothing too big or fancy," he says. I see the twinkle back in his eyes and I know what he's going to say next. "Just a little bit bigger than yours, I guess," he says, and gives me a light punch on the shoulder.

I'm sure his laugh is much more sincere than mine. And who is this guy to be touching me, ten minutes after meeting me?

"But seriously? About enough room for six hundred people."

Six hundred people? I whistle. I can't help it. That's a lot of people. A lot of Pentecostals at any rate. I try running my own numbers. I know what the books say. Of the 500 people known to be living in Grand Prairie, I have 475 either baptized or confirmed at St. Pete's. The church only holds 250. Not all of the 475—not even close—actually go to Mass, and those that do are spread out over the three services. A Pentecostal church, of course, would have to be big enough to hold them all at one time because the services are all mandatory. But still.

"Wow. Six hundred. Pardon me for asking, but are there that many Pentecostals back here?"

"Not yet," he says, again offering one of those half-joke, half-gibe responses. "Got quite a few on this end of Ville Platte. Another handful creeping out on the north end of Opelousas, near Washington." He pauses. "Got some others from Church Point and Melville buying up some property in these parts."

"Is that right?" I ask.

"That's what I hear," he says. "Don't know if that'll make six hundred. But I'm an optimist."

"Best thing to be," I say, hardly meaning it. I've got a parish full of old people. I'm afraid I'd lose half of it if a flu epidemic swept through.

"After that," he adds, "you never know who'll walk through the door."

And that remark, I know, isn't a joke at all. They took Timmy. They'll take more.

Chapter 3

I head over to Easy Time to let Miss Rita have a go at me. Of course, that means I have to bring offerings. Whatever Jesus may have thought about pork, Miss Rita is a big fan of the pig and all of its parts. "Everything but the oink," is her summation of the edible nature of the animal. "I'd eat that, too, if they found a way to cook it."

Sadly, the only pork that finds its way onto the menu at Easy Time Nursing Home are the tiny flecks of pink they sprinkle into the split-pea soup. In her first years at Easy Time, Daddy would sneak in pork every once in a while. The baton then fell to me. When I went off to seminary, it fell to Teddy, Miss Rita's favorite grandson. But Teddy was sloppy and got busted by the attendees at the front desk.

Happily, Miss Rita has found another supplier. One who takes the time to double-wrap the pork—once in foil, once in plastic. One who then puts the now less-odiferous offering into a sealable plastic container, which then goes into that official-looking black leather satchel of mine.

The white collar helps as well.

I walk past the front desk, which has now sprouted a crop of little Christmas trees, and offer today's receptionist—a humorless Nurse Ratched sort—my best smile. She waves me on.

I stop outside Miss Rita's door and put my ear to it. I can hear her cackling with laughter to some comedian on television doing a bit about the difference between black people and niggers—a favorite topic of hers.

In the time it takes me to push the door open, she's dropped her chin to her chest and gone into one of her fake stupors. Today she's wearing a shirt that reads *Hi Hater.* I don't know what it means and I'm certainly not going to ask.

"It's just me," I say. "And I still don't understand why you do that."

" 'Cause if it's one of them attendees, I don't feel like them walking in here then wanting to talk to me. I figure if they gonna treat me like a baby half the time, I might as well act like one. Besides, bad enough I have to entertain you today."

"Go on," I say. "You keep that up and I'm not going to share."

She locks her eyes on me. "Don't even play around with me, boy. I might have one leg, but one's enough to kick your ass."

I never get tired of that line. It gets a chuckle out of me every time.

"Yeah, go ahead and laugh," she says, smiling now, her eyes bright with anticipation. As I reach into my bag, she wheels over to her secret stash and produces her bottle of Crown Royal. "Getting low," she says. "Don't forget next time."

"What about Teddy?" I ask as I remove the hunk of pork shoulder from the container, then peel the wrapping from the pork roast.

"Teddy? Ha! Teddy don't drink. Doesn't approve of it. Don't know where he picked that up. That boy's lucky he's family because otherwise I wouldn't let his little butt in here."

The pork, tender enough to break apart with a plastic spork, is still warm. I put it on a paper plate, then produce two smaller plastic containers, one full of rice and gravy, the other full of black-eyed peas with chunks of real bacon.

"Oh my, oh my, oh my," she says, fanning her face. Her eyes well up with tears. "You know what they fed me last night? Steamed chicken with steamed broccoli. Chicken breast!" She spits the words out as if they were bits of the offending food. "White meat!"

I get the food plated, put the plate on a tray, and just as I'm sliding the tray onto the arms of Miss Rita's wheelchair, the door pops open. I freeze. Miss Rita, who's just raised the bottle of Crown Royal to her lips, freezes as well, her eyes grown big for a split second. But just as quickly, she swallows the whiskey, wipes her mouth, and hisses.

"Timeka, get in here and close that door, girl."

I stand slowly and turn around to find a petite black woman—she might be five feet tall if she wore heels—dressed in the white uniform of the attendees. Great.

"Miss Rita!" she stage-whispers. "And, Father. Shame on you! Getting this old lady drunk."

"Don't pay her any mind, Steve," Miss Rita says. "She just came in here to snoop." But her usually blustery tone slips a little. "You not gonna tell on me, are you?" she asks, suddenly serious.

"I should," Timeka says, looking at me. "But I don't like that old cow supervising today. Besides, you made it this far in life. I don't see how it's going to matter now what you eat and drink."

"Amen to that," Miss Rita says, raising the bottle and taking a swig. "Steve, this Timeka. Timeka, this Steve."

I offer my hand. Hers is cool and dry and small in mine. "Hi." She pauses. "Father."

"Nice to meet you," I say, casting a glance at Miss Rita, who's watching us both intently.

"Well, I best be seeing about my rounds," Timeka says, and just as quickly as she'd come, she's gone.

As the door closes shut, Miss Rita suddenly becomes very fascinated with her food and won't look up. Still, I can see the prankster's smile reaching up to grab her ears.

"Really, Miss Rita. You have to give up this foolishness about me getting a woman."

"I don't know what you're talking about," she says. But without looking up she adds, "But I hear she has a thing for white boys. Especially ones in uniform."

"Just stop it. You're wasting your time."

"All's I got is time," she says. "Might as well use it to help you."

"I appreciate it, but I don't need your help."

"No, you need a woman."

I look at her. She looks at me. It's been playful so far, but she's gauging me to see if she can keep pushing it.

"Forget you," she says, finally. "Just keep bringing me my little presents and I'll quit meddling."

"That's so nice of you, Miss Rita," I say. "But we both know that's not true."

She looks up at me, somehow managing to smile while gumming a huge mouthful of pork. She swallows and points at me with the spork. "You right about that. But do us both a favor, boy."

"What's that?"

"Hang around some people your own age. All this time with little old ladies? The rest of it sitting alone out there in the woods? That can't be good for you."

"That's the path I've chosen for myself."

"Well, you better find another one before you end up someplace bad. I'm telling you, go find some friends your own age," she says. "Now, let me eat my food in peace," she adds before turning her full attention to the pork.

"Wonder what them little old white ladies would think, they knew their prize pork roast was going to some old negress?" she says to signal that she's done and ready to get back to minding my business.

"I'm sure my parishioners wouldn't mind at all. There's not a racist bone between them."

"Yeah? Ain't that nice? How many black people yall got back there in Grand Prairie?"

I don't say anything.

"How many they got in Opelousas? About ten thousand? And in little tiny Plaisance? About six hundred-fifty out of the seven hundred people live there? And Grand Prairie? Not a damn one. Boy, I live around here a lot longer than you. Don't be fooled just because it looks hunky-dory back there now."

"Miss Rita—" I start, but she cuts me off.

"Don't Miss Rita, me. Tell me something. They still got that man back there? He'd be pretty old by now. But he spends most of his time hunting squirrel in the woods."

"That describes about half the old men in Grand Prairie."

"Oh, I know that. But come on, boy. You smart. Think about their names. There's one of those names that sticks out."

Part of me wonders how she could possibly know any of the old coots back there, but I start listing out the names in my head. Earl Vidrine. Butch Lafleur. Lem Landry. T-Chew Vidrine. Harold Fontenot. Poot-poot Arcenaux. Then I have it.

"Noose?"

"Funny name, huh?"

"I'm sure it's just a name, Miss Rita."

"Yeah? How you sure? That's an odd name just to get. And certainly no mama's going to name her baby that, even if she's in the Klan."

Noose? The one or two times I've talked to him, he seemed like a nice quiet old man.

"They mighta drawn up their truce a long time ago," she says, "but if black people staying out of a town, there's always a reason for it. Might be safe now. And I'm sure confession ain't exciting as it used to be, but black people are scared of ghosts."

"Should I even ask about anything else?"

"Not if you want to look those people in the eyes every Sunday." She pauses. "But I'll eat their food anyway. They still know how to cook."

I think she might even get more pleasure out of it knowing that it was prepared by an old white woman who's never had a black foot step across her threshold.

"So," she says after taking a nip from her Crown Royal bottle. "What about that old priest's little girl? She should be about your age."

"How do you know about Vicky?" I ask.

"Steve, everybody but the pope knew about that child. Vicky, huh? That her name? Nice name. She pretty?"

"Stop it."

"You didn't answer my question."

"Yeah. Sure. She's pretty. You happy?"

"Be a lot happier if yall start . . . well . . . you know."

"Oh, dear Lord," I say in exasperation.

"Boy, you know you're not supposed to talk like that."

"It'd be a lot easier if I didn't have you driving me crazy all the time."

"Hmmph," she says. "Seems to me if you don't want to be driven crazy, you could find someplace else to go hang out."

"Believe it or not, you're not the only thing driving me crazy, Miss Rita," I say.

"Oh yeah? That Vicky girl getting after you?"

This time I just stare at her, refusing to say anything.

"Fine, then! Deny an old lady her dreams. Now go on. Tell me what's the matter this time."

I tell her about Brother Paul and the Pentecostal invaders, that I'm worried about him coming after my flock.

"I heard about that man."

"You have?"

"Oh yeah. They talking about him all over town. He start out as Baptist, but kept butting heads with people that run that show. So he jumped to Pentecostal."

"So he's not all that great," I say.

"Oh, he is. When he went Pentecostal, he took about a hundred Baptists with him. They say when that man talks, ladies start fainting in the church. I heard him on the radio a few times. That man got a silver tongue. I could practically feel the Holy Ghost coming into the room. I guess he made himself too popular for the Pentecostals, too, because they run him off. Either that or he just took off. But he took his hundred Baptists plus another hundred Pentecostals."

"So, wait, he's not Pentecostal?"

"I don't know what he is. I guess he can call himself Pentecostal. Not like there's a Pentecostal pope gonna go out there and tell him to stop."

"So he doesn't answer to anyone?"

"Just himself and the Lord."

"Great. Now what am I supposed to do? He's building a six-hundred-person church."

"Probably stick in a community center and a bowling alley or something, too," she says.

"Shit."

"Hey, boy," she says. "You know better than to talk like that around me."

"Sorry."

She falls silent for a moment, giving my problem serious thought. She sucks on her bottom lip while she thinks.

"You need you a fair," she says finally. "A festival or something."

"What?"

"Yeah, yeah, yeah. Something to keep your people busy with your church so they don't go running off to his. You gotta give them more than a talking-to on Sunday mornings. And the Good Lord knows you ain't offering them the Holy Ghost. So give them some work to do. Show them a good time."

"In Grand Prairie?" I ask, as if this is a remotely realistic idea.

"If them boys in Plaisance can fill a soybean field with all them people, on the hottest day of the year, for that zydeco festival, you oughta be able to do something with the space you got. You know people around here just looking for an excuse to get drunk and have a good time. You get 'em drunk and play 'em some good music, they might remember all them things the Pentecostals don't let you do."

"I don't know. That sounds like a lot of work, Miss Rita."

"And that's a bad thing? Work keeps a man out of trouble. And trouble sounds like the direction you're heading in."

"Well."

"Just be sure you have it in the fall after things cool down."

"I don't know if I can wait that long, Miss Rita. He's already building a town back there."

"Well, you can't do it in the summer. Somebody gonna catch a heatstroke and die. Guess you better make it in the spring, right after Easter, when everybody had it up to here with being holy. They want to let loose after Lent."

I look at her. She takes a sip out of her fresh bottle of whiskey.

"What?" she asks, pleased with herself.

Vicky's clearing the table after feeding me her version of shepherd's pie: instant mashed potatoes spread over ground beef, canned corn, and canned green beans.

"You can pretend to be a drunken Irish priest," she told me

when she served it. Now she's telling me that my mother must have dropped me on my head when I was a child.

"A festival, Steve? You've got to be kidding me."

I follow her out to the patio, beer in hand, protesting along the way. The truth is, I do need something to focus on, something to occupy my time and distract me from the fact that the world moves on with or without me.

"It'll be something to do. Bring people to Grand Prairie."

"But why? It's not like we even have stores here to draw business to."

I tell her about B.P., that I'm worried he's going to start raiding the flock.

"Steve, you're being ridiculous," Vicky's telling me. "You think this guy will build his church and suddenly everyone's going to abandon St. Peter's and rush over there? I'm pretty sure these old Grand Prairie farts are set in their ways."

"You haven't met this guy, Vicky. He's smooth."

"Smooth?"

"Yeah, smooth. He could probably talk you out of your pants."

"Is that right?" she says, shooting me a look I can't quite translate.

"Look, I don't know. I'm just trying to figure out a way to build a community. A festival seems like a good idea. Besides, it'll be fun," I say.

"It'll be a nightmare," she says. "Either no one will show up and you'll beat yourself up over it or too many people will show up, have too good a time, and the people of this sleepy little village will be upset about torn-up lawns and trash all over the place. Or worse, Steve, what if busloads of black folk turn out?"

"Black folk, Vicky?" I know she's joking. I hope she's joking. "Black folk?"

"Well, if you don't like that, you're gonna like some of your parishioners' names for them a lot less if five thousand show up at once."

"Give them some credit, Vicky. People will like it. It'll be a good time."

"Steve."

"Vicky."

"Steve."

I play my trump card. "It's an excuse to drink."

She shrugs. "Well, I can't argue with that."

We sit silent in lawn chairs. November is having another one of its Louisiana warm fits and it feels like spring. Vicky lights cigarettes for each of us. The patch of field directly in front of us rustles to life and a scrawny rabbit hops onto the back lawn.

"Well, there you go," she says.

"There I go what?"

"The name of your festival."

"Really?" I don't know. Rabbit Festival just doesn't strike me as all that inspiring.

"Everything else is taken," she says. "Jazz. Zydeco. Cotton. Crawfish. Cracklin'. Smoked meat. Sausage. Strawberry. Watermelon. Rice. I mean, the fucking Wagon Wheel Festival, even."

"Guess you're right," I say.

"Damn right I'm right. There you go. Rabbit Festival. Better yet. Le Festival du Lapin or some French crap like that."

It's not poetry but it sounds a little more legit than just Rabbit Festival. Then again, Rabbit Festival has a certain simple charm about it. And I can spell it without a problem.

"Well, Vick, we can't turn back now."

"We?"

"We got five and a half months to make this baby."

"We?"

"Yeah. You named it. You can't abandon it now."

"Do you have any idea what's involved in this sort of thing, Steve?"

"Not at all," I say. "Not a single, little clue."

She wings her bottle cap at the rabbit, sending it off in a brown blur. "You're going to owe me big for this, boyo."

Chapter 4

And already I owe her. Plans for the First Annual Festival du Lapin are getting off to a rocky start. The Web site drew no attention. A note in the weekend bulletin raised fewer eyebrows than a fart during Saturday Mass. Finally, I had to use the old Catholic standby, the guilt trip, by making an announcement during Mass—on a coffee-and-donuts day no less (one weekend a month, makes the kids happy).

I need to work on my guilting skills. All of four volunteers have shown up to this, our first meeting. Miss Emilia Boudreaux, Miss Celestine Thibodeaux, Miss Pamela Pitre, and my favorite altar girl, Denise. Vicky's here as well, but I consider her a conscript, not a volunteer. I even called Miss Velma Richard. She said, "Oh, I don't know, Father. I'll sure think about it." Apparently, she didn't think much of it.

Even the shut-ins are too busy.

We're in my living room. I'm on the couch, Vicky to my right, Denise to my left inviting so much obvious symbolism that the little voice in my head simply says, *Well, that's just about perfect.* The three older ladies are perched on chairs in a semicircle facing the couch. With the exception of Vicky, the four volunteers all seemed a little stunned at first by being in the priest's living room.

But they put that behind them quickly enough so that they can get down to fighting, fighting about the very name of the festival. I suspect this is the first bump on what promises to be a long, substandard roadway.

And to think, just four minutes ago we were all congratulating ourselves on the Rabbit Festival, a great name for a south Louisiana festival. After all, the rabbit is not only a fine animal to eat, it's a fine animal to draw and will therefore lend itself well to T-shirts and balloons and posters and such. Also, rabbits can be petted and raced and adored. Rabbits are more fun than a wagon wheel, more hands-on than a sausage, more interesting than a strawberry. Even the French name for the festival—and every south Louisiana festival worth its salt has to have a French name—is relatively easy to pronounce.

But the rabbit's not the issue. "First Annual" is the issue.

"There's no such thing," Miss Pamela has announced to the room.

She's a scold, plain and simple, the type of woman who might chase little boys off her lawn—not so much because they'll ruin her flowers but because they might break an arm and sue her.

Her lips pinch up after she makes her announcement, and Miss Emilia and Miss Celestine go bug-eyed; they're not quite sure what's just been said. I imagine that a hundred years ago Miss Emilia and Miss Celestine would have been the sharecroppers' wives to Miss Pamela's lady of the big house. About the only thing these three have in common is a preference for sensible shoes and a fierce competitive streak when it comes to proving themselves in the eyes of the Lord. But even there, Miss Pamela's faith seems more rational—German, maybe verging on Lutheranism—whereas the other two are squarely of the superstitious French Catholic variety, a hairbreadth away from voodoo and Santeria. Miss Pamela is a tall, angular woman who favors pantsuits and carries herself like an angry librarian, always on the verge of shushing you. She's the type to invite me to lunch and serve sensible portions on matching plates accompanied by silverware. She speaks in whole sentences consisting of properly used and properly pronounced words, tinged with the slightest hint of a traditional southern accent. And while Miss Emilia and Miss Celestine have been housewives their entire adult lives, Miss Pamela, until last year, had been an English teacher at the Academy of the Sacred Heart in Grand Coteau.

Which is where the problem stems from.

"There's no such thing as what?" Miss Emilia finally thinks to ask.

"There's no such thing as first annual," Miss Pamela tells her. "It's a grammatical impossibility," she adds, looking at the rest of us, daring someone to contradict her.

Miss Celestine looks at me, confusion wrinkling her entire face, like she's just burped up something she doesn't remember eating.

She and Miss Emilia are not the sort to argue in public, much less in front of the priest. They're simple women, short and round and given to wearing the flower-print dresses of your standard-issue Cajun mawmaw. They serve huge portions, fuss over me, insist I eat more, and then send me home with all of the leftovers. Miss Emilia and Miss Celestine speak excitedly in flat Cajun dialect, butchering the English language as needed and falling into French when it suits them.

"Now, Miss Pamela," I start. For some reason, I'm afraid she's going to send me to the board and make me diagram sentences for the rest of the day. But I'm the boss. I think. "I'm sure we can be reasonable."

"Father, I'm sorry. But those are the rules. It can be the First Rabbit Festival, but it can't be the first annual. It can't be annual until it's actually been held in a subsequent year on the same date."

Before I can ask Miss Pamela what the hell she's going on about, Denise jumps in.

"But First Annual sounds better. Sounds more important," she says.

Oh, dear Lord, child, you have no idea what you're playing with here. Look hard enough at Miss Pamela and you can see she was a looker in her day. And if there's one thing an aging beauty queen hates, it's a budding beauty.

"It sure does sound better," Miss Celestine says.

"Yeah," Miss Emilia chimes in.

The two don't look at each other but I can tell they're surprised to be in agreement.

Miss Pamela, though, ignores them. "Whether or not it sounds good to you, young lady," she says, offering Denise a gaze honed over thirty years of teaching uppity young girls, "is irrelevant. It still does not make the construction correct."

"Listen, ladies," I offer. "I think we can reach an agreement."

"Rules are rules," Miss Pamela says, matter-of-factly. End of debate. The Germans will neither compromise nor surrender.

"It's a stupid rule if you ask me," Denise snaps.

"Young lady!" Miss Pamela says, her eyelids snapping up like window shades.

The other two, emboldened by Denise, jump in now and they're all clucking away like hens fighting over a worm. I'd rather try to stop a knife fight than sort this out. I stick an elbow into Vicky's ribs. She shrugs and offers me a smirk.

"C'monnn," I whisper.

She lets me twist a little longer.

"Vicky," I hiss.

"Ladies!" she shouts. Silence comes quickly.

"Yall can argue all day if you want, but apparently yall can't come to a decision." She pauses. "And as chairperson of the festival."

She looks at me to see if I have an objection to this bit of improvisation. Of course I don't. I may be a fool, but I'm not stupid.

"As chairman, I'm saying we go with First Annual."

"Told you so," Denise says. I half expect her to stick out her tongue and say, "Nyaahh."

Miss Pamela's mouth drops, the better to catch her breath before launching into a grammatical sermon. But Vicky raises her hand in a stopping motion.

"Miss Pamela, I understand your point and of course you're right. But the fact is, we do intend to have another festival at the same time next year."

Whoa, whoa, whoa! I hadn't thought of that. What has Miss Rita gotten me into here? The word *eternity* flashes through my mind, suddenly more concrete than it's ever been when I toss it around during Mass.

"And the year after that and the year after that and the year after that. Right, Father?"

"Um, yeah, absolutely," I manage.

"Which," Vicky continues, "technically speaking, means this will be an annual festival. So the way I see it, it's the Annual Rabbit Festival. This just happens to be the first of the Annual Rabbit Festivals, therefore the First Annual Rabbit Festival."

Say what?

Vicky takes out a pen and piece of paper and writes across it *First Annual Rabbit Festival.*

"See? No hyphen between the first and the annual."

Miss Pamela considers the paper.

I have no idea if Vicky's making any grammatical sense at all.

She might as well be scribbling trigonometry formulas for all I'm concerned. But I think Miss Pamela understands she's lost the argument and is being offered the only dignified way out. As it is, no one else in the room knows what's going on at this point.

"I guess I can live with that," Miss Pamela finally says. "Yes. That makes sense."

"Great," Vicky says, but goes on. "Now, Miss Pamela, do you still have that cousin who runs the silk-screening and poster place in Lafayette?"

"Yes. I do. Why?"

"We're going to need someone to do the posters for the festival."

Denise starts to protest. "But I wanted to draw the poster."

I may have told her something to that effect at some point. I put my face in my hands. I can't even look at her. When I do peak through my fingers I can see Miss Pamela's mouth twist into a satisfied smirk.

"Denise," Vicky explains. "A festival poster has to be done professionally. I'm sorry, darling, but you've seen other festival posters. People frame these things. They're collectors' items. I know you can draw, but we need a painter."

Again, I get the sense that Vicky's making this up as she goes along.

"You'll get plenty of opportunity to draw, Denise. There's the local flyers. Menus. Fund-raising stuff. You name it. Then there's the T-shirt design for the kids' T-shirts." Denise's eyes light up at this. "Trust me, kid," Vicky concludes. "By the time we're done, you're gonna have your drawings all over the place, from here to Baton Rouge."

Vicky then turns back to Miss Pamela. "So, we can count on you for running down someone for the poster?"

"Of course," she says, her grammar defeat already forgotten

and an obvious victory over Denise now under her pantsuit belt.

"And, you two," Vicky says, turning to Miss Emilia and Miss Celestine. "You're going to have to round up your troops for baking."

"Oh!" they both say, their eyes dancing at the mere thought of a bake sale.

Bake sales. Plate lunches. The plans go on and on, their voices getting more and more excited as Vicky whips them into a froth. If I slump any more, I'm going to fall off the couch. I can hear a Frankenstein's bunny in steel-toe boots clomping around in the background. Already, the monster's grown out of control.

"Would you stop it with the Pentecostals, Steve? They're not going to come and take us all away." Vicky's chastising me again.

"Crazier things have happened," I protest. I tell her about Timmy.

"Wowwwww," she says. "Your childhood was really traumatic. How you survived is beyond me."

"How about a little more respect?" I say.

"How about a little less sensitivity?" she says, laughing. "And let me be clear, Steve. I'm laughing at you right now, not with you."

"Shut up" is the only response I have.

"Quit pouting," she answers. "C'mon. Let's get these cakes out to the tables."

We're in my kitchen, boxing up the handful of cakes I stayed up baking and frosting last night. It's not another bake sale, thankfully. My festival team is outside in the parking lot holding down the front lines in our barbecue plate-lunch sale. Miss Emilia's husband—known to everyone simply by his last name, Boudreaux—drove up in his pickup at five this morning, pulling behind him a trailer with a fifteen-foot-long smoker welded to it. He's been out there barbecuing ribs, pork steaks, and half chickens since then. Miss Emilia, Miss Celestine, and Miss Pamela, I imagine, were up at the same time starting side dishes: Miss Emilia on baked beans, Miss Celestine on rice dressing, and Miss Pamela on corn bread. The three of them came to Saturday Mass yesterday so they could slave over their stoves this morning. Denise had drawn up flyers and put them under windshield wipers last weekend and last night. She also stapled them to telephone poles out on the highway—as if expecting foot traffic to miraculously appear at some point. Vicky had remembered to stop at the bank to get small bills for change on Friday and, on top of that, ran to Walmart and bought three folding tables, four large plastic garbage pails, and a stack of plastic chairs so that anyone deciding they wanted to eat in the parking lot could do so.

All of which left me feeling a little guilty about doing absolutely nothing. So last night, I ran into Opelousas, loaded up my cart with boxes of Duncan Hines cake mixes and frosting, and spent the night messing up the kitchen and making myself sick eating large amounts of cake batter. I followed the instructions, so they all came out edible even if they don't live up to the standards of "homemade." I just don't want to look at them anymore and my body is craving meat something fierce. It was all I could do to get through services this morning with the smell of barbecue wafting through the doors.

"Steve, these are steady, older people here in Grand Prairie," Vicky's saying as we leave the kitchen. "They're not exactly candidates for the born-again lifestyle. You'll probably hardly ever hear from these Pentecostals. I'm sure they'll stay on their side of town."

"Their side of town? Grand Prairie isn't big enough to have sides."

"If it'll make you happy, maybe you can install some railroad tracks across the highway to mark a clear border. Then you can have a sit-down with the good reverend and just tell him to stay on his side."

"Go on. Joke. But you don't know how these people work."

She stops next to a dirty pickup, one of the many vehicles still in the lot after Mass. There are more cars pulling in, parking on the shoulder of the highway as people line up for Grand Prairie's best barbecue. "Quit being retarded," she says, rolling her eyes.

"Whatever," I say as I brush by her, but draw to a quick halt. "Look," I whisper, as if I've just spotted danger.

"What?"

"It's him."

"Him, who?" she says.

"B.P."

"Be what?"

"Him. The Pentecostal. Right there in the line."

"Get out of here," she says. "Where?" Now she's whispering. We slide up next to another pickup so we can spy without being seen.

"See the little girl with the dirty red hoodie and the Pentecostal skirt and the Pentecostal hair? The big guy right behind her. What are they doing here?"

She stares at them a few moments longer before moving again. "I'm sure they're just here to eat, Steve. Let's go."

We walk over to the serving tables, where I plop my cake boxes down. Denise lifts the cover on one and takes a peek.

"You made these?" she asks, seemingly impressed.

"As a matter of fact, I did," I say. "Want to mark them up to ten bucks a pop and sell them for me?"

Miss Celestine and Miss Emilia are slopping their side dishes into meat-laden containers and sliding them down to Miss Pamela, who drops in a square of corn bread before closing the box, taping it, and writing a *C* (for chicken), a *P* (for pork), or an *R* (for ribs) on the lid and stacking them neatly in rows so the volunteers taking orders can hand them out. When Miss Celestine and Miss Emilia hear Denise ask me about the cakes, they drop their serving spoons for a moment and rush over to make a fuss.

"Oh, Father," says Miss Emilia, "I'll buy one of your cakes."

"I'll buy two," says Miss Celestine.

"Maybe I should get three," Miss Emilia says without even thinking about it.

Miss Pamela, waiting for the assembly line to start up again, smirks at them behind their backs. I feel like a special-ed kid who's managed to make a cardboard Christmas tree without cutting off a finger or eating all of the paste.

"No, no, no," I say. "Yall have done more than enough work, already. I'm not going to start taking your money on top of that."

"Okay, Father," they both say, sounding like two schoolgirls who've just been reprimanded. They shuffle off back to their work and Vicky takes a place at one of the sales tables and starts handing out lunches in exchange for cash and checks.

I notice she's eyeing the Pentecostals, who are about ten people back from the front of the line. I try not to stare, but it's hard to resist. The little girl—Pentecostal Cindy—is doing her own bit of staring, gawking at all the strangers walking by, no doubt fascinated by the short hair and makeup on the women. B.P. has a hand resting on his daughter's shoulder and seems to be making small talk with Bobby Trahan, a man I see in church the one Sunday a month I offer donuts and coffee. B.P. catches me looking at him and offers me a smile and a chin tilt, which I try to answer. Vicky sees the exchange, looks at me, and shakes her head.

And then he's there at the front of the line.

"I'm gonna need me, let's see . . ." He pauses theatrically. "What you say, Cindy-bell? Ten rib lunches. Ten chicken lunches. And ten of them pork-steak lunches. Think that'll do it?"

Everyone in the line stops talking. Miss Celestine, Miss Emilia, and Miss Pam stop serving and turn around to get a good look at the man who's just ordered enough to feed a football team.

The child, who I'm beginning to think is mute, looks over at Denise and points. "Better get three of them cakes, too, Daddy," she says so loudly that everyone from the front of the line to the back laughs.

B.P. laughs, too. "How 'bout we make do with just one cake, huh, sugar?"

"Okay, but it better be chocolate," she says, and everyone laughs again. They're swayed so easily.

"Father Steve," he says. "How yall doing today?"

"Couldn't be better," I answer, wishing he'd leave, but offering him my hand.

"Good to hear. Good to hear. Looks like you got a hardworking crew helping you out. Who are these fine ladies?"

Vicky smiles as if she's heard it all before, but two of the three older ladies go red up to their scalps.

"That's Denise, over on the cakes," I say.

"Vicky's the one who's about to take all your money." She offers her hand and a quick "Pleased to meet you."

"And these three are Miss Celestine, Miss Emilia, and Miss Pamela."

"Ladies," he says, tipping his hat and offering a wink. Even Miss Pamela, who I would have thought was above this cheap play for affections, puts her hand up to her throat to hide the small patch of red blushing across her neck.

And just when I think it can't get any worse, I see B.P. looking over my shoulder to the hat bobbing up and down behind the open lid of the barbecue.

"Man," says B.P. loud enough to be heard in Opelousas, "I'd recognize that hat anywhere."

He's got a point. Boudreaux's hat is ridiculous. It features a smirking raccoon offering a full view of its rear end. *Registered Coon-Ass* is written above the animal's back. Miss Emilia had fussed at him all morning to take it off. Boudreaux lowers the lid of the barbecue and looks over.

"B.P.? Mais, what you doin out here, huh?" Boudreaux's accent is about as thick as they come. "Keee-yahhhhhh. They lettin' anybody live around here now, it looks like."

He steps down from the trailer and comes around to shake B.P.'s hand. "How you doin', podnah?" he asks. Then he points his chin at Miss Emilia. "B.P., that's my wife, right there. Emilia, this B.P. Remember?" Did I not just introduce them to each other? Still, he continues. "Emilia, I tole you we grow up together . . . and I still see this old so-and-so at the Walmart on Saturday afternoons." Traitor! Miss Emilia offers her hand.

"Pleased to meet you," B.P. says. "What a woman like you is doing with an old rascal like this is beyond me."

"Oh, now, you stop," she says.

"Yeah, B.P.'s the preacher bought all that land from Jugghead and dem and's building that big ol' church up the road."

He knew this? He's been cooking on my lawn all morning, his wife's been making eyes at me for all this time, and neither have said anything?

"Isn't that nice?" Miss Emilia says.

"Sister Emilia, it is nice. But it's gonna be a while yet before that church is built," B.P. says. "But when it's done, we gonna have to have yall over for a prayer or two."

At that, I see the eyes of the entire throng gathered in the lot glancing at me to see my reaction. I just stand there and smile, wanting to smack him for using that Sister Emilia business on one of my parishioners.

B.P. hands Vicky a wad of bills. "Guess I'll be going," he says. "Brother Trahan, you think you could help me and Cindy bring these lunches over to my truck?"

He tips his hat to me. "Be seeing you, Father," he says.

Chapter 5

What does the thirty-year-old man do when he needs a break from adulthood? The straight, the gay, the black, the white? The lawyer, the priest, the rich, the poor? The Catholic, the Protestant, the Jew, the Hindu? He goes running home to his mama. That's exactly what I'm doing tonight, and Vicky's riding shotgun.

Mama's only twenty minutes away in Opelousas, but it's been a while since I dropped by. Hell, I visit Miss Rita more than I visit Mama. "I think I saw you more when you were away at seminary," she's always saying. "Such is life," I'm always telling her.

This evening's shaping up to be a beauty. The sun's riding low and there's an honest-to-God nip in the air. Winter's decided to make an appearance after all.

For some reason, I'm experiencing that feeling I used to get in seminary when the holidays approached and I knew I was going home, that feeling that I'm going to pop right out of my skin.

It's a feeling, of course, that wasn't shared by many of the other seminarians I went to school with. Prior to vacations, they dragged the halls, heads hung low, nerves on edge.

"C'mon," I'd say. "You're getting away from this hermit hole. A vacation. You're going home, seeing the folks."

But the pop-eyed response was always the same: "That's exactly what's wrong."

The seminary was a Freudian wet dream of parental issues.

There was the overbearing mother who chose to ignore the fact that her son had become a priest, a woman who still expected grandchildren and, worse, still dropped hints and comments, still talked about that nice girl who lived down the street. And there was the overbearing mother who'd harangued her son straight into the priesthood and now paraded him about like a champion show dog, a woman who invited all her friends over to see the nice, fine Catholic boy she'd raised.

On the other side was the slightly embarrassed father who didn't know quite what to make of the whole thing. A quiet man who said as little as possible and asked no questions for fear that he might confirm his deepest suspicions. Or, worst of all, the hostile old man. Oh, he knew all right, and he wasn't afraid to speak his mind. He knew why his yearbook-staff son, that glee-club boy, that National Honor Society lad, that non-football-playing, squeamish-about-hunting, didn't-want-to-go-fishing sissy joined the seminary. He knew what to blame. Too much mothering. Too much TV. Too much public schooling. Too much Catholic schooling. Too much altar-boying.

But Mama's house? It's a good time. I wouldn't want to live there, but it is a great place to visit.

I have no lingering mother issues. Once she realized I was probably going to make it to adulthood without getting myself killed, she'd let go. Sure, she worried about me. Probably still does. But she's mastered a skill shared by maybe one percent of parents. She doesn't worry me with her worries.

And Tommy, my stepdad? Well, he's my stepdad. There's always going to be that slight tension that results from two men vying for the love of one woman. But Tommy was smart enough to realize early on that if push ever comes to shove, a sane woman is going to pick her child over her man. He'd made his peace with that and done his job. And Tommy had his own theory about that job, which he'd shared with me one night when we'd both gotten a little boozy and confessional. "Love and support the woman, and don't fuck up the kid."

So it's good times all around. Spending an evening at Mama's house is like being at the sort of party that, when I was a kid, I imagined I'd have when I was an adult and had my own family. Grown-ups standing around, picking at appetizers, drinking, telling dirty jokes.

During seminary, I'd typically bring some stray home with me. And even with the inevitable off-color comments from Tommy, who had a healthy and vocal distrust of voluntarily celibate men, the reaction was always the same: "Your family's so amazing."

Tonight, Vicky's my stray. She's been spending a lot of time hammering out fund-raising logistics while I've been doing a whole lot of watching. I'd offered to take her to dinner, some place fancy in Lafayette, but she declined.

"Why spend all that money on food that I can cook better?" she'd said. A regular romantic, that woman. "Besides, didn't you spend enough buying all those unsold cakes so Celestine and Emilia wouldn't slip into depression?"

"I think the point of going to a restaurant is so you don't have to do all that work," I said.

"Well, I kind of like the work. I think the work is part of the point."

Pigheaded woman.

"I'm just trying to reward you for all your hard work."

"I don't know," she'd said. "Take me to a party or something. Put me with some people other than Emilia, Celestine, Pam, and your little sweetheart."

A priest, of course, isn't exactly big on the party circuit, so here we are, pulling up to Mama's house.

Like normal, civilized people, we walk up the carport and enter through the kitchen door without knocking. There's no one in the kitchen. Cheese cubes, chips, and dips sit on the snack bar, along with a half gallon of Seagram's 7, a gallon of Carlo Rossi white, and a bottle of E.&J.—probably burgaunet sauvignoir or some bastard child of the red grapes. My kind of people.

I give Vicky a tour of the house before heading to the back-yard, where Mama's sitting on the swing, drinking a Bud Light and watching the purple martins fly in and out of the bird-house. Tommy comes out of his outdoor kitchen and I make introductions.

"It's about time Steve met a woman," Tommy says, offering his hand.

I knew that was coming, but I blush anyway. Tommy still has that power over me, the power to make me feel thirteen again.

"Well, even a priest needs a woman to make an honest man of him," Vicky answers, sliding onto the swing next to Mama. I feel the tips of my ears turning red.

"You better go get some beer," Mama tells me.

"Vick, you want to come along?" I ask.

"No, you go," Mama says, patting Vicky's knee. "She can stay here."

"I'll be okay," Vicky says. Lucille, Tommy's Lab, runs over to the swing and hops up, taking a seat between the two women.

As I walk out of the backyard, Mama shouts after me, "And make sure you don't get mine in those twelve-ounce cans. They get hot too fast." Every time, the same thing.

Five minutes later, I'm back with two cases of Miller Lite in standard-issue cans and a case of ten-ounce Bud Light cans, per Mama's instructions. Beer brand and can size are things taken seriously in this backyard. Mama won't drink Miller Lite or

Coors Light. And she won't drink anything out of a twelve-ounce can.

"Jesus, Steve," Vicky says. "What do you plan on doing with all of that?"

"That's two Hail Mary's for taking the Lord's name in vain," I say.

She scrunches up her face and sticks out her tongue in response.

"Cute," I say. It sort of is.

We settle into a backyard rhythm. Martins fly in and out of the birdhouse in flurries while Mama and Vicky chirp away, feeling each other out. I'd call it small talk, but I learn more about Vicky in five minutes than I have since I've known her. Yeah, Vicky's a nurse and the daughter of a priest. But I wasn't aware just how unembarrassed she was about the latter. She weaves that fact into the conversation as if it were the most natural thing in the world. I thought she was unguarded around me because I was the replacement priest, but I guess I'm not all that special. It's Daddy this and Daddy that.

Vicky turns out to be one of those people who loves her job. I never thought to ask. A job's a job. You just sort of pick one best suited to your disposition and go with it. But Vicky's telling Mama she doesn't even need the job because her daddy, the priest, apparently made a number of wise investments. Left her fairly well off. I shudder to think where he got the seed money.

"So before surgery," she's telling Mama, "this little shit was giving us a hard time. Whining, crying, pitching fits. Sure, he might have been scared, but still. Anyway, we knock him out, do the surgery, and then he starts to come to. And people usually cry and talk and stuff when they're coming out from under."

"Really?" Mama asks.

"Oh yeah. You're kind of half in and half out. You can hear and take instructions, but you're not going to remember any of it. Not consciously, anyway. So this kid starts coming out and he starts thrashing around, screaming, fighting, swinging in the air. Guess he's rotten to the core. So I restrain his little ass and me and the other nurse start telling him, 'Hey, Bobby, you know Santa Claus ain't real. He's fake. Your mama's lying to you.' Things like that."

"You did not!" Mama squeals. "That's awful." But of course she's laughing so hard, the swing's shaking.

I'm sure there's a special place in hell for people like Vicky. It's probably the most fun and entertaining section of hell, but still.

Before long, the guests have all arrived and we have quite a party on our hands. After eating, Tommy lights a fire in the backyard pit, around which we gather with stiff drinks. It isn't long before the inevitable happens.

"Hey, Vicky," Tommy says. "Steve ever tell you about—"

I cut him off. "No, Tommy. I haven't." I know it's already too late to put this horse back in the barn, but I try anyway. "And everybody else here has heard it eight hundred times, so we can just skip it."

"Now, wait a minute," Vicky says. "That's not fair." And of course, everyone else is dying to hear it just one more time. "What story?" she asks.

"Ruh-ruh-ruh-Rachel," everyone else says in unison.

Ruh-ruh-ruh-Rachel—or, as she was more commonly known, Rachel—was my high school sweetheart. A two-month-long crush had forced me to ask her to homecoming sophomore year and she'd said yes. That she'd agreed to date me should have been warning enough that her judgment was sorely lacking, but so these things go. She was so beautiful that night that I looked right past the ridiculous poofy sleeves on her shiny teal dress, straight into a future of marriage, 2.4 kids, and a Labrador retriever. So did she. It was that easy. In no time, we were being overly friendly with each other's parents and picking out names

for our kids and arguing over the color of the Lab puppies—
she wanted yellow, I wanted chocolate.

Like the good Catholic girl that she was, she forced me to en-
dure a year's worth of blue balls and accidental discharges before
giving in. The night we lost our virginity, we were teary-eyed
and spoke of purity and love—as if we hadn't spent every weekend night exploiting each other's anatomy in ways that made the
good ole in-and-out seem quaint. As is often the case when
it comes to religious rules, it's the technicality that matters.
Thousands of Brazilian girls walk up to the altar wearing white
every year, precisely because night after night of anal sex doesn't
count as a loss of virginity. Which might also explain that country's fascination with the female posterior.

So, yes, in a way I was fortunate. My trouble wasn't getting
into love; it was extracting myself from its tumbled-down remains.

And on the night of my Confirmation, two months before
my seventeenth birthday, Rachel pulled the walls right down on
my head.

We were at a party at Seth Goldstein's house. What better
way to celebrate our adult entry into the Church than getting
tanked at the Jewish kid's house?

Everyone was good and drunk. Even Seth seemed unconcerned about the pot smoke, the stains on the carpet, the girl
frothing at the mouth as she puked root beer schnapps into the
pool. But Rachel was silent—to me at least. One second she's
giggling with her girlfriends, the next she's rolling her eyes at
me. It was pissing me off. Still, I was so clueless that when she
grabbed my hand and pulled me into a back bedroom, I figured she'd pulled the stick out of her ass and that I was going to
get lucky. She closed the door behind her and even let me
make out with her long enough to develop a raging boner.
Then she pushed me away.

"What's wrong, baby?" I said in what I thought was a concerned yet sexy manner.

"I think we should see other people," she said with no preamble save the snapping of her gum.

"What the fuck?" I couldn't help but ask.

"I think we should see other people," she repeated.

"What are you talking about?"

"We're too young to be serious like this. We have our whole lives ahead of us. I think we're both a little immature." She didn't stumble over her words. Even as stupid as I was, I could tell she'd been preparing this little speech. As the news settled in, as my drunken brain unraveled the words, translating them into elementary English—*You're getting dumped*—I felt my lower lip tremble.

"You're dumping me?"

"I didn't say that."

"Then what does seeing other people mean?" I demanded, hoping I could gin up enough anger to hold back my tears.

"I—I just think we need space."

"Space?" Space meant breaking up. Space meant no sex.

"Yeah. Space."

"So, we'll see each other, but just less."

"Maybe."

"Okay. So we can go out next week, then?"

She hesitated. She hadn't figured on me being so pigheaded. "I think we should take time apart."

"Time apart? Like how much time apart?"

"God," she said, stomping her foot. "Just forget it."

"So we're still together?" I was desperately clinging to any last shred of hope.

"Damn it, Steve. No. It's over, okay?"

I wiped my eyes with my sleeve and blinked at her.

"But why?" I sniffed. "I thought we were in love."

"Steve," she sighed, then threw out a line every teen girl has heard a million times in a million movies—something they consider deep, an easy and dignified letdown. "I love you, I'm just not *in* love with you."

"What the fuck does that even mean?" It should be pointed out that during this conversation I'd been holding in my right hand a forty-eight-ounce cup once filled with whiskey and 7Up. It was approaching empty.

"I don't think you need to talk like that," she said.

I was a little shocked at my own outburst. "It's just that I am in love, Rachel. I am in love with you. I'd do anything for you. I want to spend the rest of my life with you." Dignified, to be sure. "You were my first. I was your first."

For the first time in the conversation she looked away.

"What?" I asked. "What?"

"Steve."

It sank in slowly, but got there all the same.

"Oh! My! God! I wasn't your first?"

"Steve." She was tearing up, crying not for the damage she'd done to me, but for the damage she'd just done to her sweet reputation.

"You lying cow!" I screamed, pushing her out of the way and making for the exit.

In the living room, where all the other kids were gathered, I grabbed a bottle of gin that was—thankfully—almost empty. I drained it.

"My girlfriend," I yelled at the room, all eyes now locked on me. "My ex-girlfriend," I shouted. Then the gin came up as swiftly as it had gone down, the thick oily taste of it scorching my throat. It was just the gin. Luckily—or unluckily—everything else stayed down as the clear stinking stream spilled onto my shoes. A few heads turned in disgust. But I wasn't to be stopped. "My ex-girlfriend is a slut!" I shouted, and threw the gin bottle at the wall, where it bounced and fell to the sofa.

"Come on. Raise your hands. Which one of you hasn't fucked her?" They all sat in silence, afraid to move.

I grabbed a half pint of vodka from a shelf and stomped back toward home. The vodka I kept down, and at some point on the walk back, I apparently decided that what I needed to do was take my clothes off and ride my bike while crying.

"So I find this knucklehead on the lawn all covered in grass," Tommy's saying. "And I'm like, 'Steve, what the hell happened? What's wrong?' And he just starts saying, 'Ruh-ruh-ruh-ruh.' So I give him a good shake and he finally gets out, 'Rachel,' then pukes all over the place and just starts crying and crying."

Vicky can't stop laughing. "That explains so much," she says.

I blush a little, but it's a good story, I think. It shows that I was a normal, stupid kid. At least Tommy was interrupted before he could tell of the horrible events that followed.

Since Vicky's fitting right in, I take the opportunity to walk off into a corner of the yard, under an oak tree, to smoke a cigarette.

This is something I've always done, this sneaking off to a different vantage point. As a child, if there were no other kids around demanding my attention, I'd gather up my Matchbox cars, find a patch of dirt, and roll them back and forth absentmindedly as I watched the adults carry on. Standing there laughing and eating, they make it all look so natural, like it's the easiest thing in the world to do.

Am I part of this? Was I ever? Or was I always just an observer, and my job simply a natural outgrowth of that?

Vicky turns from the group and looks around. Noticing me, she walks over and takes a cigarette from the pack in my shirt pocket. "What are you doing lurking here in the shadows?"

"Smoking. Mama doesn't like it. And watching, I guess. I like to watch them carry on."

"Sounds almost dirty," she says.

I don't say anything, just finish my cigarette.

"You ever miss it?" she asks.

"Miss it?"

"The family. This scene."

"Well, Vicky, I'm standing right here. I can come back every weekend if I want."

"But you don't."

I look at her now. She turns, too, away from Mama's party, and looks at me.

"You think one day you'll regret not choosing this?"

"I've made that decision already, Vick."

"That's not what I asked, Steve." She gives me one of those smiles that says, "Okay, ass, I'll let you get away with it this time." In its own way, it's not a bad smile.

She turns away and looks back to the group.

"Your family's pretty amazing, Steve-O," she says.

Chapter 6

I'm sitting in the confessional, fighting hard to stay awake. I'm slightly hungover. I might have had a few too many drinks at Mama's party. Then I might have had another one or two while surfing the Web when I got home.

So I'm bored, tired, and cranky. Sometimes I feel like this one duty is penance enough for anything and everything I've ever done wrong in my life, this sitting in a box for two hours until my ass hurts, listening to the droning of sins, transgressions so slight that sometimes I have to fight an urge to shout across the screen.

Miss Celestine is a perfect example. There she is, right this minute, keeping her every-Tuesday-morning appointment to confess that she's sneaking drinks out of her husband's commemorative Wild Turkey bottles.

"You know," she says, "the ones shaped like real turkeys."

"Yes, I know."

"Each time, I take the head off a different turkey."

The first time I heard that sentence I almost fell over laughing. Now it's just sad. How can she look me in the eye at our festival meetings? Oh, it's not the sin—if it's even a sin—it's that she's boring me half to death. Apparently, she keeps a spare bottle hidden away to top off the commemorative bottles when they start to get low.

"Why must you drink out of the commemorative bottles?" I asked her once.

"I don't know," she said.

"Why don't you just sneak your sips out of the regular bottle?"

"I don't know," she said, a tremor in her voice.

"Well, why don't you just drink out of the regular bottle in the open?"

"Oh, because I don't drink, Father," she said without hesitation.

I'd pointed out that she was kneeling there, lying to a priest in confession. "You just told me you drink."

I could hear her sniffling. Still, I figured we were verging on a breakthrough so I pressed on, asking her what exactly she was confessing to—the theft of the whiskey, the drinking, or the lying about the drinking. At which point she had herself an honest-to-goodness sobbing fit, as if heartbroken at the realization that, at the least, this was a multifaceted affair, a three-pronged pitchfork poking her straight to hell. On that day, I prescribed two entire Rosaries knowing it would take at least that to make her feel better about herself.

Now, I don't pry. I just sit there and let her get it off her chest.

But today, I don't know. Maybe it's from seeing her so much at festival meetings. Maybe I need a vacation. Maybe it's some sort of priestly repetitive-stress injury. Whatever it is, I want to slide the wood panel shut, walk over to her side of the booth, poke my head in, and have a few words with her.

"Hey," I'd say, *"would it kill you to find something interesting or different to confess? I mean, we all drink. You should have seen me in high school, stealing from the old man's cabinet, stealing pints from the*

Wagon Wheel Truck Stop, drinking till I couldn't see, then driving the center line all the way home. Hell, I'm sure there are some people in this town who get drunk every night, then beat their kids, wives. Scream at their husbands. On the grand scale of sins, yours doesn't even rate. So c'mon. Fess up. Don't you have thoughts about killing your husband or at least wish he'd die so you could have a few nights alone? Don't you diddle your old dried-out dandy, coddle your crusty cooter while thinking of some other man, maybe even me?"

I open my eyes and my head pops up. She's still mumbling along, like usual.

When she pauses, I say, "It's okay. Please continue."

And here in my dark wood-paneled box, in this close warm air, I nod off again, then wake with a start, like a woodpecker working a tree, like a hammer hitting a nail.

I've tried bringing coffee into the booth, but the smell is overwhelming and my sipping sounds—yes, I'm a sipper, we all have our faults—my sipping sounds are amplified by the acoustics in here.

To think this was the part I'd most looked forward to when I was in seminary. My childhood fascination with watching and listening was equally matched by that southern love of gossip, that thrill of seeing what sort of pettiness and ugliness lurks just underneath the skin of seemingly decent people.

But the present reality of Grand Prairie is that life is just as boring as it looks. Sure, a priest with a child is quirky, I suppose. But much to my disappointment, I've seen no evidence that anything in southern gothic writing has any basis in reality. If people are sleeping with their siblings or poisoning in-laws or torturing lost northerners in the woods, they aren't telling me about it. Maybe they're too busy enjoying themselves to come in and file a report. Maybe people these days would just rather forsake their culture and hang out at Walmart.

You'd think I'd at least get some crazy kid practically dying from guilt because he's been masturbating every night since he was eleven and just found out that it's considered a grievous sin.

So I sit here, listening for the swish of the outside doors, the shuffling of orthopedic shoes, the clop of heels, the whispered conversations, the drone of Hail Marys accompanying the clacking of Rosary beads.

Miss Celestine wraps up and I take a sip from the can of Mountain Dew I brought in today. It doesn't have a strong odor like coffee, but the can's too small for my own liking and it's almost empty. I tried a bottle, but I have a habit of recapping after every sip. A hiss in the confessional—even if it is a carbonated one—wouldn't go over well with the penitent.

"What was that, Father?"

"Oh, that? That was just Satan voicing his approval of your heinous acts."

The door on the other side clicks open and a familiar scent wafts in. Strawberry shampoo.

My thumb, acting of its own accord, presses a dent into the soda can.

Denise. She's only here for one reason. To tempt me. There's no other explanation. Her first communion is long behind her and her confirmation a year off yet. Teens don't just come to confession. But here is the strawberry smell.

I slide back the wood panel.

"Bless me, Father, for I have sinned."

She doesn't say anything else.

"It's been?" I prompt, feeding her the next line.

"Oh! Hi, Father Steve," she says, her voice brightening, like she'd been expecting someone else.

"Hi, Denise," I reply. "So how long has it been?" Strictly business, that's me.

"Ummmm, two years. It's been two years since my last confession." She sounds like she's talking to one of her friends about a boy band. She's practically speaking in the lowercase, unpunctuated sentences of her e-mail. "How long you been in here today?"

One hour and seventeen and a half minutes I almost say. "I don't know. Since ten."

"Wow, it must get kinda stuffy in there."

"Yes, well."

"What happens if you need the bathroom or something?"

That was another problem with the big bottle of Mountain Dew. I clear my throat. "Denise, there are other people waiting. We should continue."

"Oh, there's no one out there."

Great. Just my luck. Here I am, all alone in a church with the Strawberry Seductress. I shake my head clear. "Denise, maybe we can chat later."

"Oh. Okay," she says. "Well, anyway, these are my sins." Like it's something she says everyday. *"Hi, Kerri, did you see Toby? Oh my God, he's so cute. Anyway, these are my sins."*

"Uhhmmmm," she starts. "I've lied to Mama and Daddy. I beat up Billy pretty bad the other day. But he deserved it."

"Violence is not the answer," I say.

"Well, Daddy says it answered slavery, the Nazis, and Iraq, too."

Dear Lord, help me.

"Those situations were a little different, Denise. I don't think your brother was oppressing an entire country. And you're supposed to love and honor your family."

"Didn't Jesus say you have to leave your family behind?"

Great. Tell me again who had the bright idea to switch from Latin to English and let people read the Bible on their own.

"That's a different situation as well, Denise." Before she can ask why, before I'm forced to make up an explanation out of whole cloth, I go on. "Look, plain and simple, you should not be beating up your brother."

"I know," she whines, "but still. He was being such a little—"

"Denise."

"Yeah, I know. Sorry. Okay. So, ummm. What else? I guess I dishonored Mama and Daddy a few times. I skipped church a bunch of times. That was before you started. And I kind of cheated on a test. But I would have passed anyway. So I don't know if that counts."

"Cheating is cheating."

"Yeah, that's what I figured. So. What else? Let's see. I cuh—cuh—What's that word? You want something somebody else has?"

"Covet?"

"Yeah. That's the one. I coveted my neighbor's goods. Sharon, this girl at school. She's got this new MP3 player and Daddy absolutely refuses to get me one. I swear, he makes me—"

"Denise."

"Sorry, Father Steve."

Then she falls silent.

That was pretty easy. Run-of-the-mill kid stuff. Nothing to worry about. And the way she prattled on. If I didn't know any better, I'd think she was ten years old.

"Oh, and I've had impure thoughts," she mumbles.

"Shit." The word escapes before I can stop it.

"What?" she says.

"Nothing. I just sneezed."

"Oh. Bless you."

"Thanks."

Silence again. Impure thoughts? About whom? Me? Is she more than just some passive temptation placed before me by the Lord? Is she now going to be an active agent of Satan? Is she lusting after the priest? It happens. So often in fact that there are hours of class time devoted to it. I still have the notes. Somewhere.

It could just be my ego. Yes. Probably. But there's no way for me to find out.

"Have you acted on these thoughts?" I ask. That's a perfectly proper question to ask, right?

"No! Of course not," she squeals.

Of course not? Why of course not? Was it an older man? Someone she can't approach?

Maybe I should have committed a "selfish act" before coming in here today, cleared my body of the hormones obviously affecting my mind.

"Impure thoughts are indeed a sin, Denise. A minor one." My voice sounds steady. I think. I hope. "But acting on those thoughts is something else entirely."

"Sure, Father."

We both fall silent. I'm almost afraid to move. It sounds like she's stopped breathing.

"Is there anything else?" I finally ask.

"I guess not."

"You sure?"

Okay, that's a bit much, Steve.

"Well, uh, does it matter who it is?"

"Who what is?" I ask. "I'm not sure I follow you, Denise." Of course I follow you, Denise. Now just spill it already. Let it out. You'll feel so much better.

"Do I have to tell you who it is I had those thoughts about?"

I bite down on my tongue for a second before answering. "No, Denise. That's not necessary. This is about clearing your conscience. Not about gossip."

"Oh, okay!"

She falls silent again and after a minute more, I send her on her way with twenty Hail Marys and an Act of Contrition.

Then the church falls silent. It's just me in my box. I nod off for I don't know how long, waking up when I hear the hydraulic hinges of the front doors and steps running through the church.

Now what?

On the other side, the confessional door jerks open, then slams shut with a thud. Someone plops down, his breath heavy through the screen.

"Father. Oh, Father!" an old man gasps. "You'll never believe what just happened. Never. Listen. I'm walking outside Walmart and I bump into—"

"Sir. Excuse me."

"Wait," he commands, impatient. "Let me finish. So I bump into this young girl. She's twenty-two or something. And I knock her down. *Kapow!* Flat on her ass. So I help her up and, well, I don't know. We hit it off."

"Sir," I interrupt.

"Wait, wait, wait!" he says. "Well, she asks me for a ride home and next thing you know I'm in her house in her bed. Nekkid. I'm a sixty-year-old man, Father, and here I am having wild monkey sex with someone two years older than my granddaughter. I tell you, don't that just—"

"Excuse me," I cut in. "You have to start . . ." What exactly is it I'm trying to tell him? "Well, how long has it been since your last confession?"

"Never been," he says. He sounds like he's about to pop with glee.

"You've never been to confession?"

"No," he says. "I'm not Catholic."

"You're not Catholic?"

"No, sir. I'm Jewish."

Jewish? There are Jews in Grand Prairie?

"Then why are you here, telling me this?"

"Are you kidding?" he says. "I'm telling everybody." And with that, the old man bursts into laughter and falls out of his chair. But his laugh suddenly sounds much younger than that of a sixty-year-old.

"Hey!" I say, pressing my face to the screen. "Hey." I bang on the screen. "Who is this?"

He's laughing so hard that he's having difficulty breathing.

"Who is that? This is no place for jokes. Who is that?"

"You can't ask that question in confession," he says.

"Bullshit," I say. "You just made this a fake confession, I can ask whatever the hell I want to ask."

"C'mon," he says. "You have to admit that's the most excitement you've had in this confessional since you've been here."

He's got a point.

"Yeah, okay. Okay," I say. "Fine. So who the hell are you?"

"Father Mark Johnson."

"Father?"

"Yup. From St. John's in Lafayette."

"So what the hell are you doing out here?"

"I was bored out of my head. Nothing to do in Lafayette."

"So you run to Grand Prairie?"

"Well, it's different at least. Same faces, same thing in Lafayette. Thought I'd take a ride. Heard there was a newish priest and figured no one had been around to welcome you."

"Gee, thanks." Still, that's going to make one hell of a story. And I guess I can find it in my heart to be hospitable. I look at my watch. "Tell you what. I'm done here in about five minutes. Hang out in the church or let yourself into the rectory. I'll catch up to you."

"Cool beans," he says, and scampers off.

When I get back to the rectory I find Father Johnson on his hands and knees behind the television.

"What are you doing?" Has this guy no shame, no sense of

propriety? He walks into another man's home and starts mon-keying around with his television? Why not walk into church and piss on the altar?

"Keep your panties on. I brought you something."

"What, exactly, did you bring me?"

"A cure for boredom," he says. "Comes in handy for me, but it's a lot better with two people."

Before I can say anything, he pops his head up and adds, "And no, it's not porn." He goes back to work. "You know, it'd be a lot easier if you'd organize these wires back here. I mean, dear Lord!"

Curious, I follow the wires from the back of the television to a black box, which in turn is connected to two controllers bristling with buttons. "Video game? What am I going to do with that?"

"Grow a garden. Paint a picture. What do you think, dummy?" he says, standing up and patting the dust off his pants. He's some two inches taller than me, blond hair, high cheekbones. Definitely gay. A man that good looking has no other reason to join the priesthood, I don't care how faithful he might be.

I pick up one of the controllers. "I haven't played since I was a kid. Look at this thing. It's like Nintendo and Atari had a bastard child or something."

"See, you're not so out of it. That's pretty much all it is. You'll learn as you go along."

We decide on something he describes as a first-person shooter.

"Good thing about it, it lets you work out some aggression. And God knows, with that whole celibate thing, we have plenty of the old aggression. People blame these things for school vio-lence. Bet those little Columbine fuckers would have gone berserk three years earlier if they didn't have this stuff around to keep them occupied."

What an awful, insensitive thing to say. I'm starting to like this guy.

Of course, when the game starts he clobbers me. It takes me half an hour just to grow accustomed to the controller, the look and feel of the game. As a kid, I thought Nintendo's Duck Hunt was the pinnacle of gaming technology, but this is something else entirely. I find myself almost motion sick because the graphics are so realistic.

"Wow, it's almost like really killing someone," I say.

Mark laughs. "What are you talking about? You haven't killed anything yet."

"Well, it's almost like really being killed, just without all the pain and stuff."

We make little conversation. I'm too busy biting my bottom lip, squinting my eyes, and leaning my body left or right, trying to will my character out of the way of bullets, grenades, and plasma bursts.

Eventually, I win my first game, twenty-five kills to Mark's twenty-four, and I jump up, run around the couch a few times, and jab my finger at Mark. "Yeah. Now you feel my wrath." I have an inkling of just how silly this is, but I don't care at this point.

"Oh. Dear. Lord," he says, rolling his eyes, but laughing all the same.

"Yeah, roll your eyes now," I say, "but I got your number."

I sit back down and grab my controller.

"You're not hungry by any chance?" Mark asks.

Food? Do space soldiers need food? It's a ridiculous question, but there it is, floating around in my foolish head. My stomach grumbles, reminding me that I am not, after all, a space warrior.

I look at my watch. I look back at Mark, back at my watch.

Smiling, he shrugs. "Happens to everyone their first time."

"No," I say, looking back at my watch. "Four? We've been playing for four hours?"

"Good way to waste a Saturday," he says.

"Shit," I say. "I have Mass in half an hour."

"Oops," he says, standing up. "I guess there's no place to eat in this burg."

"No," I say. "Why don't you hang out? Saturday Mass is short, half an hour. I have a refrigerator full of leftovers, some of the best stuff you'll ever eat and none of it more than four days old."

He politely protests. Myself, I can see the other side of that short Mass, me coming back here to TV and a drink or two, maybe some reading to the sound of the refrigerator's hum.

"C'mon," I say.

"Well, in that case," he says.

I tell him to make himself at home and head over to the church where, of course, there's the usual Saturday problem of Denise, her strawberry shampoo wafting around the altar. That's twice in one day. I really should see about getting some incense up here. She's got a new haircut, only subtly different from the last but just enough to make her seem older—*Or old enough,* some dirty little voice shouts from somewhere in the gray matter. *You know what I'm saying?* it says. *Old enough? Get it?*

Yeah, I get it.

But for once, I have a few other things to bump that voice from center stage. I've got a gay man and some violent video games to keep me distracted.

By the time I wrap up at the church and wave off the last parishioners, it's started to rain, a steady rain with no thunder, a Louisiana winter rain that could just keep on slow and steady for a day or two.

In the rectory's kitchen, I find Mark leaning back in a chair pushed away from the table. His eyes move but nothing else does.

"You eat like this all the time?" he groans.

"Well, I don't know if I eat like *that*," I say, nodding at his empty plate. "But the locals make offerings on a regular basis, if that's what you're asking."

He looks down at his stomach and then at mine.

"Yeah, I know. It's starting to show," I say.

Mark tries to move, but I tell him not to bother. I put on a pot of coffee, clean his dishes, then warm up some food for myself.

"You have this place all to yourself?" he asks.

"Jealous?"

"Hell no. This job's lonely enough as it is. I don't know if I could take being out here all alone."

"I'm not quite sure I can, either," I say, pulling my food out of the microwave and handing Mark a cup of coffee.

"Then again, I'm not exactly doing so hot surrounded by people, either," he says, wrapping his hands around the coffee as if he were cold.

"How so?"

"Oh," he says, shaking his head, his voice light again. "Don't pay me any mind. Just me prattling on."

I look at him and he looks back, his eyes telling me that whatever thing he's got going in St. John's parish is going to stay there for now.

Fine by me.

But that doesn't stop him from divulging his biography. He's originally from Gueydan, somewhere in the deepest depths of south Louisiana, a town so small that other backwater towns make fun of it. A promising student. Popular with the girls because of his good looks. But.

"After watching a couple of, shall we say, educational videos, I had a hint of what exactly it was that wasn't quite right. Well, I couldn't be *that!* But I was. But I couldn't *do* that, and I just wasn't *going* to do that. I wasn't brought up that way! So the only logical thing to do was join the seminary. I sure as hell wasn't going to tell my parents. So off to seminary with little Mark."

"Which seminary?" I ask.

"Notre Dame, outside of New Orleans."

"I'm sure that saved you," I say. When I made my decision to join God's army, I told the bishop it was on the condition that I not go to Notre Dame, notorious for its liberal approach to the liturgy. Among other things. I figured if I was going to deprive myself of a normal life, I didn't want to do it half-assed. I wanted tradition. I wanted a uniform. And I didn't want to have to worry about bending over in the shower.

"Exactly," says Mark. "I probably would have remained celibate longer had I not joined that seminary. Wasn't like I'd have found a man back home. Hell, I might have gone back into denial, found me a big fat wife who didn't really like men, and had a baby or two."

"Yeah, but."

"Yeah," he sighs. "That's not the way it happened. Still, I guess it wasn't so bad. Familiar people, familiar surroundings. Wasn't some back-alley New Orleans drunken thing. Not that time at any rate. And once I was in—or out, I guess—Lord, did my eyes open!"

He pauses before continuing. "I try to stay out of it, really. The back-of-the-closet drama. But."

"But?"

Do normal adults, nonpriests, slip into confessional mode this quickly? I can't imagine John the Welder unburdening his soul and unpacking his sexuality to Bob the Riveter two hours into their first job together. That takes time, and probably no small amount of alcohol.

I guess confessions are an occupational hazard.

He shrugs. He looks around the room, brings his gaze to rest on the window, like he's staring out at clouds far off on the horizon instead of last summer's moths and June bugs rotting in the screen. "You're straight. I imagine you deal with a lot of sexual frustration. Imagine being gay. Like being a kid in a candy store. I stay out of the blackmail, all that. I'm not into the power and glory like some of these guys. I'm not angling to be bishop. But with what I know, I could probably make some nice deals for myself. Then again, I only know some of this because I ain't exactly anybody's version of the unstained lamb." He pauses. "But the sexual temptation. God. All the time it's there. And even when you have it under control, maybe someone else doesn't. I mean, imagine if you had two or three women living in this place with you. Sometimes feelings get involved, and that's when things get really ugly."

Is that it, then? Is he hiding from someone in Lafayette right now, running from a broken heart?

"I see your point," is all I say.

"Anyway," Mark says, turning his eyes back to me. "Sorry to bring the party down."

"Oh no. Not a problem," I say. "Any time you need to talk." I'm not sure if I mean that or not.

"Oh, sure, riiight." He looks down at his watch. "Crap. I have to head back. But you're going to regret that offer."

"Well, I meant it." Or did I?

"We'll see," he says. "Let's just consider it payment for that video game system." On our way out to the car, it occurs to me that that system probably wasn't cheap. "How much was that thing anyway?" I ask. "I can't let you pay for that."

He gives me a sly grin. "Don't worry about it. I took it from one of the toy-drive boxes at St. John's."

We both laugh.

"What's funnier," he says as he puts his car in reverse and starts to back out, "is that you think I'm just joking."

Chapter 7

When Johnny Blackfoot drives up in his battered pickup, its magnetic signs alerting the world that he is an ambassador for Magical Amusement Company, THRILLING THE MIDWAY SINCE 1966. JOHNNY BLACKFOOT, OWNER/OPERATOR, it's a shock. A shock of red hair and foul language.

Blackfoot.

I was expecting an Indian. A Native American if you will. Some solid man with shiny black hair, a big belt buckle, and nice boots. A man of few words, who ran a tight carny. A man driven to tears by litter.

What I was not expecting was this five-foot-two hairy little red man standing in the parking lot of my church.

"Well now, Father," he says, taking in the surroundings. "You're going to have a tight fucking spot here, now, won't you?"

First words out of his mouth. He's got an Irish accent. Maybe his grandfather was Indian.

"But the good thing is the pavement. You'll have your fairgoers park their shitmobiles out in a field or something, put the rides here on the pavement. You'd be surprised how some of these cocksuckers want you to put the equipment right in a patch of fucking dirt. In this state! With the rain you people get." He says it as if the people of Louisiana were personally responsible for the weather. "Next you know, the Zipper's all leaned over and the little bastards are dragging mud all over the seats and shit. D'ya know what I'm saying, Father?"

I curse. My friends curse. But it's something else entirely for a complete stranger to start right in, especially when I'm wearing my collar. The only other people who do that are pro-choicers and, from their point of view, they have every reason in the world to be cursing at people like me.

But there's no malice in Blackfoot's voice. I get the feeling that if I'd ask him the time, he'd undoubtedly tell me that it's "Twelve fuckin' o'clock, according to this pieceashit watch here on my wrist."

Whatever his linguistic skills, he throws me off. I'm supposed to be getting estimates, seeking out the low bidder. Instead, I find myself saying, "Mr. Blackfoot, I'm sure yall will know how best to use the space." I'm halfway to just giving this guy the contract, which is just as well considering how late a start we got on this thing.

He hands me a bound portfolio with a Ferris wheel and an elephant on the cover. "Fucking right we will, Father. Damn straight. My men are the best in the business. And won't give you a whole lot of shit like these other outfits. Straight-fucking-up is what we are."

"Great," is all I can say. I notice his accent is a little more than Irish. There's an undercurrent of southern twang, a touch of white-trash phrasing.

Blackfoot pulls out a wad of chewing tobacco and stuffs it into his cheek. "Tell you what, Father. What say I look around the place a bit? See what's what. I'm sure you got shit to do."

"Yeah. Okay, Mr. Twofoot."

"Blackfoot."

"Right. Sorry."

"Ah, 'sokay, Father. Happens all the time. Better Twofoot than One-eye or some such." He chuckles and spits, leaving a brown splat on the pavement.

He begins walking the property. Back and forth, back and forth, considering the trees, eyeing the graveyard, walking to the highway, and looking in both directions.

He's disappeared behind the rectory when Vicky drives up and rolls down her window.

"What are you doing standing out here in the parking lot, Steve?"

"Mr. Blackfoot's here," I say.

"Who?"

I hand her the portfolio and she pages through it.

"Well, you actually got off your ass to do something. Looks respectable. Indian, huh?" She hands the book back to me.

"Not exactly," I say as Blackfoot comes around to the front of the church again. He walks directly toward us.

"A bit small, but it can work," he says. "I suggest you use that field across the way for parking. You'll need a cop or crossing guard, too, so nobody gets their fucking heads squashed trying to cross the highway."

Vicky's jaw has practically fallen out through the car window.

"Mr. Blackfoot, this is Vicky Carrier. She's the festival director."

"Hi," she says, getting out of the car and offering her hand.

"Right, then," he says. He ignores her hand, reaches into his truck for another portfolio, and hands it to her. She makes a show of looking at it and I look down at mine.

"You actually have an elephant?" I ask.

"Sure do," he says, smiling now. "Big motherfucker, too. But nice as a pussycat." He looks into his own folder. "And she'll be free that weekend."

"Well," I say.

"Tell you what. I'll throw her in free if you sign up today."

An elephant in Grand Prairie. To think of it.

"What exactly would one do with an elephant?" Vicky asks. She's always such a stickler for details.

"Well, ya ride the fucking thing, of course," Blackfoot says.

"Of course," she says, looking back down at the portfolio in her hands.

He offers his hand to me. After I shake it, he walks back to his truck, gets in, and starts the engine. "I'll draw up the papers and fax 'em over to you," he says before driving off.

I stand there waving like an idiot child even after the short bus has pulled away from the curb.

"Steve?" Vicky asks, not at all pleased.

I just keep waving.

"Did you even talk to anyone else?"

"Sure. Of course." Now, that's a damn lie. Technically, I hadn't even talked to Blackfoot before today. I looked at other places on the Web; Blackfoot was the first to get back to me.

"Steve!" For some reason, Vicky doesn't quite believe me.

"What! It'll be fine."

"He's a goddamn Traveler."

"Name in vain, Vick."

"Don't give me that shit."

Odd. She seems to be actually angry.

"He's a Traveler," she says again.

"What's a Traveler?"

"They're like Irish Gypsies or something. Con artists, thieves. They'll probably steal the crucifix right out of the church."

I've never heard of Travelers before. Irish Gypsies? Since when? Puh-leeze.

"Just great. The one thing I leave in your hands—" she says.

"Vick," I interrupt. "It's not as if your typical carny has a spotless reputation. And I should point out that this is all short notice. The only reason Blackfoot's available that weekend is that a church fair fell through in Plaquemines Parish. The priest embezzled half a million dollars and was caught trying to flee the country with his seventeen-year-old altar boy."

I'm surprised at my own logic, that my defense actually makes sense.

"Yeah, yeah, yeah," she says. "Jesus."

"So I wouldn't go claiming any moral superiority over Gypsies or whatever they are."

"Fine," she says.

I decide to change the subject and, hopefully, her mood.

"An elephant, Vicky," I say. "We're going to have an elephant!"

That had shut her up. Okay. Not really. But the elephant impresses everyone else. Even Miss Rita. I saved the news for the day of her birthday, a week after my meeting with Blackfoot.

"That's something else," she says. "Prolly never been a elephant in Grand Prairie. All my years I ain't never seen me an elephant."

"Hey, I have an idea," I say. "I can arrange to bring you out there."

"What? I'm gonna drag myself out there just to look at a elephant? Uh-huh."

"Look at it? You can ride it, Miss Rita."

That gets her laughing. "Lord, you a fool, Steve."

She takes a pull on her Crown Royal. We're drinking it on the rocks out of plastic cups rather than out of the bottle in honor of the big day.

"I could just see me climbing up on some elephant just like it was a old mule or something."

"Yeah," I say. "You should come out there. Probably be the oldest person ever to ride one."

"Uh-huh," she says, but her laugh trails off. "Don't know about all that. Might not be around."

"Now, c'mon, Miss Rita."

"Don't c'mon me. You know five months is a long time away for somebody my age, especially with winter coming."

Where did that come from? I try to swing the topic back around to her birthday. "So tell me again why you're spending your birthday here instead of with your family?"

Unexpectedly, she gives me a straight answer. "Too hard to come back here. Spend all day with your family fussing over you, them little kids making big eyes at you, climbing up in your lap. Then you gotta come back here, to this place, to this room. You can get used to this place, but you leave from it, go back to that other world, it's hard to come back."

She falls silent for a bit, then shakes her head clear. "C'mon," she says. "Don't want to be late for my own birthday party."

"You sure you want to wear that shirt?"

Today's shirt features the heads of six or seven African-American luminaries and the phrase BLACK POWER in huge letters.

"Let's go," is all she says.

Miss Rita's birthday is an annual media frenzy by Opelousas standards. Always a reporter and photographer from the *Daily World*. Usually a matching set from the *Advertiser* in Lafayette. And typically at least one camera crew. This year promises to be worse because some old coot in St. Louis recently died, leaving Miss Rita, however old she really is, the oldest person alive in the United States.

In reality, all it boils down to is a couple of nips of whiskey for both of us before I roll her out into the main room. There, all the other inmates are lined up in chairs, eyes lazily tracking the balloons, a glimmer of recognition somewhere in there—perhaps they're remembering a child's birthday party long ago, before that same child decided that out of sight was the best place for mom and pop to live out their golden years. A monstrous birthday cake with a garish amount of candles will be wheeled out so that Miss Rita can spray it with spit before it's sliced up and most of it thrown away—the sugar could quite literally kill many of the residents. The only people who ever eat the cake are the journalists, scavengers who gobble up anything that's free. But they have the decency to wait until the hard work of asking Miss Rita how it feels to be so old is out of the way. Most often she'll reply with incoherent coos, carrying her senile act to the viewing public. Once, she responded with a very loud demand for her whiskey, causing some confusion among the nursing home staff and no small amount of blushing on my part. And after everyone leaves, I wheel her back to her room, where she delights in having pulled a fast one yet again.

This year, the home has decided to call it her 110th birthday, and despite her mood, everything seems to be going right once we're in the common room. The cake and its admirers have been wheeled out. I'm sitting next to Miss Rita, holding her hand, squinting into the camera lights. Then Joe Brasseaux, foolish enough to do a live feed for Channel 10, asks an equally foolish question.

"So, Miss Rita, what could we possibly get for a 110-year-old woman?"

I know something is off when she yanks her hand from mine and sits up straight. She clears her throat loudly.

"Well, Joe, let me tell you. You can start off by giving me my forty acres and my mule."

A puzzled, condescending smile affixes itself to Joe's face. "Well, now, Miss Rita, isn't that some—"

"Don't 'isn't that something' me, boy. I ain't off my rocker. I want my forty acres and my mule."

"I'm not sure I understand," Joe says. And that's quite obvious. What's unclear is whether he's confused by her sudden lucidity or by the forty acres and a mule reference. Joe might be pretty enough for TV, but he's about as sharp as the handle end of an ax. Joe's cameraman is trying hard not to laugh. His shoulders are practically shaking, but he keeps the camera trained on the sparring pair.

"What's there to understand, Joe?" Miss Rita says.

"Now, Miss Rita—" I start.

"Shut up, Steve," she says, then turns her attention back to Joe Brasseaux and the camera behind him. She looks straight into the lens. "Not hard to understand at all. Forty acres. A mule, Joe. Reparations. You know what that word means, Joe? Might be surprised an old nigga lady like me knows that word. But I know, Joe. Means payback. How 'bout yall pay me back what yall owe me?"

By this point, the other old folks in the home, like animals sensing an earthquake, are upset and making noise. Even the ones who can't possibly know what's going on are rocking back and forth in their chairs, no doubt understanding the tone if not the content of Miss Rita's voice.

"Yeah, okay," Joe says in a calm voice, a voice completely out of place in this conversation. Then I realize that he's talking to the person on the other side of his earpiece. He's all business when he turns to his cameraman. "They cut the transmission. Kill the tape."

"You sure?" the cameraman asks.

"Yeah, I'm sure, Carl. Who the hell wants to see this?"

"That's right. Who the hell wants to hear some old lady talk about slavery? Go on, turn your camera off."

"Miss Rita—" I try again.

"Shut up, Steve," she snaps. "And get me outta here before I have to kick Joe Brasseaux's ass."

I do as I'm told, rolling her off while the attendants try to calm the others. Miss Rita takes a few parting shots. "I'll get them Channel Three people in here. They'll listen. Least they got a black person or two working for 'em."

I push faster and when I get her into her room, I find her bottle of Crown and give it to her.

"Calm down, Miss Rita," I say.

Her hands shake while she twists the cap off. And it's not

from old age and infirmity. Her knuckles are gray with rage. "Calm down. Don't tell me to calm down. Ain't your place. More than one hundred years on God's green earth and you gonna tell me to calm down?"

"But," I start. What the hell do I say? I have the feeling that invoking the name of Jesus at this point is only going to make things worse. "Where is this coming from? What? Why did you go and do that on TV?"

She looks at me for a good long time. I try to hold my eyes on hers, but I feel my ears turn red at about the same time I look down at my shoes.

"I don't understand," I say.

"I did it because I felt like it. I did it because somebody needs to say something before the rest of yall forget."

"Forget what, Miss Rita? Slavery?"

She'd never once said the word in all the years I'd known her.

"Yeah, Steve. Slavery. What it was like after. What we went through."

"But I don't think people are forgetting. Even now people talk about it all the time." I guess they do. Right? Jesse Jackson. Al Sharpton. They're always in the news making noise.

"Oh yeah, they talking." Her voice trembles. I've seen that tremble once before, when I was nine and had taken a machete to the just-budding rosebushes she'd worked on for an entire season. "Talk, talk, talk. Make a lot of noise. But they don't know a damn thing about it. They don't know how good they got it. They don't remember."

She takes a few more pulls off her bottle and I find myself praying that it will calm her down, put her to sleep. Her breathing slows some, but it's obvious she's not going to be nodding off any time soon.

"Why now, though, Miss Rita?" Boy, I'm just full of stupid questions today.

She sighs and I move my eyes from my shoes back to her face. She's looking out the window. "Steve, you not dumb. Why now? I ain't gotta come out and tell you, do I?"

I look at her. She looks at me. A full minute passes by and I still don't know exactly what she's getting at, but I'm afraid to say anything.

"I can feel it, Steve," she says finally. She puts her hand on her chest. "It's here. I can feel it inside me."

Absolutely not. No way. Her age is irrelevant. She's been here forever and she'll outlive me. That's the way it was meant to be. It's written in the Lord's book somewhere, I'm sure.

"Well, Miss Rita, I don't think that . . ." I pause, take a breath, try again. "I don't think death actually comes for people, gets inside them, and sets up shop. Or knocks on their door and takes them away."

I'm right, right? I think I'm making sense. Maybe she's just an old lady having a bad day and feeling sorry for herself. Maybe she woke up with gas this morning and it scared her.

"Steve, I'm not talking about some old tataille." The Cajun word for monster still has the power to send a shiver down my spine. "There's nothing under my bed or in my closet or out in the hall. I'm talking about dying. I'm not some old fool. Ya mawmaw used to tell me how she was feeling. Every little detail, she'd tell me. Sick as she was, sometimes I got tired of hearing about it. She's just lucky she died before that cancer really got hold of her. As bad as she got sometimes, lucky she went the way she did. I tried to forget all her death talk as soon as she was in the ground. But now I'm remembering. Been using this body over a hundred years. I can tell something ain't right."

"Well, maybe a doctor could come in and do something."

"Steve."

She looks at me, daring me to say something else stupid. She's right. What's a doctor going to do for someone he figures should have died forty years ago?

I reach over and take the bottle from her. Her eyes don't leave me as I take a couple of swallows. I hand it back to her. She takes a swig and hands it back to me.

It still doesn't make any damn sense. She's sitting here drinking whiskey. She was just cursing a roomful of white people. Business as usual. The death of God is one for the philosophers. The death of Miss Rita . . .

"So forty acres and a mule?" It's a risk. It's mighty stupid to say. But maybe I can steer this conversation down a more humorous road. "That'll make you better?"

"It's not going to make me better. I just feel like they owe me. And that's only a tee-tiny bit of what they owe me."

"They?"

"Well, they all dead. I guess that's part of the problem." She's not joking.

Once again, I'm at a loss. "People talk about reparations all the time. I just don't know if . . ." Ah, what the hell? I've got absolutely nothing.

"Look, Steve. I ain't talking about all their nonsense. I'm talking my own nonsense. I ain't talking politicians and Jesse Jackson and 'my people,' whoever that is. I'm talking about eye for an eye like the Bible says. I'm not one of these trifling thirty-year-old lazy-ass Negroes out of the projects asking for money because I think I deserve a chunk of free change. You know my mama was born a slave, Steve?"

"Yes, Miss Rita."

"A slave, Steve. My own mama. You think my name Rita Lincoln for no reason? She didn't even know who her daddy was. Coulda been the man who owned the plantation. Coulda been some coon-ass overseer, maybe one of your people. Nobody knows. And she never asked. She worked and kept her mouth shut. She taught me how to do the same. She wasn't a slave no more when she had me. Well, we weren't called slaves. But you can call it what you want. She was born a piece of white man's

property. And she died on that same man's land, working for
him. Working in a sugarcane field. Almost sixty and still working in a field. And when she died, they had the nerve to say she
owed them money.

"People run around talking about feelings and rights and
reparations. My mama was a slave, Steve Sibille. Let that sink in.
Not talking about discrimination. Not talking about prejudice.
She was a slave. They owned her. Nobody in your whole family's
history ever had to say that. I seen people get hung. Get
burned. You know what that looks like? You know what that
smells like? This boy I ran with when I was a girl. I seen him
crawl back to his mama's house, trail of blood in the dirt behind him. He mewled like a dying cat. They cut his nuts off like
he was a pig."

I look down and take another sip.

"That's right. This ain't no movie. This ain't Jesse Jackson
talking about people getting hired down at the plant. I watched
that boy bleed to death and nobody ever did one bit of time for
it. And we all knew who did it. And there ain't enough money
in the world to make me stop seeing that sometimes. Sometimes it just comes back to me. Sometimes I'd be sitting with
your mawmaw and it would come back to me and it was all I
could do not to blame her for it, put my hands on her throat,
and choke just one damn white person."

She pauses. "It's enough to make me want to give up on God
sometimes."

"Miss Rita!"

"I know. Ain't the right thing to say. And every day I thank
Him for my life. But still . . ."

She reaches over and takes the bottle from me. "Sometimes I
wish I was senile. Pray for it sometimes. Just want to forget. And
then I see these people on the news crying about how bad they
got it. People talking about emotional abuse and low self-esteem.
Acting like every day they going to hell and back with not a

drop of water between them. Where they going? They going to the mall. They going to jobs inside buildings with air-conditioning. They getting in their cars. They working eight hours a day. Look, I know lot of them got it hard, but they ain't got it that hard. Nobody hitting them with a stick till their back bleeds if they goof off at work. They get paid for their work. Imagine that. Getting money for working. They can own a house. Can make a million damn dollars if they want to lie and cheat and steal like everybody else. We got a black president now. A black president! Even if he is half Muslim. And they act like the white man still got 'em working the fields sunup to sundown."

I want to cry. I feel like I'm nine again, and I've done something to let her down, like I'm personally responsible for all of this.

"I'm tired of hearing about it. I'm just tired, tired, tired. I don't know why I said reparations. Ain't gonna solve anything. But if they do start handing out money, they should start with me. I should be the first one in that line, because if anybody in this country deserves a damn dollar, it's me. My mama was a slave and I saw that boy get killed and I kept on going, kept on working, kept on praying. And I kept my ass out of jail. And the whole world should know that, starting with you. I ain't even told my own family half of this. They don't need to hear it. They just need to work and look forward. But you can hear it. Gave half my life to your family, so if anybody needs to remember and the TV people don't want to hear it. . . . Well, Steve, looks like the Good Lord put you here for a reason."

And that's it. The anger drains out of her voice and she winds down like an old clock. If I had no idea what to say before, well, now I'm just wishing I could back out of the room and perhaps fly around the world backward and make the whole day go away.

"I don't know what to say, Miss Rita."

She fills her cup before passing the bottle to me.

"Tell me more about that elephant," she says, her voice changing slightly.

I'm no fool, despite plenty of evidence to the contrary. I take advantage of the opportunity.

"Well, the elephant is your fault," I tell her.

"How's that?"

"Wouldn't be an elephant coming to Grand Prairie if you hadn't suggested that festival."

"I think I told you to get you a woman first, Steve," she says, the devilish twinkle coming back into her eyes.

"Well, I got an elephant instead."

Chapter 8

"Want to do something?"

"Sure."

"What do you want to do?"

"I don't know."

"Well, aren't you a big ol' bucket of excitement?"

"Hey, you called me. You think of something."

"Want to go hang out at a Walmart?"

"You serious?" I ask Mark, who's called me on a brisk Wednesday morning. I'm standing outside the rectory, smoking a cigarette and shivering. "That's your idea of a good time? Walmart?"

"Have you *seen* the weekday Walmart crowd? It's fascinating."

The truth is, over a week after Miss Rita's birthday I still don't know what to do with myself. I need some sort of mindless distraction that doesn't involve old ladies. I tried turning inward, dealing with this in a mature way, looking to prayer for either guidance or succor. But that only leads to the comfort of resurrection of the spirit, Miss Rita's happy reward in heaven after she shuffles off this mortal coil. Screw that. If Miss Rita's in heaven she's not here with me. Jesus doesn't need her as much as I do. A few hours spent checking out the specimens at the Walmart zoo is a better option than sitting around here in a state of nervous agitation.

"Fine. Meet me at the Walmart in Opelousas at one o'clock."

"You won't regret this," Mark says.

That should have been warning enough. Not five minutes after walking through the sliding doors, Mark says, "Oh, shit," then disappears into the women's underwear section. My cell phone vibrates. It's Mark.

"What was that about?"

"Sorry," he says. "You see that silver-haired guy in the tight black jeans and the cowboy boots over by the forty-nine-dollar DVD players?"

I spot the guy. "Yeah?"

"He's actually a priest."

"That guy? He looks like the Rhinestone Cowboy."

"Yeah, that ain't the half of it."

"How do you know him?"

"Don't ask, I won't tell. Anyway, I'm gonna go hide in the automotive section. You keep an eye on him, then come find me when he leaves."

Before I can protest, he hangs up. He doesn't answer when I call him back.

"Damn it," I say. But it's not like I've got anything better to do. I'm also wearing a zipped-up jacket over the old shirt and collar so I'm not going to panic the guy if I do follow him around for a bit. He leads me through hunting and fishing supplies, making furtive glances at any single man who crosses his path. Looks like someone's stalking game in the hunting section. Eventually he gives up and heads over to the grocery section, where he picks up two jugs of Carlo Rossi—one red and one white—before leaving.

On my way to automotive, I spot a familiar red hoodie bobbing through the electronics department. What have we here? Our little innocent, all by her lonesome in the wilds of Walmart's most sinful section, where lurk R-rated movies, video games marked M for mature audiences, and CDs that may or may not have been scrubbed of their explicit lyrics. Indeed, lined along the back shelves are high-definition plasma televisions glistening with forbidden episodes of *SpongeBob SquarePants* and an action movie starring beautiful people in tight leather suits who spend far more time shooting at one another and blowing things up than they do talking.

But all of these things, she ignores, content instead to watch two other girls her age—one in pigtails, the other with a short bob—playing a video game. Red Riding Redneck doesn't look at the screen. She focuses on the girls' faces, mesmerized by their intensity. Their silent concentration is broken only by bursts of cooperative chatter.

"There! Get that one!"

"Look! A power-up. Grab it! Grab it!"

"Yes! Yes! Yes!"

When the game falls silent for a brief moment between levels, one of the players, the one with the bob, snaps out of the trance long enough to notice Red staring at them.

"What are you looking at?"

Red waits a beat. "I don't know. That's what I'm trying to figure out."

Ha! I half expected her to start spouting Bible verse.

"You better shut your face," says the girl with the bob.

"Why don't you try and make me?" Red says.

"I don't make trash," starts the other girl. But before she can finish with "I burn it," her partner shooshes the combatants as the game starts up again and draws the little heathens back into its magical realm.

Red glowers at them a moment longer. "Yall both gonna burn far as I'm concerned," she says before shuffling off to the CD section.

Without thinking, I follow. Thrilling as it was to see her spoiled-brat act, what I really want to see is her shoplifting some Led Zeppelin or Black Sabbath or—at the very least—standing slack-jawed in front of the bank of televisions. I find myself squinting and trying to shoot mind rays at her. "If you only knew the power of the dark side." It's useless; the Holy Ghost is strong with this one. Red homes in on the Christian music section.

"I don't know, Father. But I think Cindy-bell's a little too young to be one of your altar girls."

Shit. I turn to face B.P.

"She's definitely the wrong religion." He's smiling a pit-bull smile, waiting for me to explain why I'm stalking his little girl through Walmart.

"B.P.!" I say. Think, think, think. What can I say that makes it look like I'm doing something *other* than stalking his little girl through Walmart? "Was just trying to find a friend of mine. You know how easy it is to get lost in here."

"Is that right?" he says.

Then, sing Hosanna, Jesus smiles on me. Or Nokia does. My phone vibrates and I quickly answer.

"Where the hell are you?" Mark asks.

"Oh, you're in the garden section," I say loudly. "No wonder I couldn't find you. Well, you stay put. I'm catching up with a neighbor. I'll be there in five minutes."

"What?" he says.

I hang up, move the ringer setting from VIBRATE to OFF. Last thing I need is Mark meeting B.P., though now that I'm off the phone it occurs to me that it might be better if B.P. thought I was gay instead of a potential pedophile.

"So, yeah, that was my friend," I say, laughing. "I was looking for him back here and I saw Red. Uh, Cindy's red jacket. Recognized it and figured I'd say hi. Figured you'd be around here somewhere. Didn't think you'd let her loose for too long in the electronics department. Lot of off-limits stuff back here for her, I guess."

Shut up, Steve. Just shut up.

B.P. gives me a quizzical smile. "I don't worry too much about that," he says. "She's a good girl, not one to disobey her daddy or do wrong in the eyes of the Lord."

I have half a mind to tell him about Little Miss Obedient's exchange with the other girls. Then I hear my name again. I offer a brief prayer: *Please, God. Not now.* But it's futile. There's no ignoring that voice now. I have to face it if for no other reason than to turn away from the pleased look on B.P.'s face.

"Hello, Denise," I say, trying my best to sound as if I'm not absolutely mortified.

"Hi," she says, and grabs me around the waist with one arm to give me a hug. In her other arm is a basket. Both B.P. and I look at that basket, full as it is with CDs featuring scantily clad teenage girls in highly suggestive poses. One of them sports the moniker "Pussycat Dolls." Denise's basket also contains a DVD with the words JACKASS THE MOVIE in big white letters. It also sports two red stamps. One says *unrated*, the other screams WARNING!

But it's worse than that. Denise is wearing tight, low-riding shorts, a T-shirt that says KISS ME I'M IRISH, and what looks like an inch of makeup that was applied by a hooker who just graduated from clown school.

"It's my birthday!" she says. "Mama let me loose in the store with a hundred-dollar gift card."

"Well, happy birthday," I manage.

"Happy birthday indeed," says B.P., his smile a hundred percent genuine now. "And who might you be?"

He and Denise look at me.

"B.P., this is Denise. Denise, this is Brother Paul from the Pentecostal church they're building in Grand Prairie."

"Hi!" she says, and, perhaps thinking it will impress him, adds, "I'm one of Father Steve's altar girls."

"Is that right? I heard about you gals."

Denise's phone starts to ring. Or sing. Or rap. "Back that ass up," it says a few times before she answers. "Hello? Yeah. Okay, Mama. Okay. God. I said okay." She hangs up.

"That was Mama," she explains. "I gotta go. See you at Mass on Saturday, Father Steve."

And with a wave, she's gone. We watch her round the corner.

"That's a crying shame," B.P. says finally. He probably waited so long because he had to wipe that grin off his face before he could make his next move.

"What's a shame?"

"All that filth in that basket. Those shorts. That makeup."

"She's just a kid," I hear myself saying. I don't know if I believe that, but I do believe what I tell him next. "Her parents keep an eye on her. She's a good kid. She'll be fine."

"Maybe so," he says. "But it can't be any good for her soul."

"Her soul?" I ask.

"Sure," he says.

"You think shielding people from music and TV and makeup—setting up all those rules and walls—that's going to save their souls? You don't think that's a bit much? A bit extreme?"

"A bit much? You ask me, there's no such thing as a bit much when it comes to saving a person's soul, Father Steve. Besides, that's a strange thing to me, a man who's given up family life for his Church talking about extremes. But I will say this much, I will do whatever I can, whatever it takes to save as many souls as I can." He's got the knife in all the way, but he pauses a second before twisting it. "Don't you feel the same way?"

I feel the hot flush of shame spread up the back of my neck, over my scalp, across my face. "When you put it that way," I force myself to say.

"Wouldn't know how else to put it," he says. Then he hitches up his pants and stretches to his full height. "I guess I best be scooting." He collects his daughter and makes for the exit.

What a self-righteous son of a bitch. I'm sure he's such a saint. Yeah, maybe I wanted to see his daughter sully herself, give in to modern temptations. But he's not fooling me. I saw how happy he was to see my altar girl loaded down with a basket full of filth. He wasn't so worried about her soul that he couldn't take delight in seeing me embarrassed.

"Who the hell does he think he is?" I mutter.

"Who?" Mark slides up next to me. "And where the hell have you been? I need to get out of this place. Now."

"What the hell's wrong with you? And who was that priest you were trying to avoid?" I ask. Lot of hell going around in the last few minutes, it seems.

"I don't want to talk about it," he says. "What crawled up your butt?"

"Nothing. I don't want to talk about it."

"Fine," he says. He looks at his watch. "Looks like it's Miller time."

"Sounds good to me," I say.

Mark and I drive over to Pizza Shack and work our way through a couple of pitchers of beer while avoiding any honest discussion about what is bothering us.

Back in Grand Prairie, a blinking answering machine is waiting for me.

The first message is from Blackfoot. "Father, I've been trying to reach you. We need to talk. You have some decisions to make. And soon."

Decisions? I thought he just made everything appear. Granted, I haven't given him any money yet. Crap in a bucket. The thought of money and fund-raising is immediately depressing.

The second message is from Mark. "Hey, Steve. Just thought

I'd see if . . ." There's a pause. "Well. Never mind." What's that about? Didn't I just leave him about half an hour ago.

The third message is Blackfoot again. "Father. Give me a call. Please." His tone is sharp. The time stamp says 9:00 p.m. Five minutes ago, and not exactly business hours.

Shit. This is the last thing I want to deal with. Still, I find the carnival folder. Might as well see exactly how it is I've screwed up before I return the man's call.

The phone rings again. Who is it this time? Blackfoot or Mark? I let the machine answer.

"Steve, it's Vicky."

"Vick!" I say, picking up. Maybe she'll want a drink.

"What the hell? I just got off the phone with Blackfoot."

Son. Of. A. Bitch.

"What the hell have you been doing?" she asks. "You need to get the ball rolling."

"Wait. What? Slow down. What did he say?"

"He's been trying to call you for two weeks to figure out the details."

Two weeks? Have I been avoiding his calls for two whole weeks already? "What details?"

"How we're going to pay for this. The rides we want. Who's going to control the rides. How to split the money."

"I thought they handled all that."

"Have you even looked at the material he gave you? I mean, aside from your precious elephant. Which you're going to lose at this rate if you don't make these decisions soon."

"Well."

"No, you've been playing video games, fucking off with Mark. You're not in junior high any—"

"Fine! Okay!" I say. "Jeez. I'll go through it all tomorrow and figure it out."

"No," she answers. "I have to work tomorrow."

"I said I'll take care of it."

"Excuse me if I don't trust you. I think we should do it tonight. Get it over with."

Great. Just great.

"Well?" she says.

"Fine. You want to do this over the phone or you want to come over?"

"Hell with that," she says. "You can drag your ass over here."

"Now?"

"No, at midnight. Yes, now." She hangs up.

As I'm driving over, my stomach clenches up. I think I'm actually nervous. As an adult, I've never had a woman pissed at me. Say what you will about the seminary, about the celibate life, but it does have that lack of a woman-scorned-thing going for it. As a priest, you really have to screw up big time to get a woman on your case. Funerals, maybe. But that sort of anger is directed more at God. And weddings definitely. Woe be to the priest who awakens Bridezilla. But I've escaped both of those situations so far. No deaths, no weddings in my fair village since arrival.

But that leaves me more than a little clueless as to how to deal with this. What do I say? What do I do? Should I apologize? Should I get her flowers? Not that there's a florist in Grand Prairie.

On impulse and possibly because I still have too much beer in my system, I pull over to the shoulder to look for some sort of flower, maybe a dandelion or something. It's December and I know damn well I'll find little more than rye grass, but I'm terrified of facing her. Better to cast about in the damp grass and face potential armadillo attacks. I'll grab something tall and green, make a joke of it. Maybe that'll disarm her, I'm thinking when I spot an odd cluster of plants, about knee high. There are no flowers, but the stalks and leaves look a little more interesting than plain grass: thick stalks and, though it's hard to tell

between the dark and the glare of the headlights, some reddish
tint to the leaves. I reach in and squeeze tight around the base
to break the stem and—

"Holy shit!" I scream, pulling my hand back immediately. It
feels like I've put it in boiling water. "Shit, shit, shit!" I hop
around waving my hand in the air. Tears stream out of my eyes.
Burning grass. Stinging nettles. Indian brush. Whatever the
hell it's called. When we were kids, we knew enough to stay
away from it. But here I'd gone and wrapped my hand around
it and squeezed as hard as I could.

I get back in the car and drive to Vicky's house as fast as I
can.

"Vicky! Hurry up! Let me in." I pound on the door. I wipe
my nose with my left hand. "Shit, shit, shit."

"Jesus, Steve. Hold your goddamn horses."

That's right. She's pissed at me. She swings open the door, a
glower fixed on her face. "You don't need to be so loud."

"Yeah, yeah, yeah." I barge in, run to the sink, and turn on
the cold tap.

"What the hell?" she says, a touch of confusion in her voice.

"Burning grass."

"Burning grass? How?"

Yes, Steve, how? Go on. Explain that one to her. "Don't worry
about it."

"You come running into my house with your hand swollen
and red from burning grass . . ."

Damn it. And it occurs to me, too, that if I don't explain, the
only rational explanation for this is that I stopped to do my
business roadside and made a bad grab when it came time to
wipe.

"Fine. I was trying to find flowers for you to apologize for
being such an idiot."

She shakes her head.

"What?" I ask.

She starts to smile a bit. "So this is how you try to make up for being an idiot?"

I clench my jaw. I can feel my face turning red. "Yes. I am aware of the irony."

"You dumb-ass," she says, laughing. She grabs a couple of beers from the fridge. "Here, hold that. And don't think this lets you off the hook."

"Yeah, sure. Can we just do this now?"

"Oh, now you're the one in a hurry all of a sudden?"

I back off. Contrary to all evidence suggesting otherwise, I'm not developmentally challenged. The sacrifice of my hand was enough to erase her anger, but it will only go so far.

"Sorry. It just hurts."

"Sissy," she says, leading me into the living room. "You know, Jesus had spikes driven through His hands. Both of them."

"I've never claimed to be anything close to the kind of man he was."

Vicky drags her feet across the carpet and flops down on the couch. She's wearing slippers, sweats, and a hooded zip jacket. It's halfway open, revealing her collarbones and a bit of cleavage dipping into a tank top. Her hair is pulled off of her neck into a short ponytail.

We sit side by side on the couch. The light, the feel in the living room is drastically different than in the kitchen—or any room in my place. In place of the glaring fluorescents and white tile, there is a dimmed lamp and earth tones. It makes me want to whisper . . . or take a nap.

"So what's the deal?" I ask.

"Have you looked at this at all?" She waves Blackfoot's literature.

"No," I say. "Not at all."

She gives me a look, shakes her head.

"The first decision is how to handle payment." She flips to the appropriate pages.

We have two options, it seems. One is called a traditional carnival. Blackfoot and his crew would come in full bore and run the show at no cost to us. They take their cut, we take ours. The second option would be to pay for the equipment and manpower, rent it so to speak, and then take one hundred percent of whatever we took in.

"Well, that's a no-brainer," I say. "Option one all the way. Let them do all the work. Then we don't have to worry about these stupid fund-raisers."

That was easy enough.

"Not so fast, chief," she says.

Of course.

"But, Vick—" I start.

"But, Steve," she says, mocking me. "Look. I thought option one would be the best way, too. But there's a catch."

"What? Is the cut too small?"

"Well, thirty percent isn't the best cut in the world. But, no, that's not it. Option one gives them control of *everything*—that includes placement of our booths and stages. They also get a cut of everything, including *our* food concessions and *our* event booths. And you can bet your ass our food concessions are going to bring in a lot more money than theirs will."

"You go over this with Blackfoot already?"

"No. He didn't want to deal with me," she says, biting her bottom lip for a second. "Asshole. Just wanted to know where the man was."

"Oh," I say, wondering if I should poke at that wound to her pride. I decide not to. "So what are we looking at with option two?"

"On average, five hundred per ride for Saturday and Sunday. Two fifty per ride for Friday."

"In American dollars? Per ride! Per day!" I stand up and start pacing. "Aw, crap, Vick. We'll never be able to raise enough money. What can we afford, the elephant and a merry-go-round? Shit."

"Sit down and shut up for a second." She pats the couch. I throw myself down next to her and fling my head back. She turns to face me and her leg ends up pushing against mine. "We just put down a deposit and we'll pay him the difference with what we take in on the rides."

"But what if we don't make enough? What if it rains? That's been known to happen in Louisiana." I'm whining now.

"Have some faith," she says, and pats my knee. "Now sit up straight. Your nostrils aren't exactly your best feature."

"Fine," I say.

"Good," she says. "Now the fun part."

"Oh yeah?"

"Yeah. We pick the rides," she says, and flips to those pages.

Of course, this leads to another argument. But this one I don't mind so much, silly as it is. I immediately draw up my list: TurboForce, the Flume Ride, Gravitron, Space Loop, Twister, Zipper, Bullet, Bumper Cars, the Yo-Yo, the Screamer, the Murderer, the Mangler and the Strangler, and Quadzilla.

At which point, Vicky calls me crazy for any number of reasons. "Two seconds ago, you were worried about pricing and now you have the most expensive rides and no room left over for the kiddie rides."

"Ah, fuck the kids," I say, my inner teen slobbering over the possibility of a backyard full of my very own thrill rides.

"Steve!" She slaps my knee. "Besides. You don't have room for these tall rides. Unless you rip out all the trees."

"To hell with the trees."

She shoots me a warning look, but doesn't really mean it. She lets me keep the Zipper and the Gravitron and suggests a

Ferris wheel, swings, Super Slide, the Hurricane, a merry-go-round, and the Tilt-a-Whirl.

"Honestly. How could you have forgotten the Tilt-a-Whirl?"

"I didn't forget," I say. "The Tilt-a-Whirl makes me sick."

She laughs at me. "You *are* a sissy."

"Hey, the Tilt-a-Whirl probably would have made Jesus his own self sick. I'll take crucifixion over the Tilt-a-Whirl any day of the week."

"Whatever." She then adds to her list a few kiddy rides: Crazy Planes, Dragon Wagon, Spin the Apple, Helicopters, Granny Bug.

"And the biggest damn moonwalk they have," I add.

"Ohhh. Good idea," she says.

She rewrites everything in a neat and orderly fashion and hands it to me. "Make two copies. One for me. One for Blackfoot. Then call him for a meeting."

"Yes, ma'am."

I find myself on her doorstep, heading for my car.

She's leaning against her door. "See, Steve? That wasn't so hard."

"No, I guess it wasn't," I say.

"We make a good team, even if you are a slacker."

"Yeah, yeah, yeah," I say, waving off her comment as I climb into the car.

I drive back to the rectory with the radio blaring, the window rolled down, letting the wind blow the thoughts out of my head.

Chapter 9

A fit of paranoia is always a good way to start off the day—especially Christmas Eve. This morning I received a call from the bishop's office requesting me to drive to Lafayette immediately. Wasn't told what it was about, just to get there. So of course I was having heart palpitations for the entirety of the drive to Lafayette. What was it? The altar girls? I'd been spending too much time with Vicky? I didn't get proper clearance for the festival? The Xbox lifted from the toy drive? Oh no. I'd deprived some kid living in a shelter of the Christmas gift he'd been praying for all year long!

But Bishop Flemming had cleared everything up quickly.

"We seem to have a problem," Flemming said the moment I stepped into his office. He was grinding a cigarette butt into a Notre Dame Fighting Irish ashtray.

At which point I almost confessed not only everything I'd done wrong since my first day in seminary, but everything I'd ever thought of doing.

"It's your friend. Mark," Flemming said, saving me from myself.

That stupid video-game console. I decided to play dumb.

"What seems to be the problem?" I asked.

"You don't know?" Flemming countered, arching an eyebrow at me. The old "you can't shit a bullshitter" look.

"To be honest, I don't know Mark all that well," I said, which was true enough.

"Really?" Flemming asked, genuinely surprised.

"Yes, Bishop Flemming. He's stopped by a couple of times, called a couple of times, but that's about it."

"That's odd," Flemming replied. He waved me farther into the room. "Sit, sit."

I sat.

"We thought he might have called you. According to word around St. John's, he'd taken a shine to you. They say he's been out your way a few times and that he talks about you quite a bit."

Had they been following Mark? Spying on me? Did they think I was gay?

"Well, I mean we did hit it off, Bishop, but." I stopped. "I, uh, don't. Well. You know."

"Steve, it's okay. I'm not trying to get at that."

"Oh, of course not," I said weakly.

"But Mark did have some personality issues with a lot of the men here in Lafayette. And he did seem to like you, to be on good terms. So we thought he'd at least call you when he ran."

"Ran?" I asked.

"Yes, I'm afraid so," Flemming said. "It happens. People have a moment, a crisis of faith and all that. We just want to get him back home, into the fold so to speak."

"But, Bishop, I had no idea," I said. I didn't quite know what he expected me to do. "He never even called. I wouldn't know where to find him."

Flemming leaned forward and fished a cigarette out of a gold cigarette case on his desk. "Oh, we know where he is at the moment. We were just hoping you could go and talk to him. We think he might listen to you."

So here I stand, in the doorway of this dark, throbbing place, a gay disco preposterously set off a highway in the middle of Cajun country halfway between Lafayette and New Iberia.

Smoke is thick like fog in the low-ceilinged darkness of the room. When the air conditioner cycles on—my hopes for a white Christmas dashed yet again—I can practically feel something . . . sin? temptation? . . . swirling in the smoke. I stand just inside the door, letting my eyes make the transition from the white glare of sunlight behind me to the indoor dusk in front of me. A few heads swivel my way, then back, with little pause in the conversations.

Mark's in here somewhere among the mumbling midday shadows.

Immediately behind me, the door opens. The shaft of sunlight splits the room, landing on Mark, giving him the appearance of a persecuted saint—a saint perched on a stool in a gay bar, hunched over a beer, a neglected cigarette burning to the filter between his fingers.

The door closes, bringing us all back into darkness. I make my way over to Mark, who doesn't acknowledge me.

"Jack on the rocks," I say into the smoke.

"There you go, Father," the bartender says.

I had no idea the word *father* could be made to sound so dirty.

I put a hand on Mark's arm in greeting.

"So, how we doing today, Father Johnson?" I say in a bad Irish accent.

He turns and looks at me, his eyes unfocused, more red than white.

"Mark," he says. "The name is Mark."

"Get off the stool, Mark, and let's get the fuck out of here."

A woozy grin creeps across his face and he turns to me.

"You coming on to me?" he asks, and grabs a belt loop, yanks

me closer. His head swivels a little and a sour cloud of cigarettes, booze, and body odor envelops me. His hazel eyes focus
suddenly, and his voice shifts, more a threat now than a joke.
"You want a piece, Steve? You want to take me home and fuck
me? Tired of jacking off? It's a sin either way, right? Might as
well get some ass, no?"

I grab him by the collar of his dirty T-shirt and pull him even
closer. "Don't start this shit with me, *Father*." I'm hoping the "father" makes a dent, reminds him of his office, that he's something more than just a drunk in a bar having a tough time of it.

"Mark," he says in a whisper, his eyes swimming out of focus
again. "My name is Mark." He loosens his grip on my pants and
turns back to the bar to fumble with a crumpled pack of cigarettes.

"Shit." I snatch the pack from him. I light one for each of us
and turn back to my whiskey. A conversation bubbles down in
the smoke at the end of the bar, the bartender and bar-back
bantering in a foreign language. The words filter in while I try
to figure out what to do next. I recognize the language but
don't understand it. The words and structure are just on the
other side of familiar—like something struggling not to be Latin.
Maybe they're talking about how tough it is to pay the electric
bill for this place. Maybe that's why it's so damn dark in the
joint.

"One thing I want to know," Mark slurs. "Been coming here
every day for a week and still don't know what language they're
speaking."

"Didn't think to ask?" I say, and immediately regret it.

"No. No, Steve. I didn't think to ask."

"It's Esperanto."

Like a dog who's heard a barely perceptible noise, Mark lifts
his head slightly. "Huh. That's the name of this place." He
seems amused. "Go figure."

"Yeah, it was supposed to be this scientific thing. Rational. Simple, straightforward, rules that everyone would understand. It was supposed to be the universal language."

"I thought Esperanto meant hope," he says.

"Yeah, that, too."

He takes a drag off his cigarette. "Well, I guess this is where it all ended up." He waves his hand in the air to indicate our surroundings.

I've got no response for that. We fall silent and stare into our drink glasses, looking for answers.

"You know what I been thinking about lately? Thinking about a lot?" Mark says suddenly.

"I don't know, Mark, the years of school, seminary, service you're throwing away?"

"I been thinking about Uncle Charlie's cat," he says, oblivious of my comment. "Uncle Charlie's old black cat. What was that damn cat's name?" He stops as if he expects either me or the beer to provide an answer.

I turn from the bar and wait, staring at the empty dance floor. Suddenly the music kicks on, Beethoven's Ninth set to a ludicrous disco beat, complete now with electronic chirps and beeps, dry-ice smoke, and strobe lights. At noon, no less. The loud, driving thump of it all hammers at my chest. A handful of men move to the dance floor and start dancing and grinding.

"Can I get another Jack over here?" I call a bit too loudly into the smoke. "Double. Please."

New drink in hand, I down half before my gag reflex kicks in. The warmth rushes through me.

"Chase," Mark says. "That was the cat's name. Chase. Black cat. Had a little white patch just under his neck. Old as dirt. I was just a kid, fifteen or something, and I'd gone to stay with Uncle Charlie for a couple of weeks in New York. Lived in the Village. Don't know what the hell my parents were thinking."

Mark orders another beer and a shot, but leaves the tequila

standing untouched on the bar. He lights a cigarette with no problem. He takes a drag, then holds the cigarette away from him, considering the burning ember as if he'd only now discovered fire. After another drag, he begins talking, the smoke pouring out of him, making him look like an overworked machine.

"So I'm in the apartment alone one day. Hanging my head out of the window, checking out the cruisers on the street below. It was hot. I didn't have a shirt on." He chuckles, shakes his head. "At the time, at that age, I didn't even allow myself to see that the men walking by were checking me out. I didn't even allow myself to think that Uncle Charlie was . . . you know . . . Anyway. I'm sitting in a window in the Village, half naked, sweat running down my little tan body."

Mark waves at the air in front of him, clearing away an unnecessary part of the story.

"Anyway, I'm watching all the men go by when I hear this meowing, almost a howling. I know it's the cat but it doesn't sound right. He sounds like he's in pain. So I go into Uncle Charlie's bedroom and there's Chase. It's almost hard to see him, 'cause he's black as night and tangled up in this black sweater. I call his name. 'Hey, Chase. Hey, buddy. What's the problem?' And he looks at me with this, this look on his face. Like he's been caught with blood on his paws or something. He tries to run off but his claws are caught. He's hunched over the sweater and his claws are caught and he looks confused so I decide to help him. I'm walking toward him when I notice it. His little kitty cock is out, red and swollen. I stop and stare at him. He stares at me, pissed off or guilty or something.

"So Uncle Charlie and his roommate walk in and Chase frees himself and runs under the bed. 'I think Chase was humping your sweater,' I tell Uncle Charlie. And you know what he does? He tousles my hair and he and his friend laugh. 'Oh, that's not my sweater, Mark,' he says to me. 'That's Chase's special friend.

Cats get lonely, too.' 'But it's a sweater,' I say. 'You make do, kid,' he tells me. 'Sometimes you just make do.' "

Mark mashes his cigarette out and shoots the tequila as if washing the story out of his mouth.

I stare into the smoke and try to make sense of this cat story. Is it some sort of repressed, mixed-up memory? Was Mark the sweater, his uncle the cat? But the music thumps on and the Jack is catching up to me. Someone slides up next to me at the bar and shouts, "Cosmopolitan," into the smoke. The bar to either side of us is empty, but here's this clown brushing up against my arm.

I don't want to turn and look, but out of the corner of my eye I can see the man turn to me, twirling the straw between his teeth, looking me over like a piece of meat.

"What are you drinking?" He leans in close over my drink and actually sniffs it. "Whiskey?"

Against my better judgment, I turn to him. Deep brown, hungry eyes look into my own. He's a young-looking forty and sports a deep orange spray-on tan. A light sheen of sweat glistens on his forehead.

"Thanks, but no," I say.

He gives me a knowing smile, as if he's heard that one before, and turns back to the bar. When the cosmo arrives, he leans over the bar, disturbing the smoke, revealing the shirtless bartender for a moment. Whispers are exchanged; then my orange friend walks away.

Another double appears in front of me. I stare at it.

"For fuck's sake, Steve, have the drink," Mark says quite clearly. "Have the drink, grab a fucking stool, and say your piece. Try to talk me out of it. I know you have to. And to be honest, I want to hear what you have to say."

I turn to Mark and our eyes meet again. They've come back into focus.

"Just sit," he says. He exhales a cloud of smoke and smiles.

"And no, I wasn't molested by my uncle." He laughs and shakes his head. "If you only knew how much I want you to convince me, how much . . . I don't know . . . how much I want to see the light or whatever and go back with you."

I grab a stool. "I know," I say, more to myself than to Mark. I take a swallow of Jack and light another cigarette.

"It's only sex," I say. The words ring hollow. I don't even know why I'm saying them, but something needs to be said, even if it is bullshit. I push on. "Sex is only one facet of the human experience. It's something sacred, reserved for marriage between a loving man and woman." I stop, unable to go on. For some reason, the image of the cat goes through my mind.

"You've got to do better than that," Mark says. "I've gone through all that already. I've given that little speech myself." There's a hint of desperation in his voice now. "Tell me you've got something reserved for emergencies, some great secret, a mystery, something that will heal me."

"Think of the years you've invested, Mark," I begin again. Maybe practicality can win the argument. "Look at it that way. All these years of education and preparation and service. And you're gonna throw it away for what? For a little taste of sexual freedom? Don't do it. Reconsider."

Mark looks at me for a moment. He seems angry almost, let down that I can't come up with something better. "Why? Why reconsider? Why did they send you out to catch me? Why this need to stop us from leaving the fold? Do they think it'll cause a mass exodus? That everyone else will realize how much of their lives they've wasted and priests will just start heading for the exits, run to the nearest hooker or singles bar?"

"Mark, they're just worried about you. And you know it's more complicated than that."

"Is it, Steve? Is it?"

"Yes. Yes, it is. You know how few of us there are these days.

Just . . . just don't quit." I mean that. In that moment, I discover a little protective spot in my heart for the priesthood. We can't just surrender, can't let go of people like Mark. We're growing fewer by the day. "Listen. It's understood." I search for the right words. "It's understood that there will be transgressions. That's what confession is for. Just because you make a little transgression every once in a while is no reason to quit. I mean, we're only human. Hell, you know that."

"Confession?" Mark says, astounded. "Are you serious? Listen to yourself. Did it occur to you the main reason they sent you is not that they give two shits but that they're afraid I'll rat some of them out?"

I don't say anything.

"So what? Now that I've made my little break, you guys talk me back into the fold. Things are forgiven. We reach an understanding. Feel better because we're all human, because even the best of priests have their weaknesses, need to get drunk, need to get laid?"

"Something like that. Yes," I say, almost embarrassed. That is what I'm saying, right? That is what I was sent here to do.

"Unless it has to do with money, right?" Mark counters. He's whispering, but the anger is evident. "We wasted no time in shunting David off for skimming money off the top. I tell you about that one? If they could have crucified him, they would have. But a little sex is okay as long as no one knows about it. Hell, feel up your altar boys—or girls." He shoots me a look. "Do that and they'll bend over backward to cover for you. Fucking another person is okay, but fucking the Church isn't." He stops and lights another cigarette. "Can I get another fucking beer over here!" he yells.

I light yet another cigarette. I have no idea what to do with myself. I'm afraid that if I don't keep my hands occupied I'll punch Mark in the face. We can't afford to think this way. It's like Miss Rita leaving the home for a weekend, only to realize how depressing it is when she gets back to it. We spend so much time squashing our urges that being celibate becomes second nature. Almost. But start tiptoeing across the line and it isn't long before biology reasserts itself, reminds you just what kind of freakish existence you're living. Quite frankly, I don't need this.

"I have another question for you, Steve," Mark begins after getting his beer. "Why here? How did you find me so easily? Why do none of these people seem surprised to see you here? And your lecture. You're talking about sex, yes. But you seem to have very little to say about my choice of partners."

"Listen, Mark. We've all been through it."

Mark turns to me. I can feel my cheeks flushing in the dark of the bar.

"You?"

It was nothing. Most people wouldn't even count it, but . . . But what? I freeze for a bit. "You know how hard it is to escape seminary clean," is all I can think to say. My voice drops to just above a whisper. "You know that."

Mark almost sputters when he speaks again. "Are we broken, Steve? What the hell's wrong with us? You make it sound . . . I don't know . . . almost natural. Tell me. Do we come in twisted up like this or does the system twist us into deviants?" The desperation in his voice is growing and he's beginning to speak louder. "Are we all faggots and pedophiles when we come into the priesthood or is it just something about putting on the robe, strapping on that collar, sitting in those little dark booths listening to other people's sins—"

"Damn it, you know better than that," I cut in, my voice rising now, smoke spilling out of my mouth and nostrils. "Yeah, okay, you're right. A lot of confused and repressed people join the priesthood. They have urges. But you know what? We . . . they deal with them, goddamn it, and they still manage to do good work."

Mark interrupts. "Oh yeah, we're all fucking saints, aren't we? Because we wear black and wear a collar and say Mass and don't get laid most of the time. That makes us special, makes us any less sinful?"

"No," I say firmly, regaining control of my voice. "It's still a sin. It is still wrong in the eyes of the Church. But it's something we have to deal with on a personal level. We are all born with sin, Mark. And you know we have counseling for this sort of thing. Yes, you'll have your transgressions. Yes, sometimes you will feel guilt, overwhelming amounts of guilt. For your own actions." I pause. "And for standing up in public and saying that what all these people . . ." I motion to the people around us. "That what all these people do every day, how they choose to live their lives. That that's all wrong. Hell, Mark, you don't even have to believe that. This is a job. And the good we do far outweighs the damage. Don't look at it as you being unable to live a life of God just because you've got this weakness."

"Weakness," Mark says with a chuckle. "Sin. Good versus bad." The anger is gone from his voice now. He's almost on the point of crying. "You're missing the point. God, you're missing the point by a mile. You think this is a mere matter of conscience? Yeah, sometimes I feel guilty about these urges I have, guilty about supporting a faith that says men will burn in hell for loving each other. But you know what? I think I could live with that."

I look at him. "Then what is it, Mark? I don't understand."

"Hell, Steve, I don't know if I understand. I feel like every day I spend in the Church, some little part of me breaks. Like this loneliness . . . I don't know how to say it." He pauses and looks at me. "It's like this loneliness is accumulating, getting more and more unbearable every day." He pauses and throws back the shot of tequila that had appeared at his elbow. "I don't want to be like my uncle's cat, Steve. That cat lived his entire life in that fucking apartment and he lived a long, long time.

And all he ever had was that sweater. His little transgression was the sweater. And lately . . . every time I jerk off, every time I even consider another person as simply a release, a transgression, I think of that damn cat." I notice his eyes watering now, his Adam's apple working up and down. "Damn it, I don't want to be that cat. I don't want to get more and more twisted. I don't want this loneliness building up day after day after day, driving me crazy until I come to in the rectory one rainy morning and find myself humping an altar boy."

He stops and turns back to the bar, makes a slight motion with his hand. Yet another beer and shot are produced. I stare at him, unable to say anything. The image of the cat comes clearly to my mind now.

"Steve," Mark says.

"What?" I turn to the bar and peer into the mirror behind the bottles. Another Jack appears in front of me.

"Say something," Mark says. "Please."

I try to look at him, but can't. I came in here to save him and now I can't even look at him. I hate us both right now. I finish the Jack in two quick swallows and throw money on the bar. The air conditioner kicks on again, sending the smoke swirling around the room.

"Steve," Mark says, reaching toward me.

A shudder goes through my body and I force myself from the stool and toward the door. As I walk by his table, the little orange man who'd bought me the drink wiggles his fingers in a good-bye gesture. I ignore him and push the door open, squinting against the light.

Christmas morning finds me not on the altar of St. Pete's standing in front of a hundred somber white faces, but in a pew at Zion Baptist Church surrounded by the shouting faithful and their even louder clothes. Who knew that a woman would wear a purple dress and gold shoes for something other than

an LSU game? I'm hemmed in by Miss Rita, sitting in the aisle
to my left, and Vicky to my right. Vicky, the only other white
person in the church, looks slightly amused.

This isn't exactly how I pictured Christmas morning, but
pain in the ass that it is, I'm happy to take my mind off that little scene with Mark. I'd managed to get back to St. Pete's and
cram in a nap and shower before the Christmas Eve children's
Mass. I don't know that the nap helped any as I felt hungover
and I was practically sweating whiskey. "Something smells
funny," Denise kept saying. "Yall smell that?" The other altar
girl, Maggie, shot me a look. "It smells like my daddy when he's
about to yell at me."

Father Sibille, bringing joy into the lives of his parishioners!

Miss Rita, though? This morning, Miss Rita is beaming,
pleased as punch with her Christmas gift.

Every year, she demands something slightly absurd—sometimes something small and inconsequential, sometimes something ridiculous and extravagant. Every year she gets what she
wants.

Last year, it was a bright orange Mr. T T-shirt. Mr. T's Mo-
hawk was made of some sort of puffy material. Under his face
were the words *I Pity the Fool.* The only other thing she asked
for was a matching battery-powered key chain that repeated
Mr. T's most famous phrases. For the whole week of my visit
from seminary I couldn't utter more than two sentences without hearing the phrase "Quit yo jibba-jabba" coming from the
key chain and accompanied by Miss Rita laughing so hard
she'd almost slide out of her wheelchair.

Three years ago, she requested a handheld GPS unit.

"For what?" I asked. "You're in a chair in a nursing home.
You can barely read and I don't think you can even see the
numbers on a screen like that."

"You sure know how to make an old lady feel good about
herself," she told me.

"But what do you need a GPS for?"

"Just in case," she said. "You never know."

Of course I bought the thing. After it was out of the box and powered up, she thrust it at me. "Tell me where we at."

"We're in your room."

"Don't make me get out of this chair. Tell me what that GPS says."

"Fine." I read off the longitude and latitude numbers. Then I showed her the map.

"Ain't that something," she said. "Now show me where your mawmaw's house was."

This year, I wasn't going to let her catch me off guard. While I should have been planning for the festival, I pored through catalogs trying to guess which absurdity she would wish for. A robotic monkey head? A seven-foot-wide Thomas Kinkaid painting? A two-man tent? An English saddle?

But no. Nothing that easy.

"I want you to come to church with me Christmas morning," she said.

"What? I can't do that."

"Why not? You shamed of me?"

"It's Christmas morning. I'm a priest," I stammered. "It's— it's. It's Christmas."

"Boy, I know you got that old Cajun priest doing a French Mass at eight thirty."

"How do you find these things out?"

"Don't you worry yourself about my business."

"Your business?"

She changed the subject. "It ain't going to kill you to come to early service with me. You can drop me to Teddy's house afterward, be back in Grand Prairie in time for your other Mass."

How convenient. "Wouldn't you rather have an iPhone?" I asked.

"An iPhone? What the hell I'm gonna do with an iPhone?"

"What the hell do you do with a GPS?"

"I get plenty use out of that GPS. I never get lost going to the community room. Besides, I don't see what the big deal is."

"I don't know," I whined. "I'm a white Catholic priest. Don't know if I want to start off Christmas morning in a Baptist church hearing about the white devil."

"Please," she said. "They ain't going on about white devils in that church." She paused. "Not on Christmas, anyway."

"Ugh."

"Look, boy. It ain't that much to ask. Just come to church with me. One time. Could be my last Christmas, you know."

She had me there.

"Okay. Fine. I'll go to church with you. Anything else you want? A pogo stick? A pool table?"

She smiled. "Now that you mention it, there is one more thing."

Then she demanded I bring Vicky. After five minutes of arguing, she really laid it on, said it was the dying wish of an old woman on her last Christmas on earth. Hadn't she helped to raise me since I was a child? After a century of hard living, it would do her heart good to see me with a woman just once.

"Even if it is just pretend," she threw in.

After I finally agreed to ask Vicky, Miss Rita insisted I call her right then and there to get an answer.

"If she says no, tell her I got stage-ten cancer."

"There's no such thing!"

"You ain't a doctor. Now shut up and call that girl."

Thankfully, Vicky agreed immediately.

This morning, when we drove up to Easy Time, Timeka told us Miss Rita was in her room dressed and ready to go. "She's been up since five this morning," she said as she let us into Miss Rita's room.

"I couldn't wait to see my Christmas present," she said without a trace of embarrassment. "Now get over here, girl, so I can get a look at you."

"Hi, Miss Rita," Vicky said, offering her a hand. "I'm thrilled to meet at least one other person trying to knock some sense into Father Steve's head."

Miss Rita laughed. "I must not be doing a good job if he's still dressing up in that monkey suit with a pretty girl like you running loose back there."

"Okay. Let's go," I said, but otherwise kept my mouth shut. To open it would have been to invite more scorn from both of them. They did well enough without my help.

"You never told me she was pretty," Miss Rita said as I pushed her chair. "And that dress. That's something else."

Indeed, the dress was something else. Vicky is a jeans-and-shirt sort of woman, so seeing her in a dress—even a conservative navy blue knee-length one with a white collar—had thrown me for a loop. It clung to her in places that I typically tried not to notice.

"Pretty cold out today, Vicky," I said. "Sure you don't want to button up your coat?"

She and Miss Rita looked at each other and laughed.

Now here we stand in Zion. So far, the minister hasn't launched into a white-devil tirade and people have quit staring at us. Once the service started, there just wasn't time for it, what with the call-and-response prayers, the singing, the shouting. It makes my parishioners look like a bunch of tree sloths who'd gotten into the Ambien. So no time for staring. No time for reflection or contemplation, either. Maybe they think enough during the week.

It is Christmas, after all, why not really celebrate the coming of Baby Jesus? He's the savior, right? Makes more sense to sing and shout and dance than to choke on incense for an hour while murmuring through the liturgy. Not that I plan on making any changes to today's services back at St. Pete's.

Miss Rita elbows me in the hip, motions me to lean in.

"Get your head out of the clouds," she says. "Quit thinking and sing."

She grabs my hand, lifts it and hers over her head, and sings a few lines in a high, off-key voice. She stops, yanks me down again. "Sing, I said. And grab that girl's hand."

"Miss Rita."

"Don't Miss Rita me. And don't make me tell you again."

She raises our hands over her head and starts singing.

I turn to find Vicky laughing at me, her hand already waiting for mine. She leans in. "It's not going to kill you," she says. "Besides, look how happy she is."

As I take Vicky's hand, Miss Rita squeezes my left hand hard.

I whisper to Vicky, "I guess you're right. But it seems a bit dishonest. It's just pretend."

Vicky looks down at Miss Rita. "She's a hundred years old, Steve. I think she knows what she's doing."

"I guess," I say.

"Now shut up and sing," she says.

I don't have to be told four times.

Chapter 10

The tent is thick with the smell of gumbo and the murmur of voices. It's a brisk Saturday night in Grand Prairie and half the population seems to have turned out for our gumbo fund-raiser. Many of them are the exact same people who buy the cakes and plate lunches, the same ones who give their kids change to drop into the box decorated with brown bunnies that sits in the entryway to the church. I'm afraid of asking how much more money we need to raise.

I've got a fake smile plastered to my face and if I have to drink a gallon of beer to keep it there, then so be it. I'm tempted to go inside and drain half a bottle of whiskey, but that would lead to very bad things. So beer it is. And the fake smile is staying there, regardless of the infantile thoughts zipping through my head. Christmas was two weeks ago and today I got another call from the bishop, telling me Mark hadn't been seen. No one knows where he is. Not even his parents. Screw Mark. Screw him for dredging up the sorts of things that should stay buried deep in the mind. Mark is wrong; an adult lifetime of repressing our most basic urges is perfectly healthy.

"I have to wonder, Vick. Wouldn't it have been easier just to ask each of these people for a hundred-dollar donation and be done with the whole thing? You know, 'Give us a hundred bucks, we'll hire the carnival, and then we'll charge you again for the rides.' " I might have a fake smile on my face, but that doesn't mean I can't be a pain in her ass.

She takes a swig of beer out of a plastic cup. She'd decided today to pick up a couple of kegs—I don't know when she became copriest, but there it is. Now Denise is selling beer for a dollar a cup while my three old birds dish out the rice and gumbo. I've noticed Denise take a few swigs, and I've also noticed her parents watching and doing nothing about it. It's a fine Louisiana ritual, watching your child sneak her first beers—even if it's at a fund-raiser in the church parking lot.

"Boy, Steve, you have a special talent for missing the point," Vicky says, pushing her bowl away and tipping her chair back. She's wearing cargo pants and a camo army jacket with the name Stinson over the breast pocket. Her blond hair's pulled in a tight ponytail and her eyes glint with satiation. It takes a rare woman to be so comfortable—and look good doing it, if I must admit—under the glare of the naked hundred-watt bulbs we used to light the tent.

"What do you mean?" I ask, knowing full well what she'll say.

"This was never just about the money. And it's not just about the festival, remember? You've got yourself a community on your hands."

I put my fingers together in the shape of a cross, stick them out toward her, and hiss.

"Shut up," she says, laughing. "Seriously. Look around you. You got practically the whole town out here, even the ones that don't go to church. I used to nag Daddy to do things like this, but he was just too damn lazy."

"Really? You? Nagging? Say it ain't so."

I do feel something resembling pride. It's either that or a bad piece of sausage. I look around. Everyone is laughing and smiling. Old ladies are clustered in circles, clucking like hens.

Children dart in and around the tables, rush out of the tent into the cool night air, and dare each other to go into the cemetery. At the back end of the tent, Boudreaux and a crew of old farts stand around on his cooking trailer.

"I guess you're right," I say.

"You should be used to that by now," she says. "Besides, for someone so paranoid about B.P. raiding your flock, this is the exact sort of thing to keep the Pentecostal wolf out of the fold. You're being a good shepherd."

"Wow. Bonus points for using Christian imagery," I say. "But let's not mention B.P., please."

"Too late," she says.

"Well, don't mention him again."

"No, I mean too late," she says, rocking her chair forward and motioning toward the front flap of the tent.

There, conjured by the mere mention of his name, is B.P. In the flesh. He surveys the scene before him as if he's gauging the crowd, determining their worth before stepping all the way into the tent. Filing in behind him are his wife, his youngest boy, Little Red Riding Redneck her own self, and another seven or eight Pentecostals.

A second of silence washes through the tent as the flock stops eating and talking long enough to assess the intruders. Most of them go immediately back to what they were doing, but a few stare.

Good. I wish they'd point and laugh as well.

"This is better than TV," Vicky says.

"Shut up," I say.

"Aren't you going to get up and say hi?"

"No. He can come to me."

"You are so, so ridiculous. Paranoid, ridiculous, and a bad host."

The last comment is the only one that stings, but before I can get up, B.P. and his posse are closing the distance.

"Father Steve, it sure do smell good in here tonight," he says, shaking my hand with his right paw and grabbing my shoulder with his left. Sure do smell good? There he goes with the aw-shucksterism again. He's probably got a degree in English, the jerk. "How yall doing tonight?" he asks, his eyes sliding over to Vicky, who's still sitting down, then back to me. He's probably starting to think we're attached at the hip.

"A lot better now that yall are here," I lie. "Glad you could join us."

"You kidding me? We was gonna eat macaroni and cheese tonight, but we could smell the gumbo all the way down to the church."

Church. Right. Fancy name for a big pile of dirt and a trailer park.

"Sister Vicky, good to see you again," he says, acknowledging her.

"Same here, B.P.," she says, raising her glass of beer to him. His eyes narrow some, but his smile remains fixed to his face. "Who are all these fine people following you around tonight?" she asks.

"Just my little bit of family," he says, hitching up his pants and looking like a rancher who's about to give a tour of his thousand-acre spread. He begins the introductions and I immediately forget all their names. With the exception of his oldest son, they all look like clones—ruddy-faced, thin-lipped polite people. The men are in jeans and flannel shirts. The women are in denim ankle-length skirts, sensible shoes, and floral-print tops. They wear no makeup and their yards of uncut hair are twisted into buns.

His son, though—the older one—he's a different story entirely. He's wearing designer jeans. A well-worn black leather jacket over a just-wrinkled-enough blue-and-white-striped shirt, the sleeves of which are French-cuffed. Silver cuff links. Italian leather loafers. His hair is moussed into one of those perfectly mussed bed-heads. He looks like something his plain-jane wife accidentally ordered out of a J.Crew catalog one rainy day and never bothered to send back.

The only reason I forget his name is that I immediately think of him as B.P. Junior. And Junior he shall remain.

"Mind if we join yall?" B.P. asks, both he and Junior pulling out chairs and sitting down before I answer. B.P. reaches into his pocket, pulls out a roll of cash, and hands it to his wife, who, along with the other women, is still standing. "Yall go get us some food," he says, and they move off silently.

Vicky's left eyebrow arches as she watches them go and come back with bowls for the men, then go and come back with bowls for the children, then finally go and come back with bowls for themselves.

When they're all seated, B.P. interrupts the stream of small talk and grabs the hands of the two Pentecostals closest to him and says, "Let us pray," which causes them to all bow their heads. "Dear Lord, we thank You for the blessings You've put on this table before us. We thank You for our health and this beautiful night. We thank You for blessing us with these neighbors."

That's nice of him.

"And have mercy on their souls," he adds.

As he says "Amen," I look at Vicky, my eyes big in a "See? I told you so" gesture. But she just puts her hand over her mouth and looks over her shoulder to hide her laughter.

"Let's eat," says B.P. He and his family tear into their food as if it had personally insulted them.

The nerve of this man, to come to my church and tell *his* God to have mercy on *our* souls! He and his pack of dogs who eat as if they hadn't in five years, who were probably stuffing their pieholes just minutes before arriving.

Then Denise lopes over to our table, doing her best to impersonate a Labrador retriever puppy, what with the gangly legs, the flopping hair, the dopey grin. She throws her arms around my neck and I freeze in horror. I can smell her shampoo, but what I really notice is the beer on her breath.

"Hey, Father Steve," she says too loudly. "Can I get you another beer?"

The entire B.P. clan stops in midslurp, like feasting hyenas who've just heard the growl of an approaching lion. Their eyes turn to Denise and me.

Denise, looking right back at them, says, "Hey, yall want some beer, too? It's just a dollar a cup."

"Excuse me," Vicky says before pushing away from the table and running off, no doubt to fall on the ground and laugh herself into a stroke.

B.P. lowers his spoon and considers the both of us. His lips slide into a sly smile that makes me want to punch him.

"No, thanks, honey," he says.

"Really?" she asks, then drops her voice to an exaggerated whisper. "It tastes good, though."

B.P. casts his eyes around the place as if noticing for the first time all the plastic cups of beer, the lit cigarettes. Those eyes come back around to me, to my plastic cup ringed with foam, the pack of Camel Lights in my black shirt pocket, which sits about six inches south of my white collar.

"Well, honey," he says. "Temptation often tastes good. But some things are bad for a man's body and, more important, his soul."

Her grip on my neck loosens. She's confused. "Oh," she says, then, God bless her, shrugs off B.P.'s words as if they meant absolutely nothing. "Okay. But how about you, Father?"

B.P.'s smile grows. That son of a bitch is daring me to make a move.

I look him right in the eye and say, "I'd love another one, Denise. Make sure you fill it up all the way."

As she skips off, Vicky comes walking back. B.P.'s eyes slide over to her for a moment, but I'm not done yet. I look at his wife, old what's her face, and the other women.

"I know yall aren't partial to alcohol," I say, "and beer certainly isn't everyone's thing. But I got plenty of wine in the house if yall want."

They all look down at their bowls.

"No, thanks, Father," B.P. says, trying to keep his greasy smile on his big fat face.

"Really? No wine, huh? Funny thing, that."

"What's so funny about avoiding the sins of alcohol, Father?"

"I don't know. Seems a pretty harsh thing to call something like that a sin, considering Jesus's first recorded miracle was turning water into wine."

His ears turn a touch red. "Bible don't say he drank it."

"You know, B.P., I think you might have me on that one." I look at Vicky, who hasn't managed to sit down yet. "He's got a point, Vicky," I say, standing up. "But that's an awful lot of sin to be throwing around for free. I wonder, though, what it was He was drinking at the Last Supper." I shrug. "Anyway, don't want to turn a fine meal into a theological discussion, and I should probably go make sure Boudreaux ain't burning the gumbo. So thank yall for coming and good night."

But I don't go check on Boudreaux. I head toward the rectory and get myself a real drink.

How did I get here in the first place? I mean, a priest. Really.

In junior high, I looked at the adults around me—teachers, bus drivers, crawfish farmers—and wondered "Why that?" Surely, as children, they didn't think to themselves, *I want to be a crawfish farmer when I grow up.* I grew a little older, and I chalked it up to gender or education gaps. My parents' generation, the lower-class folks at any rate, clawed their way into the middle class as quickly and efficiently as possible, dreams be damned. Middle class was the goal, not a dream job. The man would take what he could get and the woman, if inclined to work, would either teach or become a nurse. They'd set up a base from which the kids could aspire to better things, be lawyers, doctors, and bankers and such. Which is what we did, my generation. We hit the playground running, promising to get big, important, adventurous jobs and leave this place and never come back.

It never occurred to us that people sometimes simply fell into jobs and houses and families. That, unless you're particularly focused and driven, life sort of has its way with you.

When I was fifteen, I figured people became priests the same way prophets became prophets, the way Joan of Arc became whatever it was that she was. One day while walking through a field of flowers or one night while you slept wrongly imprisoned, God tapped you on the shoulder, gave you the lowdown, and that was it. You just didn't say no when called up to the majors.

That didn't happen with me. I wonder if it happened with B.P. He certainly seems sure of himself. He certainly seems to think he's on a mission from God.

There's a knock on the door. "Padre! You okay in there?"

Vicky.

"Just a second," I say.

"You okay?" she asks again.

"Yeah, yeah. Just needed the bathroom is all."

"Look, everyone's leaving, so be a good boy and come say your good-byes."

"Is he still here?"

"No, they left already."

That established, I venture back out to my flock and help with cleanup. After they've all gone, I ask Vicky inside for a drink.

"Nahhhh. It's too nice out," she says. "Let's go see if that old swing still works." She points her chin at the swing.

She holds the screen door open for me.

We fall onto the swing and she opens a couple of cans. "Kegs were kicked," she explains. The beer's near freezing; little flecks of beer ice dissolve on my tongue.

The slow thrum of crickets is punctuated by moths and other bugs ticking and tocking into the security lights. We push at the ground with our toes and the swing squeaks as we move back and forth. I wonder, if someone saw us from a distance, if we'd look like an old couple, or two ridiculously oversized children. I'd venture the latter, considering the way Vicky's dragging her boots in the worn patch of dust below the swing, causing an imbalance in our motion. The groove under her boots is a good inch deeper than the one under my shoes.

"You and your dad use this a lot?"

"Yeah. When I was a kid. Not so much after I grew up," she says, smiling up at me. I think it's the first time she's given me a straightforward smile. Not a hint of sarcasm. "But you're sitting on my side."

"Want to switch?"

"No. Figure I'll sit on this side." She points to her feet with the beer can. "Dig Daddy's ditch a little deeper."

We lapse into silence. I feel like I've been alone for weeks, like I haven't spoken to another soul for years. It makes no sense, but there it is. I want to talk, to babble. But I've got no idea what to say or how to start.

"You know, long as I've been here, I haven't used that path through the woods yet." How's that for scintillating conversation?

"Ohhh, my little path."

"Your path?"

"Yeah. I made it. Hacked my way to the bayou with a chainsaw and machete. Took a tractor and shredded it all down to stubble. Then I plowed what was left." She shakes her head. "That last part wasn't such a hot idea."

"Why?"

"It rained right after I plowed. Huge mess. Call it my little lesson in soil erosion. All that loose bare dirt. It was muck from here clear to the bayou. Daddy got a kick out of it. Hell, he'd encouraged me, helped me out a little. I think he would have liked to open it up for the parishioners."

She pauses and looks in the direction of the woods.

"But Lord, everybody else wanted to kill me. Well, the old farts who hunt back there, anyway. Not happy at all. So I waited till it dried up some, then packed it down best I could by running the tractor back and forth, back and forth. Hell, I dreamed about driving that tractor for weeks after that. I vibrated in my sleep. Then I seeded the path with rye grass and anything else I thought might take root long enough to stop a swamp from forming. I was scared those old coots were going to shoot me off that tractor or string me from a tree."

Now, why don't I get stuff like that in confession?

"You should have seen my original plans. I was fourteen and plenty big in the head. I was going to pave it or something. Cobblestones. An elevated boardwalk with railing and lights. How I planned to afford that, I don't know. Guess I figured I could pass the collection plate or hold a bake sale."

"Bake sale?" I groan. "Don't say that again."

"Oh, c'mon." She elbows me in the ribs. I'm glad she's in good spirits considering how behind we seem to be with the festival. I've been having nightmares that, come April, I can't pay Johnny Blackfoot and he comes riding after me on a very upset elephant.

"Fine," she says, and hops out of the swing. She grabs four beers and slips them into the various pockets of her pants. She cracks two fresh ones and hands one to me. "Let's go for a walk."

"Sure thing," I say.

So we walk straight for the woods without a glance back at the security light. And when the undergrowth rustles to life, I hold my breath rather than scream.

"Rabbit," Vicky says.

"Really?" I'm impressed.

"How the hell should I know?" she answers. "What am I, Marlin Perkins?"

We move on without talking, our shoes whispering through the occasional patches of grass or crunching on leaf litter. We round a curve, and Vicky says the bayou's not too far off. It's a pleasant walk, the darkness and the sounds of the forest and the beer and the company are working together.

And then a scream. A high-pitched shriek.

"What the fuck?" The crimped metal edge of my now-squeezed beer can bites into the flesh between my thumb and forefinger.

"Shhh," she says. "Quiet."

Well, that it is. Whatever it was scared everything else in the woods silly as well. Just as the forest comes back to life, the sound comes again.

"Listen," Vicky says.

"Shit, Vicky. It's kind of hard not to."

What the hell? The only logical answer, floating somewhere at the edge of my mind, a fear trying to make itself known, is that it's a cougar, which supposedly makes a sound like a screaming woman. No one's seen a cougar back here in a hundred years or more, but that does little to put my mind at ease.

A third scream, this time more faint.

"I think it's moving away," I say, unable to hide the relief in my voice. *Please, Lord, let it be moving away.*

"It's floating down the bayou," Vicky says.

"What?" I replace the cougar in the bushes with a baby in a basket, a bayou Moses.

Now that the thought's occurred to me, as the fourth wail comes in, it does indeed sound like a baby in distress. People abandon babies in Dumpsters, leave them in cars in the hot sun, flush them out of the womb with saline and suction.

But here in Grand Prairie?

I start ticking off a list of parishioners. Who's pregnant? Who's capable of such a thing?

"C'mon," Vicky says, moving quickly into the darkness. I can't see her, but I imagine her hand waving me forward, her shoulders hunched over as she shuffles away in a creeping military posture.

Despite my instincts, the little voice in my head guaranteeing me that absolutely nothing good can come of this, I follow her. She stops and I pull up short. Two feet in front of us is the drop-off to the bayou. I can sense the barely moving water below.

"Be still," she whispers.

Be still? I'm having to force myself to breathe. I can't see. I've lost track of time. And I feel foolish, like a faithless coward.

As if in agreement, another scream goes out, directly in front of us.

To my right, a beam of light reaches out, strikes the water, and moves left until it spotlights two glowing red eyes. No sooner do I see them, no sooner do I register a paralyzing fear gripping my tailbone, than they're gone with a loud sploosh, an almost comical sound that dissipates quickly, leaving behind silence and the taste of copper in my mouth.

"What in holy hell?"

Vicky's laughing. "Need to change your under-roos?"

"Well, excuse the fu—excuse me for being scared shi—" I stop. Then start again from a different approach. "And you had that flashlight the whole damn time!"

"Calm down. It was just a nutria."

"Nutria?" Say what? I've been scared witless by a big, dumb rodent? "I've seen nutria, Vicky. I've seen them in the park in Lafayette. Since when do they make noises like that?"

She's laughing again. "I guess since they've been floating around in the dark back here."

The only thing I can think to say is, "Well, doesn't that just make perfect sense?"

She tosses her beer can into the bayou, grabs one from a pocket, opens it, and passes it to me. It's warm now, but I take two large gulps anyway. I remember that there's a crushed empty in my right hand. Not feeling particularly charitable toward Mother Nature, I wing the can into the water. I take another swallow of beer and imagine it working through me, calming me down.

And with the calm comes a feeling. High school. That's the only phrase that comes to mind. Creeping around in the woods. Warm beer. Being scared silly. And more. Hope? Potential? Optimistic uncertainty? Those emotions that come flooding in immediately after fear is successfully vanquished, after a light is shone under your bed to reveal no monsters there, after your finals come back and you do indeed have a future. The feeling that you still have options, rather than a track you've set yourself upon.

"Padre?" Vicky disturbs my little reverie.

"Yeah?"

"Come here," she says.

"Where?"

Her light clicks on, spotlights an iron bench with an S of a spine and one seat facing the bayou, the other the woods. I take the seat facing the water. She clicks the light off.

While my eyes readjust to the darkness and the black indentation of the bayou becomes more fact than imagination, I drink warm beer and listen to Vicky breathing. After what seems like several minutes, she speaks.

"So, Father Steve, why the priesthood?"

"That's a good question," I hear myself say. I must be drunk if I think that's a good question.

"I'm sure it is a good question," she says. "How about a good answer?"

I don't think I'm that drunk. "Can I have another beer?"

"Hell yeah," she says.

I open the beer and lean forward, away from her, looking at the bayou.

"I don't know," I finally say. "It just sort of happened."

I know what she's going to say.

"Steve, janitors sort of happen. Priests don't just sort of happen."

"I think your dad may have disagreed."

"Touché," she says. "But really."

"No, but really," I answer.

It's all right here on the surface, ready for me to spill, but I go through the motions of remembering anyway. I scrunch up my brow for effect as if she can see me, as if she wouldn't see right through that.

"Well. I planned on the job and the marriage and the kids."

"Like everyone else," she says, finishing my sentence. "And then what? You gay or something?"

"No." I sigh. "That might have made more sense, been a better explanation."

"To who? Your mom?"

"No. More to myself."

In no hurry to go on, I take a few sips of beer.

"So what happened?"

"It just didn't work out."

I can feel her turn and look at the back of my head, an impatient gesture.

"Oh, was that all?" she asks.

"Sure." I shrug.

"Steve."

"What?"

"Steve," Vicky says again. "You just don't up and join the priesthood because college wasn't working out."

She's not going to let this go.

"It wasn't college—not the grades or whatever."

I stop again. Now I can definitely sense her neck and shoulders tightening with impatience. She's getting tired of pulling teeth, so I anticipate her next question.

"And it wasn't a woman." I add, as an afterthought, "Or a man."

"Well?"

I sigh and run my fingers though my hair, and for some strange reason say a little prayer of thanks for still having all of it. *Thank you, God, for letting me keep my hair.* The way my mind works sometimes, trying desperately to run itself out of tight situations, fight or flight, daze and confuse, shuck and jive.

"Okay. It wasn't *one* woman. It was all of them. Remember the other night how Tommy told everyone that story about that girl dumping me and me riding around half naked on my bike?"

"You mean Ruh-ruh-ruh-Rachel? How could I forget?"

"Well, the story didn't end there."

After being so unceremoniously dumped by Rachel, I had to face her every day of the week at school. Seeing her made me want to cry and vomit and cut myself all at the same time. There was simply no escape. She and I were both in advanced placement, meaning we were in the same eight classes, sitting right next to each other.

Worse, perhaps because she felt guilty or felt she had the upper hand, she was trying to be nice. Worse still, either because she was forgetful or because she was the evil, manipulative sow I suspected her to be, she'd put her hand on my shoulder or rub her fingers through my hair while walking by, then say, "Oh. Oh my God. I'm sorry, Steve. I'm so sorry."

Other than an under-the-breath "fuck off" here and there, I kept it together for a week. And when the weekend came, I was relieved that she didn't show, allowing me to get drunk with my friends and accept their condolences. That is, until Cicily Gautreaux—who'd always hated Rachel and had a bit of a crush on me—let the cat out of the bag. Rachel wasn't hanging out on the back roads of Opelousas because she was at a frat party.

"God, she's so stuck up. All she's talking about is Brad and his stupid frat house. Two weeks of that. I can't take it anymore."

Two weeks? That meant she was seeing this Brad before she dumped me? And a frat house?

I had a sudden very vivid image of Rachel naked on her back in some squalid room, a blond jock type with a backward-facing ball cap, pulling up his pants as he walked out of the room, high-fiving one of his buddies and saying, "Your turn, bro!" In this vision, Rachel smiled and said, "You know, I can do more than one at a time, yall."

I was so angry I shook. But I did nothing. I went home that Saturday night and stared at the ceiling. Every time I shut my eyes, visions of my ex-girlfriend fellating half a football team pranced across my head.

Sunday was the same.

Monday, when I went to school I wanted to punch Rachel right in the nose. But there are rules about such things. Then she dropped her pen. It fell right under my desk, but I sat there staring straight ahead.

"Steve," Rachel said finally, in a tone indicating that I was being a jerk. "Can you get my pen, please?"

"Why don't you call Brad and ask him to get your fucking pen, you whore?"

Dr. Crane stopped writing on the board and looked over her shoulder. Rachel burst into tears and ran out of the room.

"Yeah, go ahead and cry. I should be the one crying!" I shouted.

In religion class, I raised my hand.

"Yes, Steven?" Mr. Hitchens asked.

"I have a question about the story of Rachel, Leah, and Jacob."

"Steven, I can't see for the life of me what that has to do with Saul on the road to Damascus, but okay."

"I guess I'm just confused. I mean, Rachel is pretty much a liar and backstabber of the worst sort. Shouldn't God have smote her or something?"

As it turned out, I was wrong. Leah was the liar. But it was still enough to get Rachel to run out of the class crying.

She didn't come back for trigonometry.

But I wasn't done with Rachel yet. Revenge didn't satisfy me for long, and it didn't do much for the visions of her sucking off the entire Kappa Alpha house. I spent another entire week without sleep and Friday night found me strung out, exhausted, and sitting with "Fudge Round" Arcenaux under his carport, doing tequila shots and watching him work through a box of Little Debbie Fudge Rounds snack cakes.

I didn't hang out much with Fudge Round. He was a neighborhood kid who went to public school and didn't seem to have much use for socializing beyond the extent of his yard. His parents were never around—his mom worked nights, his dad worked offshore when he wasn't in jail—so Fudge Round was content with sitting in the drive watching the world go by, smoking pot, drinking, and, when the urge struck him, huffing gas. If people showed up, he was happy to entertain. If no one showed up, he was equally happy to enjoy his substance abuse and Fudge Rounds in peace.

Fudge Round was steady—steady and loyal. He might not have been the brightest guy in the world, but he was always eager to help a friend in need. And spending large amounts of time alone in various states of intoxication gave him a unique approach to problem solving.

I happened to have a problem and Fudge Round was working on a solution. We'd already given lip service to being adult, taking the high road. He even told me, "Cuz, it's like I heard dis one time. If you love somethin'—really, really love it—you gotta let it go. And if it come back, you know it's meant to be."

"And if it doesn't?"

"Well, it's time to go fishin' for somethin' else, my friend. There's plenty of fish out in the sea."

"Fuck a fish," I said. At that point, the sea looked like little more than a stagnant pond and I was too angry to consider any more mixed love metaphors.

Though a peaceful guy by default, Fudge Round brooked no treachery. So he sat in silence for a while.

"I think I got it," he said finally. "She scared of the devil?"

I laughed for a good five minutes. We'd been smoking as well as drinking and it just struck me as funny. "The devil?"

"Yeah, cuz." He called everyone cuz. "You know, the devil."

"I know who he is."

"Well, she's probably scared of him, right?"

"I don't know. I guess."

"Me? I'm scared to death of that devil." He shook his head and interjected a "Kee-yahhhh" to show how serious he was. "Scared, scared. Think about it. Eternity. Forever. Pass your mind on that for a little while. For. Ever. That devil poking you in the ass with that pitchfork. I tell you what, that keeps me up at night sometimes. You don't worry about that, do you?"

"I guess," I lied.

"Everybody must at some point," he said. "So that devil's probably the scariest thing in the whole world."

"Okay," I said. "So?"

"So, c'mon," he said, and led me to a storage shed, from which he pulled out a roller, a paintbrush, a paint pan, and a can of firehouse-red latex exterior paint.

"Take your clothes off," he said.

"Say what?"

"You heard me. Take your clothes off. We gone put the fear of the devil in that girl."

It made no sense. It made perfect sense. I stripped. He handed me the paintbrush. "You do your privates. I'll roll the rest."

If I wasn't already high enough to be considered clinically re-tarded, the paint fumes quickly finished the job. The paint was cool, thick, and went on sticky. In awed silence, I watched Fudge Round work. His tongue poked out of the corner of his mouth as he concentrated. After he was done, he took his own clothes off.

"Fudge Round, what are you doing?"

"Mais, if there's something scarier than one devil, it's two devils!" he explained as if I was the stupidest man alive.

"But you never leave your yard," I protested.

"Shoo," he said. "You don't know all there is to know about Fudge Round. Besides, you're my friend. And this is what friends do."

If my ducts hadn't been clogged solid with paint, I would have cried. Instead, I painted Fudge Round. After we were done, we smoked another bowl. By the time we left his place, it was near three in the morning.

We rode our bikes, somehow making it three miles without being seen. Upon dismount, a layer of red paint stayed with the seat, leaving our blinding white asses exposed to the night air.

Other than painting each other and scaring Rachel, Fudge Round's plan was short on details. But when I saw her house and her car in the drive, things sorted out on their own. I dropped my bike and ran across the lawn, dew tickling my ankles. I ran as fast and as hard as a drunk and stoned boy covered in red paint could run and then spread my arms and threw myself against the front door with a startling *thwap*.

I backed away from the door and considered my work—a big red splot resembling a crow or perhaps a crucified midget who'd been detached from his head. I turned to Fudge Round and smiled.

"Cuz, you crazy or something? Get your ass back here before her daddy wakes up."

As if on cue, a light turned on in the master bedroom.

"Shit," I said. "Run around the back."

We crouched on the side of the house, laughing into our arms. After five or ten minutes, the lights went off.

"Where her window at?" Fudge Round asked.

I led the way. It was a single-level ranch, with windows that practically stretched from window to ground. I raised my hand to knock.

"Wait," Fudge Round said. "Let me think a bit." Finally he snapped his fingers and broke off a handful of branches from a shrub. "Now roll in the grass."

"What?"

"He just cut the lawn. Get some grass all over you. It'll make you scarier."

So I did.

He handed me a branch. "Now take this and scratch on the window. Not too much. Not too hard. Just enough she'll hear."

While I started on that, Fudge Round rolled himself in the grass. He looked ridiculous.

It was only thirty seconds before the nails-across-chalkboard sound of branches on glass woke Rachel, who turned on a light, probably her bedside lamp. I stopped and held my breath.

"Do it again," Fudge Round whispered as he slid up right next to me. I did it again, once slowly, then a frenzied brushing motion. From the other side of the window came a muffled "Eeep" then a "Shhh" and what sounded like a male voice.

"Cuz, is somebody in there with her?"

"Brad," I hissed. My gut clenched and my heart hopped into my throat. My hands started to shake, so I occupied them by brushing the branch across the window again.

"You sure it's not her daddy?" he asked.

"I'm fucking sure."

I heard more muffled whispering, then the vertical blinds snapped open, revealing two pairs of eyes. Rachel, in an over-sized T-shirt and a pair of old boxers—my old boxers. And some guy, Brad, shirtless and sporting his own pair of boxers, bulging slightly in the middle.

I snapped.

"Rawr! Motherfuckers!" I screamed, and started pounding on the window. Brad stumbled back and Rachel let out her own scream, the likes of which I hope never to hear again. It went on and on. But I wasn't done. *"Rawwwwrrrr! Rawwwrrr! Mother-fuckers! Rawwrrrrr!"*

Fudge Round chimed in as well. *"Wooooooooooooo! Booga-booga-woooooo!"* he shouted.

We were all still screaming when her bedroom door flew open and her dad burst in. He wore white briefs and a pair of untied work boots and carried a very large handgun that ze-roed in on Brad's face. Brad fell down into a crouch and threw his hands over his head. "No, no, no, no," he yelped, pointing out the window. To this day, I shudder to think how close we came to getting Brad shot in the face.

But I didn't have time to process anything that night. It took all of half a second for the old man's pistol to swing toward the window.

"Run!" Fudge Round shouted.

He didn't have to tell me twice. We dived from the window just as the glass exploded from the first shot. Just to be safe, the old man fired twice more. By that point we were stumbling madly over our bikes, trying to force our fear-stricken limbs to quit imitating Jell-O and start doing the serious work of getting us the hell off that lawn.

Rachel still hadn't stopped screaming.

I heard the old man say, "Whoever the hell you are, call 911. And put some damn clothes on before I shoot you, too."

Finally perched on my bike, I took one last look over my shoulder. Rachel's dad was walking through the remains of the broken window like some unstoppable movie monster, his fish-white belly glowing in the dark.

We made it five blocks and were safely out of the old man's reach when I stopped to throw up. Pizza, fear, tequila, beer, and rage came pouring out of me. The bitterness, though, that was going to stick around for quite some time.

"You okay, cuz?"

"Yeah, I feel better, I think," I said. "Look, man, this meant a lot to me, Fudge Round."

"Awwww, shit," he said.

"No. Really," I started.

"No," he said, pointing at the police cruiser making its way down the street, its spotlight sweeping the neighborhood like some devouring eye searching for prey.

I imagined the 911 call.

"Two devils were outside our window."

"Two devils, you say?"

"Yes, devils."

"Can you describe these . . . devils?"

"You know, red and, um, covered in grass."

"Really?"

"And they're riding bikes."

Then the same thing had to be repeated as the dispatcher radioed the cruiser. And there it was, seeking out two devils riding their bikes through the night.

Fudge Round shook his head, wrung his handlebars in his hands. His eyes had gone big, as if he were the one seeing Satan. "Cuz, I can't get picked up. I can't. It'd be the end of old Fudge Round. I just can't."

I'd never seen him worried about anything.

"Just ditch your bike and go hide behind that house," I said.

"What you gonna do?"

"Don't worry about me."

I saddled up and rode. I rode right by the cruiser and waved when I sped by. "Evening, gentlemen," I called out in a British accent, then pedaled like hell.

Of course they caught me.

But it was worth it. Brad was scarred for life. Rachel was grounded for the rest of the school year. And I was forced to go to Confession. From behind the screen, I heard the priest gasp in laughter no fewer than five times.

Vicky was laughing. Hard. I can see where others would find it funny. I get that. But even now, I'm still frightened by just how unable I was to control the feelings raging through me, my complete inability to handle rejection.

"And then there was Stephanie. In college," I said.

"There's more?"

"Oh yeah."

The short version was Stephanie and I were nineteen and, being nineteen, stupid. We thought we were in love. We moved in, played house, bought a dog. JuJu, a yellow Lab. Then she dumped me. Thinking it was the mature thing to do, I let her keep both the dog and my heart. Of course that kind of thinking is folly. After working my way through a bottle one stormy night, I drove to our old place to visit my dog. I parked on the street and stepped out into the rain. She, at least, was happy to see me. And because it really had nothing at all to do about the love between a boy and his dog, I called JuJu out into the front yard, where we played in the rain. I stumbled around drunk, calling her name manically. She barked in the pure unadulterated delight of finding a playmate in the middle of the night.

"Lightning flashed, thunder rolled, and I yelled, 'JuJu' at the top of my lungs."

"Oh. My. God," says Vicky, clutching her knees, hardly able to breathe. "That is so not funny."

"Even less hilarious was that Stephanie and her new boyfriend called the campus alcoholic hotline instead of the cops." And what followed was three weeks' worth of mini interventions and counseling that totally missed the point. I wasn't an alcoholic. Alcoholism—as twelve-steppers are fond of saying—is a disease. My drinking wasn't a disease, it was a symptom of a worse malady—inability to deal with women in a rational manner.

"Wow," says Vicky, "it's all starting to fall into place."

I finish my beer, throw the can into the bayou.

"Here, have the last one," she says.

I take it without protest and drink half of it in one swallow.

"But, Steve, just because it's not working out with the ladies, you gave up and joined the priesthood?"

"Well, don't go looking for sense where there is none to be found. And that's only the half of it. After that, the mere thought of going on a date was enough to give me panic attacks. The minute a girl said yes to a date, she stopped being this pretty object and became someone who was one hundred percent bound to crush me. I actually got so nervous, I threw up on one girl. Therapy didn't work. Drugs didn't work. And not to sound young and stupid—which I was at the time—but the ladies were the whole point. I mean, why bother with college and finding the job and earning the money if not for that one lady and to provide for the family and all?"

"Wow, that's romantic."

I can't tell if she's being sarcastic or not.

"Then one day, I was going to a wedding in Opelousas—a high school friend of mine—and there was a mix-up or I was spaced out or something and I went to St. Landry instead of Queen of Angels. I realized my mistake in the parking lot, but went in anyway and just sat for a while. I hadn't been to church in years and I felt, well, I guess at peace. No voices. No calling. Not much of anything. Just this blissful emptiness. A lack of commotion more than anything else. Silence. And, I don't know, I think at that point I started to realize I couldn't be in love—or anywhere near it—in a balanced or quiet way."

"So, what?" she asks. "The Voice of God is actually an absence of noise?"

"Something like that."

I finish off the beer, look into the middle distance where I imagine the bayou's opposite bank to be. There's more to it than that, I'm sure. There has to be, right? I've been doing a bang-up job of not giving it much thought since making the decision, and I don't necessarily feel an overwhelming need to change that right now.

"You know, Steve, I have to say I'm a little disappointed."

"About?"

"I can't believe you never told me you were the Painted Devil of Opelousas!"

I laugh. "You knew about that?"

"I wasn't the only rumor floating around these parts, bub."

After a moment or two of chuckling, I turn it around to her. "So what about you?"

"Me and God are square."

"That's not what I'm talking about."

"Well, Steve, you're the one changing the subject, so why don't you be a little more clear?"

I can't tell if she's teasing or not. She doesn't sound upset.

"What are you doing out here, in Grand Prairie . . ." I let it trail off. I don't say "in the woods with a priest."

Now there's a little edge in her voice. "You mean all alone without a man?"

"It is sort of an odd place for a single young woman to call home."

She lights another cigarette, exhales. "I guess so. But I'm not just any single young woman. I'm the daughter of a priest and get a little tired of explaining it over and over again when I move beyond my little world."

"What about dating? What about men?"

"Oh. That," she says.

"Sorry. Just asking."

"Let's just say it's been a while. Will probably be a while yet."

"What happened?"

"Why did something have to have happened?" she asks.

"Just an educated guess," I say.

There's another long pause before she speaks. "James Stinson happened."

I suddenly remember the name on the shirt she's wearing. "Oh," I say.

"Yeah," she says. "He was in the 256th. Just one of those guys you hear about on the news getting blown up by IEDs."

The emotion has gone out of her voice.

"Were you two serious?"

"Had the dress picked out and the caterer booked."

"I'm sorry. I had no idea. None at all." I guess the gossip-mongers of Grand Prairie have some respect for her misery.

"Not your fault. Nothing anyone could have done. Damn

fool loved his army almost as much as he loved me. He died doing what he loved."

She stands up suddenly, flicks her cigarette off into the trees.

"How about we go get a couple more beers?" she says, and offers her hand to pull me up.

The conversation, it seems, is over. We walk slowly, in silence, back to the rectory.

Chapter 11

A warm weekday evening finds me standing in the middle of St. Pete's cemetery, smoking a cigarette while working on next Sunday's homily. We're two weeks from Lent, itself forty days from Easter, forty-five from the festival—and full of musings on death and resurrection. We're getting to the business end of Christianity. And while I'd like to avoid the subject, maybe talk about elephants or roller coasters or something, I'm not a Protestant, so I can't just haul off and sermonize about any old thing. I'm a Catholic priest and that means sticking to the topic at hand, which is set by the Gospel reading for that particular week. So I'm standing in a cemetery and, impossibly, finding it hard to think about death coherently.

"Steve," a man's voice says, hesitant but expecting.

I wonder if he saw me jump.

I turn to find Mark, in jeans and flannel shirt, stepping out of the shadows of the church. Great. I wasn't planning to host a pity party for two.

"Mark, you kinda scared me. Didn't see a car."

"Oh, I had Mama drop me off."

"Drop you off?"

"Yeah. Look, I'm a bit of a mess and I just couldn't stay with Daddy and Mama. She's brokenhearted about me quitting and Daddy . . . well, let's just say he had a strong suspicion that the reason I quit and the reason I joined might be one and the same."

We both look down and contemplate the cracks in the driveway. I know what I have to do. I don't have to ask myself WWJD.

"Where's your stuff?" I finally ask.

"You don't mind?" he says.

I look at him. "No, Mark." And I realize the next sentence is true only as it comes out of my mouth: "To be honest, maybe I could use a roommate out here."

"Yeah. It is spooky," he says. "I was getting a little creeped out by it. I saw one car pass by in the last half hour."

"That busy, huh? Well, we can go inside and crank the TV up all the way."

"Sounds good."

We walk around to the church entrance to grab Mark's luggage.

"Why'd you put it up here?"

Mark laughs self-consciously. "I don't know. I kinda pictured me throwing myself down on the steps before the heavy wooden doors and screaming 'Sanctuary' or something. But I forget what a low-rent operation you have out here. Glass doors. No steps."

"Well, you should have gone to St. Landry if all you wanted was effect."

"Not just effect, Steve. Drama!"

"Just because you're completely out of the closet doesn't have to mean you have to actually be a stereotype." I'll say this much for guys, gay or straight: it's easy to pick up a friendship and act like nothing's happened. I can only imagine how quickly Christianity would have collapsed had Jesus and the Apostles been a bunch of women. Jesus would never have got-

ten over the fact that they abandoned him during the Crucifixion. "I can't believe you guys would *do* that to me. I'm never
speaking to you again. *Ever!*" Then, out of spite, he would have
run off and joined up with the Zoroastrians.

I stop short at the sight of Mark's luggage: an army-surplus
duffel and a pet carrier.

"Look, Steve," Mark says. "I hope you don't mind."

I, in fact, do mind. It's one thing to be babysitting him. I
don't want the complication and aggravation of a pet. But it's
the first time Mark's voice has wavered. He sounds almost des-
perate at the thought that I might say no.

"Well, I don't think I mind," I lie.

"I promise you, it won't be a problem at all," Mark replies.

"Yeah, and that's what you said about that goldfish I bought
you when you were nine."

"Shut up, Steve. Look. He's the most adorable thing." Mark
opens the door and reaches in. "Come out here, you," he says
in that voice people get when talking to children and pets. He
pulls out a black puff of fur, just bigger than his hand, and
thrusts it at me.

I take it—a black kitten with a white patch at the throat. It
opens its eyes, looks at me, yawns, then goes back to sleep. Well,
put a fork in me, I'm done.

"What's its name?"

"I named him Chase," Mark says, running his finger gently
over the kitten's ears.

I scratch Chase under his chin and look at Mark's face. He's
thoroughly absorbed in the kitten. I hand it back and he places
it into the carrier slowly, closes the door quietly while holding
his breath. I've seen that look before on some priests' faces as
they close the tabernacle doors.

"Well, let's get Chase inside," I say. "See if we can set yall up
with a place to rest your weary heads."

After we've settled in, there is a brief nightmarish moment in which silence settles over the rectory and nothing seems to move.

"So," says Mark.

"So," I say.

It's not just the conversation from Esperanto standing between us, it's the fact that he's gone from the guy who stops by to the guy who will be living down the hall. I feel the pressure of months of awkward silences.

"Sit tight," I say. "I'm going to make a phone call."

Vicky, never one to disappoint, shows up with a case of beer.

"So, this is Mark," she says. "Good to meet you finally. I've heard a lot about you."

As she loads the beer into the fridge, Mark raises his eyebrows at me.

"Well, Steve certainly didn't tell me his girlfriend was hot," Mark says.

"Oh, please," Vicky says.

"I'll tell you one thing," Mark starts, intent now on making me blush. "I sure wish I could be hearing Father Steve's confessions to see just what exactly goes on between you two."

"Unless a wet dream is a sin," she counters, "I don't think there'd be too much to hear."

"Oh my," Mark responds. "I like this one already."

"Okay, you two, knock it off." I can feel my ears going bright crimson, but I'm pleased the two of them hit it off. "And give me a beer."

So we start drinking. They pick on me. We play drinking games. We play video games. We taunt the kitten.

"You're not going to get stuck with a lousy old sweater, are you, Chasey?" Mark says over and over. "We're going to get you a nice foxy lady cat."

"What's that all about?" Vicky asks.

"Long story," I say.

We start in on tequila shots. And when we are so drunk that

we can no longer keep our video-game cars on the video-game roads, we do the smart thing: we wander off into the woods, making crow noises in the night and laughing so hard we can barely walk. The sky is just turning gray with morning when we finally make it back to the rectory.

Mark scoops up Chase and goes to the guest room.

Vicky throws herself on the couch. "I'm staying here," she says.

"Fine by me," I say, a wee little voice in the back of my head making a wee little noise about the fact that her car has been parked out there overnight. What will the parishioners think? Whatever. I grab a blanket from the hall closet and spread it over Vicky, who's got her arm thrown across her eye.

"You run a weird show, Padre," she says. "Daddy would be proud."

"Yeah," I say, somewhat touched. "Wonder what Bishop Flemming would think?"

"Well, don't worry your pretty little head over that," she slurs. "Now go to bed."

I'm pulled up through my hangover by a clanging in the kitchen. Sunlight streams in through the windows and it sounds like someone is beating on a pot with a wooden spoon. It's two in the afternoon. I stumble into the kitchen, on the way noticing Vicky trying to bury her head under a pillow.

In the kitchen, Mark is beating on a pot with a wooden spoon.

"Mark! What the hell are you doing?"

"I'm trying to wake you people up. The day is getting old. We have work to do."

The kitchen reeks of bacon and eggs and coffee.

"The Lord does not smile upon the lazy," he says, banging on the pot again. "Bring out your dead!" he yells.

"Okay! Okay! We're up," I say. "Now stop it before some old lady in the parish hears all this and decides to call the bishop or something."

"Oh," Mark says, suddenly stopping. "Guess that wouldn't be too good."

"No. Not at all."

He puts the pot and spoon in the drain board. "Anyway, you and Vicky need to wake up and eat so we can get to work."

"Work? Work on what?"

"Everything," he says.

"Jesus," I say, stumbling off to the bathroom.

"I heard that," he shouts. "Name in vain. That's ten Hail Marys for you."

As we sit down to Mark's afternoon breakfast, he begins to prattle on about his plans. His first order of business is to "do *something*" to the rectory, which he considers a travesty of late '60s design. "This wood paneling and toothpaste-colored paint. That's just got to go."

"Okay, Queer Eye, slow down. I don't have that kind of budget."

"First of all, Steve. It doesn't cost that much. Secondly, I got plenty saved up and it'll give me something to do."

Vicky and I look at each other.

"And speaking of money, how are things going on this festival?"

That's right. At some point in the night, we'd filled him in on that.

"We're almost there," Vicky says.

"You got the carnies?"

"Yeah."

"You got the booths lined up?"

"Just the carnie ones," I say. "Haven't gotten around to fooling with the rest."

"What!" Mark shrieks.

Vicky rolls her eyes. "I tried to tell him."

"Steve, you need the local booths. Arts, crafts, yadda-yadda-yadda. And what about the food?"

"Well, we have some volunteers," Vicky says.

"Volunteers!" Mark practically shouts. "Are you nuts? You crazy? No volunteers. No. Doesn't work that way."

"Well, we are sort of new to this," I say. "And since when did you come out of the festival heavens with knowledge direct from Festivus?"

"Hey, the one thing I did right at St. John's was run these things for the Catholic school fairs. Anyway, hell, you don't need any more fund-raisers. You'll get the rest of your money from the caterers."

"Really?" Vicky and I ask.

"Think about it. They pull up a trailer for the weekend and sell little itty-bitty tiny bowls of food for five bucks a shot. Then they gouge on the sodas and beer. And most of that money stays under the table."

"But this is our first year," Vicky says. "Why would they want to take the risk?"

"Are you kidding?" Mark replies. "These guys go to festival boards every year begging and pleading and weasling and bribing to be let in. But once a festival gets going, board members like to stay with what works. So if some of these newer guys smell a chance to get in on the ground floor? Forget it. They'll fall all over themselves to pay you an up-front fee *and* give you a cut of the profits."

He's not done yet.

"Now. Rabbits? You get rabbits?"

"Rabbits? For what?"

Mark rolls his eyes. We could get a marbles tournament going with all the eye rolling going on at this table. "For what?

Hellloooo. It's the Rabbit Festival. You think the Good Lord is just going to send a fuzzy plague of little white bunnies to Grand Prairie?"

"But wouldn't the caterers take care of that?" Vicky asks.

"Yeah," I chime in.

"Not the eating kind, you morons." Mark shakes his head as if he were an unwilling teacher instructing a couple of slack-jawed students.

"Then what?"

"The petting bunnies. Think of the children. The precious little children and the dollars that follow them. Parents come for the music. It's the kids who get them to spend the money. So you'll need bunnies. Lots of little white bunnies. Bunnies for racing. Bunnies for a petting zoo. In fact, call some farmers, get some sheep and goats and stuff for a petting zoo. It'll stink a little, but hey, it's open air. Hell, we can even sell bunnies. The parents will hate you, but it's all about the precious little children."

"But this is a church," I counter, finally confident that I have at least one good point. "We're not Barnum and Bailey. We're not in this to turn a profit. It's for the community."

"Firstly, this is Louisiana and a festival is a festival is a festival. You attach that word to something, you have a responsibility. Secondly, this is the Church. Profit, my boy, profit. Besides, do you really feel like starting over from scratch next year? Bake sales and plate lunches and all that crap."

That phrase again. "Next year." And the year after. And the year after. But I hear these words coming out my mouth: "Actually, some of those things were kind of nice. I felt like we were all coming together as a parish."

Mark stares at me, his mouth slightly open.

"Well, you can kiss my ass if you think I'm starting over from scratch," Vicky says. "You might have had fun walking around like lord of the manor, but those things were a lot of work, Steve. It's all you next year. If it's up to me, and I'm chairman of the festival board, I say we go with Mark. Hell, I say I resign and give it over to Mark."

Boy, did she wake up on the wrong side of the couch this morning! Talk about yin and yang. I've got the Martha Stewart of hangovers on one side and a bitter woman on the other.

Mark puts up his hand. "Oh no, sweetie. No chairman for me. Let's call me a festival consultant."

"A consultant?" Vicky asks.

"Sure." Mark then looks at me. "That way, if the natives start asking questions about your new boyfriend, you'll have a perfect excuse. The Lavender Mafia man is here to take care of a little business."

Makes sense to me.

"Okay. So there we go. We'll set all that up. Any money left over, we'll stick it into an interest-bearing account. And who knows? If I've got free time and I'm still puttering around here, I can do some day-trading with it. By next year at this time we'll be able to fly in the Rolling Stones if they're still alive.

"Speaking of," he continues without much of a pause. I wonder if he's ever going to stop talking. "What kind of music yall got lined up?"

Vicky and I look down at the table, sheepishly. This has been a point of contention on the board. It was the one thing that Miss Emilia, Miss Celestine, Miss Pamela, and Denise had agreed on. There absolutely had to be music at the festival. But we had fought long and hard to convince them that it was just too much, too soon for such a small village. It would be too expensive, too much of a hassle.

"Tell me you have music," Mark says, exasperated.

"No," Vicky says, getting defensive. "We don't have music. We don't have the budget for music. Besides, we got such a late start, we figured everybody would be booked. We were just going to get a DJ."

"A DJ? Oh no, no, no. What exactly are you spending all this money on, then, if not music?" Mark asks. "Where's it going?"

I look at Vicky. I sure as hell don't know.

"Well, actually, most of it's still there. I don't know. Expenses are bound to come up."

"Yeah," Mark says. "Like music. You gave the carnies their deposit, right? You'll get at least half of the lumber and stuff needed to build the booths donated. Even if you don't, it doesn't cost that much. You'll have to spend some money on the bunnies. But all the rest is volunteer work."

"I guess," Vicky says.

"Trust me," Mark says.

Suddenly I'm reminded of the serpent in the garden. "Well, how do we go about getting bands?"

"We're going to have to do it the old-fashioned way. But that's the fun part," he answers with a smile.

In the same way people want to get a good look at a car crash, I want to see what the inside of El Sidos looks like during broad daylight. I'm sure it's the very picture of sanitary. El Sidos is a juke joint. No other word for it, with the possible exception of honky-tonk. A low-slung building located on the wrong side of the tracks. The actual wrong side of the tracks. We're the only white people in the house. In the dark, though, El Sidos seems clean enough. That's all I've ever asked of a bar. The floors are swept, air-conditioning humming, no puke in the bathrooms, and my arms aren't sticking to the table. Neon signs—notably Hennessy and an old Schlitz Malt Liquor Bull— buzz behind the barkeep. But there's part of me that still wants to see it in broad daylight, with the lights blazing.

El Sidos is part of Mark's "the old-fashioned way," in which we hit every juke joint we can find and beg musicians to play. We've already lined up most of the bands—a country cover band, a rock cover band comprising high school kids from Opelousas (lousy, but we're "doing it for the children"), and three Cajun bands, each made up of men so old I'm convinced that at least one of them will die of a heart attack while onstage. Those bands, though, are just fillers. What we're doing now is lining up the acts that will get people shaking, the zydeco bands.

And what Mark says, I do. In two weeks, he's taken care of all the remaining details of the festival, has won over the festival board without a problem, has somehow become the point man with Johnny Two Shoes, Black Toes, or whatever his name is. And, most important, has gotten Vicky to stop nagging me about all of this stuff.

He's also managed to rip out the wood paneling in the rectory, repaint every room in the house, and retile the bathroom floor. I'm starting to wonder if I should search his room for meth. And he's still found time to sit on the couch with Chase in his arms and watch obscene amounts of bad television. He's become addicted to Thursday nights on NBC, Sunday nights on FOX, and won't leave the room if he comes across reruns of *Hunter* or *The A-Team.* "Stephen J. Cannell is a genius," he keeps telling me.

At least he doesn't watch reality TV.

And when he's not too busy with the tube, he's dragging Vicky and me across the wilds of Cajun country.

Our adventures have taken us through the Louisiana of Louisiana, the things that were right in front of me my entire life: truck stops, bars, honkey-tonks, and diners, some right there in Opelousas where I grew up. I came of age during the great Americanization of America, caught up in a sweep of malls, fast-food joints, Walmart, and pop radio. I embraced it all. Give me my Big Mac, my Filet-O-Fish, my Quarterpounder, and french fries. Let Michael Jackson thrill me. Fling open the doors of Walmart and everyday low prices. All this talk of the death of the small town? Fine by me. Main Street? As if. The few occasions Mama didn't have time to drive to Lafayette and thought she might possibly find something in one of the stores in downtown Opelousas, they seemed like they hadn't been re-stocked since the late '60s. For the first MTV generation, Main Street was some embarrassing old relative that wouldn't die fast enough.

And we were worse when it came to music. Cajun and zy-deco? Perish the thought. Country dance halls? As if. Zydeco was too black. Country was too white trash.

Luckily, though, what we thought didn't matter. Our culture managed to survive, partly because of the older generation, partly because there will always be kids who aren't embarrassed of where they come from and who don't spend their nights lying in bed mouthing words in an attempt to sound like Peter Jennings.

Mark, apparently, had been one of those country kids, so he was our tour guide. "If I'm going to repair this damage you've so obviously inflicted upon yourself, I might as well get it all in one shot."

Since Mark arrived a week before Mardi Gras, that seemed at first as logical a place as any to start. So off we three went to Mamou for the Courir de Mardi Gras, which involved us wak-ing up at the crack of dawn and driving around the countryside following costumed men on horseback as they went from house to house getting chickens for the communal gumbo. If there's anything sillier than a full-grown, half-drunk man wear-ing a purple hood and robe and chasing a chicken before most people wake up for breakfast, it's a full-grown, half-drunk priest doing much the same thing. Which is exactly what happened when one of the riders spied me—stupidly wearing my collar—sitting in Mark's car. I did manage to catch a chicken, which garnered me a spot on the back of someone's horse for the remainder of the run. So it was that while Vicky and Mark drove around Mamou looking for a place to park, I got to ride into town like a hero—if a hero meant someone who held on for dear life as his stupendously drunk host struggled to stay on the horse as he waved and threw beads to the folks lining the parade route. We learned nothing of practical value for the Rabbit Festival, but learning nothing had never been so fun.

And then it was on to the nightclub tour. We went to Slim's Y-Ki-Ki, the most famous zydeco club in Opelousas, to watch Chris Ardoin and Double Clutchin'. When I was a child, Daddy muttered to himself as we drove past on Saturday nights, slowed to a crawl because of the traffic and the people darting across the highway. I remember peeking my head out of the window, wondering what all those black people could possibly be doing in that little windowless building. I remember how, in high school, we were all somewhat amazed that Charlie Muntz, a white boy, hadn't been beaten to death after he hit one of Slim's patrons while driving home drunk.

We went to the Brass Rail on Landry Street for Pabst Blue Ribbon specials and a few games of pool. Frank's Liquor Store, which turned into a bar in the evening. We Cajun-waltzed at Richard's on Highway 190 somewhere just outside Eunice. In Eunice, we did the white-man shuffle at the Purple Peacock, rife with twenty-something kids obviously under the thrall of Ecstasy and God knew what else. Drank too many beers at Bada's, a bait stand by day, nightclub by night.

And now we sit in a dark corner of El Sido's while Lil Pookie sets up. It's oddly silent in here. The other patrons talk loudly, laugh, but something about the place makes it obvious that it's accustomed to a good seventy percent more noise. The waitress brings over a bucket of ice, a pint of Crown Royal, three cans of Coke, and three plastic cups.

"Yall from Texas?" she asks.

"Nope," Mark says.

"Yall students over at the college?" she guesses.

"Nope. We're from Opelousas."

"Well, ain't that something," she says, surprised that native white people would cross the tracks and pay five bucks to get into a place like this when we could just as well wait two weeks and see the same band at Grant Street Dance Hall or some other venue more in line with the taste of nice white folk.

I'm ashamed to admit that I've always imagined these places seething with resentful black men nursing drinks and grudges against the man. Reality, of course, is slightly different. Whatever their problems, like anyone else, anywhere else on a Friday night in America, they're here to put all that behind them—a matter of business too serious to be interrupted by a few white people. The looks wandering over in our direction so far have mostly come from men who are checking out Vicky. A few women have shot cursory glances as well, but these were only to check out their competition. Mark and I don't even rate.

And once the music starts, none of it matters. We dance. Vicky and Mark are masters. I've become something resembling proficient. I have the basics down and move as well as any of the Texans that come through on their dance-tour groups. Still, though, I stumble, and often catch the counting in my head leaking out of my mouth: "One-two-three-four, uh, one-two-three-four" or "One-two-*three*-four, five-six-*seven*-eight."

Mark and I prefer zydeco dancing to Cajun. The music is faster, wilder, the dance more frenetic with more room for interpretation (and, in my case, mistakes). Vicky, while good at it, still has a special place in her heart for Cajun waltzes and two-steps.

We start out dancing in rotation, Mark and I taking turns with Vicky. But it isn't long before men are breaking free from the bar to cut in. Mark and I laugh and applaud the moves we'll more than likely never master—there's good; then there's what these guys do.

"What say we go find a couple ladies to dance with?" Mark yells over the music.

"Why not?" I yell back.

Mark picks out the prettiest woman in the room, a dark-skinned, golden-eyed lady with a severe look about her. She has close-cropped hair covered by a cowboy hat and wears impossibly tight jeans that run down into a pair of maroon snake-skin boots. She knows damn well how fine she is and she's continually faced with the task of deciding which men are good enough to spin her around the dance floor. All of this, of course, is a waste on Mark—and me. I've asked him before why he only dances with the best-looking women and, with his usual stereotypical flair, he told me, "If you must accessorize, accessorize with only the highest quality."

I go for the friendliest-looking woman I can find, someone who looks like the type to take sick puppies in. My dance partner is a short woman with long extensions, long false eyelashes, and long acrylic nails with zigzag designs. She, too, sports tight jeans and snakeskin boots, as well as too-red lipstick on a mile-wide smile.

We don't talk much, simply exchange names and careers. I lie (forgive me, Lord) and tell her that I'm a counselor. Her name is Rosy and she has her own band just starting at the smaller juke joints. I'd ask her more, but between counting out the dance steps and spying on Mark and Vicky, I really don't have the time or the mental capacity. I'm sure if I tried to chew gum right now, I'd fall down and break my leg.

Mark has already defrosted his partner. She's laughing, pressing her forehead to Mark's shoulder one moment, then throwing it back, the cords in her neck dancing, the fillings in her back teeth glinting in the light from the disco ball. Vicky, too, has her partner laughing. She's returning the favor, aiming that straight smile of hers right into her partner's face.

But because I'm getting to be a chubby slug who does little

more than stand at a podium and eat the massive amounts of food cooked for me by little old ladies, I'm winded and sweaty by the end of one song. I pass Rosy off to a more able partner and shuffle back to the table, where I throw myself at my chair and pour the last of the Crown into a plastic cup of melting ice.

Still, Mark was right. This is fun.

Chapter 12

Knocking on my bedroom door wakes me from a rather explicitly sexual dream about Eleanor Roosevelt. I once thought that after a couple of years of celibacy I'd get used to some of the more disturbing couplings in the sleeping world, but I wake up with a start, thankful for two things: I didn't break the vow and I didn't break it with someone of Eleanor's appearance. It's 4:00 a.m.

"Time to get up, Steve."

It's Mark.

"Looks like the lynch mob is here."

"Already?"

"Early bird and all. Besides, who knows how long this is going to take?"

He hangs in the doorway, hair combed, fully dressed: black shirt, collar, black priest pants stuffed into steel-toed boots. Big puffy hunter-safety orange coat.

"Why are you dressed already?"

"Kind of figured you'd have a lot more explaining to do if I answered the door wearing nothing but my boxers and bedhead."

I fall back in the bed. "Shit."

"It's okay. I told them I was just a visiting priest here to help you leading up to the festival. They seemed happy to let it go at that."

"Thanks," I say. "Now get out of here so I can get dressed." I pull on thermals, jeans, a flannel shirt, and a ragged seminary sweatshirt. It was supposed to get as low as thirty degrees overnight, and I can feel the cold seeping through the windows. I throw a camouflage coat over the ensemble. Too cold for priest clothes. Besides, I look a little more manly this way. But not nearly as manly as the fifty or so boys and men who are waiting for me out in the parking lot, smoking cigarettes and murmuring to each other at a low pitch. It sounds liked a well-tuned diesel engine, one that shuts down when Mark and I step out into the frigid night air.

Boudreaux, Miss Emilia's husband and the commander of this ragtag battalion, greets us with a wave. "Morning, Fathers," he says, removing his *Registered Coon-Ass* cap and rubbing the top of his bald head as if to warm it up.

"Boudreaux," I say. "Everybody. Yall met Father Johnson?"

They all wave and mumble an affirmative.

"We best get started," says Boudreaux, placing his cap back on his head. "Fathers, yall want to move yall's cars? We gonna try to do this as close to the carport and rect'ry as possible. Stay out of the wind."

Still sheltered in the door, I hadn't noticed until now the treetops leaning over in the dark. It looks bone-biting cold beyond the glow of the parking-lot lights. I bet it'll feel ten degrees colder when I actually get out of the house, which I aim to avoid as much as possible without coming off as a sissy.

"We can do that," I say. "Yall want us to make some coffee?"

Boudreaux smiles. "Oh no, Father. Yall gonna help us this morning. Miss Emilia can make the coffee." He turns to his truck and bangs on the rear fender before shouting, "Emilia! Wake up! You can get out the truck now. Go on in and make us some coffee."

Miss Emilia climbs slowly out of the truck, wraps her arms around her body, and shuffles over to the door. "Morning, Father Sibille. Morning, Father Johnson." Staring up at us from the bottom of the steps, she looks like a teacher's pet who's been asked to clean the blackboard.

"Get in here before you freeze to death," I say as Mark and I give up the warmth of the rectory to join the men at their work. The door closes behind us, leaving Mark and me in a world we both thought we'd long ago left behind.

Boudreaux puts thumb and forefinger to the corners of his mouth and gives a shrill whistle, setting the men jogging to their trucks. A ballet of pickups—each of which has a blue tarp covering its bed—ensues as they all move to the side of the lot closest to the highway. Boudreaux's leaves the line and backs slowly toward the space assigned for this morning's task, pushing a trailer on which sits something shrouded in yet another blue tarp. The outlines suggest a sarcophagus built for a giant. The truck stops and out steps Boudreaux, who unknots the strings holding the tarp down. The others watch in silence.

"Thibodeaux," he says, "grab a corner."

Thibodeaux does so.

"Ready?" Boudreaux asks.

"Mais, I guess so," says Thibodeaux, not quite sure what to expect.

They whip the tarp back, revealing a cypress-paneled box about ten feet long and three feet high. Its lid, edges, and bottom shine silver in the parking-lot lights. Someone lets loose an appreciative whistle. Just when I think there's no possible way they'll be able to lift the thing, four of them hop in the trailer and make short work of unloading it. The rest gather around as

Boudreaux and Thibodeaux remove the lid, revealing an empty hollow lined with more shining stainless steel.

"Mais, goddamn, Boudreaux, you outdid yourself this time, yeah!" says someone.

"That's what you been locked up in your shop with the last week?" asks another.

"That's it, right there," he says.

I reach out and touch the wooden side, a shiver rushing through me. It's like touching a coffin. "What is it?"

"That's our microwave," says Boudreaux with a smile.

Boudreaux's "microwave" is simply a monster-sized version of what's known in these parts as a Cajun microwave. It's a cypress box lined on the inside with stainless steel. On its lid is situated a tray meant to hold hot coals. Meat goes in the box. Lid goes on top of the box. Coals go in the lid. No-muss slow cooking.

And apparently Boudreaux figured we needed a king-sized version for the next step in the war of mutually assured destruction we've been waging with B.P.

No sooner had Mark moved in and told me we didn't really need any more fund-raisers than I called a halt to the bake sales. Bye-bye to the barbecues. Good-bye to the gumbos. And good riddance. Then one Sunday after Mass, I watched as nearly all of my parishioners made a left out of the parking lot and headed in B.P.'s direction. I stomped over to my car, intending to follow. Wedged under the windshield wiper was a bright green piece of paper.

Food! Faith! Fun!

Worse: *Stop by the future home of the Holy Bible Fellowship Pentecostal Church of Christ for a day of barbecue and community. Games for the kids!*

"Son of a bitch," I whispered. Judging by the name of the

church, he'd gone rogue, breaking off from any of the real Pentecostal communities in the area. And now he was going to poach my parishoners.

Sure enough, when I cruised by the place, there was my entire parish, a sea of camo and LSU purple, milling about B.P.'s property. A thin plume of white smoke seeped out of a large barbecue contraption set in the middle of the field. It appeared to be twice the size of Boudreaux's trailer rig. Between two trees, I spied Little Red Riding Redneck, her brother, some other kid, and my very own Denise, hands tied behind their backs, jumping up and down, participating in some sort of born-again depravity. I made a U-turn, headed back to St. Pete's, and started working the cell phone. It was time for an emergency meeting of the festival committee. That night. No excuses.

They all showed up on time. Miss Celestine, Miss Emilia, and Miss Pamela looked like they were sick with guilt—or sick with eating some other church's filthy barbecue. Vicky looked mildly amused. And Denise, simply too young to know any better, immediately started bragging about winning a hot-dog-on-a-string contest.

"It was pretty cool," she gushed. "They tied this string between two trees. Then they hung some wienies from the string. Then they tied our hands behind our backs. Then we had to hop up and down while we—"

"Denise," Miss Pamela said, trying to cut her off.

"What?" she answered, ready to go toe-to-toe with her arch enemy.

"Denise," Vicky cut in. "I don't think Father Steve wants to hear about the barbecue."

"Oh," I said. "That's not true. Not true at all. I want to hear all about B.P.'s barbecue. Looks like yall all had yourselves a good time."

Even a deaf monkey could have interpreted my mood. Denise fell silent and looked to the old women for guidance, but they were all looking at their shoes. All Vicky had to offer was a shrug.

After a few minutes of silence, Vicky spoke. "I'm sure Father Steve called us together for some other reason."

In truth, I hadn't even thought that part through. If I didn't come up with something, I'd just look like an angry and jealous boyfriend. Panicked, I blurted out the first thing that came to mind.

"Bake sale. Next Sunday. Get the word out."

"Yes, Father," they replied at once, in unison, as if saying "amen."

"Okay," I said. "Okay. That's all I wanted. I have some work to do. Thank yall for coming."

With that, Denise, Miss Celestine, and Miss Emilia hurried out, tears in their eyes. Miss Pamela took her time, leaving with her back straight and head held high. Still, I knew she'd been chastened. Vicky, of course, stayed behind.

I shut the door behind the guilty and rested my forehead against the windowpane.

"That was a fine performance, Padre. Really, another bake sale?"

I didn't look up. "You have a better idea? Obviously, I just can't sit back and wait for the festival."

"Hey, look at that," she said, walking over and grabbing me by the shoulders. She gave me a brief massage, releasing perhaps ten pounds of tension. "Looks like you're realizing this is a year-round job."

She squeezed again. I groaned.

But that was it. She patted me on the back three times. "But it's your job, boyo. You handle this one." She grabbed one of my belt loops and pulled me away from the door so she could make her own exit. "And you make damn sure you call each one of them old ladies tomorrow to apologize. And Denise, too."

An hour later, before I had a chance to even think about apologizing, there was a knock on the door. I opened it to find Boudreaux standing in the dark. I thought he'd come to kick my ass for humiliating his wife.

"Boudreaux," I said, looking around to see if any other old men were hiding behind the trees waiting to pounce.

"Father."

"How can I help you?"

"Hear you having another bake sale."

There it was. He was going to beat me like a redheaded stepchild.

"Yeah, looks like it." I felt the less I said the better. No need to provoke him. Boudreaux may have been thirty years my senior and he didn't look like much, but I figured he had the deceptive strength of a chimp—he'd break my fingers, tear off my testicles, then pull my shoulders out of their sockets and beat me to death with my own arm.

He took off his hat and looked down at it. Was that a sign of aggression? Was he going to bare his teeth next? Pound his chest?

"You don't think we've had enough cake out here for one year?"

I forced a chuckle. "Well, it sure has been a lot. And I'm sorry if I'm taking up too much of Miss Emilia's time."

He crammed his cap back on his hand and put a hand up to stop me. "Look. It's like this." That four-word phrase was a Cajun signal that the speaker had decided to stop dancing around an issue. "Emilia got nothing better to do. And her and them ol' gals will bake you a million cakes if you ask them to. And their friends will buy every single one of 'em. Hell, Father, they'd jump off a cliff for you."

"Well—" I started.

He put his hand up again. "Look. You gotta realize something. You in a fight now. B.P., he done called you out. And you gonna have to do better than a bake sale. I know that man. He don't stop unless you make him. He's what you call a one-upper."

"A one-upper?"

"Yessir. He always has to know better than you. Always has to catch a bigger fish, drive a bigger car, have a bigger scar, have the worst problem. Tell that man you got ten fingers, he'll look you in the eye and tell you he had twelve just yesterday but two fell off in his sleep."

I couldn't help but laugh, but Boudreaux didn't.

"I guess it's funny at first, but that gets aggravating after a while, yeah." He'd taken his cap off again and was twisting it in frustration. "Kee-yahhhhh!" he exclaimed, and slapped the cap against his thigh to clear his head. "Look," he started again. "That man means business. He got you in his sights. Not just you, but the whole church, too. Them old ladies love you, but it's like he's bringing them roses and you just giving them a handful of clover you found on the side of the road. After a while, they might start doing more than eating his barbecue."

"Shit," I said, forgetting I was in front of a parishioner.

"That about sums it up," he answered.

"What do we do?"

"Well, that festival's a good idea. I thought you were crazy at first, but now it almost looks like you saw him coming. Problem is, we smack in the middle of winter with nothing to do until then."

"And bake sales aren't going to cut it?"

"Nope."

"Any suggestions?"

"We should try a couple more main courses, something a little more involved than some cupcakes in a box."

"Like?"

"We could start with fried turkey."

I thought about it. "That isn't cheap, Boudreaux. And it sounds like a lot of work."

"No, it ain't. It ain't cheap. But how much you willing to pay to win? As far as the work goes, me and the boys will take care of that."

He was right. He knew it. I knew it. He knew that I knew. I wasn't going to let B.P. win, even if it meant bankrupting the church.

"What can I do?" I asked.

"Make up some flyers. Rent one of them fun-jumps for the kids and pay the bill when I send it to you."

With that, he drove off into the night.

The turkey fry was a rousing success. After a week of dreary Louisiana winter rain, the clouds broke on a Sunday morning to give way to a sixty-five-degree day of kids jumping and grease splattering. The only hiccup was that Mark and Vicky absolutely refused to let me give away the food for free. "You can bankrupt your church, but you're not bankrupting my festival," Vicky said. I thought, as the priest, I had some sort of veto power, but she quickly cured me of that delusion. I even tried to rope Boudreaux into the fight, but in yet another sign of the man's wisdom, he said he'd have none of it. "Besides," he added, "they don't mind paying a little for the pleasure. Makes it feel like a sacrifice."

I didn't have much time to gloat. Two days later, the smell of fried turkey still hanging in the air, Boudreaux drove up. His entire face was pulled down into a frown.

"What's the problem?"

He handed me a flyer.

"Son of a bitch," I said.

B.P. had stepped it up. *All the turducken you can eat,* the flyer read.

"Turducken! How much money does he have?"

For most of us, turducken—the Russian nesting doll of poultry—was a once-a-year novelty served up at Thanksgiving or Christmas. For do-it-yourselfers, deboning a duck and chicken, then stuffing them into a turkey was too much work. To buy one ready-made typically ran fifty bucks or more.

"He's gonna have pony rides, too," Boudreaux said.

"Oh, c'mon!" I ripped the flyer in half, ripped it again, then balled it up and threw it on the ground. "What do we do now? At this rate, we'll have to have a festival before the festival."

We stood in silence for a while. Finally, Boudreaux spoke.

"I think I have an idea."

"What is it?"

"I don't want to say."

"Why not?"

"Don't want word to get out. I want to catch that sumbitch off guard. He won't know what hit him. If this works, he'll have to have a full-on circus to top us."

"How are you going to keep something like that a secret?"

"You just going to have to trust me, Father."

"Okay. Fine. But what do I put on the flyers?"

"I don't know. Just go crazy."

So I did. *February Surprise!* I wrote. *A Winter Wonder! Boudreaux and crew present a meal so stupendous, so amazing, so colossal, so mouthwateringly delicious, you'll want to* SLAP YA MAMA! *It's so beyond the limits of imagination, we can't even tell you what it is.*

I used big letters and sprinkled exclamation points liberally throughout. Heading off all arguments at the pass, I typed the word FREE in a 72-point font across the bottom. I printed them and Denise distributed them before Mark and Vicky could do anything to stop me.

Now here we are in the predawn darkness and I have no idea what's unfolding around me.

"Boudreaux, what's going on?" I ask.

"Yeah, what kind of koo-koo you got us up to this time?" asks Thibodeaux.

I turn to Thibodeaux. "Yall don't know what's going on, either?"

"Mais, no. He wouldn't tell. He call me up on Tuesday and tells me to find fifty pounds smoke sausage and chop it up. I still got no damn idea what we doing."

Another old man, Felix Arcenaux, pipes up. "You think that's crazy, he called me on Tuesday, too, and made me swear on my mama's grave not to tell anybody. Then he axed me to bring—"

Boudreaux puts up his hand, cuts him off. "Okay. That's enough for right now. It'll make sense soon enough." He looked around the crowd. "Now. T-Chew, you back your truck up and let's unload those tables. And, CaCa, you get some charcoal going in that barrel pit. Once it's ready, start preheating that box."

While the men set out about their tasks, Miss Emilia carries out a tray of coffee.

"Yall about ready to start?" she asks.

"I reckon," says Boudreaux.

Miss Emilia works up the courage for her next question. "Can I call Celestine, tell her to come?"

"Now c'mon, Emilia. You do that, half the town's gonna be here in half an hour."

By the way he's smiling, I can tell he wouldn't mind that so much.

"No. I'll just call her. I swear. And maybe Pamela."

Boudreaux waits, makes her suffer. "Fine. But nobody else."

She's already got her cell phone to her ear by the time he shouts after her, "I don't want a bunch of women and kids out here getting underfoot."

With his wife back in the house, the fire going, and the tables set up, Boudreaux surveys his troops. Clad in camo caps and hunting clothes, hands jammed into their pockets, they stand shivering in the cold.

"Yall about ready?"

Mark whispers to me, "Ready for what?"

"Not even God knows what this one's all about."

Boudreaux claps his hands together. "Allons! Let's go. Thibodeaux, you get that sausage and put it on that table. Arcenaux, you and Toby, back your truck up, get what you brought and slap it on that table. See if you can do it without telling anybody."

Arcenaux and his grandson head for his truck. The rest of the battalion mutters its disapproval at being kept in the dark. One shouts out, "Arcenaux, what you brought, man? Just tell us!"

Arcenaux, now caught up in the theatrics, shouts back. "Yall hold yall horses. Won't be but a minute. Now get out of the way so I can back my truck up."

Said truck backed up, Arcenaux hops out and drops the tailgate. He and Toby grab hold of the blue tarp and whip it off.

"Kee-yaaaahhhhh," someone exclaims. "It's a whole damn cow."

That it is. Not just a side of beef, but a whole damn cow, gutted and skinned and glistening under the lights like an autopsy-ready alien at Roswell.

Kenny Wyble slaps the side of the truck. "Mais, Boudreaux, if you had him bring a whole damn cow"—apparently whole damn cow is now the thing's official name—"why you asked me to bring—"

"Kenny," Boudreaux says. "Just hush your mouth and go get your truck. Rest of yall get this on the table."

That done, Boudreaux looks to Mark and me. "Fathers, yall ready to get busy?"

We both shrug. "Sure."

"There's some seasoning in these bags," he says, pointing to some gallon-sized zip-tops. "Want yall to rub this whole damn cow real good on the outside. Then, yall take that sausage and put about a quarter-inch layer all over on the inside. Pack it in good."

"Don't we need gloves?" I ask.

Boudreaux looks at me.

"He's just joking," Mark says, elbowing me in the ribs. "C'mon, Steve. Time to get to work." Ten seconds later, he's rubbing the cow like it's had a long day at the office. "Boudreaux, yall going to inject this thing with marinade or what?"

"Nah. I thought about it, but it'll be plenty moist. You'll see."

The others jog off to Kenny Wyble's truck to harass him, leaving us to our work. Arcenaux, after parking his pickup, has climbed in the back of Kenny's bed and is waving a rake handle at the other to keep them away. As I rub a handful of spice into the whole damn cow's haunch, I look at Mark. "Since when are you one of the boys?"

"You kidding me? I passed as one of the boys for eighteen years. I made damn sure I was always first to volunteer for this kind of thing. I guarantee you I was twice the man you were in high school."

"Please."

"How many deer did you kill in high school?"

The fact was, Mama had never let me go deer hunting. Duck, squirrel, dove—all of that was fine. Deer? No. Too many kids were killed deer hunting, she said.

"How many did you kill?" I ask.

"Ten."

"Ten? In four years? Is that even legal?"

"Not hardly," he says.

We stop talking as Kenny Wyble's truck backs up to the table with a throng of men jabbering excitedly around it. Not even the appearance of Miss Pamela and Miss Celestine calms them down. They're on the verge of rioting. Arcenaux and Boudreaux, stationed in the back of the truck, are laughing so hard they're having problems standing up, much less fending away the gang. When they finally do whip off this blue tarp to reveal a whole damn hog, all hell breaks loose. Cheers rise up in the air.

"I knew it," someone shouts.

"Aw, you didn't know a damn thing, you," he's promptly told.

"I told yall Boudreaux done lost his mind," says someone else.

"B.P. can keep his damn turduckens," one of the others says.

"No, he can't," says Rocko Castille. "Boudreaux made me bring fifteen of them, too."

"And me, I brought a whole damn sheep," says Tommy Carrier, running off to get his truck.

The crowd breaks out into another round of cheers as they realize that we're about to assemble some sort of Frankenstein version of the turducken.

Boudreaux puts his hands up one more time. "Okay. Okay. Might as well get moving. CaCa, start getting that box warmed up. Rest of yall, get the heads off the pig and the sheep. Fathers, I figure yall got the rest figured out."

"Yes, sir," says Mark.

"Any questions?"

I can't help myself. "Boudreaux, how did you think of this?"

"I read it in a book," he says.

"A cookbook?"

"Hell no!" Boudreaux says as if I offended him.

"Boudreaux! Watch your mouth in front of Father Steve!" It's Miss Emilia, who's been standing on the steps huddled with Miss Celestine and Miss Pamela watching the madness unfold.

"Sorry, Father," says Boudreaux. "But no. Not a cookbook. Just a regular book. Can't remember the fella's name who wrote it, but it was something in Czechoslovakia." He pronounces it "checkasluhvakyuh." "And a bunch of Africans use all sorts of animals—even a zebra—to do something like a turducken. I couldn't get that out my head."

"You don't say?" I say. Boudreaux reading a novel. I just can't imagine it.

"Aw, yeah," says Thibodeaux. "That fool always got his nose in some book or other. Ever since he was a kid."

"Yeah," says Arcenaux. "Used to call him Book-Book Boudreaux before he got big enough to beat us up."

Boudreaux, by now, is blushing. "I'm still big enough to do it," he says. "So everybody shut up and get back to work."

So says Boudreaux, so it is done. After Mark and I get a good coat of sausage spackle into the whole damn cow and season the outside of the whole damn hog, Boudreaux and Thibodeaux heave up the swine—exhaling like steam engines in the predawn cold—and try to wedge it home. It fits only after some on-the-fly surgery that entails Arcenaux removing the hog's ribs and Mark sawing off its feet with a hacksaw. Figuring the whole damn sheep will require the same treatment, Mark leaves me to stuff the hog, while he goes to work with efficient fury.

"Shooo! They taught you how to do that in priest school?" one of the younger men asks, teasing Mark.

"Hardly," he says, standing up from his grisly task and wiping his hands on his jeans as if born into butchery. "That's old-fashioned Gueydan education, right there," he adds.

The mere mention of the town sets off fifteen minutes of duck-hunting talk, in which Mark reveals that he knows practically every hunting lease within fifty miles of his birthplace. The men of Grand Prairie, who grew up here in the higher grounds of Cajun country with only a measly little bayou or two pulling in wood ducks, are jealous of a marsh Cajun who grew up with mallards, teal, canvasbacks, and geese practically nesting in his backyard.

While they prattle on about hunting, I keep stuffing ground sausage into the hog, fighting the overwhelming urge to ask for an apron, or maybe even a high-pressure hose, to get the cold pork grease off my hands. Thank God it's cold; otherwise I'd have no excuse for the shivers that periodically rack my body when I realize I'm elbow-deep in two different animals and applying more meat to their insides.

Soon enough, the meat monstrosity is assembled and ready to go. Boudreaux positions two men over the microwave, ready to lift and shut the lid as quickly as possible to minimize heat loss. He, Arcenaux, Thibodeaux, and Mark take places near each leg of the overstuffed cow.

Arcenaux grabs a hoof and says, "C'mon, let's go."

"Now, you just wait a minute," Boudreaux says, then looks to me. "Father, want to say a quick word before we lay him to rest?"

"Sure." Figuring the gathered army has little patience for long-winded sermons, I go with a standard grace even though it'll likely be some time before we actually eat. "Bless us, O Lord, and these thy gifts, which we are about to receive through thy bounty, through Christ our Lord."

They all chime in on "Amen."

"And please don't let our roast beast burn," I add.

"Amen," they all say again, more heartily this time.

With that, the beast is placed into the box, the lid clamped down tight, and more coals shoveled on top. The sun is just reaching pink fingers over the trees to the east.

"Now what?" I ask.

"That's it," Boudreaux says. "Sits in there for eight hours."

"That's it?"

"Yup."

"When do you check it?"

"As long as the thermometer says three hundred, we don't."

"So you're not even going to peek?"

"Not till two o'clock, I ain't."

I'm not man enough for that sort of self-discipline and I don't mind telling him so.

Boudreaux laughs. "That's okay, Father. Most of these others aren't, either. That's why I'm going to have to sit here and keep watch."

My work done, I head back to the rectory to take a nap before eight-thirty Mass, leaving Boudreaux and the gang to pull lawn chairs up around the Cajun microwave and break out a silver flask.

Both Masses come and go in a blur, neither a fine performance by anyone involved. Like kids keeping an eye on the clock the day school lets out for summer, we fidget and keep looking toward the windows as if we could see through the stained glass. The smell doesn't help. I think the parishioners have it worse than I do as they have no idea what's in the box. Those who come for eight-thirty Mass refuse to leave, content to gather around Boudreaux and his men, begging to be told what's in the box. The only answer they get is, "Just some old leaves and trash." Folks arriving for the eleven o'clock Mass have to park on the side of the road and in the field across the highway.

By the time eleven o'clock Mass ends and we've cleared enough cars to set out tables and chairs, it's coming on two o'clock and the day has warmed up to a balmy fifty degrees. The crowd is buzzing by now. A photographer from the *Daily World* has materialized.

"You the priest?" he asks.

Resisting the urge to ask him if he's seen anyone else running around in a long white robe, I say yes and ask him what brings him around these parts.

"We got five calls at the paper this morning."

"So you know what it is?"

"I know what they told me. I don't know if I actually believe them."

"Have a little faith," I say.

At two on the dot, Boudreaux pushes himself out of his lawn chair and walks to his truck. He returns with a game-dressing tripod, which he sets up between the microwave and the crowd.

"Yall ready?" he asks Arcenaux and Thibodeaux, Kenny Wyble and Toby.

"You not even going to check? See if it's done?" asks Thibodeaux.

"Nope," answers Boudreaux, pulling asbestos gloves over his raw hands. He orders the lid lifted, reaches in with a length of chain, and has the whole damn cow hoisted up and hanging upside down from the tripod within five minutes. Juices drip off the cow's snout onto the driveway.

"Roast beasts!" he announces. And verily, the crowd erupts into Hosannas and Hallelujahs to such a degree that I worry God might mistake it for idol worship and smite us all.

Boudreaux waves me over. We stand on either side of the stuffed beast, our backs to the parishioners, like fishermen who've just hauled in a thousand-pound meat shark, as the photographer snaps away.

The beast is delicious, a good time is had by all, but most important, on Monday afternoon the photo runs on the front page of the *Daily World* above the fold.

For now, B.P. is vanquished.

Chapter 13

It's a moment I never could have imagined back in Seminary. I'm in front of a church—my church—with an Irish Traveler carnival man on my left and a self-exiled gay priest on my right. We're measuring for our fair that's just over a month away. The Lord's work, indeed.

"That's one way of looking at it," says Mark.

"Say what?" I ask, confused.

"You just said it's the Lord's work."

"I did?"

"Sure did."

Blackfoot spits on the concrete. "I don't know about all that, but work it is and sure ain't gonna get done all by its fuckin' self, now, is it, gentlemen?"

"Fuck no," says Mark, smiling at his recently found freedom to curse like a sailor in front of laymen.

"That's the answer I was looking for," says Blackfoot. "Let's walk."

We walk to the northeast corner of the property. Blackfoot hands me a pad and pencil. "Just write down what I tell you," he says. He hands Mark the end of a tape measure poking out of a monster-sized spool, one of those jobs with a handle on it. "You just stand there lookin' pretty," he tells Mark.

"I was born for this job," Mark says as Blackfoot stomps off through the grass, the tape unspooling behind him.

"Father, you really need to cut this fucking grass," he says, as if insulted by the state of St. Peter's lawn. "It's a fuckin' sin," he adds.

"I like him a lot," Mark says. "He's just beyond belief."

"He's something," I say, a little perplexed by Mark and Blackfoot. Blackfoot, who'd seemed mostly unwilling to work with Vicky, hasn't had any problems dealing with Mark over the phone. I'd thought maybe Mark was dialing the gay down a notch, but this morning—the first time the two men met face-to-face—he had it blaring at the usual volume. Blackfoot would have to be blind not to have noticed it. But some people, I guess, have no gay-dar.

"Okay, Mr. Fancy Pants, you come stand right where I'm standing and bring the fuckin' tape with you," Blackfoot shouts from the end of his tape.

"Fancy Pants?" Mark says, arching an eyebrow. "I think he likes me, too!"

So much for the no-gay-dar theory. We walk toward Blackfoot, who's standing about three-quarters of the way toward the tree line. The tape spools back up on its coil as we go.

"How long is that thing?" I ask.

"Three hundred feet, Father."

"Oooh, that's a long one," says Mark.

Blackfoot looks up at him from under his bushy eyebrows. "Always the same thing with you people, ain't it?" he says, but there's no anger or disgust in his voice. He seems sort of amused, in fact. "One might be a no-count midway man, can't read the fuckin' comics section, and the other's a fancy-pants college man, taught by the church its own fuckin' self, but same thing on their minds. Same. Exact. Thing."

"Well, it is so hard to deny nature, Mr. Blackfoot," Mark says. Did he just bat his eyelashes? Is he flirting?

"Don't go that way myself," says Blackfoot, "but trust me, lad, I know what it is to have a one-track mind about certain things." He winks at Mark, then looks at me with a crooked smile. "Now, it's these that don't have a fuckin' outlet I don't quite trust."

"Don't worry about him," Mark says. "He'll come around one day. For one team or the other."

Blackfoot takes his spool and walks back toward the trees, chuckling.

"I can't stand people who laugh at their own jokes," I say.

"Aww. Did someone get his widdle feelings hurt?" says Mark.

"Shut up."

But I'm smiling, too. Better they get along than not. In fact, I'm surprised how swimmingly some of this decompartmental-ization of my life is going. Mark gets involved with the Rabbit Festival—things flow smoothly. Vicky meets Mark—they like each other. Mark meets Blackfoot—they get along. This keeps up, maybe I can drag Miss Rita out here.

"Five hundred fifty!" shouts Blackfoot.

"Five hundred fifty!" I shout back, and start to scribble on the paper. "Wait. That another five hundred fifty on top of the three hundred or five hundred fifty total?"

"C'mon, Father. Use yer eyes, would you? You got a nice piece of land out here, but it ain't a fuckin' landing strip."

"Sorry," I shout back, and bend back to the notebook.

"So that would be five hundred fifty total," whispers Mark. "Just in case you were still confused."

"Shut it," I say.

We've finished measuring up both the unpaved and paved portions of the property when a bright yellow Hummer with tinted windows drives into the lot and pulls up next to Black-foot's ramshackle pickup.

"Who is that?" Mark asks.

"I don't know," I say.

The passenger door opens and out he hops.

"B.P.," I hiss.

"That's him?" Mark asks.

"The one and fucking only," I answer.

Blackfoot walks up beside us, spooling his tape measure. "Everything okay, Father?" he asks.

"Yeah," I sigh. "Everything's fine."

B.P. waves, hitches up his pants, and starts sauntering over, that hundred-watt grin of his visible all the way across the lot. B.P. Junior, dressed like a male model, hops out of the driver's side, waves our way, but stays put by the Hummer.

Mark takes a quick breath. "My God! Who is *that*?"

"B.P. Junior," I say.

"Dear Lord," Mark says, "that is a fine piece of man."

"Don't even think of going there," I whisper. "Now shut up," I add as B.P. gets closer. "And this time I mean it."

I fix a fake smile to my face and add a dash of false cheer to my voice. "B.P., how the heck are ya?"

"I tell ya, Father, the Good Lord's been treating me all right. I think He mighta been listening to my son a little harder than me, though, because I sure prayed for the boy not to buy that thing." He turns and looks at the Hummer, shaking his head. But his consternation strikes me as false. I have a feeling the first chance he gets, B.P.'s going to take that thing off-roading himself.

"Boys will be boys," I say. Jeez. Every time the man shows up, I find myself in a cliche arms race.

"I guess they will," B.P. says, and for a split second, he sounds sad or angry or a little of both. But he shakes it off quickly enough. "So what we got going on out here today?" He seems to have forgotten our little standoff at the gumbo fund-raiser.

I make my introductions. "B.P., this is Johnny Blackfoot of the Magical Amusement Company. And this is Mark Johnson, a, uh, friend of mine who's been staying with me here at the rectory."

"Is that right?" B.P. says, giving Mark a good look.

"Yup, that's right," I say. "Mr. Blackfoot, Mark, this is the Reverend Paul Tomkins of the soon-to-be Pentecostal church just up the road a bit."

"Yall just call me B.P.," says B.P., puffing his chest up a bit.

"Pentecostal church?" says Blackfoot.

"That's right," says B.P. "That's one big prayer of mine the Good Lord has seen fit to answer."

"Well," says Blackfoot, "I guess congratulations are in order all around, then. That's something, there. Guess there's fuckin' room for everybody out here." Then Blackfoot does three things. He launches a greasy glob of dark spit onto the pavement. He then sticks his index finger into his cheek, pulls out the wad of tobacco, and chucks it over into the grass. Finally, he reaches into his shirt pocket and produces a crumpled soft pack of Winstons.

"I must say, Reverend, it sounds like you have a little more luck with the Old Man upstairs than old Blackfoot here," says Blackfoot. "I keep trying to quit these fuckin' things. Get down on my knees and ask Him for some help. Every damn night. But no fuckin' doin. They'll be the fuckin' death of me, no doubt. But I guess that's the hand dealt to me." He lights up and takes a long slow drag, his lips curled around the filter in a smile.

B.P.'s chest deflates just a little and my own smile becomes that much less fake.

And just when I think it can't get any better, Mark chimes in. "Handsome son you have there," he says.

For a split second, B.P.'s ready to take this as a manly compliment, but then he notices Mark has his hand to his throat—much the way a woman would—and hasn't taken his eyes off of Junior.

"He looks familiar, too," Mark continues. "Does he work in Lafayette? Maybe I've seen him around there."

B.P.'s trying hard to hold the smile on his face. "No. He ain't got much time to get into Lafayette. Ever. He's either busy helping me build the church or he's with his pretty little wife."

I've seen Junior's wife and she may be many things, but pretty and little aren't among them.

"So what brings you out today, B.P.?" I say. I have to say something, anything to bring this conversation to someplace that doesn't make me feel like laughing hysterically while dancing a jig.

He seems happy to be thrown a rescue line. "My boy was showing me his new truck and I saw yall out here with the tape measure and was just wondering what yall was up to."

Yeah, I think. *And now you wish you'd told him to keep on driving.*

"Yall ain't thinking of expanding?" he tosses in.

"No, nothing like that," I say. "Our humble little church is all we need. Something big and showy probably wouldn't fit the parish."

Take that!

"I'll give you that, Father. She is a plain one for a Catholic building."

Ouch.

"Anyway. We're just making plans for the festival."

"Festival? So yall still plan on having that little fair?"

Perhaps he thought he'd build his own flock out in the boonies, away from temptation. Now here I am messing the whole thing up. And he's contributed at least seventy-five dollars to the cause so far.

"Sure thing, B.P. First Annual Rabbit Festival. Rides. Food. Contests. The usual."

"Well, ain't that something?" he says.

"And bands, too," adds Mark. "Lot of live music. Zydeco. Cajun. Country. Couple of teenage rock bands from Opelousas. When the flyers are printed, I'll be sure to drive by and give you some. Maybe you and your son can get the word out."

Blackfoot clears his throat. "You know, Father, before I forget . . ."

"Yes, Mr. Blackfoot." I can't wait to see where this is going.

"I was thinking that while the beer garden is a nice touch, what would really spice it up would be a casino night."

I want to hug this man, but I dig deep and find the strength to restrain myself.

"That might be a bit much, Mr. Blackfoot. Trouble with the gaming commission and all. But a bingo night might be a good idea. It's not *real* gambling, but we can still give out cash prizes."

B.P.'s smile is fading again and I know that whatever it is I'm feeling at this moment, it's a sin.

"So when's this little festival going to be?" he manages to ask without gritting his teeth.

"First weekend after Easter," I say, fighting the urge to scream, *"In your face, old man!"*

But suddenly his oily smile is back, and watching it creep from one side of his face to the other, I know I'm not going to like what's coming next.

"You don't say?" He nods, pretends to count some numbers on his fingers. "Turns out that's the weekend we're having a big tent revival up at the property there. Sort of our way of starting things off on the right foot."

Bastard.

"I guess it'll be a big weekend in Grand Prairie," I say. *Bastard. Bastard. Bastard.*

"Reckon so," he says. "Of course, I'd already been in touch with the sheriff's department about redirecting traffic and dealing with parking up on our end. Hope it doesn't block things up too much for you."

Oh, you Holy Rolling son of a bitch. I can just see cars trying to get down from Ville Platte stuck in his little traffic jam or, worse, thinking his boring tent revival is my festival and just turning around and going home. Or worst of all, some of them poking their heads in and catching the Holy Ghost and converting.

"I'm sure it'll be fine," I say. "Just hope I don't block things too much up on my end."

"Oh, I wouldn't worry about that too much, Father. None of my people will mistake a fairground for a revival."

We'll see about that. Maybe I'll park that elephant right in the middle of the road. Or better, I'll have it stampede the tent.

"Well, I best be off. Gotta go show that truck off some more."

I'm hoping that Mark says something cute about Junior, but B.P.'s latest move has taken the wind out of his sails. I can tell that his mind's already working on the ramifications, processing the next move, mapping out alternative routes.

"And just to be safe," says B.P., "I'd check with the gaming commission about that bingo night. Rules have changed a lot in the last couple of years."

"I'll do that," I say, and wave him off. He and Junior climb into the Hummer and drive off.

"Shit," Mark says.

I say nothing for a bit. Blackfoot offers me a cigarette. It calms me down a touch, but I'd like nothing more than to stub it out in B.P.'s eye.

"Don't worry about it," I say halfheartedly. "We'll deal with him later."

We walk over to Blackfoot's truck.

"Fuckin' Pentecostals," Blackfoot says before spitting on the concrete and climbing into the cab. He cranks down the window and waves us closer. He looks around as if someone could possibly sneak up on us out here. He whispers, "I can take care of that one, Father, if you want me to. No extra charge. Just say the word and it's done. You don't have to answer now, but there it is. It's an offer." He shifts his truck into Drive and moves off, hawking a monster loogie at the stop sign at the end of the drive.

"Holy shit," says Mark. "That was intense."

"Yeah," I say, afraid to admit I'm battling with some very mixed emotions at the moment. I don't know what Blackfoot meant by his offer, but I had to bite my tongue not to give him the go-ahead.

"What religion are his people, anyway?" Mark asks.

"I don't know," I say. "But I do know that I need a fuckin' drink somethin' fuckin' fierce, ya know what I'm fuckin' sayin', ya fuckin' cocksucker?"

"Wow," Mark says, laughing. "Don't do that again. Ever."

I leave Mark and Chase alone in Grand Prairie and drive to Opelousas to file a report with Miss Rita. Overall, it isn't so bad. Sure, B.P. is trying to make trouble, and if he ruins my festival I might have to let Blackfoot burn down his church. Then again, I have Blackfoot on my side. And the parishioners, for now. Mark, too. And Vicky. Nag that she is, she means well and I couldn't do it without her. Zipping down the highway on a sunny winter day, I offer up a little prayer of thanks.

But as I'm walking into Easy Time, my mood changes immediately—and not just because it's full of lonely, old people waiting to die. My brisk "Hi" to the usually bubbly Marie is met with a curt "Hey, Father" and a dirty glance at my bag. She's got one hand on the phone and it looks for all the world like she's going to dial 911 to report me for getting an old lady drunk and jacking up her cholesterol.

"How's Miss Rita?" I ask.

"Oh, she's awake," she says, an edge in her voice.

"Is she sick?"

"No," she sighs. There are tears in her eyes. "That's just the nicest thing I could think to say about her this morning."

"That she's awake?"

"Yes," she says, then puts her hand over her mouth and dashes for the bathroom, crying.

I stand in front of Miss Rita's door a full minute. "Jesus, give me strength," I say before pushing it open and walking into her room where I find her sitting like a spider waiting for its next victim. An angry, sullen spider wearing a neon-green T-shirt that reads *I'm not your Magical Negro*. She's got her "You did it this time" rays shooting out of her eyes.

I know better than to say anything. I open up my bag and reach for the Crown Royal and cracklin's, try to hand them to her.

"Just put them down there," she says, motioning to the night-stand but keeping her eyes on me.

I stand up straight and try to meet her stare. It's high noon at the old folks' home, and I know for certain that I'm going to get shot down by this old lady. I break first.

"New shirt?"

"Brand-new." Her eyes glint.

I've walked right into her trap. I might as well make it quick. "What's it mean?"

"What do you think it means?"

"I have no earthly idea."

"Guess you're not as smart as you think you are."

Again, we fall into a silent stare. Again, I cave.

"You going to tell me what it means?"

Without taking her eyes off me, she reaches over to the nightstand, fishes the Crown Royal from its purple sack, frees it from its plastic seal, unscrews the cap, and takes a slug. She doesn't say, "Ahhhh," and neither does she wipe her mouth. Her lips glisten with whiskey when she presses the call button and speaks again.

"Yall get Carl in here," she demands.

"Timeka's free," Marie says.

"Did I stutter?" Miss Rita asks. "Now tell Carl to get his chubby butt in here."

Carl comes trotting into the room.

"Hey, Miss Rita," he says. "Father." He nods.

"Hi," I say. I haven't dealt much with Carl. He's a soft, pudgy white guy with spiky white hair, a goatee, and a diamond stud in his left ear.

"Carl, can you make my bed?"

He looks at it, a bit confused. "They didn't make it this morning?"

"Guess they forgot," she says.

He shrugs. "Okay, then. No problem."

"Dropped my pillow on the floor, too," she says.

"Okay," Carl says, reaching to grab it. When he bends over, a massive expanse of white back fat and ass crack slip out of his waistband.

I turn away to spare myself the sight, and see Miss Rita watching me closely.

"Like what you see, Steve?" she says.

"What?" I say. "What's that supposed to—"

Carl straightens up, interrupting. "What's that, Miss Rita?"

"Nothing, Carl," she says, not taking her eyes off me. "You know what, though, Carl. Father Steve, here? Maybe you two could get together sometime. Occurs to me, yall might have a thing or two in common."

Carl and I look at each other. He's turned the color of boiled crawfish and I'm sure I have, too.

"Well, Miss Rita," he starts, a nervous smile fixed on his face. "I . . . Um . . ."

"Don't worry about it, Carl," I say. "She's just in a mood today. Thanks for making the bed."

He takes that as his cue to leave and hightails it out of there.

"Don't you dare talk about me like I'm not in the same room," she says as Carl closes the door behind him.

Suddenly I'm twelve again, and in deep, deep trouble. It's not the inevitable beating I'm scared of, it's disappointing Miss Rita, suffering that irrational childhood fear that your bad behavior will make someone suddenly stop loving you. It's a powerful, primal fear. But I try not to give in. If I start crying now, I'd lose any shot of escaping this conversation with a modicum of dignity.

"What was that about?" As if I didn't suspect.

Her words rush out in an angry flood, starting out low and fast and building to a righteous shout. "I told you to get you a woman, Steve. I told you a hundred times it wasn't natural living like that. Told you to start a festival to keep you out of trouble and now come to find out you're living with a man. A man! Doing Lord knows what! That is a sin, Steve. One of the worst. And you know what else? It woulda killed your mawmaw if she knew. It's enough to make me want to die! I'm sick. Sick to my stomach and I just want to drop dead right now!"

She's reached such a volume that Marie and Timeka come bursting through the door. Before either can speak, Miss Rita—again never taking her eyes off me—shouts, "Get the hell out of my room, Marie. I said I'd call you if I needed you. Now get out."

Marie runs off crying for the second time today. Timeka shoots me a dirty look before pulling the door shut quietly.

So Miss Rita thinks I'm gay. Is that it? That should be easy enough to clear up. Still, I need a shot of courage. When I move for the Crown Royal, she snatches it away and kicks her wheelchair as far as it will go into the corner, knocking over a lamp in the process.

"Miss Rita!"

She says nothing more, just clutches the bottle of Crown to her chest as if it were a life preserver, or perhaps a jug of holy water.

"First of all," I start. "Gay people aren't vampires."

Which is exactly the wrong way to go about this. She starts rocking back and forth, shakes her head from side to side, and whispers to herself, "I knew it. Lord. I knew it. I knew it. I knew it. I tried to stop him, Lorine." She's talking to Mawmaw now, apparently. "I tried. Nothing I could do. See what your church got him into? You *see*? Now he's going to burn in hell. Burn in hell for all eternity."

A small part of me wants to laugh, but that could prove fatal for one or both of us. "I'm not going to burn in hell," I say.

She stops rocking. "No? You got some fancy-pants reason why not? I know what the Bible says. Go on. Grab it out of my nightstand. Leviticus 18:22. 'Thou shalt not lie with mankind, as with womankind. It is abomination.' English don't get any plainer than that. And there's more where it came from."

"Okay, now just hold on a minute."

"Get that Bible."

"Miss Rita."

"Get it."

I pluck it from her nightstand and hand it to her. She waves it away.

"No, you read it."

"C'mon, Miss Rita."

She smacks the arm of her wheelchair with the flat of her hand. "Read it, I said. Leviticus 20:13 this time."

I read it. "If a man also lie with mankind, as he lieth with a woman, both of them have committed an abomination: they shall surely be put to death; their blood shall be upon them."

"Your church got some way around that?" she asks.

"No," I sigh. In fact, St. Paul heaps plenty more coal onto the pile, calling the practice unclean, impure, unnatural, and the act of a depraved mind. "It doesn't. It hates gay people just as much as your church. I'm sure if there was a contest for gay-hating, it would be a tie."

"Least they got one thing right," she mutters.

"We need to set a couple of things straight," I say.

"You need to get a wet-nap and wipe off the covers of my Bible."

Unable to stop myself, I laugh.

"Don't you get smart with me," she says, her voice rising again. "If I have to, I'll find a way to get out of this chair and slap the white right off your face. Now wipe the filth off my Bible."

"No." Sadly, this is one of the bravest moments of my life.

"What did you say?"

The icy tone in her voice is almost enough to change my mind. Twenty years ago, that phrase would have immediately preceded a switching that would have left my legs welted for a week. Which is why I made it my business to learn never to provoke it.

"I said no."

"That's it," she says. She caps the whiskey bottle, puts it on the floor, then starts struggling to lift herself out of the wheelchair. She's going to kill herself.

"Damn it, Miss Rita. Sit down."

We're both shocked. I half expect God himself to reach down and smack me across the face.

"I'm not wiping your Bible down. Even if you think gays are disease carriers, it doesn't matter. I'm not gay. You hear me? I'm not gay. Not that it should matter, but I'm not."

Of course, saying I'm got gay sixty-five thousand times is an odd way of demonstrating that it doesn't matter. She doesn't believe me. That much is clear.

"I don't know what else to say. Mark is a friend. And yes, he's gay. Gay as the day is long. He needed a place to stay. But I'm not gay."

She breathes heavily, trying to figure out her next move.

"I want you to swear," she says.

"God," I say, sounding like a petulant fourteen-year-old. "I swear."

"I want you to swear to me, to your mawmaw. I want you to swear on that Bible."

"Oh, now I can touch it? Now it's okay to swear on your precious Bible with my filthy hands?"

"Boy," she says in a way that tells me I've reached the limit.

For all intents and purposes, this is a court of law. She takes the Bible, I put one hand on it, raise the other. I pluck up the courage to once again stare her in the face. "I, Father Steve Sibille, swear to Miss Rita, to Mawmaw, to God and Jesus and the Holy Ghost—"

She interrupts. "Swear to Mary, too. Doesn't mean anything to a Catholic if she ain't in there."

"And I swear to our Holy Mother Mary, Queen of Peace, Lady of Mercy, on the Holy Bible, that I am not gay and have never been gay. So help me."

I stand there for a full minute with one hand up in the air before either of us speaks.

"Put my Bible away," she says.

"Like I'd lie to you, anyway." I tuck it back into her nightstand.

I motion for the Crown and she hands it over.

"It's just wrong, Steve." She's confused now more than angry. "Bible says God put man and woman on this earth to make babies."

"If that's true, then why did God make them gay in the first place?"

"Steve!"

"Miss Rita!" I say, half mockingly. "And you of all people."

"Me?"

"That doesn't sound familiar to you? Being picked on? Threatened? Shut out? Let me ask you something, considering when you grew up and where, the things you went through, would you have chosen to be born black?"

"That was in God's hands. Not up to me."

"Wasn't up to Mark, either. Look, he's just a friend. He grew up in Gueydan, out in the country. You think he woke up one morning and said, 'I want to be gay. I want all the other kids to pick on me and beat me up. I want my daddy to stop loving me. I want to make my mama cry. I want everyone in my town to whisper behind my back'?"

"Hmph," she says again. "He doesn't have to go fooling around with men. That's a choice he has."

"I give up," I say, throwing myself into a chair. "Thought you'd be smart enough to see that."

She's silent for a good long time. This may be the only time a Catholic priest has defended homosexuality to someone of another faith—or any faith. I'm so far off script, I wouldn't be surprised to go outside and find a papal tow truck taking away my car and a bishop standing in the parking lot demanding my collar.

Finally she looks up. "I'm sorry," she says. I half expect her to choke Fonzie-like on the word.

What? I keep very, very still, afraid to ruin the moment. Miss Rita doesn't apologize.

"I understand what you're trying to tell me. Maybe you're right. Maybe I'm wrong. It's what I been taught, what I believed for a hundred years."

"I understand," I say. God only knows what it took for her to apologize. She's right. A hundred years of an unchallenged prejudice doesn't just disappear.

"Hope you happy," she says. "You made an old, dying lady feel ashamed of herself."

I just can't help it. "Maybe you should," I say. "A little, at least."

"Hmph."

"Besides, this is the first time in my life I got you to admit you were wrong about something."

She smiles a little. " 'Cause it's the first time in your life I *was* wrong about something."

"Well, I'm certainly going to mark it down on my calendar."

"While you at it, might as well mark it down as the first time you had the nuts to stand up to me. Though I wouldn't go bragging you stood up to somebody in a wheelchair."

We both force a chuckle at my expense, glad we're back in familiar territory of laughing at Steve rather than fighting over his immortal soul.

She offers me a weak smile. "This is all your fault, anyway."

"How so?"

"You'da found you a woman in the first place, I wouldn't have had to embarrass myself like that."

"Oh, you're going to start that again?"

"I never stopped."

"Miss Rita."

"What about that girl we went to church with on Christmas? The one always hanging around, helping you with the festival? The one keeping you too busy to come visit me more often?"

I pause just a moment too long before saying, "She's just a friend."

"Uh-huh," she says, with a smile. "Thought you said you couldn't lie to me."

I'm blushing again. Damn it.

"Ha!" she shouts, slapping her thigh. "We gonna get you straight yet."

Exasperated, I find myself back on script. "We've been through this all before, Miss Rita. I'm a priest."

She throws her hands up. "Just stop it right there. You can bend all of them church rules for your gay friend." Her smile grows a little stronger. "Seems you could bend one or two for yourself."

"Lord," I say. "There won't be any bending of the rules."

"So don't bend them," she says. "Just break them. You know you want to. I know you want to." She pauses, as if thinking something over. She claps her hands, pleased with herself. "And if that girl's spending that much time foolin' with you instead of going out with other men, she probably wants to, too."

"I'm not breaking my vows. End of story."

"Not even if it was an old lady's dying wish?"

"Not even. And stop saying that."

"Fine," she says. "Be that way. Not that it matters. If that girl gets it into her head to go after you, you won't be able to fight it forever."

"Just stop it," I say, trying not to blush any more than I already am, trying not to show any more emotion at all.

"Okay, Steve, you don't have to pout just because I'm right."

"You're not."

"Of course not." She shakes her bag of cracklin's and picks around for a good one. "You get on home, leave me alone," she says, dismissing me without looking up. "And I'm sorry for calling you gay."

I stand up to go. "That's not what you should be apologizing for."

"I know," she says, still picking in the bag. "Sorry for letting that hate in my heart. I'm never gonna say this again, but you right. I'm wrong. Put that in your scrapbook."

I might have to start scrapbooking for just this occasion.

Miss Rita rolls her chair over to the wall and pulls down her calendar, closes the cover on Mr. March's gleaming black body. She hands it to me.

"What's this for?" I say, getting defensive again.

"Go on and give that to your friend. That Mark fella," she says.

"You don't have to do that," I say. But the truth is, Mark will likely wet himself in glee over the gift.

"I feel bad," she says. For a split second, she sounds almost like a child that's been scolded. In fact, she sounds like I used to when she'd scold me. "I'm glad you have at least some kind of company out there. A person shouldn't be alone." Then she changes her tone. "Besides, I already looked at all the pictures. Figured at my age, better look now. Might not make it through the year."

"Okay, Miss Rita," I say, walking out the door. "Bye."

"And you tell Vicky I said hi," she shouts after me.

Chapter 14

I didn't expect to see a crowd at a roadhouse on a Wednesday night, but it's amazing what a rock-blues band and five-dollar pitchers can do for business. The place is crawling with unattached men on the prowl for the next victim. But I'm good and drunk by the time I realize that none of these hard-legs has asked Vicky to dance. Weird. Well, their loss, I guess.

We haven't been dancing, either. Mark's usually the ringleader. But I left him alone in Grand Prairie tonight. I didn't tell him I was going out with Vicky, even though he's sure to find out about it soon enough. After Miss Rita's fit, I needed a little break from Mark. When I gave him the calendar, he ran directly to his room to hang it up and went on and on about how he wanted to meet her. I couldn't find it in my heart to tell him it might not be the best idea. She'd said she was sorry, but I imagine there are limits to how much a person can change. And, to be honest, there was that little dark corner of my heart that was ashamed she thought I was gay—which in turn made me ashamed to be ashamed.

So I left him behind. So we haven't been shouting over each other and laughing. And we haven't been mingling with the locals.

What I have been doing is drinking a little faster, a little more than usual. Maybe even a lot more.

"Hey, stud, you gonna ask me to dance or what?" Vicky says.

I turn toward her. It feels like an exaggerated movement, as if my neck turns; then my head and eyes catch up a few seconds later. She's looking at me and there's this, I don't know. It's not quite her usual smirk, but not quite a smile. Her eyes dance in the candlelight. Red candles. She looks positively saintly in red candlelight.

"Huh?" I reply.

"We gonna dance or sit on our asses all night?"

This, I know, is a rhetorical question, yet my mind, dulled by booze, cycles through the available answers.

I offer my hand, she takes it, and at that point a wee little voice in the back of my head says, *Excuse me, Father Steve. Not to be a stickler here, but you've never danced to this music before.* But before the voice can lodge any further protest, we're moving along easily, and as far as I can tell, I have it all under control. I'm not counting out loud, not stumbling over my feet—just moving, gliding.

"Damn, Padre. You're cutting a rug tonight," Vicky says, looking down at my feet.

I blush a little, but I don't care. I, too, look down at my feet sliding across the floor, turning me around seemingly without input from my brain.

"I guess I was due," I shout over the music, enjoying my Navin Johnson moment. I've found my rhythm for once. I'm leading and she's following and we don't show any signs of stopping, even between songs. We're red-faced and a little sweaty when the band downshifts into a cover of "You Look Wonderful Tonight." My first inclination is to step off the dance floor, but for whatever reason I pause, frozen by a clear flashback to high school. I'm standing on a cul-de-sac in a soon-to-be-developed suburban neighborhood. Some guy in an amped-up van is playing DJ, and pops this same song into the tape deck. And there I am, slow-dancing with Ruh-ruh-ruh-Rachel, happy as a clam at high tide, gulping down the summer air, heavy with the scent of fresh cut grass and entirely too much Drakkar Noir.

Vicky pulls herself into me, puts her head on my shoulder, and we rotate slowly.

Now that we're not moving at such a frantic pace, I can feel how drunk I really am. That little blast of nostalgia has knocked me into one of those fugue states in which I can watch myself from a higher vantage point, something akin to astral projection.

There we are, turning slowly below me, looking like any couple in the world, no different than the others on the dance floor. So that's why no one else asked her to dance. We looked like a couple. A regular deductive genius, I am.

And there's Vicky lifting her head just a bit, enough to get me to pull back a tad to look down at her. She lifts her head up a little more and looks at me, her eyes heavy-lidded as if she's just waking. She stands slightly higher on her toes, moves her face closer to mine.

I expect to be pulled back down into myself, made more aware of my surroundings as I'm flooded by memories of all those long-forgotten kisses.

But no. I stay up here, watching, waiting, wondering. The only thing close to a fully formed thought going through my head at the moment is: *Huh. That's not what Jesus would do.*

The kiss ends. She puts her head on my shoulders.

I didn't tell Mark.

I woke up that morning earlier than I had any right to. After the kiss, I'd suggested shots. Lots of them. Perhaps it was the first step in erasing the event. At any rate, the rest of the night is now forever gone from my memory. Yet there I was at nine that morning, putting coffee on, humming to myself, waiting for Mark to get his ass out of bed so I could tell him.

But just as suddenly, the hangover showed up and along with the sour stomach, my head began throbbing with pain. And common sense. And propriety. And a touch of "What have I done?"

So I didn't tell him. If I'd told him, it would have made the whole thing real, made it that much harder to put it behind me. Of course, there were two tangoing that night, and if Vicky told Mark, well then, I'd have a drama on my hands.

A small part of me wanted to see if she would tell him. Because if she did tell him, that would have meant . . . I don't know. That it was something more than drunken stupidity? That she was excited that it had happened? That she was mortified, wanted to make sure I hadn't taken it the wrong way but was too embarrassed to ask me directly?

Yet since that evening Mark hasn't come running in, half squealing and half screaming at me for not telling him about this, the biggest development since the invention of fire. Nothing from him. Vicky's been silent all week long as well. And, it goes without saying, nothing from me. Nothing all around.

Nothing except a loud clang as the shiny gold saucer that is held under the chalice of the wine slips out of Denise's left hand and hits the gleaming strip of marble at the edge of the altar.

I wake up as if from sleep. I'm in the middle of Saturday evening Mass. And there's Denise with this satisfied look on her face. She's still got the chalice firmly gripped in her right hand and looks me straight in the eye as Maggie falls to all fours to grab the saucer. Denise shrugs as if to say, "Shit happens. Sue me."

She knows! The thought flashes through my mind and I feel a blush coming on. But I regain control quickly enough. The only thing Denise knows is that this week and last I've been distracted by something—something so distracting that it distracts me from her distractions. And that's pissed her off, it seems. Or maybe it was simply an accident.

Either way, I'm back. And there's Vicky sitting in the third pew from the door, right next to Mark, whispering to him from time to time.

Maybe she's telling him right now.

No. She knows better than that. Mark wouldn't be able to stop himself from blurting out an "Oh. My. God. No, you didn't!" and smacking her on the thigh right during the middle of the Eucharistic Prayer.

So I muddle through the rest of Mass as best I can, wrap things up, and head for the door, where I'm mobbed by the usual gaggle of old geese. Denise takes off without saying good-bye. After my old birds fly away home, I walk over to Mark and Vicky, who are waiting for me at the edge of the cemetery. Mark hands me a cigarette.

"What a beautiful, heartfelt Homily," he says. "I thought it would never end."

"Shut up," I tell him. "Hey, Vicky."

"Evening, Padre," she says. "I have to say that cymbal crash during the Eucharistic Prayer was a nice touch."

"Yeah, well."

"It's almost like Denise was angry at you for something," she adds.

I look at her. She looks me in the eye and smirks, shrugs her shoulders.

Mark looks at each of us in turn, his eyebrows knitting in confusion, as if he's just about to connect a few dots.

"So where are we headed tonight?" I ask.

"Excellent question," he says. "I say Hamilton's."

"Sounds good to me," I say.

"I'm not going to make it tonight, fellas," Vicky says.

"What?" I say before I can stop myself. I'm sure it sounds entirely too defensive, perhaps even wounded.

"Does someone have a hot date?" Mark asks. "Do tell."

"Just a previous engagement is all, Mr. Busybody," she answers.

So it's going to be like that.

"Fine," Mark says. "Be coy. I guess we can't expect you to spend all your time with a couple of eunuchs."

Speak for yourself, is on the tip of my tongue, but I swallow the words.

"You don't have to be so dramatic, Mark," she says. "I'm sure you two studs can have fun without me."

But we don't, really. After Vicky leaves, I lock myself in the bathroom for a good fifteen minutes then tell Mark I'm not feeling well enough to go out. I don't know what I'd do if I actually spotted her with a guy somewhere.

Did I just allow myself to think that?

"Oh, so your girlfriend can't go and you suddenly develop a mystery illness," he says.

"What's that supposed to mean?" I ask.

He gives me a hard look before answering. "It was supposed to be a joke. But if you get that defensive about it, I might start wondering."

"Oh, shut up." I'm finding that to be the best answer for everyone tonight. "I might not be up for going out, but I'll still whip your butt on Xbox."

"Fine," he says. "But I'm going to need some alcohol if I'm going to sit around here with you all night."

"Fine," I say.

And it is, mostly. The video games almost keep my mind off whatever it is Vicky's doing. And when that doesn't work, I start drinking.

*   *   *

After another week of mostly avoiding each other, and with no official agreement of any kind, Vicky and I are almost back to normal.

Almost.

She seems not as quick to laugh at my jokes. To be fair, I seem unable to make many. It's as if I can't help but take myself seriously in her presence. And if I notice that, surely she must. And Mark? If he notices, he doesn't say anything. Hell, he's probably tickled to be getting all of the attention. When we go dancing, she dances with him. She'll make a show of asking me, but I just beg off. She seems to find Mark the funniest man alive, laughing at all of his jokes as if they're funnier than they actually are. And they're not that funny.

The two of us also talk through Mark rather than directly to each other. I'm half expecting her to lean into him one night and say, "Mark, tell Steve that I think the weather's pretty good tonight."

And then tonight Mark gets sick and decides he can't go out. Judging by the inhuman smells and sounds wafting from the bathroom, he's not faking.

"So I guess we'll just stay in," I say through the door.

"No," he groans.

"Mark, you're in no condition to go out."

"I'm not going out," he says, then flushes the toilet. After the noise subsides, he continues. "But you have to go. I promised this band's manager we'd give him a check and a contract tonight. *Tonight.*"

"Seriously?" I ask, suddenly facing the prospect of going out with Vicky unsupervised.

"Yes, seriously." He pauses. "Oh, Jesus, this is just so gross." He flushes again. "Anyway, Vicky's got the check. So give her a call. I'm going to be in here a bit longer."

I walk, slowly, toward the kitchen phone. I pick up the receiver, start to dial, then stop. I pour myself a drink, finish it, then pour another before picking up the phone again. No big deal, really. I'll just tell her Mark's sick and she'll volunteer to go drop the check off by herself. She's not going to want to deal with me, I'm sure.

"Mark's sick," I tell her when she answers.

"He's not coming out?" she asks.

"Nope."

A moment of silence.

"Well, what time you picking me up?" she asks.

Another, longer moment of silence. My stomach drops. Why couldn't she just volunteer to go alone?

"Steve? You there?"

"Uh. Yeah. I'm here."

"What time you picking me up?"

"Half an hour?"

"Sounds good," she says, then hangs up.

I put the phone back in its charger. It's slick from the sweat on my palms. I finish off my drink and pour myself a third. I'd have a fourth, but I have to drive and I'm afraid it might push my stomach a bit too far. Already it's doing flips, acting like it might start an export business in one or both directions. I drive to Vicky's house in a daze, trying to ignore the telltale signs of an anxiety attack.

"Not good, not good," I mutter to myself. I even try to pray, mouthing the first words that pop into my head. "Lord Jesus Christ, please have lightning strike my car and kill me dead right now. Amen."

But no such luck. I pull into her drive and blow the horn, convinced that if I get out of the car I'll puke. She runs out, flapping in flip-flops. She's wearing a sundress that just happens to highlight her womanly figure.

I force a smile onto my face and reach over to open her door. Through the buzz of bees in my head, I hear myself say, "Well, hello there, sexy."

Hello there, sexy? What the hell is that about? Am I suddenly a Vegas lounge lizard?

"Hey to you, too, Padre," she says before hopping in and kissing me on the cheek.

I swallow hard and needlessly adjust the rearview mirror. Just as I notice the smear of lipstick on my cheek, she reaches over and rubs it off with her thumb. It's all I can do not to pass out.

"Got something for the drive," she says, and pulls a flask from her purse.

"Excellent," I say. *Oh, thank you, Jesus,* I think, and take a long pull.

How I make it through the evening is a mystery. I'm in a complete state of panic for the first half, I get blind stinking drunk for the second half.

When I wake up the next morning, I'm certain we didn't have a heart-to-heart, I'm fairly sure we didn't kiss, and I have no I idea how I got home.

Mark tells me, while laughing at my hangover, that she drove home, that they put me to bed and she slept on the couch, waking him up at six in the morning so he could bring her home.

"What did she say?" I ask.

"What do you mean?"

"When she dropped me off last night. What did she say? Was she pissed off or anything?"

"I don't think so. She just looked tired. She said you obviously can't handle your liquor."

"That's all?"

"Yeah. Why?"

"No reason," I say. "Just wondering."

Chapter 15

I'm in the kitchen of Mama's house, scrubbing a pot so hard I might go straight through its bottom. I'm not ready to go back to the empty rectory.

Mama had her "Get out of Lent Free" party tonight, an affair she hosts right smack in the middle of Lent. She tells everyone they're completely free to break whatever fast they've imposed on themselves. Mama's not exactly a model Catholic. I invited Vicky and Mark. It was our first outing together in a while—I haven't done anything with Vicky since the night she dropped me off. I simply can't bring myself to go. I get panicky just thinking about being in a bar with her. I don't need to do that to myself. Oh no. Much better to give myself other complexes. Like jealousy. Of Mark of all people. No, I haven't been going out. But they have. And to hear him tell it, it's just a blast. And when she does stop by the rectory, she and I are distant, while she and Mark seem to grow closer and closer. It's a regular Mark and Vicky show.

And tonight, after all the other guests had gone home, Mark decided he was going to Esperanto and Vicky decided she was going with him.

"Fine, yall have fun," I told them.

"You don't want to come?" Vicky asked. Maybe it was my imagination, but she seemed like she was just going through the motions, just being polite.

"Some of us have to work tomorrow morning," I said. "Besides, I'm not really allowed in places like that," I added, looking at Mark.

"What. Ever," he said, rolling his eyes. "Come down off your cross. Jesus needs it back."

"Watch it," I said, feeling suddenly sanctimonious. "Remember where you sleep at night."

"Yes, Father," he said, mocking me.

"Don't make me separate you two," Vicky said, laughing, as if this were all just some sort of joke.

So now they're on their way to Lafayette and I have my hands in the sink and Mama won't leave well enough alone.

"I think Mark and Victoria make a cute couple, don't you?"

I see her sneak a glance at me, gauging the impact of her jab. Can't hide anything from good old Mom. She's like one of those people who knows exactly what time it is but insists on asking you to check your watch anyway. The thing is, she's not so sure I know what time it is, she's not sure I can see the clock right in front of my face. As far as I'm concerned, we're in two different time zones entirely. I'm in one of those countries, like Afghanistan, that has an extra eighteen minutes thrown in there somewhere, screwing up all the timetables.

"Vicky deserves a good man, and God knows he could use a woman," she says.

"I think Mark's the one who could use a good man, Mama."

"Now, Steve."

"Mama," I say, exasperated, "the man's as queer as a three-dollar-bill."

"I'll tell you something, boy," Tommy says, coming into the kitchen to pour himself a drink and pour me some unsolicited advice. "I know queer and that boy ain't it."

Of course. Tommy, the professional on male sexuality, probably still harbors lingering doubts about me. He wouldn't know queer if it snuck up behind him and fucked him up the ass.

"Hell," Tommy goes on. "Them two probably in the backseat of that big old car of hers right now."

I tighten my grip on the glass I'm washing. Mama looks down at my hands and I follow her gaze. My knuckles are turning white, so I loosen my grip and finish the dishes hurriedly, in silence. Tommy makes three more comments about knowing what gay looks like and how Mark isn't it before going to bed.

"I'm going to take a bath, then go to bed," Mama says.

"Good," I say. "I mean good night."

She looks at me, waiting for me to say something.

I stare back at her.

"I'm gonna finish this beer," I say.

"Okay." She sighs. "Lock the door when you leave." Before slipping down the hallway she throws one more glance over her shoulder, but neither of us says anything.

Alone in the kitchen, the fluorescent lighting looking not quite right in the old house, the refrigerator ticking, the pipes stirring to life as Mama turns on the hot water in her bathroom, I peel the label off my bottle. It's almost empty and I want another. Then another. And another. My eyes come to rest on Tommy's bottle of Seagram's 7. I reach for it, turn it around on the counter so the label faces me. My fingers twist off the cap while the other hand pries a red plastic cup from the inverted stack on the counter. I fill the cup halfway, look up to make sure no one's coming, and toss the whiskey back.

I pour another half glass and toss that back, recap the bottle, throw the cup in the garbage, and grab a beer before walking out to the car.

The beer is long gone by the time I get to the rectory, where I find all the lights are off. No surprise there. It's only nine thirty. Even if Mark and Vicky leave the club at midnight—

which isn't Mark's style at all—it will be one before they get back to Grand Prairie.

Walking into the kitchen, I stumbled over Chase.

"Goddamned cat," I say, and instantly regret it, thinking for a brief second that the cat, like the cursed fig tree, will shrivel up and die. Instead, Chase gives a plaintive meow, rubs some hair on my pants, and runs to his empty food bowl, where he meows again.

"Fine," I say, and pour food for the cat and a drink for myself before plopping down in front of the TV to watch Friday night television, programming designed to appeal to people who have no social lives. I suffer through the late news and work my way through another drink. I find a small prayer escaping my lips, asking that the *M*A*S*H* reruns be funny enough to drive all this melancholy away. But Hawkeye just seems silly, Radar pathetic, and the clock's hands make their merry way around its face and still no Mark or Vicky.

"And fuck Klinger, too," I say to the TV.

Chase rambles into the room and hops up onto my lap.

"Off," I mutter, pushing him down immediately to fetch another drink. Stumbling into the kitchen, I try to remember how many I've had, but can't. All that matters is that I'm drunk. But I'm not so drunk I don't know what time it is. It's almost 2:00 a.m. and still no sign of the prodigal priest. Still no sign of the Virgin of Grand Prairie. And I'm definitely not drunk enough to drown out the voice of Tommy saying over and over again, "I know queer and Mark ain't queer. Hell, they're probably in the back . . ." And so on. It's as if there's a scratched CD stuck in my head.

Back in my chair, I pick up my cordless phone and study it, no doubt looking like an ape trying to figure out how to get to the inside of a coconut.

I can call them, they both have cell phones. But under what pretense? "Hi, I'm drunk and I'm having issues and I hate you both right now but could you hurry home? Please." Still, just as I'd watched my fingers work the Seagram's bottle at Mama's house, I watch them dial a number, Vicky's number. As the phone rings, I try momentarily to think of something to say. I'll keep it light and airy. It's not like I'm checking up on them. I'm just bored is all. Just bored and want to say a simple "Hey."

Her voice mail picks up. "Damn," I whisper, and hang up without leaving a message. Crap. Will that seem weird that I didn't leave a message? I start to dial again, but stop myself. She's already got one "missed call" from this number. What's it going to look like if I call more than once? Stupid caller ID. How do stalkers and prank callers do it these days?

I'll call Mark. That's what I'll do. Better that way. Hell, I can actually check up on Mark, right? He's living under my roof. Yeah. Sure. Perfect.

Voice mail.

Have they turned off their phones? Maybe they can't hear them. But it's after 2:00 a.m. The club is closed now. Besides, Vicky always keeps her phone on vibrate so as not to disturb anyone. "And to get a little tickle," she sometimes adds.

"To get a little tickle."

The phrase goes caroming about my head, turning the lights on in all of the little rooms I like to keep locked up and dark.

"Get a little tickle," her voice says.

"I know queer. He ain't queer," Tommy's voice answers back.

For a moment, I can actually see the pink elephants on parade, or worse, their cousins, the heffalumps and woozles.

Their phones are off. They've turned their phones off and are doing God knows what in the backseat of Vicky's car. Or they're dead, trapped in a ton of crumpled steel wrapped around a telephone pole. And here I am accusing them of the worst.

Or they're simply in a no-service area.

Ha. No-service area, my ass. I know damn well what's going on.

I stumble back into the kitchen.

Meow, says Chase.

"Shut up, I said," says me. I throw an ice cube at him, but miss. I refill my glass and go back to the living room, this time taking the bottle with me.

An infomercial has replaced *M*A*S*H*, so I do a quick loop through the basic cable channels. Jews killing Arabs. "Go, Jews!" I say. The pope apologizing for something the Church once did. "Fuck that. Never say you're sorry," I advise the pope. Pakistan and some other Stans threatening to invade India. "Gandhi will rock your world," I warn them.

The Disney Channel is showing a *Herbie the Love Bug* movie. One of the originals.

"Stupid fucking Volkswagen," I say, but don't change the channel.

It doesn't matter. My mind is shutting down now. I can see it. It's like the lights being turned off in a large auditorium. Way, way down at the far end, the first row goes black. *Thunk!* Then another row. *Thunk!* Then another. *Thunk!* And so on. And up here in the foreground, in the only light still available, are Vicky and Mark pawing each other and grunting away. Otherwise, *thunk! thunk!* It can't come fast enough.

It seems I've just nodded off when the phone springs to life in my hands.

"Where the hell are you two?" I growl into the phone.

Silence on the other end. I hold the phone away and blink at the caller ID. *Out of area.*

"Hello?" I say again. "Who is this?"

"Father Sibille?" The man's voice on the other side is confused, tired.

"Yeah," I say. "Yes." I try to call up the sober reserve. This could be a parishioner. This could be serious.

"This is Dr. Prejean."

Oh no. They've been in an accident. A drunken Mark drove them right into a telephone pole. I'll kill him.

"It's Miss Simmons. She'd asked me to call."

"Miss Simmons?" It's all I can think to say. Who the hell is Miss Simmons? I try to remember the parishioners, but can't.

"Yes, Father. Miss Rita Simmons."

Rita Simmons? Rita Simmons? Simmons? Simmons? Rita? Rita.

"Oh, God."

"She started to go and they called me and she asked me to call you."

"Oh, God," I say again. I mean it as a prayer, I think. "Oh." I try standing up, but the room swoops in on me, pushes me back into the chair. "I'll be right there."

How the hell am I going to drive all the way to Opelousas in this condition?

"Just give me a minute," I say.

"If you want, Father. But she's already passed."

"What?"

"She's gone, Father. About five minutes ago."

"Oh."

"I'm sorry, Father."

"Yeah."

"I'll have someone call you in the morning."

"Yeah, of course." My voice is a whisper now. My mouth has never been drier. My stomach is churning, sour.

I press the Talk button to hang up the phone. The beep seems impossibly loud. I press the button again.

But who am I going to call? Who?

I press TALK a few more times, then force myself out of the chair and into the kitchen and return the phone to its base. I notice Chase in his kitty bed and shuffle over, pick him up, and hold him in my arms, slide down against the wall. The cat squirms some, then settles down. I don't know what I would have done if he'd squirmed free and abandoned me. I pull Chase in closer, bury my nose in his fur, and cry, a little for Miss Rita and her family but mostly for my own sorry self.

When the sun comes up, I force myself out of bed. I vaguely remember Mark coming in, finding me on the floor. I can't remember if I told him anything.

I call the diocese to find a substitute for Saturday afternoon and possibly Sunday.

"Well, did you try finding a substitute yourself?" the secretary asks me.

"Excuse me?"

"Did you try to find—"

I cut her off. "I heard you. No, I didn't try to find one."

"Well, Father, it would probably—"

"Listen, you take care of it. It's your job and I don't have time."

"But, Father—"

"Look, do whatever you want. I've got funeral arrangements to make. So if my parishioners show up today and tomorrow and there's no priest, well, so be it." This is insanity, talking to a church secretary like this. She can make life difficult for me later on down the road, but I can't help it.

"Father, I don't think that tone of voice is necessary."

I can tell she's already planning to obstruct every phone call I ever make to the diocese again, will screw up my requests for appointments with the bishop, will make sure I get the worst seats at big dinners, exclude my name from parties. Every church lady has a shit list and I'd just worked my way to this one's top ten.

"Hey, one of us gets fired, so be it. But we both know the

Church is far too short on priests and there's enough power-hungry little snits just like you to fill up seven circles of hell," I say.

"Father!"

I hang up the phone. Then call back.

"You know what?"

"Listen, Father."

"No, listen. Forget it. I was wrong. I'll take care of it. No sweat."

"Father, are you—"

I hang up again and walk into Mark's room. "Mark, wake up for a second."

"Huh," he says from under the blanket.

"Look, you're gonna have to do something for me."

"What?" He blinks. "Oh my God, Steve. There's something I have to tell you."

"About you and Vicky?"

"Me and Vicky? What are you talking about? No, something else. Last night—"

"Just save it." It's not about him and Vicky and I don't have the time or energy for any of his cute-boy bullshit. "I gotta go see about Miss Rita and her family and I need someone to say Mass this afternoon and tomorrow. They're giving me a headache down at diocese, so you gotta find someone for me. I know it's a pain but—"

"Steve." Mark pulls the blanket away from his face.

"Mark, let me finish, I know you probably can't be bothered and you were out all night and—"

"Steve, I'll do it. Just go, already."

"You'll do it? You'll find someone? Don't fuck this up, Mark." Suddenly I'm acting like I'm the one with my act together, like I've been running a tight ship in these parts.

"Yeah, just go."

We look at each other. I start to ask what time he got in last night, where he and Vicky had gone after the club.

"God, Steve. I'm so sorry. I know how much she meant to you," he says.

For the briefest of moments, the demons that have taken hold of me lately are convinced he's talking about Vicky, confessing something about last night. And just as quickly I realize what I'm thinking and am disgusted with myself. I want to cry again. I leave without saying anything more to him.

I'm five minutes down the road when I pull over to vomit. My spat with the secretary had chased off the hangover, but now it's back in full force. I squat on the gravel shoulder, one hand against the fender for support, sweating and almost crying from the pain of what are now dry heaves. The sun is bright, impossibly warm for this time of year. The greens of the field are gaudy and the blue of the sky looks like a ridiculously large and inviting swimming pool. The chirps of the birds pierce my ears. I don't need a mirror to know what I look like: a man in black hunched over in the dirt, pasty white with just a hint of yellow, a tinge of green, sweat beading on his forehead, tears leaking from his bloodshot eyes, a bead of snot hanging from his left nostril. After the first wave of vomiting is over, my body cycles through the hangover and I start shivering. It's all I can do not to crawl into the backseat and sleep, or better yet, slink out into the field and stretch out, the cool grass beneath me, the warm sun above.

But I have work to do. After a few more rounds of dry heaves, I climb back into the car and drive to the nursing home. There, Timeka offers her apologies and leads me to Miss Rita's room. I see Timeka's nostrils flare, her eyes slip into their corners to consider me, the smell of my hangover so strong it's cutting through the antiseptic.

The halls are mostly silent and the few people out of their rooms don't make eye contact with me, as if embarrassed by the presence of Death, that they were so weak that no one put up a fight when he showed up to take Miss Rita off.

I'd expected the room to be stripped bare, everything boxed up. But nothing has been touched. Photos, knickknacks. Everything is still in its place. Except for Miss Rita.

"She didn't want us to touch her stuff," Timeka says. "Said you was the only one who could touch it."

"Thanks," I whisper. "Can I be alone?" I can't get rid of her fast enough.

"Sure, Father."

When she's gone, I walk into the bathroom and go through another round of dry heaves. That take cares of that. It's over. I can tell by the ache in my stomach and the exhaustion that overcomes me. I want nothing more than to curl up around the toilet, the cool tile pressed against my face. I wash my face in the sink three times. For some reason I say, "Hooo boy" to myself before walking back into the room.

It takes me a few hours to box everything up. There isn't much, but I move slowly, partly because of the hangover, partly because I drift off whenever I come across something I'd given her. She'd kept everything, every card, every photo, every little knickknack, all in neat piles. Into one box, I put things her great-grandchildren and grandchildren and children had given to her. Into another, a smaller one, go things my family had given her.

In the nightstand by her bed I find a microrecorder and neatly stacked tapes. It's an odd little thing, out of place here. Then again, it's now out of place in the outside world, where tapes have gone the way of the gramophone. There's one loaded into the recorder. I press PLAY. Nothing. I rewind the tape all the way and press PLAY again.

"Steve, why you listenin' to my tapes boy!" she shouts, then starts cackling.

I flinch at the sound of her voice, press STOP. Her voice—the voice of the dead, of a ghost—frightens me on some primal level. But I press PLAY again.

"You can have the tapes or Teddy might like them. But they yours first if you want them. I just didn't want to forget nothing."

There is a long pause. I look at all the other tapes stacked in the drawer. She couldn't possibly have filled all of them. They were probably part of that old instinct to save up for a long winter. She and Mawmaw used to make fig and pear preserves before every winter—as if Louisiana ever suffered more than a week or two of below freezing temperatures, as if they didn't each have a refrigerator, a freezer, and access to the Piggly Wiggly produce section. "You never know," they always said. "You just never know."

Her voice starts up again. "Had it in mind to make a good-bye tape, but I ain't got much to say that I ain't said before." Another pause.

"And I'm tired, too, I guess."

She pauses again.

"Tell the kids I love 'em and all that. Love you, too, Steve, but you smart enough to know that, I hope. Your mawmaw woulda been proud of you. I am, too."

One final pause.

"But I still say you need you a woman," she says with a chuckle. Then: "I mean that."

And that's it. I try to hold myself together, keep it all in, but a *whumph* sound escapes me and I draw a sharp breath. I bite my bottom lip to stop it from trembling and wipe my eyes as the tears come. I want to get biblical, to sob or wail or gnash my teeth and rend my garments. I don't. It's not that I realize at this moment how selfish, how melodramatic I'm being. It's just the hang-over, last night's anger, has taken all that out of me. So I'm content to let my eyes leak a little as I play snippets from each tape.

There isn't much to them. They aren't dated as such. Each is labeled with a number, 1–40, written in crude, trembling lines. The one empty case, presumably for the tape already in the player, hadn't been numbered.

Number 40 starts out as a conversation with one of the attendants.

"Hi, Miss Rita."

"Hmph."

"Well, someone's testy today."

"Hmph."

"Looks like it's time to change them sheets."

"No."

"Now, Miss Rita. Why not?"

"I want a white girl to do that."

"Miss Rita," the girl says, a little shocked, but laughing all the same.

"You heard me, Tilly. Git one of them scrawny-ass white girls in here."

"Girl, you crazy."

"Maybe so. Maybe so." They're both laughing now.

"Well, much as I'd like to help you, none of the white girls are on shift today."

"What about that fat girl? Tiffany?"

"That's not nice, Miss Rita."

"Well, girl's fat as a tick on a dog's butt."

"I guess that's one way of looking at it. But she's on vacation. Went to Florida."

"Hunh! Who wants to see that bloated thing on the beach? Hooo!"

They both laugh again.

I smile. I don't know when tape 40 was made, but she seemed to be keeping it up until the end. I take 40 out and slide in the first cassette.

"Go on, say something Mawmaw." It's the voice of a young man, probably her grandson Teddy.

"Say what? I ain't talking into that thing."

"Aw, c'mon. You can talk into it. Like a diary. Every day."

"Now, why in God's name would I want to do that?"

"You just took God's name in vain, Mawmaw." *Good one, Teddy.*

"Shut up, boy. Is that thing on?"

"Yeah. You want to listen?"

There's a click and I imagine Teddy rewinding the tape, playing it back. Then more clicking and clacking, some "Testing. Testing" from Teddy, then a tentative "Hello" from Miss Rita.

I can see Teddy showing her how to use it, thinking maybe he'd hit the jackpot. Teddy had been at the University of Southwestern Louisiana, majoring in English or folklore or history or some such. He probably fancied himself the next Ernest Gaines, with Miss Rita his own personal Miss Jane Pittman. A real one.

I can more clearly see Miss Rita putting up a fuss, swearing up and down she wasn't going to fool with such nonsense, but secretly pleased at the attention. What I can't picture is her actually talking into the recorder every day. It just wasn't like her. Maudlin self-analysis was the mark of younger generations. And she surely wouldn't want it to sound to the attendants like she was talking to herself.

But a taped diary isn't exactly what she'd kept. After that introductory course from Teddy, she'd only taped conversations. Attendants mostly. Maybe she hoped to catch one of them on tape doing something wrong. The attendants, though, are well-meaning people, southern kids with deep-rooted respect, possibly some healthy fear, of their elders. They suffered her abuses with good humor, mostly because it was her way of showing affection to the people in her daily world—and the attendants were those people, her new family.

The tapes make Miss Rita's own family and me and my family seem like alien visitors who dropped in once a year to see how things were going. But even though the tapes were crude and the family appearances apparently few and far between, I could tell who Miss Rita's favorite was: Kanita, her great-granddaughter. When Kanita stepped into a scene, Miss Rita's voice sang.

"Come here, girl, come sit on my lap."

Then the sound of running feet, the child apparently unperturbed by her surroundings.

Then an "umph" from Miss Rita as the child lands. I've never met Kanita, had only seen posed pictures of a little girl in pigtails and pink. And that's how I still imagine her—pigtails, pink dress, four years old—even though she's more than likely wearing sneakers, jeans, and a dirty T-shirt.

And then there's tape 17.

I'm startled by Daddy's voice.

"I'd like to bring Sally and Jonathan around." His second wife and my half brother.

"Why?"

"Why? I think they should meet you."

"Why?"

"I don't know."

"Yeah, well. I don't want you to."

"But, Miss Rita, why not?"

"Because I don't want you to."

"But I don't understand."

"Don't expect you to."

"But I thought it would be good for the boy. He's heard so much about you."

"Well, let him keep hearing. Besides, that kid don't wanna be coming up in a nursing home."

"Well."

"Well nothing. Your new wife and kid, that ain't part of me. Now, you and your brother and sister and that first group of kids, I know yall through your mama and I feel like I owe yall. Don't know why, but that's the way it is. But this new wife and kid, I got no connection there and I ain't a museum exhibit. Show your new boy some pictures. Don't need him up in here gawkin' at the old colored lady. I got enough people in my life as it is. Enough white people for sure. Lord knows I got enough with your other boy moping around here half the time."

I feel a stab of guilt and indignation.

"Well, he's always been like that, Miss Rita."

My own father betraying me.

"Uh-huh. I wonder where he gets it from. Just like you when you was a boy, mooning around over some girl."

"Well, Miss Rita, boys will be boys."

"Exactly. He ain't a boy no more."

"Besides, he's a priest now."

"Uh-huh. Yall couldn't have talked some sense into him before he run off and do that? Rather he be in the army if you ask me."

There's a pause in the tape. Then Daddy again.

"Miss Rita, Steve hasn't been moping about any girls recently?"

She pauses. "No."

"You sure about that?"

When was this tape made?

It's weird that Daddy even asked. He never pried, seemed to assume that once I hit sixteen, I had things pretty much figured out. I see him less than I see Mama.

"Yeah, I'm sure. Like you said. The boy's a priest. Don't pay no attention to me. Time slips around on me sometimes. He's a good kid. See him more than I see my own family."

"That where you get your whiskey?"

"Don't know what you talking about," she answers. I can picture the twinkle in her eyes as she dares Daddy to call her a liar to her face.

A knock on the door disturbs my reverie.

I clear my throat, find my voice. "Yes? Come in."

Timeka pokes her head in. "Hey, Father. Some of Miss Rita's family is here."

"Okay," I say, looking down at the recorder in my hands.

"Um, Father?"

I look up.

"Yes?"

"They'd like to come in."

"Oh. Yeah, sure."

"Okay, I'll go get them."

"Great."

Then without considering propriety, morality, or roasting for all eternity in hell, I close the drawer, lock it, and put the key in my pocket.

Stupid, I know. I blame it on the hangover. Besides, what am I going to do if Teddy asks me to open the drawer? Say I lost the key or couldn't find it? Wait until Teddy goes to the bathroom and dump the cassettes in the box marked *Steve?*

Still, she said I could have them. Then again, the right thing to do would be to give the tapes to the family. I start to sweat again, the whiskey smell apparent even to me now.

Another knock and a head pokes through the door. "Father Steve?" It's Teddy.

"Oh, hey, Teddy," I say, walking toward him, holding out my hand. As Teddy takes it, I pull him in for a hug, a manly one, a priestly one. My first death hug, I realize.

"You holding up okay, Teddy?"

"Yeah, yeah. How about you?" He eyes me cautiously. I see

his nostrils working. I wonder if he's thinking that all Catholic priests are drunks.

"Yeah, I guess so." I stop, wipe my forehead. Now that I'm standing again, having to talk again, the hangover seems intent on coming back. "Well, I don't know."

"Exactly," Teddy says.

We stand in silence for a minute, doing what men do best— not communicating. Then the door creaks open, revealing a girl of ten or eleven. She wears slightly baggy jeans and a distressed Run DMC sweatshirt—vintage, no doubt. How can something from my teen years already be considered vintage? How fast is the world moving?

The child moves slowly, like she's just been given a heavy dose of valium. Her bloodshot eyes seem unfocused and she stands in the middle of the room looking around as if the concept of four walls and a ceiling was an alien one.

"Come here, baby girl," Teddy says, reaching to her. "Angela and Carl were taking care of stuff at the funeral home, so Kanita came with me," he says by way of explanation. "They just flew in from Texas. That's why I couldn't make it sooner."

Kanita shuffles over and rests her head against Teddy's hip.

"Hi, Father Steve," she says, and sniffles a bit.

"Hi," I say, then look at Teddy, confused. "This is Kanita?"

"Yeah." He says it like a sigh.

"Man, she's grown," I say, still processing. "I don't remember. Did we ever meet?" I look at both of them. Teddy answers.

"Probably not. But Mawmaw talked about you enough, I guess."

Then Kanita speaks. "I got a picture of you and Grandmawmaw."

I look at Teddy, try to swallow the lump in my throat.

"It was the only recent picture of herself that Mawmaw liked. She gave it to Kanita," Teddy explains.

Oh, that was it. Vanity, thy name is Rita. And Steve.

"We got other pictures, too, at Mama's house," Kanita says.

We look at her.

"Grandmawmaw gave 'em to Mama. Photo albums. One, she's holding you when you were a baby. One of your first communion. One of you in a purple robe."

"Graduation," I say. "High school." My eyes are stinging now.

I feel guilty all of a sudden. Guilty about not visiting enough, guilty about not being here at the end, guilty about being in the midst of a self-pitying drunk instead, guilty about being hungover this morning, about hiding the tapes.

I am a worthless piece of shit, I feel like saying to them.

And Kanita's just standing there, staring at me as if I have an answer, something to make sense of this, to explain why her great-grandmother was not in her room, was instead being placed in a silk-lined box somewhere. I have a direct line to God and Jesus, after all, don't I? I should be able to simply look up, mouth a few words, listen, and then translate.

But here I am, hungover and strung out on self-pity and self-loathing. I look to Teddy, who's eyeing me closely, quite possibly praying that this white guy can keep his shit together and not scare his niece.

I swallow the lump in my throat, choke down as much of my selfishness as I can stand, and cough out the rest. "Well," I say, slipping the key to the nightstand out of my pocket.

"Teddy, there's something in the nightstand," I say, handing him the key. "I thought you'd want it."

Teddy walks to the nightstand, places the key in the lock. "It's not her bottle of Crown and a bag of—" he starts, but stops when he sees the drawer's contents.

"I listened to a couple just to see what they were," I say, fingering the unlabeled tape still in my pocket. That one's mine.

It's Teddy's turn now to struggle with his emotions. I want to tell him not to get too worked up over them. But, hell, let him savor the moment.

Teddy fingers one of the tapes, places it into the recorder.

"Um, Teddy," I say, shooting a glance over at Kanita. "Probably not now."

"What?" Kanita says, quick enough to catch on to adult subterfuge.

"Nothing, baby girl," Teddy tells her, and closes the drawer. "Why don't you go get that box out of the car?"

She eyes us suspiciously, but does as she's told.

"She seems to be taking it well," I say.

"Not really. Usually, she would have fought me to see what was in this drawer." He pauses. "You sure I can have these?"

"You're her family, Teddy." But I want them, damn it, want them all. What else did she say about me? Which conversations did she tape? How much of my own voice is on those tapes, how many of my confessions? "You'll have kids you can pass them on to or something."

"You okay, Father?" Teddy asks.

"Huh? Yeah. Yeah, Teddy. Rough night last night," I say, and offer an impish grin, thinking Teddy might give me one of those little shocked looks, say something like "Aw, now, c'mon, Father Steve. C'mon now." And I would say, "Well, priests gotta have fun, too." And the two of us would chuckle knowingly.

Instead, Teddy says, "Hmph."

I can't tell if it's a judgmental "hmph" or a dismissive "hmph." Baptists.

"Well," I say finally, "I sorted everything, took some of the stuff Daddy and us gave her if yall don't mind."

"No. Not at all." Teddy drifts off somewhere and I fall into my own little world until Kanita comes back, wrestling with the cumbersome box.

"I guess I'll be going," I say.

"Yeah, okay," Teddy answers.

"You'll call me about the church arrangements?"

Teddy looks down at his hands sheepishly.

"Teddy?"

"You knew she wanted to be buried out at Zion, right?"

My heart lurches. "Yeah, Teddy. I knew." But I hadn't. I'd never asked. I'd assumed for the last year or so that when the time came, I'd be the one.

It's like being told my own mother is being interred by the ayatollah.

"Yeah. No, I knew, Teddy," I say again. "Just let me know when."

"Sure thing, Father. Sure thing."

Chapter 16

For lack of a better idea, I drive to Daddy's house, where I find the family gathered.

Daddy's is a beast of a house vaguely reminiscent of Mawmaw's old place. It's elegant in its own way, but seems slightly ludicrous just sitting out here in the middle of nowhere. Even though it's an hour and a half from anything remotely resembling a town, they've all come.

All told, counting me and the spouses and children, twenty-nine people are clamoring about Daddy's house. My uncle Red and his wife, Joanne, and their children, Bubba, Tiffany, and Johnny. Bubba, who's my age, is married with two kids, Tiffany married with one child, and Johnny's girlfriend is pregnant with what everyone assumes is his first child.

My aunt Belinda has four children, all girls, through her first marriage. Her second husband, Donald, added another two. Of Rachel, Jessica, Jenny, and Wendy, Belinda's original four, Rachel has two boys and Jenny has two girls. Wendy's pregnant with her first and Jessica is in college and, even more surprisingly, single. Lisa and Lucy, the stepsisters, are so far without child.

Here they all are, as if they were animals and the presence of death had prompted a herding instinct. I bring the box of reminders in and they offer me coffee.

At some point we all settle in. Even the grandkids—who are usually tearing around the yard like small tornadoes—trickle into the living room and, like lions after a hunt, seek comfortable refuge for their weary bones—the little ones in the laps of their mothers, the larger ones in front of the fireplace, at odd angles in easy chairs, draped over the backs and arms of couches like cats on branches.

It's time for what I call the Book of the Dead.

The Book of the Dead is not reserved only for sad days like this one. It's trotted out at every family gathering, usually right after a heavy meal and immediately before we start in on the really tall tales. In essence, it's a catalog of all those distant relatives and local legends who've died since the last clan meeting—with the true standouts getting repeat tellings.

These stories aren't so much a running obituary column as they are a celebration of just how, shall we say, interesting some of our relatives were. Nonc Enios, for example, who, aside from having what I always thought was a silly name, was blind as a bat but insisted on driving his '73 Ford pickup everywhere, lurching to stops, zigzagging across roads, accelerating too fast but never going above thirty miles per hour. Everyone called him "speedy," and it never failed to get a rise out of him. "Aw, go on. Yall go to hell," he'd say. "Dat's about twice as fast as dat ole mule-drawn wagon used to go, so it's plenty fast for me."

Aunt Irene, Uncle Albert's wife, who never visited except for funerals and only then after being heavily sedated. She was deathly afraid of the bridges over the Mississippi and Atchafalaya rivers. During their construction, the Mississippi bridge had taken a brother, the Atchafalaya a cousin. She was convinced that they would get her, too, if she tried crossing.

Uncle Koko, who—well, suffice it to say that the story about him and the cow isn't fit for mixed company.

There are more. Great-aunts and uncles, third cousins by marriage, the retarded kid who used to live down the street and would chase Daddy and them home from school every day. Everyone will get a turn eventually.

Most of the dead have met their ends at the hands of "the cancer." Runner-up is heart attack and third is "catching a stroke." And if those don't get you, be sure that freak accidents—hungry farm machinery, exploding tanks, falling trees—will.

For the first time in my life, I'm a primary participant in this ritual, having put in my time with Miss Rita over the past few years.

But I find myself talking about Mawmaw's death instead of Miss Rita's, perhaps because the pain is too close to deal with, perhaps because Mawmaw's death is what had really bonded me and Miss Rita together.

It seemed from the day I was born, Mawmaw was locked in battle with the cancer. In the final go-round, doctors had told her she probably wouldn't see 1987. But the summer of '85 found Mawmaw, in a burst of good health and spirits, puttering about in her garden. I was twelve and more than a little resentful at having to spend the time with her—she didn't seem sick, seemed perfectly fine, was probably faking it for the attention from her grandchildren who were running off into adolescence and leaving her behind as if she were some sort of embarrassing relic from childhood, a stuffed animal, a security blanket.

So while Mawmaw moved about under her wide-brimmed hat, I sat on the back porch reading adventure stories about a boy lost with his dog in the wilderness.

Then she yelped from behind a four o'clock bush.

"Fils de putaint!" she yelled.

"You okay, Mawmaw?" I called, not looking up from the

book. Never in a million years would she curse in English in front of us, but she was quick with the Cajun French swears. That she'd just screamed out "son of a bitch" probably meant little more than she'd scratched her arm on a branch.

There was a brief silence before she answered.

"Jus a lil' bee sting, cher. Nuttin' to worry about."

I rolled my eyes. Even when no one was around, I found her heavy Cajun accent embarrassing beyond belief.

Looking back, I always wondered if there was something in her voice at the time to betray her lie, a wavering, a sharp inhalation. I looked up for a brief moment. She was walking from the shrub she'd been working on to another, clenching and unclenching her fist. The sun was so bright it hurt my eyes.

"You sure you okay, Mawmaw? You want one of your cigarettes to rub some tobacco on it?" I held up her pack of Winstons.

"No, cher. You stay up there and read your book." Then, "Always wished I could read." Then, "I'll be okay. Just stay up there."

Five minutes later, though, the four o'clock bush she was tinkering with shuddered heavily, some of the petals falling to the ground. When I ran over to see what had happened, I found her facedown in the bush, her breathing shallow.

"Mawmaw!" I hissed at her. "What's wrong?"

"Leave me be, Stevie."

"But, Mawmaw."

"Stevie, leave me be, I said." She gasped for air. "Go on in the house and get Miss Rita and tell her to get a shovel."

"What?"

"You heard me. Now go. Tell her to get a shovel."

And those were her last words. I ran off into the house and straight for the kitchen.

"Boy, what's wrong with you?" Miss Rita yelled at me. "Quit runnin' in the house before I grab that switch," she added, her hand already reaching for the three-foot length of crape myrtle branch above the fridge.

"Mawmaw. Bee stung her. Shovel. She said to tell you grab a shovel."

"What?" Miss Rita answered. "Slow down and tell me what happened." But she was already turning the stove down to a simmer, wiping her hands on a towel, and following me out to the flower garden.

Mawmaw hadn't moved. She was still facedown, her breathing shallow.

"Didn't have the sense to turn her over," Miss Rita said. Then we saw the puncture wounds between the thumb and index finger on the right hand. The area was a mixed rainbow of purple and black, with red streaking up the arm.

"She got stung twice?" I asked.

Miss Rita looked at me for a second. She didn't have to say it out loud, but I could tell what she was thinking: "Boy, you stupid or something?" Instead, she said, "Stevie, you go to your mawmaw's bedroom, get that shotgun in the closet, and bring it back. Make sure it got some shells in it."

"You want me to call an ambulance or something?"

"Just do what I said," she screamed.

I ran back to the house. It was the first time I'd ever heard it silent during the day. No humming. No talking. No wash being done. No dishes being banged. Something was seriously, seriously wrong. I ran to the closet, reached an arm through the clothes, and felt for the shotgun. I cracked open the chamber and saw two shells nesting in the barrels. I ran it back to Miss Rita. She cracked open the chamber, then snapped it shut again.

"Now go get a shovel," she said.

"Don't you think I should—"

"You should go get a shovel like I said."

Halfway back from the garage, shovel in hand, I heard a shot. I sped up, convinced that Miss Rita had shot Mawmaw to put her out of her misery. Country people did that all the time to their animals. Why not to people, too?

"What did you do?" I screamed. "What did you do?"

But she was standing over that first four o'clock, the one Mawmaw had been fooling with when she screamed out. Miss Rita put a hand over her eyes, squinted into the bush. She lifted the gun to her shoulder and fired the other shell. A flurry of leaves exploded into the sunlight.

She held her hand out. "Just hush and bring me that shovel." She took it from me, parted the bushes, and drove the shovel through like a spear. Her forehead glistened with sweat and I suddenly realized how hot it was, that I was sweating, too. My shirt stuck to my back and I could feel the itch I always got on my legs from running through tall grass.

"Son of a bitch," Miss Rita whispered, dragging first the head, then the shot-riddled body of a two-foot-long rattlesnake. It was so ridiculously small. How could that take someone's life?

But everyone agreed, it was a much better way to die than the cancer. None of those messy drawn-out good-byes to deal with.

"She went in her garden," Daddy says, "doing what she liked to do."

We stay up late into the night and I sleep in the guest bedroom. I wake up the next morning before everyone else and head back to Grand Prairie, hoping to catch a snippet of Mass, see who Mark has lined up. I don't feel like dealing with him right now, but Mass will do me good, help me to clear my mind, even if it will be a bit jarring to see someone else in my church, leading my flock.

About four miles from Grand Prairie, I see a telephone pole wearing a couple of Rabbit Festival posters. Oh yeah. That.

About three miles from Grand Prairie, I see a pole covered

from the ground up to about eight feet with bright yellow posters. I slow the car to a crawl. TENT REVIVAL screams the headline right above the dates—which, sure enough, are the same dates on the Rabbit Festival posters.

"Son of a bitch," I say. I don't know how the mind works, but mine had done a good job of pretending the revival was just something to worry about at a later date. The posters drive the reality home.

The next pole is covered in neon-pink posters. The one after that in yellow. Just past that pole, an army of yard signs shouting TENT REVIVAL: APRIL 15–17 march off over the horizon.

"Fuck me," I say, before following them all the way back to my own church.

At least the cars in St. Pete's parking lot indicate that Mark came through with a substitute. Either that or the congregation is hanging out in the church for lack of anything better to do on a Sunday morning. I pull into my parking space—why didn't the visiting priest take it?—and enter the church through the entrance near the rectory. The church is silent. I must have walked in during the meditation after the Eucharist. I hang back and wait for the priest to speak, not quite certain I'm ready to look at all those upturned faces, looking for guidance, needing.

"Please rise," an all-too-familiar voice says.

It can't be. I stick my head into the entrance to the altar and there stands Mark, blessing my parishioners, offering them the sign of peace. It's all I can do not to walk out onto the altar and drag him off by his hair.

Enraged, I stomp back to the rectory.

Ten minutes later, Mark comes in whistling. "Steve-o?" he calls out. "You home? How you holding up? Boy, do I have some news for you!"

I'm sitting in the recliner, staring at the blank TV. If I stand up, I'll start punching him.

"Hey, Steve."

"Get out," I say.

"What?"

"You heard me. Get your stuff, pack your bags. Get out."

"What are you talking about?"

"What am I talking about? How about you, no longer a priest, going out on my altar?"

"C'mon. I couldn't find anyone. No one could get out here yesterday. So I figured—"

"You said Mass yesterday, too?"

"Well, someone had to do it."

I stand up, shouting. "Someone? Sure. How about a real priest? You quit, remember? Did that occur to you before you went traipsing out onto my altar in my church?" It feels good to scream. And Mark happens to provide a welcome target.

But he's not taking it without a fight.

"Your altar? I thought that belonged to the parishioners, not to you."

"It's my ass on the line once the bishop finds out I let some Lavender Mafioso ex-priest say Mass."

"Fuck you, Steve. You think the bishop gives a rat's ass what goes on in this backwater? What with your altar girls, your whenever-you-feel-like-it morning prayers, your half-ass way of doing everything. And hell, even Vicky. It's not like you're a bunch of saints back here."

"What the hell is that Vicky comment supposed to mean?"

"Oh, I don't know. You tell me."

There's only one way to answer that. "Just shut the hell up, Mark. Just shut the hell up and leave."

"Where am I supposed to go, Steve?"

"Not my problem. Why don't you call up Mommy and Daddy? I'm sure your daddy would just love to have his strapping young lad back home."

I immediately regret saying it, but probably not as much as I should.

Mark storms off into his room, packs a bag, then walks into the bathroom to gather his hair product and skin creams and whatever the hell else is taking up all the shelf space in there. After throwing his bag into the car, he comes back in and makes a teary phone call.

"Yeah, right now. I have no idea," is all I can make out. I don't know who he's called.

After Mark puts the phone down, he starts calling for Chase.

"What do you think you're doing?" I ask.

"I'm calling my cat, is what I'm doing."

"Your cat, huh? I feed him. I pay for most of his food."

Mark stops in his tracks. "Don't even try that. He's my cat, damn it."

He's got a point there. Fine. He's taking the cat. Fine with me. I don't care. I don't need either of them.

"Just leave," I say. "Please, just get out of my face."

"Fuck you," Mark whispers. "Just you fucking go to hell."

He walks out to his car, cranks it up, guns the engine, and leaves a spray of gravel behind him.

I walk over to the phone and hit the Redial button. Vicky picks up.

"What the hell's going on over there?" she begins.

I press the Talk button, shut her voice off.

Chapter 17

Whatever my problems, the show must go on. Church business must be attended to. So I sit snoozing in the confessional, Miss Emilia on the other side, murmuring like a setting hen warm in her nest. She's fretting over her treatment of her husband, how she pinches his nose at night to stop him from snoring, how she used to lace his food with saltpeter to stop him from groping her at night, but now she's thinking of getting some of that Viagra stuff because he just doesn't seem interested at all anymore.

"I have needs, too, Father. A woman does."

I wonder which soap opera she lifted that line from. It would be funny—if this hadn't been the seven thousandth time I've heard Miss Emilia say it. That contented, almost purring sound she is making tells me that this talking obliquely about sex to a priest in a closet-sized room is one of her life's little pleasures.

That purr also lulls me to sleep.

"Father?"

Her voice wakes me. But by now, I'm a pro at these things. "Yes?"

"I think that's about it."

"Of course. Of course. Anything else?"

"No, Father." But before I can send her off, she starts again. "Well, I don't know if this is the time or place."

"What is it, Miss Emilia?"

"What are we going to do about that tent revival?"

I want to slap her for bringing it up. I was zoning out in here—drifting away from anything having to do with rabbits and Pentecostals. Now my chest is tightening up, my heart racing.

"Don't worry about it," I say.

"But it's less than two weeks away."

"Yes, I'm aware of that," I answer, unable to take the edge off my voice.

How could I forget? Signed contracts from vendors are showing up in my mailbox. Phone calls from other vendors that didn't make the cut are pouring in, too. They want to know if there've been any cancelations. They want to know if I can save them. Denise drops by repeatedly for more petty cash to pay for more posters to paper more telephones poles and any other blank surface she can find. And Blackfoot's calling me every single day. "You might think it's overkill, Father, but I can't fuckin' emphasize e-fuckin'-nough that you've got to stay on top of this," he says.

"So what are we going to do about the Pentecostals?" she asks again. The only silver lining here is that B.P.'s got my Rabbit Festival parishioners so worried, none of them will be turning into Pentecostals any time soon.

"Let me worry about it," I say before dispatching her. I sentence her to a paltry ten Hail Marys and an Act of Contrition, knowing it will stick in her craw that her offenses were deemed so trivial in the eyes of the Lord. I know as well that it doesn't matter what sort of penance I give her, that she will march out to those pews and have a kneel-off with Miss Celestine, each woman praying loud enough under her breath so that the other is sure to hear. I could tell Miss Emilia to run out, buy some Ecstasy, wire her husband up, and suck him off until her dentures fall out and his cock breaks. And she would do it. But only after stopping in the pew and praying the Rosary until Miss Celestine left.

Miss Emilia walks out and no one else comes in. Helen Dauterive, one of the regulars and usually the last in line, is at home sick. I can enjoy a few minutes of peace if I can just clear my head of bunnies and B.P. I remember my sophomore year in college. I pulled eighteen credits, worked two jobs, and was a 2:00 a.m. DJ for the campus radio station. During breaks from my shift at the college bookstore, I'd go to a seldom-used men's room and take a catnap in one of the stalls. That second semester was the time things had first gone wrong with my head, when I couldn't sleep at night at all unless I drank myself stupid fast enough to get through the rage and jealousy chewing my insides, getting myself to pass out before I started seeing vivid images of Stephanie and her new boyfriend going at it while JuJu the dog watched.

And now? Now I'm fighting the battle all over again. I've secured myself in the safest profession I know and locked myself up in a tower guarded by rules and vestments and sacraments, but here I am all over again. Worse, infinitely worse, this time around I have to pretend, even to myself, that it's not happening.

Mark and Vicky come to Mass together every Sunday. I deliver my homilies, staring off into some neutral space so that I don't have to see the two of them sitting there.

After this past Sunday's Mass, the parishioners herded us into a tight circle to pester us about festival details. We smiled as politely as possible at one another, answered the questions, cracked jokes. I don't know about Vicky and Mark, but it made me sick to my stomach. I couldn't stand to look at them. And then Denise started in on the tent revival. "They've covered up some of our posters," she said. I was just about to give her a "There, there, child" when everyone else joined in. "I seen posters all the way on the other side of Opelousas," somebody said.

"We have some out there," I answered.

"I ain't seen any," someone else responded.

"Well, they're there," I said.

"My son works for the sheriff's department," proclaimed another voice in the crowd. "He said Brother Paul's asking him for a police escort. Said they're going to have a hundred-car caravan coming in on Friday evening. Right when our festival's supposed to start."

The crowd fell silent.

"Oh, I wouldn't worry about that," said Vicky, shooting me a smirk. "I'm sure Father Sibille has it under control." I went to one festival meeting after the fight with Mark and informed the board that, because of other duties, I was passing the reins over to him and Vicky.

So it goes without saying I don't actually have anything under control. The most I'd done is make a mental note to call someone at the sheriff's office but haven't gotten around to it. Less than two weeks to go and I haven't gotten around to it. Instead, I'm sitting in the confessional trying to wish it all away.

There's a knocking at the screen. I gasp awake, thinking for a moment that I've come to in a coffin, that someone has declared me dead, sealed me up, and tossed me in a hole.

It doesn't sound like such a bad idea.

"Steve-o? What are you doing, sleeping in there?"

"What? Yeah. I guess I dozed off."

"Poor form, Padre. Poor form."

When the reality of her voice, the smell of her perfume sinks in, I feel my shoulders tense up.

"What are you doing here?"

"I've come to make a confession."

Great. What am I going to do about this?

"You fall asleep in there again?"

"Um. No," I whisper.

"I can see how that would happen. Stuffy. Warm. Boring. Daddy used to bring a pillow, prop his head up."

"Vick?"

"Yes?"

"Can we do this?"

"Do what, Steve?"

"The confession, Vick."

"Oh, that? I was just shitting you. That'd be a little uncomfortable, no?"

What did that mean? What's she been doing? Who's she been doing? A green bolt of envy streaks through me. I pause, steady myself, steel up for some old-fashioned denial.

"Uncomfortable? Why?"

"Oh, c'mon, Steve."

"What?"

"Uncomfortable, I guess, for the same reason you've been hiding from me."

"I don't know what you're talking about, I'm just having a spat with Mark." I suddenly feel like a rat in a cage. It's all I can do not to start clawing at the door and run out screaming.

"If you don't know what I'm talking about, you got bigger problems than I thought."

Figuring anything I say will be the wrong thing, I keep my mouth shut.

"Steve, wake up."

"I'm awake."

"Steve." Her voice sounds like it's on a fine line between anger and laughter.

"Vicky, what are you doing here?" I almost sigh. This is the part where she tells me what a fool I'm being, tries to figure out some way to let me down easily because, of course, it would just never work. She's right. And, now that we've arrived at this, there's no point in arguing. It is being resolved. Why not skip directly to the end?

"I wanted to talk to you," she says.

"You don't have to come here to talk to me. You know where I—"

"Cut the crap. You've been avoiding me. You don't answer when I call. You don't answer the door when I drop by. How does that make me look, getting snubbed by the priest?"

"You? How does it make me look?" A hint of anger creeps into my own voice. "I mean, just what does it look like to have you coming over every day, staying for so long, me going to your place all the time and then Mark coming in and then now he's living with you? Just what the hell does that look like? What are people going to think about me? What's worse? That they thought I was fooling around with a woman or that I'm being cuckolded by a gay man?"

For a moment, there's complete silence on the other side of the screen. Then a slow leak of air as she exhales and a slight tremble in the wood paneling as if she were shaking, as if the whole thing were about to come down.

"You!" she spits.

My head jerks back at the force of the word. For a full thirty seconds after that, nothing. Just as I'm about to speak, she starts.

"You son of a bitch, you," she hisses. "What will people think of you? You? It's always about you, isn't it? Steve needs some altar boys. Steve doesn't know what to do with the altar girls. Steve needs a distraction. Steve needs a festival. Steve needs a friend. Wait, what's that? Steve can't even wipe his own ass? Miss Emilia, can you help him out there? Mark, do this. Vicky, do that. What do people think of you, Steve? If they could see beyond that collar of yours, they'd think you're a selfish prick."

It all comes out in such a rush that I don't have the time to process any of it before she circles back to her original question.

"And what about me? What do people think about me? What do *you* think about me?" she asks.

"I just thought you needed some attention." I hear the words stumbling out of my mouth and immediately regret them.

"Fuck you," she growls. There's a loud *thwack* on the screen. "You self-absorbed bastard. You have some nerve. You're going to sit there and call me a whore for attention?"

"That's not what—"

"If this screen wasn't between us I'd haul off and slap the living shit out of you."

With that, she leaves, slamming the rickety door of the booth behind her. Then my door is yanked open and she's standing before me in all her red-faced, tear-streaked fury. I've never seen anything like it before. It terrifies me. Then she does haul off and slap me. The report echoes through the church.

"And that gay man you're referring to is one of the best friends you have in the world. He's been moping around my damn house, feeling like he's got no family left. But I guess your head is too far up your ass to realize that. You're like a goddamn teenager. You think you're the only tortured soul in the whole wide world who goes to bed at night alone."

She wipes her nose on the back of her hand, turns, and walks away.

Miss Emilia and Miss Celestine, still on their knees, spin their heads to watch her go. Their Rosaries fall silent.

Vicky stops at the front door and turns around. "Ladies, I'm sorry to interrupt. And don't forget we have our last meeting next Wednesday. Miss Emilia, it's your turn to host."

With that, she's gone.

Miss Emilia and Miss Celestine look at me. I can think of nothing better to do than shrug.

Miss Emilia looks down at her Rosary for the briefest of moments, blinks away any crisis of faith brought on by my obvious fallibility. Then she and Miss Celestine, at the same time, cross themselves and shuffle hurriedly after Vicky.

Not quite sure what to do about Vicky, I resort to the only other person I know who can help. Besides, judging by what she told me, he's just waiting by the phone for me to call and take him back.

"Mark," I say into his cell phone's voice mail. "I'm sorry. I was an ass. A major, major ass. I want to apologize. And . . . well, call me."

Two minutes after I flip the phone closed, it vibrates.

"Steve?" he says, as if expecting someone else to answer.

"Hey," I say.

"Hey," he says back.

There's ten full seconds of silence. It feels like half an hour.

"So," I say.

"So," he says.

"I guess we should talk."

"You guessed right." He sounds wounded and angry.

So he's not going to make this easy.

"Look, Mark. I'm sorry—" I start, but he cuts me off.

"That'll do for now." Men are so much easier than women. "I'll make you suffer for such extreme asininity at a later date, but boy, do we need to talk!"

"But . . ." I don't know what's going on. So I ask, "What's going on?"

"I'll explain in about ten minutes. Just fire up your computer, I'm coming over."

Fifteen minutes later, he's bursting through the kitchen door without knocking, and he's carrying an armload of posters. An equal mix of bright red and brighter yellow, they're all torn at the corners. Some still have staples hanging from them. I take one from him as he tries to crumple up the rest and fit them into the garbage can.

"Hey, these are posters for B.P.'s revival," I say. Train to Glory shouts the headline on this one. The locomotive looks more possessed than holy, like it's heading right for me, intent on barreling over everything I've half-assed tried to accomplish.

"That fucker," he responds. "I keep stealing them. But as soon as I tear them down, he's got that Little Red Riding Freak of his back stapling them to telephone poles."

"How long have you been tearing them down?"

"About five minutes after the first ones went up."

"I'm surprised he didn't come blaming me," I say.

"Probably would have, but I told him to his fat smiling face it was me."

"What? Why? When did you do that?"

"First time he caught me."

"And he didn't beat you senseless?"

"I'm sure he would have loved nothing more," Mark says, straightening up from the garbage can, and sticking his right leg in it to stomp down the posters. He's got a wide smile on his face. "But there have been developments."

"What's that mean?"

"Come," he says, heading over to my computer. "I would have told you sooner, but you were having your fit or whatever it was, and I was just too pissed to deal."

He pulls up the Web and surfs over to a Gmail account. He clicks on an e-mail weighted down with attachments and begins moving picture files to my desktop and opening them. He's moving fast and windows are popping up all over the place, but I can see that some of the photos are clearly, as the kids say, not safe for work.

"What is that?"

"Southern Decadence. Last year."

"Southern what?"

"Humongo homo-fest in New Orleans at the end of the summer. Imagine Mardi Gras, but less inhibited."

"Less?" I can't even picture that. "Less?"

"Whatever it is you're imagining right now, multiply it by ten. Swinging dicks. Public fornication. Varying degrees of prostitution. It's a grand old time."

"I don't understand," I say.

"Here we go," he says, dragging one of the photos up to the front and expanding its window. This one looks harmless enough. Three buff guys with too-pretty hair and too-tight T-shirts holding neon-pink drinks and assaulting the camera with thousand-watt smiles. The one on the left catches my eye for some reason. "This one on the left is a guy named Timmy," Mark says.

"What the fuck?" I say.

Mark, who was set to move onto the next guy, stops, confusion on his face.

"I know that guy. I went to elementary school with him," I say.

"Get out of here," Mark says. "I used to fool around with that guy."

"Wow. Just . . . wow. We were best friends in grade school and then the Pentecostals took him."

Mark smiles again. "Buddy, you don't know the half of it." He turns back to the computer. "Now, this second guy, believe it or not, was a roommate of mine in seminary."

I do my best to drag my eyes off Timmy and onto the guy in the middle. I'm happy to realize I don't know him and look back over at Timmy. He's aged well, I'd say. Very well. If he grew his hair out, he could try out for the cover of a romance novel.

"Now this one." Mark's finger drifts over to the right. My eyes follow. Instead of sliding back to Timmy, they stick.

"Now, why does that one look familiar?" I ask.

"Take a moment," Mark says, focused on the screen.

I'm drawing a blank. He looks vaguely familiar, but because of the shock of Timmy, my mind's stuck in a rut, trying to dredge up other names from grade school.

"No idea," I finally say, exasperated.

"Oh, c'mon, Steve."

I look again. "Nope. He looks familiar, but I just can't place him."

"I guess it's all about context." He clicks on the next photo. Gone are Timmy and the former seminarian. The guy on the right in the previous photo is now all by his lonesome, visibly drunk and shirtless, his chest beet-red from too much sun.

"Pretty sure I've never seen this guy with his shirt off," I say. "So it's not exactly helping."

"You're right, you're right," Mark says. "How about this one?"

Same guy, still outdoors, still drinking something pink, still sunburned, but now wearing boxers. Boxers, I might add, that are parting in the front to reveal an erection.

"Now, c'mon," I protest.

"Quit being such a prude," Mark answers. "Trust me, this is going to be so worth it."

"Really? How? This doesn't exactly do anything for me."

"Oh, I know you're batting for Team Vicky, Steve."

"What's that supposed to mean?"

"Okay, Steve. Make you a deal. You quit insulting my intelligence and I'll quit teasing you with this."

We stare at each other for a moment.

"Fine," I say.

"Very well, then," he says, then opens a photo of the same guy completely naked, standing with his arms outstretched. It's dark now in the New Orleans of the photo, which makes his crab-red chest and his moon-white ass look even more absurd. Of course, the group of guys standing around him, laughing and pointing at his monstrously large and erect penis, adds a dash of, I don't know, surrealism to the photo.

"I give up," I say. "Really."

"I know. That wasn't fair. But I couldn't help myself. Try this. Take a good look at him. Now imagine him in designer jeans, a tight T-shirt, sunglasses—"

"But what's the point?" I say.

"And he's climbing out of a bright yellow Hummer, with his prick of a dad smiling away and threatening to ruin my god-damn festival," Mark says, turning back to the computer.

Now it's my turn. "Get out of here!" I'm not sure, but I think I may have shrieked. "Junior?"

"His actual name is Lester. I don't know how you forget a name like Lester, but if you'd called him that instead of Junior, I might have made the connection sooner. I told you he looked familiar that first time I saw him!"

"Wowwwww." Now I'm whispering.

"It only gets better."

Mark begins to click on more photos and the computer starts to look like a fornication flip-book, with Junior—sorry, Lester—pleasuring and being pleasured by any number of different men.

"I can't believe you have photos of this," I say.

"It's called Southern Decadence for a reason," Mark says. "A few thousand drunk men with not a bit of estrogen around to shame them? Forget it."

"Jesus," I whisper.

"Name in vain," Mark says. "Name in vain. Let's not have this little session corrupt you."

Corrupt me? I'm about to have a stroke. I don't know what to do.

"Does B.P. know?" I ask.

"I'm sure he suspected, which is probably why my charms didn't work on him that first day. Especially after I made the crack about Lester looking familiar. And let's just say he's a little more suspicious." He clicks open the photo of the three guys again. "I actually showed this one to him."

"You did what?"

"I *tried* to tell you. That night Vicky and I went to Esperanto, I saw 'Junior' there. Well, I thought I did. So when I got home, I looked through some photos, made a few calls, and pieced it all together. And when B.P. caught me ripping down his posters, I just happened to have a printout of this one."

"What a coincidence," I say.

"I know, right? So I showed him the photo—just this harmless little one where everyone's smiling and dressed—and I haven't heard a peep from him since."

I stand silently for a moment looking at the screen, then at Mark. Then I look at the ceiling. Then I look out the window. Then I look at my hands and notice I'm still holding B.P.'s poster, the one advertising his revival that's directly challenging my festival, my authority, my flock's ability to have themselves a good time.

"Move," I say to Mark.

"What are you doing?"

I pull up my own e-mail and key in the address written on the bottom of the poster. I attach the photo of his naked, sunburned son standing on a dark New Orleans street, a pack of ravenous men leering at him. I type:

B.P. . . . . thought you and I should have ourselves a little talk. I need a favor or two and I think for any number of reasons you're just the man to help me out. One reason is attached. If you don't find that one convincing enough, I have plenty more. And trust me, the others are much, much more convincing.

Mark is jumping up and down and clapping his hands. "You are so not going to send that!" he screams. "No way."

I type two more lines—Yours in Christ, Father Steve Sibille—and hit SEND.

Chapter 18

I'm sitting on the back steps of the rectory enjoying a cigarette and a final moment of silence before the festivities begin when I hear my name.

"Father Steve."

It's Denise. She's wearing a Rabbit Festival T-shirt, one of the ones she'd designed, and black jeans and bright red sneakers. In the sunset, she looks like what she is, a thirteen-year-old girl with not a great deal of worry in her young heart. She's a good kid, one who helps around the house, one who volunteers at her church, one who wants to please adults. Looking at her, I feel more than a little embarrassed that I'd made her out to be such a temptress. Coy, maybe. A young girl trying out her new flirting abilities on the safest thing around, possibly. But a temptress? Hardly.

"Is it time?" I ask.

"Yeah, your turn." She looks nervous. She has a lot riding on the success of this thing, I guess. This is her first almost-adult undertaking. She wants desperately for it to go well.

I follow her through the gathering crowd and up onto the stage. I see the same look of apprehension and excitement on the faces of Miss Emilia, Miss Celestine, and Miss Pamela as they stand watching me climb the steps. How much of their lives have they put into this?

The crowd in front of the stage is growing quickly. My parish. All of them in the same place at the same time. I've never seen that before. It's always broken into thirds: Saturday evening, early Sunday, regular Sunday, each with its own personality. Now they're all here, standing before me, looking at me expectantly, as if I have the power to give them something.

I do have a power, in a way, to stand in place and let people make of me what they will, to project upon me whatever it is they think they need. I don't have to do much, really. Just show up, listen, offer a nod of understanding, a word of encouragement, let them know that there is always at least this much, a priest. After all, the most important job of the shepherd is to stand there and watch, provide comfort. There they all are, my flock.

And the carnies. They're here, too, a scraggly lot of tattooed predators, probably drunk, possibly stoned. But even the carnies are behaving themselves for now.

And Mark and Vicky, standing off to the side, arms crossed, looking at me. Mark is smiling. Vicky looks tired.

I haven't spoken to her since the confession. I figure we needed a little time to figure out our next moves, whatever those will be. I have a vague notion of what I want to do, but it's going to be a test of faith and courage to say the least. And, to be honest, I'm afraid of Vicky, afraid she's still angry and will never be able to forgive me.

They look at me. I look at them, smile sheepishly. Mark's beaming with pride. Vicky's expression doesn't change, but her eyes challenge me. *Your move, boss,* she seems to be saying.

I step up to the microphone and tap it. There's no feedback.

"Testing?" I say, and my voice comes through loud and clear.

"Well, it's a beautiful evening. Looks like someone's smiling down on our little festival." Being good parishioners, they laugh at this. "And I think we should start off with a little prayer."

There's a general commotion as the men remove their hats and heads are bowed. The carnies fidget some, at a loss for what to do.

"We want to offer up thanks today, God, for You providing us with such a strong community and with this opportunity to gather in one place and celebrate one another, celebrate Your gifts. You have a good flock down here in Grand Prairie and I want to personally thank You for that right here in front of them. They need to know I'm proud of them for coming together like this and working so hard." A rock star would simply have said, *"Hello, Grand Prairie,"* but it serves the same purpose. It's a shout-out to the hometown crowd. "And we all want to thank You for the weather, and the music, and the food."

After the prayer, they look up at me expectantly. How much longer am I going to hold up the festivities, they want to know.

"Before we start, I want to thank the volunteers who set up and those of you who volunteered to help clean. And I also want to especially thank our Festival Board, Miss Emilia Boudreaux, Miss Celestine Thibodeaux, Miss Pamela Pitre, and Miss Denise Fontenot. Yall come up here." The four of them come forward and the crowd applauds loudly as I hand each one a bouquet of a dozen roses. A few of the men even whistle. I look over at Mark and Vicky. Mark's smile has grown a little larger. He's a sucker for drama. Vicky seems surprised that I had the presence of mind to get something for the three women and Denise. She doesn't need to know it was Mama who "reminded" me that I should make the gesture.

"These ladies did a lot of hard work, so yall give them a hand," I say. The crowd goes about as wild as a Grand Prairie crowd can. Denise is smiling so hard, I worry that her teeth might fall right out of her head.

"And there's two more people I have to thank," I tell the crowd. They all turn to Vicky and Mark. "While I was off doing whatever it is I do, these two people were the ones running around getting these fund-raisers together, working the phones, and finding the music so we can dance from tonight straight through until Sunday evening."

The crowd breaks into applause again, with the carnies even contributing a few hoots and hollers.

"So if Vicky Carrier—she was the director of the board—and Mark Johnson, our consultant, the one who really got this thing to where it is—if they could come up here."

Vicky and Mark look at each other hesitantly before moving forward and climbing the steps.

"Mark," I begin, "well, Mark. I didn't know quite what to get him. But I do know he has a little black cat, about this big." I hold my hands up about six inches from each other. On cue, the crowd lets out an appreciative "awwww."

"So," I continue, "I got the cat something instead." I motion to Denise, who comes forward with a cardboard box with holes in the side. "I got that little black cat a little girl cat." I lift the kitten out of the box, hold it close, and stroke its fur. I can feel its heart thumping quickly against my chest.

"Mark?" I say, turning to Mark.

Mark comes forward, biting his bottom lip. I don't know how the parish is going to react if a grown man starts crying in public over a kitten. I hadn't thought of that. But Mark holds it together even as I give him a firm, manly, heterosexual hug.

"Mark," I whisper, careful to step away from the microphone. "I'm sorry. This is the proper apology I owe you. Really."

"You did good," Mark says. "But I think Chase might be gay."

"Shut up," I say. "And look. Not that you'd want to, but you can move back in whenever you want. If you want."

Mark's smiling again. "Would tonight be too soon?"

"Tonight?" I say, surprised.

"Yeah," Mark whispers. "Living with that woman's getting to be a bit much. Lord. She's been nuts since you went AWOL."

I don't mean to, but I smile. "Yeah. Sure. Tonight's fine. Yeah."

I turn back to the microphone. "Big hand for Mark."

After the applause dies down, I start again. "Now, yall all know Vicky Carrier. She's been part of the parish for a long, long time." Everyone murmurs approval. "And she's a hard woman to buy for. She's got pretty much everything." A number of people nod, but I flash a knowing smile at the audience and add, "Well, except a husband." It's a risk, but I'm trying to uphold the false impression that everything is normal. Nothing to see here. Everyone in the crowd laughs. Real laughter this time. I look over at Vicky. She's not smiling. "Anyway, they were out of those at Walmart." Again, the crowd laughs. "So I talked to some people around the parish and we put our heads together and we all came up with an idea."

And that idea involved B.P. He'd responded to my e-mail within the hour by driving up in his son's bright yellow Hummer.

Before I could even say hi and ask about his health, he was making threats. Seems he'd forgotten his aw-shucks charm at home.

"I could just call up the diocese and rat you out. You and your gal and that little poof you got there and whatever it is you got with them little altar gals—the whole damn lot of you."

So it was going to be like that.

"I suppose you could. Guess you'd have to ask yourself who has more to lose. Whose family would be hurt most by this? That's what I'd ask myself. But I don't know if that's all that fair, considering I don't have a family." All that living alone had finally paid off!

He'd glared at me, his nostrils flaring.

"And to be perfectly honest, B.P., though I don't have a son of my own, I think the rest of these photos would break your heart to a million tiny little pieces. I think these photos might be the sort of thing to come between a man and his God. In fact, I'm inclined not to show them to you at all. But you push me, you'll see them, but not until after everyone else from Ville Platte to Church Point has gotten a good look."

He huffed like a bull and I thought for sure he was going to drive one of those sledgehammer fists of his right into my face.

Finally, he said, "What do you want?"

"What do I want? Well, B.P., luckily for you, I'm not a greedy man. I only want three things. I want you to postpone your tent revival for a week."

"Look here, you know I can't do that. I got five preachers coming down from—"

"I don't care where they're coming down from. Fake a stroke. Fake a death in the family. Just call them and tell them to come the following week. Or never. Or would you rather them be the first to see these photos?"

His face had grown so red by this point, I was afraid he would have a heart attack. "What else?"

"Second thing's much easier than the first. Just keep your mouth shut about what happens out here and stay on your side of town."

"My side of town."

"I know. It's not really a town, but you get my drift. Don't come around trying to convert my people and I won't go around trying to convert yours. Don't drive into Opelousas spreading my business all over town and I'll be kind enough to do likewise. Hell, at some point, maybe we can have some of those interfaith things that seem to be all the rage these days."

"Over my dead body," he'd said.

"Yeah, well, maybe you'll come around." I couldn't help myself. I was half tempted to hit him up for money to see how far I could take things.

"What else?"

"Last thing is the easiest one of all," I said. "Might involve a little sweat, dirt, and hard work, but, hell, it'll be fun."

Denise walks up to me and hands me a covered plaque.

"Now, we're an odd little parish, we know that. Some of our secrets are not so secret." I pause before continuing. "And while I didn't know the man too well, I know you all had a lot of love for Father Carrier, almost as much love as Vicky did."

The entire crowd, with the exception of the carnies, who by this point have wandered off to their rides and games, aim a smile Vicky's way. "So I got this plaque made, and it says 'The Father Paul Carrier Memorial Trail. In Loving Memory of Father Paul Carrier, the Parish of St. Peter's Church in Grand Prairie.' " Again the crowd applauds.

Vicky's hand has gone to her chest and she seems to be clutching the buttons on her shirt. It strikes me as such a lady-like thing to do.

I push on. "Now, I know this isn't going to make Mr. Robichaux and some of the others too happy, but I also went ahead and took the liberty to lay gravel on that path from the back of the rectory clear to the bayou." And by that, I mean I took the liberty of telling B.P. to get his fat ass on his big yellow bulldozer and get working. Which he did with minimal complaint. "Put some benches back there, too. And Jimmy Vidrine built a little deck overlooking the water and everybody's welcome to it all year long."

Vicky's crying now. That shocks me some, but not half as much as the fact that I managed to surprise her with this. I thought for sure some old bird in the parish would have squawked before today.

I hold the plaque out to Vick. When her trembling hands reach for it, I pull her in tight for a hug.

"You are one nervy son of a bitch," she whispers, her arms dead at her side.

"I know, Vicky," I say. "I'm a no-count bastard, too, but sometimes I can't help myself."

"Shit."

"It's okay, right? This is a good thing?" It's almost as if I'm trying to convince her. I hadn't thought of it before and suddenly I'm worried that I've gone and made everything worse.

She tries to compose herself, wipes her nose on the heel of her palm. So much for ladylike. "Just get this party started, damn it. I need a beer," she says while smiling at the crowd and waving.

"Can do." I turn back to the microphone and put on my own false cheer. "Okay, folks. I'm going to shut my trap now. Yall go and have a good time."

We descend into the crowd. As parishioners mill around us offering congratulations and compliments, Vicky maintains a breezy air. But I can see the cold glint in her eyes, a tightness in her face when she's forced to acknowledge me.

When the first strains of accordion wash over the crowd and the Zipper jumps to life, people suddenly remember they're here for a party, not simply to jabber the night away. A few couples spin off onto the dance floor, the teens make a mad dash for the scary rides, the smaller children drag their parents toward the kiddie rides, and the largest contingent—of which I am one—amble toward the beer and food booths.

I tug on Vicky's sleeve, and she stops to consider me. I'm not sure where to start.

"Seriously, Vick. Thanks for all the help."

"You're welcome," she says, her face stony, her body language guarded.

"I just want to—"

She cuts me off. "Not now, Padre."

"But—"

"Just drop it. We have to get through this weekend. We have to put on a show. Whatever it is you're going to say isn't going to help. So drop it."

"Fuck," I say, more to myself than to her.

"That about sums it up," she says. Then, "C'mon. We have to judge the rabbit stew contest."

Side by side, we walk down the midway. The sun is setting over the cemetery, and the blinking lights of the carnival games and rides are a sight to behold. It's a cool night and the sounds of zydeco and screaming girls mix easily in the air; they can probably be heard all the way in Plaisance. Children, their faces already covered in cotton candy and face paint, run by, kicking up dust behind them. I'm struck by such an overwhelming sense of nostalgia that I have to stop. For a moment, it hurts to breathe. I remember clearly the sensation of heartbreak. Not the anger and envy and self-loathing that immediately follow a breakup, but the pure, almost sweet sadness at the bottom of it all.

Vicky stops, too. "What is it?"

I put a hand on my chest and shake my head clear. "Nothing. Let's go eat some bunny."

Of course, it's not that easy. On one hand, it's nice to be back with Vicky and Mark. Even though our little triumvirate is broken, we manage to play nice, largely through the efforts of Mark. On the other hand, I imagine this is what hell must be like—being so close to something that once seemed ideal, knowing that you'd reached too far and fucked it all up.

I'd like nothing more than to sneak off to the rectory and down half a bottle of whiskey, but I'm tapping reserves I didn't know I had and resisting the temptation. I'll have enough headaches this weekend. Adding a hangover to the mix isn't going to help things any. If nothing else, I learn that ice-cold Dr Pepper pairs well with nine out of ten rabbit stew recipes.

By eleven o'clock, it's all over.

What a strange sight, to see a carnival empty out. The families with small children are the first to go, the children asleep in their parents' arms before reaching the parking lot. Next are the families with older children—the nine- and ten-year-olds hopped up on adrenaline and junk food, but exhausted all the same. Many of them have to be dragged screaming through the dust, "But I'm not ready to leeeeavvvvve," their common battle cry. Then the dancers, who scatter into the parking lot sweaty and happy as soon as the band stops. And then, finally, the teens, who hang on until ten thirty, when the rides and midway shut down. The taillights of their cars join the dragon's tail of dust snaking out onto the highway.

Once they're all gone, the carnival seems to let out a long, slow breath as a hush falls over the grounds and the lights and rides go dark.

Then noise again. The food vendors start to break down their equipment, and the carnies, who'd sat sullenly by their rides all night revving motors up and down, suddenly come to life, shouting at one another, laughing, cracking open their first beers.

I'm standing in the midway watching it all, distracted, when Vicky slides up next to me.

"We need to collect the cash and receipts," she says, pulling her hair back from her face with both hands, leaving her elbows pointing out like the guns of a ball turret. She looks beat. She wears it well.

"Go home," I say. "I'll take care of it."

She looks at me as if I've just promised to build a church by hand in three days. "Do you even know how to do this?"

"I'm sure it can't be that hard," I say. "You've done enough. It's the least I can do. Just show me what to do."

She walks with me to the "Boudin Ball" booth and talks me through the process. Look at their receipts, take our cut, write it down.

"When you get back to the rectory, just count it all to make sure it adds up."

"Aye-aye, Cap'n."

"You're sure you can do this?"

"Vicky."

"Okay, okay."

Mark jogs up to us. "Hey, party people. Need help?"

"I got it," I say.

"Yeah," Vicky says, raising her eyebrows. "Apparently, Steve has it under control."

Mark looks at me. "Really?"

"Oh, c'mon," I protest. "I'm not retarded, you know."

"I guess sometimes we forget," Mark says, laughing at me. "Anyway, I'm going home with Vicky tonight. I have to get Chase and the rest of my stuff. I'll bring it over tomorrow."

"Sounds good. And yall try to sleep in. If anything needs doing here, I'll take care of it."

With that, they're off. I walk the grounds, collect the cash, and return to the rectory to count it. One night of business has us three-fourths of the way to the break-even point. Satisfied with a job well done, I decide to walk the midway one last time before turning in.

It's a cloudless night and now that the rides have shut down, I can see the stars above. Instead of chirping crickets, I hear machines cooling and settling, the beginnings of a party over in the circle of trailers across the highway where the carnies have set up.

I find myself in front of the elephant enclosure. It's vacant. I'm not quite sure why. I haven't had a chance to catch up to Blackfoot for more than a minute or two. I lean on the railing and consider the empty circle. I wonder if Miss Rita would have been disappointed. She'd seemed genuinely excited to see one. Hard to imagine living that long and never seeing an elephant up close. Then again, I'm sure she'd be quick to tell me she'd seen plenty—and an elephant wasn't going to make or break her life either way.

She'd definitely be disappointed with the mess I've made for myself. She'd grab me by the collar, give me a good shaking, and tell me to quit my whining and get on.

"I'm trying," I'd say.

Then she'd reply, *"And you still need a woman."*

"She'll be here tomorrow," a man's voice says.

I jump a little at the sound of it. It's Blackfoot.

"What was that?"

"I said she'll be here tomorrow."

"Who?"

"The elephant," he says, and laughs. "Who'd you think I was talking about?" He laughs again. "You got it real fuckin' bad, don't you?"

"What?" I counter.

"I don't know what, exactly. But whatever it is, it's got a tight hold on you." He walks over and leans on the fence. "Been watching you all night. Walking around, doing your job like a man who knows what he's doing."

"Something wrong with that?"

"Wrong? Fuck no. But—and no offense—competence ain't exactly the first fucking word that jumps to mind when I see you."

"People can change, can't they?"

"Depends on what you mean by change. I think they can become what they were supposed to be in the first place. Or they can deny whatever the fuck it is that's bothering them in the first place—distract themselves with work or chasing money or some such."

I'm a little freaked out. It's like he's crawled into my head and started peeking around. I don't dare look directly at him, so I sneak my eyeballs over to the periphery. He's done the same thing, his reptilian right eye nestled in the corner of its socket, considering me. A wicked little grin creeps across his face.

"So tell me, Father. How well is this little festival of yours keeping your mind off that woman? I imagine this evening you survived fine. But tonight? Ahhh, the fucking night. You're more than a little afraid to go back to that room of yours. All that silence. Can't fucking sleep, no matter how hard you try, no matter how dead tired. Tormented soul and all that."

I back away from the fence slowly. "What are you? Satan or something?" I ask. God has never said a single word to me, but the devil is suddenly more than happy to oblige. And instead of offering something really cool in exchange for my soul, he's content to scare the shit out of me.

Blackfoot starts to shudder. His shoulders pump up and down. He pounds the fence with a closed fist and his eyes are squeezed shut, tears rolling out of them. His breath comes out in quick little grunts. He looks like a bullfrog with something lodged in its throat. I figure he's about to hurl a stream of bright green vomit or turn into a werewolf.

I'm just getting ready to run when he grabs the fence, steadies himself, catches a deep breath, and releases a high-pitched "Heeeeeeeeeeeeeeeeeee." Then he starts shaking again, bends over, and puts one hand on his knee and another up toward me.

"Don't," he says. Then: "Heeeeee. Huh. Heeeeee." He's laughing. And trying to breathe. "Oh . . . Heeeee . . . Dear . . . Heeeeeee. Fucking. Lord!" He gets out the last two with a shout, shakes his head. "Fuck. Fuck. Fuck."

The fucks bring him back to himself. He straightens out and wipes the tears off his face.

"Fuck me, Father." He pounds his chest, trying to dislodge the last few laughs. "Didn't mean to make you shit yourself."

"I wasn't," I start to say.

"Don't get me started again, Father. Please." He looks as if he's just finished a marathon.

Fine. I'll grant him that he scared me nearly shitless. "But how?" I want to know.

"If you asked my mother, she'd say it was 'the gift.' But it's just carnival tricks is all. Or, if you go to a fancy fucking college, I guess you could call it something like deductive reasoning or psychology or something."

I just look at him.

"It's like this," he continues. "I run a caravan. I'm judge and jury of this group. I watch. I listen. I pay attention. I also seen thousands of people march through my midways. I also watched my grandmother—may she rest in peace." Here, he crosses himself and spits over his shoulder. "Watched her read palms and cards for fifteen or so years. People ain't all that complicated, Father. It always boils down to the Four *F*s: fucking, fighting, family, and funding. That's it. That's people in a nutshell. And, man of the cloth or no, you're still people. And you ain't exactly hard to read."

"Oh, really?"

"You're a man. You live alone in the woods. You got no worries about funding. You got no family. So that leaves fucking and fighting. And those two almost always travel together. And despite your little poof of a friend there, I figure you bat for the right team. So a healthy young lad such as yourself needs to get laid something fucking awful. And the pinched way you carry yourself, I can tell it's been a fuck of a long time since you've had a good roll in the hay."

"You could say that about any priest," I counter.

"Well, most of them—and I've seen a lot—aren't spending half their time with single members of the opposite sex barking up their tree. Much easier to defy nature, Father, when you remove all the temptations."

It's like Miss Rita all over again. "You're not the first person who's beaten this dead horse."

"Doesn't surprise me any."

"Besides, what am I supposed to do? I'm a priest. I've taken vows. I'm married to the Church."

"Vows, huh? How are those treating you?"

"They're not supposed to be easy. The sacrifice is the point."

"Still sacrificing things to God, are we? I think a fucking goat would do just as well," he says. "Certainly cause a lot less trouble. Where does that sacrifice for God get you, Father? Ever think of that? A sacrifice He didn't ask for, mind you. All them other clowns in the Bible were married, had children. And yet here you are. How many fifteen-year-old boys were part and parcel of this sacrifice you people make?"

"That has nothing—"

He cuts me off. "Fine. Cheap fucking shot, that was. Sure. Your hands are clean. For now. But my point remains. Nothing fucking good ever came of denying nature."

"We're not animals," I say. "We deny our nature all the time."

"C'mon, Father. You know better than that. We channel it. That's what the rules are for. Even in a caravan, you channel nature. You manage it. Now, when you try to deny it? Like you people do? That's where the trouble starts."

All my years of education and I'm having circles talked around me by a man who cheats kids out of their quarters with bent basketball rims, short-lived goldfish, and blunt-tipped darts.

"That's all well and good," I say. "But at the end of the day, I have to make my peace with God."

"Ha!" he shouts. "Make peace with God? Really? Make peace with yourself, Father. The Good Lord sure as hell can take care of Himself. Besides, I think He'll be a lot less forgiving if you finally snap and find yourself in a back room with one of them altar girls of yours. And if He don't notice, for fuck sure her daddy will."

There's a glint in his eyes as he says this, but he's not joking. I shudder to think of the things he's seen in his years of running that caravan of his.

But all of this is beside the point, isn't it?

"Fuck it," I say, draping my arms over the elephant fence and putting my head down on the top crossbar. "It doesn't matter anyway. Even if I were to throw all caution to the wind and risk my job, it doesn't matter. It's too far gone. She's pissed. She hates me. She's made that clear enough."

Blackfoot walks over and pats me on the back. With a good-natured chuckle, he says, "You're a goddamn fool, ain't you? She's giving you that much trouble, she ain't fucking done with you yet."

And with that, he walks off into the night, whistling.

Chapter 19

I'm woken at an ungodly hour by a pounding on the door, a thumping so loud that it cuts through the fog of a medicated sleep. I took three Tylenol PMs last night, but fell asleep before they had time to kick in.

The pounding continues. I pull black pants over my black boxers and shuffle toward the door. From the weak light filtering through the windows, I can tell that dawn is just breaking.

"Coming," I shout, thinking the drumming will stop. Instead, it's joined by a voice.

"Get your ass out here, Father. She's fucking here, ready and waiting." Blackfoot. It's a hell of a voice to wake up to. "Early bird catches the worm, Father. Get the fuck up. She's not going to wait all day."

"I'm up!" I yell back, and swing the door open to find Blackfoot and a three-ton elephant standing outside the rectory.

"Want a ride?" He smiles, revealing his tobacco-stained teeth.

The elephant expels a burst of air. It sounds like the sigh of a woman grown accustomed to her husband's foolish ways.

"Right now?"

"Early bird catches the worm," he says.

"Shouldn't that thing be in a pen?"

His smile grows bigger. It's approaching a leer, but it's an infectious one. After all, there is an elephant in my yard, and Blackfoot and I seem to be the only two people on the planet awake.

"Where's her driver?" I ask.

"He took the truck to get washed," he says. "You got an hour all to your fuckin' self."

"What about you?"

"Me? I ain't that selfless, Father. I already took her for a spin in the woods. Knocked a few trees over."

"Really?"

"Fuckin' A, she did."

"Awesome," is all I can think to say.

"Now you go get a proper shirt and shoes on," he says. "You ain't got all fuckin' day."

It takes me all of two minutes before I'm back outside and climbing a ladder to the box on the elephant's back. Her real name is Gertie, he tells me. The signage and the contract call her Simba, but the name she answers to is Gertie.

"Nice to meet you, Gertie," I say, scratching the top of her head. From my perch, I have a clear view of the rectory's roof. There's a Frisbee on it. "I only wish Miss Rita was here to meet you."

"Who?"

"Old friend of mine," I answer. "She passed a month ago."

"Fuckin' sorry to hear that," he says

But you wouldn't know it. We're both wearing goofy grins on our faces. I feel like a ten-year-old who's just been given a flying car equipped with a flamethrower and rocket launchers.

"I'm sure you could think of someone else to share this once-in-a-lifetime opportunity with," he says.

"I don't know about that," I laugh. "If I called her at this time of the day . . ."

"Who said anything about calling, ya fuckin' sissy?"

"No."

"Why not?"

"Well, first of all, an elephant on the highway," I say, searching for excuses.

"Oh, don't blame it on Gertie," he says. "She's walked through the Lincoln Tunnel in New York. I think she can handle herself on an empty road."

That was all the excuse I had.

"Just do it, Father. Who fuckin' knows? You get to her before she has her morning coffee, she won't be awake enough to resist."

"Well, aren't you the optimist this morning?" I say.

"Maybe," he says, climbing up the ladder. "Maybe. But let me show you how to steer, just in case you grow a pair of balls in the next thirty seconds."

Five minutes later, I'm riding an elephant down the highway with the sun rising to my left. Gertie moves at a leisurely saunter, her breath the only sound on an incredibly still morning. I do wish Miss Rita were here to see this. I can hear her clapping her hands in delight. That would have been a more fitting end to her life—riding like a queen on the back of an elephant, looking down on everything around her. Maybe she could have just kept on riding, free of that home, with a couple of bottles of Crown Royal and a week's worth of cracklin's.

But the closer I get to Vicky's, the harder it is to hang on to that vision. Instead, my chest tightens, my palms get clammy, and it feels like something's stuck in my throat. Perhaps sensing that something is wrong, Gertie stops. Should I turn her around and head back home? Miss Rita's voice comes to me: *"Quit acting like a sissy and get on over to that girl's house."*

But—

"Don't 'but' me, boy."

"Okay, Gertie," I say. "Let's get a move on." That's all there is to it.

Gertie's not the fastest mode of transportation. Fifteen minutes after leaving St. Pete's, I'm only halfway to Vicky's house when I hear the sound of clopping hooves. In the distance, heading toward me, is Lem Landry and his mule-drawn wagon. That figures. With the number of out-of-towners bound to come in for the festival, he would break out the wagon—whether to get attention or simply hold up traffic, I don't know.

He slows as he draws up to Gertie and me, puts a hand over his brow to block out the sun.

"Lem," I say.

"Father," he says, looking up, down, and around. "That an elephant you got there?"

"It sure is, Lem."

"Kee-yawwwwww!" he shouts, slapping his knee and smiling. "I done seen it all, me. Mais, watchoo doing with it?"

"Riding it, I guess."

"I see. I see."

This has got to be the most absurd conversation either one of us has ever had.

"Well, I'll be seeing you, Lem."

"Okay, Father," he says, then puts a hand up. "Wait! Let me take a picture of yall." With that, he takes out a cell phone and snaps a shot. "That's a good one. I'ma have to e-mail that to you."

"You do that, Lem," I say, gently nudging Gertie into gear. Lem stays parked in the middle of the road. As I move away I hear him talking into his phone. "Mais, yall got to see this. Father Steve done got him an elephant and he's marching it around town. No lie! Like I would lie about something like that." He listens in silence for a bit. "Well, yall hurry up and come on. And call CaCa, tell him bring his horses."

Ten minutes later, Gertie and I—and Lem and half the geriatric population of Grand Prairie, including CaCa and about twenty other men on horseback—arrive at Vicky's house. I look over my shoulder at them and wave.

"Hey-hey!" shouts one of the old men, and the crowd erupts into applause and whistles. That brings Vicky to her door, coffee mug in hand.

"What's going on, Steve?" she asks, her face stone stiff.

That's a tough one to explain. "I guess I took Gertie for a ride and accidentally started a parade."

"Gertie?"

"Yeah, this is Gertie," I say, leaning over to scratch the top of her head.

"Isn't that nice?" she says. "You got your elephant."

I'm not going to get control of this conversation by myself, so I decide to play dirty. Loud enough for the gathered crowd to hear, I say, "Go get some jeans on, Vicky, and come for a ride on my elephant!"

The town folk erupt into cheers once again. "All right, Vicky!" someone shouts.

She waves, smiles, and closes the door.

My cell phone rings. It's Mark. "Are you insane?" he says, glee in his voice. "You're totally insane."

"Maybe."

"You look totally hot up there," he says.

I scan the house and see him peering out from behind a curtain in the bathroom.

"Is she pissed?"

"Well, she's stomping around and muttering to herself. I'm afraid to come out of the bathroom. . . . Oh, shit! There she goes. Bye."

He hangs up just as Vicky opens the door. She walks up to Gertie and puts a hand on her gray flank. "How am I supposed to get up there?"

I look back at the crowd. "Go climb on top of Mr. Melancon's truck. I'll spin her around and pick you up."

The crowd parts for Vicky, every one of them giving her a

good morning or a tip of his hat. They part even wider to let Gertie through. Some of them reach out and tentatively touch her hide. "Just like a big ol' horse," somebody says.

After a few minutes of navigating and nudging, I've got Gertie nestled up to the side of the pickup.

"Where am I supposed to sit?" Vicky asks, all business.

I hadn't thought of that. I'm going to be doing the steering, but I don't want her behind me where she can easily smack me in the back of the head. "Sit up front. Blackfoot said that's the safest way to do it," I lie.

"Is that right?"

"Yes, Vicky. That's right."

She climbs on and sits down, her legs warm against mine. I close my arms around her, grabbing what passes for reins. Vicky's tense, her back stiff, her head straight. But I've got this overwhelming feeling that I could melt into her right here. I can't remember the last time I've touched a woman like this. I get lost for a moment.

"We going to move or what?" The edge in her voice brings me back to the moment.

I look down at the crowd. "All right, yall. Let's get this parade started. Back to the church!"

They cheer again. Those in cars turn their radios to KBON and crank the Cajun music. Others work their cell phones. Within minutes, those who haven't joined the parade are parked along the side of the road ahead, their children standing on top of the cars and screaming and pointing. The once-silent morning has given way to a rowdy celebration loud enough that they couldn't possibly hear me talking to Vicky.

"So I was thinking," I start. I'm nervous, but manage to keep a smile fixed on my face and one hand in the air, waving. Vicky does as well.

"How's that working out for you?"

"You're not going to make this easy, are you?"

"Make what easy, Steve? What, your whole life isn't easy enough, with everyone doing everything for you?"

"I'm sorry. I'm trying here."

"One night of collecting cash isn't going to make up for it."

"I know. I know. This isn't about the damn festival anyway."

"Then what's it about?"

I wave and smile in silence for a minute before working up the courage. She knows what this is about. She just wants me to say it.

"Us," I finally manage.

"Us?" she says. "Us? Ha! What about us?"

"C'mon, Vicky."

"No. You c'mon. What about us?"

"There's something here, isn't there?"

"Define 'something.' Define 'here.' You don't even know the first thing about me, Steve."

"I know you're lonely. I know you've been lonely out here. And you're afraid of living your life like that."

"Wow, you like to lead with charm, don't you? Besides, sounds to me like you're projecting."

"That doesn't make it any less true."

She pauses for a bit. "And what? You're going to solve that for me? Just because you're horny, I'm supposed to throw caution to the wind for a six-month fling. Then twenty years later, I'm spending Saturday nights playing cards with the few old ladies who weren't completely scandalized by my run-in with the priest. And you're back in the arms of Jesus, pretending nothing happened?"

"I'm not your dad."

"You got that right."

"And this isn't about sex."

"No? Then what's that poking me in the back? Or is that a banana in your pocket?"

"Jesus," I say. I hadn't even realized. For the first time in the conversation, I drop my waving hand. I adjust myself and scoot back a little. I haven't felt this peculiar shame since fourth grade math class when I went through the rite of passage of being called to the blackboard in the midst of a Vanna White daydream. "Never mind that," I say. "I'm not talking about sneaking around. I'm not talking about hiding."

"Then what, pray tell, are you talking about?"

In need of a moment, I shout out to the crowd. "Good morning, Miss Robichaux! How yall doing, Mr. Deville?"

"Pathetic," I hear Vicky mumble.

I take a deep breath. "I love you," I say. "Now? You happy? I said it."

She reaches into her pocket, pulls out the cell phone, and flips it open. "Hi. *Daily World?* I've got a front page story for you. Steve Sibille just told me he loves me. And, really, if I wasn't on the back of an elephant right now, I'd fall down to my knees and sing praises to the Lord." She closes the phone and puts it away. "Jackass," she says.

If I didn't have one hand on the reins and the other in the air waving, I'd choke her. But I remember what Blackfoot said, that she's giving me this much trouble because she's not done with me yet. I only hope he's right.

"Go on, Vick. Keep that wall of sarcasm up. But I'm not going to stop. I've made up my mind. I don't want to grow old alone. I want to grow old with you, even if it means losing my parish. Even if you are a royal pain in the ass. And I'm not giving up just because you've got a smart-ass answer for everything I say. The only thing that's going to stop me now is a restraining order."

For a few minutes, she says nothing. She simply waves at the crowd and tries to smile. My heart's beating a hundred miles a minute and I feel completely naked.

"That's real fucking romantic," she says, shaking her head.

"Real fucking romantic." But as she says it, the tension goes out of her shoulders and neck, and she leans back into me. The scent of her shampoo—it's medicinal, perhaps even dandruff-control, but certainly not apple or strawberry—nearly knocks me off my elephant.

When I wake up at three o'clock Monday morning for a drink of water and a trip to the bathroom, the rain has slowed considerably.

It remained clear and cool all weekend and the First Annual Rabbit Festival had pulled in a steady stream of visitors from Opelousas, Ville Platte, and beyond. But late Sunday afternoon, as the last band was setting up, a frontal system began to poke its thunderheads up over the horizon. It moved slowly and the band, Chris Ardoin and Double Clutchin', seemed unconcerned. They played for half an hour while the storm inched its way in from the north, a growing wall of purple clouds lit from within by strobes of lightning. I felt at times like I was at a tennis match, my eyes zipping to the band one second, the clouds the next. Who was going to win? I was beginning to feel smug—God had blessed the entire festival, He was holding back the rain, allowing the band to finish while providing a natural fireworks show.

The air went still for ten minutes. The band played on. Then the wind picked up suddenly, leaves blowing through, the banners and pennants on the festival grounds whipping violently back and forth, dust coming in from the surrounding fields. The band looked up nervously; it kept playing. But when a bright flash of lightning struck—it was a couple of miles away, but looked and sounded like it had hit right behind the stage— Double Clutchin' stopped in the middle of the song. Chris Ardoin leaned into the microphone. "Well, folks, I think the man upstairs trying to tell us something, and we not ones to say no to Him."

Everyone laughed, applauded, then ran for the cars. No horns were blown, no fingers proffered as they filed out of the parking fields and the rain started coming down in sheets. In the time-honored parlance of church bulletins across the country, "A good time was had by all." More importantly, no one was killed by lightning, which had happened at the Zydeco Festival on two separate occasions.

I stand over the kitchen sink, staring out at the makeshift skyline of the carnival rides, their spindly frames becoming more distinct, strong black lines materializing from gray curtains as the rain slows to a light patter, then stops. No birds call, no rabbits shuffle, no dogs bark or growl or yelp, no cats creep. Since Mark has come back, Chase and the other cat, Rabbit, have been sleeping in his room. The carnies, so loud earlier in the night, are all in their trailers deep in chemical comas. This is as silent as it gets back here. Even the wind has ceased, the leaves giving one final sigh as the back edge of the front finally slips over Grand Prairie. The only sounds are the *plinks* and *plonks* of water drops landing on trailer roofs and Tilt-a-Whirl carts.

I nod dreamily as I stand there, slightly amused that I've become reacquainted with sober sleep. I'm drowsily thinking how awfully nice it is of nature to cooperate with this mood, when a rooster crows somewhere in the distance.

I jolt awake, wide-eyed.

"Stupid rooster," I mumble, smiling.

I pour myself a glass of water, drink it, then walk back to my room and climb into bed next to Vicky.

The First Annual Grand Prairie Rabbit Festival

Ken Wheaton

ABOUT THIS GUIDE

Turn the page for some
Rabbit Festival lagniappe—
a little something extra.

Gumbo for Dummies

I'm the sort who makes vast pronouncements about Cajun cooking. As I am from Opelousas, Louisiana, and most people outside of Louisiana think a Cajun is either (a) a mythical being, (b) Emeril, or (c) Adam Sandler in *The Waterboy,* I'm not exactly shy about telling most people they don't know what they're talking about and they likely haven't had Cajun food. The sad reality is that in most places, Popeyes red beans and rice is the closest thing to authentic you'll find (and it's actually pretty good). After an exchange about gumbo on Twitter, I figured I'd quit mocking people for not knowing any better and would provide you with a roadmap to true gumbo bliss.

The following is for chicken and sausage gumbo. Note that I don't use okra because I don't like it. Also note that Seafood Gumbo is a different beast from this (and in some ways easier to cook). What you should not do is mix seafood and chicken/sausage gumbo.

Finally, don't you ever put any of the following in your gumbo: tomatoes, corn, peas, carrots, or mushrooms.

I will find you. I will slap you.

Before starting, a word about ingredients.

Roux. In Cajun cooking, roux is usually made with vegetable oil and flour. Never, ever use olive oil as it has a distinct taste that does not belong in this dish. You can make your own roux (see pages 299–301) or, like many time-pressed Cajun mamas and mawmaws, just use the jarred stuff. After all, it's flour and oil and contains no secret techniques or ingredients—not even "love," though "impatience" is often thrown in.

Sausage and andouille. This will be your biggest ingredient challenge. My suggestion is to order it (and your roux) from cajungrocer.com or something similar—at least for your first time out, so that you can see what this sausage is supposed to taste like. Both Cajun sausage and andouille are typically smoked pork. Most people can't tell the difference between the two. After roux, this is probably the most crucial ingredient in getting non-seafood gumbo to taste like gumbo. *Do not* substitute Italian sausage. There are some kielbasas that come close, but they tend to be greasier. In a pinch, the safest substitute to use is Aidells Cajun Style Andouille, which you can typically find at gourmet stores.

Tasso (pronounced tah-so) is smoked pork with very little fat. It's almost like ham. If you can't find it, don't worry about it. Just double your sausage.

Onions. Use yellow or Spanish onions. Don't use white or red onions.

Tomatoes. Don't use them. Ever. I don't care what anyone says. If I find out you're using tomatoes, I will come to your home and revoke these recipes! (Sorry if I'm repeating myself, but I feel strongly about this.)

Serving. Gumbo is a soup, not a stew or a gravy. While it is served over white rice, the rice should be covered almost completely. (For a pretty serving, pack the rice into a small ice-cream bowl or some such, then flip that into your soup bowl. Pour enough gumbo so that the top of your little rice island is just sticking out of the brown ocean of goodness.)

For a quick-and-easy gumbo recipe, buy a jar of Savoie's Roux and consult the recipe on the label. It's not going to be the best gumbo in the world, but it's pretty good and it's certainly better (and more authentic) than anything you'll find in a restaurant (or in New Orleans). It's a good place to start before trying to experiment later down the line.

If you feel up to it and want bragging rights, make your own roux. (I've long given up on doing this.)

1 cup vegetable oil
1 cup flour
(Note that handy dandy 1:1 ratio if you're making smaller or bigger batches.)

In a cast-iron pot or skillet, heat the oil over medium-high heat. Slowly whisk in the flour, stirring constantly for three to five minutes until the roux is caramel—almost but not quite chocolate—in color. To be extra careful, I actually use a lower heat and just sit there and stir it until it's done, because if you burn even a little bit of it, you have to throw it all out. Don't be afraid to take it off the heat a little bit before it's done, and *keep stirring* it as it will continue to cook even when it's off the flame.

Now, on to the gumbo.

1 large chicken (cut up and seasoned)*
vegetable oil
1 large onion, chopped
1 green pepper, chopped
4 pods of garlic, minced
3 stalks of celery, chopped
4 huge tablespoons of roux
1 pound smoked pork sausage or andouille
1 pound smoked tasso
4 quarts water
½ cup of green onions, chopped
cooked white rice

*For extra-tasty results, skip the whole chicken and get yourself legs and thighs. Dark meat is better. All of this is better if the bones are still in. If you cook gumbo long enough, all the meat will pull away from the bones, anyway. But if your guests are squeamish, feel free to use boneless thighs. Do *not* use boneless breast meat.

First step: Season and brown the chicken.

Generously rub down your bird parts with either Tony Chachere's Creole Seasoning, Slap Ya Mama Seasoning (both available at cajungrocer.com), or a mixture of salt, black pepper, and garlic powder (and just a dash of cayenne).

Cover the bottom of a large black iron pot (or a soup pot—two gallons or more) with a thin sheen of vegetable oil.

Set to medium-high heat.

Brown the chicken pieces to a golden brown. If parts stick to the bottom, hit it with some water and scrape the bits up. That's extra flavoring.

After the chicken is brown, remove it from pot. If the bottom of your pot is small, feel free to do the browning in batches.

Next: Lower the heat a notch and chuck in all the vegetables *except* the green onions. Toss in a touch of salt and black pepper and sauté for two minutes or so. Chuck in your roux and stir it all together, letting it simmer for another three minutes or so.

Blend chicken, sausage, and tasso into the mix and sauté for fifteen minutes. (You might want to add just a little water—or even white wine—if it looks like your roux is sticking to the bottom.)

Next: Add your water.

Do this slowly, stirring constantly. (Note: Some folks will substitute part or all of the four quarts of water with the chicken stock. As I let mine cook forever, stock isn't necessary. And if you're using store-bought stock, you'll have to watch out for salt content.)

Bring to a rolling boil.

Reduce to simmer.

Cook anywhere from 1.5 hours to all day.

For another layer of flavor, add one bay leaf and/or one sprig of thyme. (Be careful with thyme. It can overpower pretty easily.)

Again, you'll need to salt (and possibly pepper) it at some point, but wait at least an hour after simmering starts before you start salting to see how much the sausage is bringing to the party.

Skim off the fat or grease as it cooks.

Add water if you think you need it, as quite a bit of it will boil away . . . which is fine. While you don't want it to cook down to stew consistency, letting it cook longer gets it a bit thicker and gets in more flavor.

Add green onions immediately before serving.

Serve over cooked white rice. (Don't be afraid to drown the rice.)

Ken's Crawfish Etouffee

Crawfish is almost always the first thing to come up in a discussion with non-Cajuns about Cajun food—unless it's Thanksgiving, when the talk turns to turduckens or deep-fried turkey.

Let me say first that Crawfish Etouffee (Ay-too-fay) has little to do with crawfish boils—in which people stand around in the backyard drinking beer and getting their hands messy cracking those little buggers open and eating all the tail meat. Unless you have an outdoor space, the proper equipment, and access to live crawfish, you can just forget about boiled crawfish. It's only good fresh. And though you can get live crawfish delivered in season (generally February through June), it's ridiculously expensive. And take it from someone who boiled crawfish in a New York City apartment—just don't. The horrible ditch-water smell will be with you for weeks and stray cats will come from miles around to investigate. At any rate, if you want the great taste of crawfish, go with etouffee.

Crawfish etouffee is a rich, buttery crawfish dish served over rice. The below recipe is easy . . . so easy, in fact, I'm not certain I transcribed it correctly! I wrote this version down for a friend's wedding quite a few years ago (hence the vaguely inspirational-sounding notes toward the bottom). Cooking time varies, but it shouldn't be overly watery, and the end product should come out with a reddish-yellow color. Traditionalists out there will point out that it's better first to make a roux and do it the slow way, but you can find those sorts of recipes on your own.

1 big yellow onion
1 medium-sized green pepper
couple of stalks of celery

2 pods of garlic (or more, if you can stand it)
1 stick of butter
1 pound of cleaned and cooked crawfish tails
1 bay leaf
3 or 4 Roma tomatoes, diced (otpional)
1 can of Campbell's Condensed Cream of Mushroom soup
1 bunch of green onions
salt and black pepper to taste; cayenne pepper, if you want to spice it up

Chop yellow onion, pepper, celery, and garlic. Sauté in butter over medium heat until onions are translucent and green peppers have wilted. Chuck in the crawfish tails, the bay leaf and, if using, the diced tomatoes. Add salt and black pepper. (Go easy on the salt, because Cream of Mushroom soup is fairly salty.) Let cook on medium low for about ten minutes. Spoon in Cream of Mushroom soup—about half the can, to start (this depends on how liquid-y the dish is so far)—until you have a thick, creamy sauce. Put on simmer. Chop up the green onions and chuck those in for color and taste. Let simmer for another ten minutes or so. Do not leave heat on high or overcook because crawfish will get rubbery. Adjust salt and pepper to taste.

Serve over cooked white rice.

Notes:

1. This is an extremely simple dish. Cooking time takes perhaps thirty minutes (of course, playing around and cooking longer usually makes things taste better). There are much more complicated ways to make this dish. But, sometimes, shortcuts do work. And notice, too, the ratios are pretty much all 1:1, so if you want more, it's pretty simple for even math dummies like me to figure out.

2. The crawfish is best ordered from Louisiana. Cajungrocer.com is a good site for such things. Like most things in life, the crawfish tails can be found in Chinatown for much cheaper and much less effort. But they taste awful. Just because something (or a reasonable facsimile of something) can be found in Chinatown, it does not mean you should purchase it. Your guests will not be impressed with your nose for a good deal if your dish smells like water from a drainage ditch.

3. Butter. Butter is important. Everything is better with butter. You can cut the butter amount a little if you want the dish to be a little less rich. But under no circumstances are you to use oil of any kind, margarine, or butterlike substances.

4. Campbell's Cream of Mushroom soup. Not to sound like a midwestern housewife, but you should always have a few cans of this in your pantry. Like a lot of the much-maligned values of the red states, Cream of Mushroom soup seems hopelessly trite, outdated, and square. But it works. It's something that, used in the right way, can help you make an exotic dish like this and do it quickly and simply. The old-school version of this dish calls for a roux. But that's awfully French sounding and, as usual when involving the French, is overly complicated, time-consuming, and likely to fail—all for an end result that tastes the same.

5. Tomatoes. Everything above this line is my mama's recipe. Mama doesn't use tomatoes. I do. Why? Partly to jazz up the taste. Partly to be different. Sometimes you can tweak tradition without throwing it all out the window.

Discussion Questions

1. Did Father Steve ever stand a chance against Vicky? Discuss the struggle he had with his vows.

2. At one point, Father Steve refers to the "Americanization" of America. In other words, with the spread of chain stores and fast-food franchises, the country became more homogenous. Though some people bemoan the loss of American subcultures, many people in unique areas of the country want their Walmarts and Burger Kings. Indeed, Walmart is a gathering place for some of the folks in Grand Prairie. Has this homogenization robbed south Louisiana of its unique character, or, from what you gather from the book, has that character survived?

3. Do you think Father Steve has "church envy"? He may have issues with other religions, but does it seem that he wants a bit of that community and dynamism offered by less traditional religions? Was he jealous of B.P.'s church because it was larger and had more parishioners? Discuss the size of a church as it relates to community.

4. At what point do you think Steve first sees Vicky as a woman rather than as a sidekick or an assistant?

5. Does Mark's story in the bar resonate regardless of sexual orientation? Does he seem less concerned with the Church's stance on homosexuality than with the fact that, gay or straight, living alone, detached from society, may not be emotionally healthy? Do you feel that such a lifestyle is antiquated, or does it have its merits in contemporary society?

6. Does Vicky make a good point? Has Father Steve, aside from detaching himself from society as a whole, become lazy and self-absorbed? What about him has changed since organizing the Rabbit Festival?

7. Father Steve and Miss Rita seem to have a pretty open relationship and could almost be seen as a hopeful sign in race relations, yet other than their interaction, their worlds appear to be fairly segregated. Do you see them as a sign of racial progress or as a holdover from a time when black and white were thrown together by unequal working relationships?

8. Did Father Steve join the priesthood for the right reasons—i.e., as a refuge from his own inability to deal with regular relationships? Do you think this is a motivation behind some who seek a cloistered life, regardless of religion?

9. Is Blackfoot right when he says that denying the sexual urge is ultimately a futile gesture? Or are there arguments to be made for the focus and discipline necessary to maintain a celibate lifestyle?

10. How do you think the Church will respond to Father Steve's actions at the end of the book? What about Father Steve's congregation?